ERUPTION 2085

BY JORDAN HAMPTON

The story and characters in this novel are purely fictitious and are entirely the fabrication of the author. Any resemblance of these characters to actual persons, living or dead, is purely coincidental. Certain long-standing institutions, agencies, and public offices are mentioned, but the characters and events involved are wholly imaginary.

theonlymrh33@gmail.com

www.authorjordanhampton.com

ISBN (Hardcover): 979-8-9858346-2-8

ISBN (eBook): 979-8-9858346-3-5

Cover design by Jay Koala Photography and Jordan Hampton

Edited by Kenne Stu

Printed in the United States of America

A Conversation Between Present and Future

My son, I love you so much.

Let nobody convince you

That your melanin isn't a source of pride.

Your darker complexion is a badge of honor,

Because where our ancestors were cut

And beaten

And bruised to the point where their skin broke,

Yours is clear. You are the sum of every hope

They ever had for their legacy.

You're brilliant and strong,

Compassionate and insightful,

Resourceful, artistic, and tougher

Than they ever imagined you to be.

My son, I expect from you so much

Because you're not where the dream ends.

In you is my hope that you'll pass on Everything I've taught
You about goodness

And hope

And love, that you'll show

A generation newer than yours

The best in mine but none of the worst.

You may not always see it,

But that darkness in your skin

Is a light to the eyes of many,

So lead them in the strength and intellect

Synonymous with you.

My son, I speak life to you so much

Because as mine fades by the day

I will that it fills you, that in you they see

The generations that came before,

That they know the names of the lost

By the swagger of your walk

And your head held high

Despite the weights of the world

Thrown on your shoulders in bulk.

The weak moments will come, so draw from

The well of your forefathers' strengths and Mingle them
With your own.

Rise above the many -isms that rage against you and claim
Your throne,

My little prince,

My son,

My hope.

My son, I love you so much.

I only pray that you love yourself as you should.

To every black child like me that was ever made to feel inferior because of the melanin in your skin. You are my inspiration for all of this!

Prologue

January 3rd, 2085, 9:09 p.m.,

Nine days had passed since the Reds launched their assault. Scarlet patrols increased throughout the Southern Wastes. Whatever remained of the Yaiba and Kabuto in the region was to be hunted down and exterminated by order of the King of the Reds. It was strategic. Mechanical. If John didn't know any better, he would've thought that King Shane had grown a brain in the last few days. This sort of tactical advancement was usually beyond his reach, mostly because he tended to take his idiot advisors too seriously and put too much trust in his idiot son Nash, Prince of the Reds.

But uncovering the background of this conundrum would have to wait. Now he wasn't the Director of the Yaiba. He couldn't afford to get distracted by the many maybes or what-ifs that surrounded this bomb-blasted moment. No, he needed to focus, because in this moment, he was the Rairyu he once was, the black-ops leader he was known to be, a Violet Shadow if ever there was one.

"This is horrible," Ryan Morrisey whispered into the comms. "Everything looks so…" He trailed off, no doubt distracted by the broken buildings and bodies that lay scattered about the scorched earth. They were everywhere. Scarlet uniforms and Yaiba Hanzo Gear mingled together, joined in the fraternity of death. It was enough to make John question the point of this war. Then Emiko's face gripped his mind and reminded him.

“Don’t worry about that, kid,” John replied. “Focus on why we’re here.” They weren’t far from the mark, now, anyway. After the comms network was restored, the central computer picked up the signal of Bill’s Hanzo Gear in Yorktown. If there was any chance that he was alive, they had to take it. The Insurrection’s military might had been reduced to a quarter of what it once was. So many lives were lost. So many friends. So many children.

“Target is in range,” came the cold voice of Serenity Crawford. Hearing her over the comms was weird for John, because in all the unpredictability of war, he still never expected to be in a position to work with the former leader of the Scarlet Scourge. Strange though it was, he witnessed her sacrifice her station and even her ideals for the person she loved. That, in John’s mind, was respectable. “Get ready.”

“Don’t have to tell me twice,” Cal Richmond cooed. His new prosthetic eye was, as he’d explained it, “in need of more of a field test,” though John couldn’t imagine what could top the destruction of the Kingdom Drone Network. He knew that that wasn’t the only reason why he’d come along on this mission, though. Bill had always been like an uncle to Cal and Darius. To them, almost as much as to John, the new Lightning Dragon was indispensable.

Ryan, Serenity, Cal and John, each of them perched atop one of the last few remaining structures in the city of Yorktown, waited patiently and watched the road below as two boys, neither of them a day older than 18, sprinted through the debris. A cell of Kingdom Scarlet patrolmen gave chase on their transports, but strangely enough, the experienced soldiers kept their distance. The moment the pursuers began to encircle their prey, the taller of the boys would lash out at them. He whipped his arm around, and to the surprise of the Yaiba operatives that looked on, a metal chain followed its path and whipped the blade at its end through a combination of metal and flesh and bone.

"We should help them," Ryan spoke over the comms. Despite his brutality on the battlefield and knack for Tsuchiryu, he was a kind, ultimately compassionate soul who endured the kind of combat that he did only to secure a future where all men truly were seen as created equal. John always admired his youthful idealism and the unwavering foundation that Ryan had been able to create for himself from what usually amounts to the fleeting feelings of the inexperienced, but was mindful that it led the young Shadow to more reckless actions than not.

"Wait," commanded the Director. "Let's see what they're capable of first."

"You can't be serious," Serenity challenged. She had grown a conscience in the last few months, and John surmised that in her mind he was just leaving these children to be massacred by hardened Red soldiers.

"I am," John replied firmly. "The tall one has a knack for the kyoketsu-shoge, or at least enough instinct to keep him alive. I want to see more."

"But pops," Cal spoke, his tone reasonably reserved so as not to incur the wrath of his superior and adoptive father, "what if they can't hang?"

"Then we'll step in," John assured him. "I have no intention of watching any further Scarlet slaughter." This put the others at ease, but the rattle of the distant chain resurrected Serenity's fear. The taller boy, dark skin with a slim but muscular build, curly hair shrouded in a blue hooded sweatshirt that covered his elongated torso and an unimaginable intensity in his eyes, had attacked their pursuers once again. The kyoketsu-shoge pierced the windshield of an oncoming transport, and then the heart of the driver. The vehicle accelerated, but just when the boy looked to be finished, he retrieved the chain and rolled out of the way. The transport collided with another that had hoped to cut off their path, and at the recoiling of the weapon to the tall boy's arm, the shorter one (who by all counts was still fairly tall) brandished a sword.

The sum of the Shadows that watched the skirmish were bewildered to say the least. This boy, thin-built with a tattered flannel button-down draped over a dirty white hoodie, alabaster skin and a focused expression, charged enemies proficient in modern warfare with a simple sword. It was Serenity who looked through her visor, mostly to confirm what she already couldn't believe.

"Hold on," she said when she saw it.

"What?" John's expression was focused, intense, as befits a former Lightning Dragon.

"The hilt," Serenity replied. John focused his visor as well and saw it too. The hilt of the sword was outfitted with a compacted power generator that was impossible to see from that distance without the help of their tech. The boy charged the oncoming vehicle, sword rested at his hip. The transport sped on, fully intent on mowing the young man down. Then there was the rattle of heat-treated chains. The blade of a kyoketsu-shoge pierced the engine of the car, and as it started to spin out of control the occupants jumped from its cabin. The boy with the sword only narrowly dodged the now pilotless vehicle. His form was sloppy, but despite the fact that he nearly died, John found the dodge and intensity of his movements to be mildly impressive. The two Scarlet aggressors regrouped, and as their guns raised to take the boy down he ran in irregular patterns to only briskly, narrowly avoid the gunfire. The fearsome rattle of chains echoed on the battlefield again, and one of the Scarlet Troopers fell split by the mighty whip.

The young man with the sword closed the distance much faster now, and as the pistol in his opponent's hand aimed for his head, there was a swift slice and a brilliant flash. The former gunman howled in pain at the sudden loss of his hand. The boy turned from him only briefly, and with another bright burst of light he pierced the man's chest. As the victim fell to his knees the boy withdrew his sword and decapitated the Trooper without mercy, a move that made the eyes of the Shadows widen with awe and a tinge of fear.

"Bring them in," John spoke into the comms. There was a moment of pause, but then the boys were surrounded.

****

January 3rd, 2085, 11:17 p.m.,

The Insurrection base was, at the moment, an abandoned factory surrounded by a few equally desolate warehouses. The only power that ran through the circuits of their makeshift dwellings was courtesy of the portable generators that the engineering techs supplied for this mission. The stretch of land from the Roan Mountain down to Atlanta had been cleared of Scarlet invaders, and the Waste Raiders were free to resume their way of life. It was that restoration of freedom, as well as the foundational attempts to help them rebuild that fostered newfound respect between the Raiders and the Shadows.

The ambience of the old factory was as could be expected: dimly lit, covered in layers of dust that probably dated back to before the Second Civil War, saturated in a scent that emanated oil, rust, and the tedium of days long forgotten. Little by little, though, the Yaiba endeavored to bring new life into the place, especially since it wasn't clear how long they would be there. That subtle flame of life became a quiet blaze upon the return of the Director and his team. The others, caught in their work, watched as John, Cal, Ryan and Serenity ushered in two young men, one light and one dark, both covered in tattered clothes and enough dirt to grow a plant.

Ryan and Cal took them to the showers to have them cleaned, an ordinance that none with noses objected to, and when they'd been sufficiently cleaned (which in this case meant that they'd been power washed like a house in the North Carolina spring), they were brought back before the Director in his makeshift conference room with Ryan and Cal positioned by the inner door for added security. They could feel the aura of his presence even before they entered, and truthfully it was that fear that prevented them from attacking him on sight upon their apprehension. Something in them knew that these people were not to be taken so lightly. They stood motionless as the Director, a tall man with natural curls, skin like burnt sienna and piercing dark brown eyes shrouded in a mystery indecipherable to the two young men. He sat on what was left of an elevated platform of the dimly lit warehouse shipping room, silent as his eyes shifted from one of the boys to the other.

"I want to know," John began slowly as his gaze fell upon the taller of the two, "where you found those." He nodded to the kyoketsu-shoge wrapped around the boy's lengthy arms. He was roughly six foot seven, six foot eight, and now that John had seen him up close he noticed that the curls atop his head were as matted as the flat strands of his companion, his form was gaunt with the shadow of muscle and his eyes betrayed something of the horrors he had seen. He looked about 17, maybe 18, though there was no way to tell for sure without due conversation, something that the young man currently failed to provide. They watched the Director, distrusting anything about their present surroundings. Their hesitance made the corner of John's mouth curl upward into a rueful grin as he assured them, "I don't bite you know."

"You sure you won't do something worse than that to us," asked the giant, his voice a smooth tenor disrupted by the rattle of fear. John, in this moment, remembered the boy that Darius had been upon his first major assignment. He'd lost his grandmother, battled the Scarlet Scourge, and had been betrayed by his uncle to a mission that risked his life long before he was ready. There was so much fear in his boy's eyes, so much sadness, and that was what he saw with this young man.

"I know it'll likely take more convincing, but I have no intentions of hurting you," John assured him. His eyes cut to the young man's companion, who looked younger than the giant and twice as fearful. The former Rairyu surmised that there was little use in trying to talk to him.

"Nine days ago, my older brother went missing in a Scarlet bombing run somewhere around here in Yorktown. I want to find him and bring him home."

"You just said it was a bombing run," spoke the swarthy youth, "how do you even know he's still alive?"

"The day the bombs dropped over Yorktown, his life signs fell but they didn't stop," John replied. It was the one glimmer of hope for the Yaiba Insurrection's upper ranks after they'd lost so much. So many. Bill was alive, he just hadn't been found yet. That knowledge was the only thing that kept John from breaking down over it.

"Yeah, well, a lot can change in nine days," said the young man, his voice as dark as his skin. John cut his eyes at him and the boy clammed up.

"I want to ask you again," John muttered with a reptilian hum to his voice, "where did you get those kyoketsu-shoge?" The sudden sharpness to his expression led the young man's body to quake in a fear that he'd never experienced before. His muscles suddenly tensed as his terror reached its peak, and as John moved forward, the boy moved back.

"There were a lot of bodies after the bombs dropped. You could smell it, you know. All the death and destruction. When us survivors came back above ground, we salvaged what weapons we could from the people that died. Not like they had any use for it," explained the kid. John's expression relaxed from its prior intensity, though the deeper furrow of his brow showed that he was still troubled. He paced for a moment, silently wrestling with the thoughts in that flickered back and forth in his head.

The whole reason he'd brought these two back was that he thought it would lead to Bill.

"I see," the Director finally said. There was a heavy sorrow to his voice that, in that moment, *for* that moment, dispelled the innate wariness of the two young men. John noticed this, and in a split second his demeanor changed, and their distrust had returned in full force. "Well then in that case, what are your names?"

"I'm Leo," spoke the giant with a calm that reminded John of the fiercest warriors. The boy nodded in the direction of his silent comrade, whose focus had never once shifted away from the Director. "He's Al."

John smiled at them warmly. "Get some rest," he told them, and motioned for the two attendants to escort them to the barracks. "You've had a long day." Surprised, the boys followed the two underlings, curious and a little afraid of what would come next.

****

January 4th, 2085, 8:45 a.m.,

There was a warmth to the Scarlet Throne that Bryan Piccio had never expected, a feeling of power about it that he had never known, and yet now felt belonged to him and none other. It'd been a number of days since his ascension to his new role as the head of the Scarlet Kingdom, and that through the craftiest plan that he'd ever concocted. The Yaiba in him was extremely proud to have screwed with the Reds in a way as massive as this, but the Monarch that oversaw the inner workings of an entire nation could hardly be bothered with the petty grudges of the past.

The last nine days had been busy enough for Bryan. The varied levels of ricin that he'd administered to the other Scarlet nobles had taken effect. Each noble of the King's Court had died at staggered intervals, just as planned, and when the poison was discovered by the coroners, Bryan made sure to place the blame on the only member of the Court to escape with his life: Prince Nash. All threats and opposition to his power had been properly accounted for, which left the work of sustaining the Kingdom largely in the hands of Bryan and any allies he managed to secure.

That was the purpose of his present engagement. He looked down from the Scarlet Throne at the four individuals that knelt where the former Court's table once stood. The marks on the floor where it had once been fastened lingered still, doubtless a reminder to all who stood before the new King of the Reds that the old manner of doing things had been done away with. A new order had taken its place in the palace, and Bryan hoped that with these people by his side he would be able to cement its strength.

His azure gaze shifted between them in kind. First in line was a woman of voluptuous curls of brown velvet hair that draped over the caramel skin of her face. She he knew to be his daughter, once thought lost but very much alive—and well taken care of. That much he could thank his predecessor for, though it was foolish of him not to realize that her loyalty to him would fade as soon as those beautiful brown eyes met her father's face.

At the other end was Serafina Leyva, daughter of the late Viscount Leyva, a woman who had proven her worth through her confrontation with Emiko Ishikawa, late leader of the Yaiba Insurrection. Serafina had since been named the default leader of the Scarlet Scourge and had been charged with recruiting new members. At first indifferent, Bryan had come to view the young woman with a kindness not unlike that that he showed Lyla. Perhaps it was because he was so vividly reminded of Lyla when he looked at Serafina, or perhaps it was because the lupine hunger often reflected in the new Scourge leader's eyes warned him of her untrustworthy nature. Either way, as long as she served him with the same fervor as she did his predecessor, he would have no reason to put her down as well.

To Serafina's immediate left was Kyle Crawford, brother of Serenity (the former Scourge leader) and Ryan Crawford. From what King Bryan had been told, they came from a prestigious military lineage that at the very least went back to the night of the Hanzo Gear field test some 39 years ago. His father, Alan, was the legendary sniper that not only witnessed the whole thing, but survived the first-ever encounter with a Yaiba Rairyu. The mere thought of Dre Hamlin leaving someone from that night alive was enough to send a chill down Bryan's spine. It'd long been reported that there were no survivors to speak of. It's almost as if the Reds' national treasure had colluded with the enemy. But Bryan's reason for this summons had more to do with Major Crawford's personal military history.

Kyle Crawford was the number one intelligence officer in the Kingdom, and had the skill of command like his older sister Serenity. He was more than an asset to the war effort, and was likely the reason the Reds knew the location of the Roan Mountain base. More interesting to Bryan, though, was the fact that this man was likely the one responsible for the death of his son Jaden. His eyes narrowed, but only for an instant. Besides, someone much more interesting had taken his place in the King's audience chamber.

Zachary Smithfield knelt between Kyle and Lyla, head bowed before his new ruler with the utmost sincerity and humility. Zachary was an older gentleman, but not by much. Bryan pegged him at not a day over 43. In any case, Bryan was pleasantly surprised when Smithfield not only welcomed the Yaiba outcast into the Kingdom's central tech hub, but demonstrated a level of engineering expertise that rivaled that of old man Masamune or that wierdo Kaneuji. He was a mastermind of machinery, but he deferred all authority to Bryan even from their first-time meeting. There was a mutual respect between them. Brilliance recognizes brilliance after all. Bryan smirked with all the smugness of a fresh and unchallenged ruler as he realized that perhaps Mr. Smithfield had been the first to recognize the legitimacy of Bryan's reign, not from his devotion to the word of the former King—Zachary was uncharacteristically intelligent for a Red—but from the respect of one technological innovator to another.

Quiet musings aside, now was the time for him to address his audience. He eyes them for a moment longer, as if to savor the uncertainty in each of their expressions, and then he began. "You may rise." They did as much, not willing to test the meaning of the severity of his tone. Even Lyla was unsure of her standing with her father. She had seemed something off about him when she'd brought him back to the Kingdom, but she was in the dark as to what it was. All she knew was that she cared nothing for it. "Relax. I didn't call you in here to kill you or something insane like that."

"Respectfully, why did you summon us if not for a show of your new power?" All eyes fell on Serafina, the only one bold enough to speak so carelessly before a monarch. The moment grew tense as the King refrained from speech. Lyla, who had never seen her father with this much power before, was left to wonder if he'd already gotten drunk with it in only nine days. Serafina, on the other hand, hardly cared what this old man believed he could do to her. Better than him have tried, after all, and all of them had met their end before the wily nobleman's daughter.

"My power has already been demonstrated in the air raid across the southern parts of this continent. To flaunt even further would be a waste and an abuse," spoke the King calmly. His answer came as a shock to everyone in the room, and was delivered with such a distinct air of regality that Kyle had to wonder if the man had really come from the barbaric Yaiba Insurrection. While the others in the room looked relieved by Bryan's words, Serafina's face contorted in visible disgust.

"Well, the former King—"

"—was an incompetent egoist who gave no thought to what the Kingdom could be beyond an accessory to his own fragile self-image," Bryan finished pointedly, and the Scourge leader bit her tongue with a scowl. It was almost enough to resurrect the jokester he'd been before. Almost. Her disdain was to be expected. Bryan did intend to keep her on a much shorter leash than he'd have allowed for Serenity Crawford. "I have no interest in wasting the bodies of my soldiers in this war." He paused for a moment with a contemplative look about him, but then the new King of the Reds deigned to rise from his seat and pace the floor, an action that only exasperated the nervous feelings of the four in the room. "Niccolò Machiavelli once posed the question, 'To be loved or to be feared: which is better?' Since the untimely death of my predecessor and the rest of his Court at the hands of Prince Nash, I've been thinking about my response, both to the combination patricide/regicide as well as the state of affairs in the Scarlet Kingdom."

"Majesty," Kyle was the one to speak now, wasting no time in accepting the even-tempered state of mind through which his new King conducted himself, "with all due respect, weren't you a Yaiba Insurrection operative until recently?" Bryan raised a curious eyebrow, impressed with the Major's intelligence network. As it stood, only a select few knew of his origins with the Insurrection. Most of those who had known the secret were dead now. Time would tell if Major Crawford would join them on the other side. "I simply mean to ask, why give so much consideration to how you would deal with a people you saw as your enemies only until a month or so ago?"

"I think the answer is a rather simple one," Bryan replied nonchalantly, as if Kyle and the others should already know the answer. "Everything the light touches in this Kingdom is now mine. Should I want for my territory and its people to suffer just because of our history of conflicts? Moreover…" his tone grew darker with the pause, and suddenly even Serafina tensed with his every footstep. He came to a halt now and turned to face them.

They could all see that beneath the elegant bravado of a king, there was a pain that Bryan had kept well-hidden up to this point. "The Insurrection has scarred me in ways that the Kingdom wished it could have."

There was another moment of uneasiness before Zachary spoke up. "What is it that you have brought us here for, Sire?" Bryan sniffled, then quickly put away his authentic self to don the façade of the King once more. The sudden steel in Bryan's expression, that ineffable quality that reminded her of the ferocity of the old King Shane, struck Serafina as a mark of respectability, and in this moment, she was the only one who saw him for the master performer that he was.

"I want to repay those who have wronged me, I will not lie to you, but I also want to preserve the only place that not only gave me a home when I was cast out of my old one, but gave me a crown and more dignity than has ever been extended in my direction. Without the Court in place the operations of the Kingdom wool stagger and then halt. If that happens, then we would be giving our enemies the advantage over us. But if you all join together with me, if you work with me to tend to the people as the greatest assets to this kingdom that I know you are, then together we can create a new order that reaches from one end of Prevalence to the other, a civilization even greater than that of old." He grounded himself again. His passions had found their way through his words, and as the looks of his audience shifted from frightened and nervous to thrilled and hungry, he waved his hand at the lot of them. "Take a few days to think about it. You're dismissed."

Bryan turned from them and walked out, and as his potential new Court kneeled as was the custom, the King smiled a devilish smile.

****

January 4th, 2085, 9:00 a.m.,

He jolted awake the moment he felt the warmth of the sun on his cheek. His breathing was heavy, his body was covered in sweat, and everything on him hurt. He rested on a makeshift cot of ruddy fabric and rusted metal that sat surrounded by debris in the shadows of an abandoned building. He looked over to the crack in the wall that allowed the sun entry. *Where—*

"You're finally awake," interrupted the surprised Southern drawl of a man, momentarily shrouded by the shadows. "We were all beginning to wonder how much time you had left." The man in the shadows moved forward to look him over. He placed a hand under the injured man's chin and carefully moved his head around from one side to the other for inspection. When that checked out, the shadowy man, whose brunette hair ran to his shoulders and whose pale skin clung closely to his bones, moved to flex the injured man's arms. "Name's Hank Davis. And you?" The man on the cot opened his mouth to answer, but closed it almost as soon. He thought about the simplicity of the question, and the longer it took him to answer the more frustrated he became until…

"I'm…" his voice trailed off as the silhouette of an elderly man filtered into his mind. The silhouette grew younger, stood straighter, but the voice he used to call him never changed despite its muffled intonation. "I'm…" the injured man repeated, and closed his eyes to better focus on the man in the depths of his mind." *Easy, now! I'm not as young as I used to be, Billy Boy!* The words came back to him almost as clearly as if they'd only just been spoken, and suddenly the man—Bill— was filled with a profound sorrow. He ignored that feeling for now. Now he couldn't seem to remember anything about himself or anything else. Now he was stuck in God knows where with this Hank person. He needed answers first. He could deal with his feelings once he found out what he needed to know. "I'm Bill," he answered a bit more frantically than he'd intended.

"Seems like you had a hard time with that," Hank responded with an air of suspicious contemplation. Hank continued to check his condition as they spoke. "You're still a little banged up but you should be fine as long as you continue to rest."

"What happened to me?" Hank paused a moment at that, his hands still testing the flexibility of Bill's arms. The look that Hank assumed did anything but fill Bill with optimism.

"Reds dropped all sorts of bombs on us outta nowhere. The city up top was left in even more ruins than what we started with. Found you lying in the remains of an old church building after all the chaos was over." Hank's eyebrows lifted for a moment in recollective admiration. "The suit you were in must've been enough to keep you alive during all that. Took us three days to get you out of the damn thing."

“Suit…” Bill murmured as he scanned the makeshift infirmary. It was clear that he had no memory of anything, save for his name. Hank assumed that it would all come back to him if given the time. For now, the most important thing for him to do was to relax.

Relaxing, though, was far from Bill’s mind. He returned his attention to the man who had been kind enough to treat his wounds and asked in as much calm as he could, “Did you happen to find an elderly man anywhere in the area?”

“We found a little bit of everyone in the aftermath, more dead than alive,” Hank replied with his best sympathetic voice. Bill’s throat clenched from a worry that, at present, remained unfamiliar. He wanted to say more, he wanted to supply his caretaker with every detail he could muster so that the old man—whomever it was—could be brought back safely. But he couldn’t. Bill knew nothing of his past. He resolved to get up, to go on the search for this man from his past, only to be halted by his injuries and the doctor before him. “Whoa, hold your horses there, pal. Can’t have you wandering off before your wounds have healed. You stay here and get some more sleep. We’ll sort everything else out when you’re in better shape.”

“Alright,” Bill replied reluctantly after a moment’s pause. Hank eased him back down onto the cot, and once Bill had elected to rest his eyes, the doctor made exited the room.

****

January 4th, 2085, 10:11 a.m.,

It was busy here, but there was a certain tranquility about it. Al was impressed by the way the Yaiba worked together to accomplish even the smallest goal. When they'd come to retrieve him an hour ago, he'd already been watching them from the shattered window of the drafty old room they'd stuck him in. He'd been brought before their leader—John Hamlin—just as he had been before. Leo stood beside him, and then they were told to kneel. There was a structure here among these people, one built on the kind of respect that Al could tell came from close relationship and affection.

They loved their leader, but there was something that Al couldn't quite grasp about that. His time in the Southern Wastes had taught him that people couldn't be trusted, and so he watched the Director with a degree of skepticism that constantly showed on his face. Even so, John only smiled at him as warmly as he would his own son, and told the two young men that they would assist the others in their chores. Based on how they handled that, they would be given the choice to begin training in the ways of the Yaiba Insurrection.

"What?" Al couldn't believe it, so much so that he spoke for the first time in the presence of what was veritably their king. John merely raised his eyebrows in delighted surprise as he waved his hand. The attendants, Cal and Ryan, moved to escort them out and John simply responded with a strangely dismissive yet intentional, "Work hard."

They pulled him along and guided him to the water prep station. At first Al had no idea why they even needed one when the Insurrection was obviously so well-equipped for a drought. They not only had transports with tanks full of fresh drinking water, they built a well at the heart of their camp.

"Everything you need is right here," Ryan told him in his best attempt to sound helpful. "We have a heated tub to boil the water in on the other side of that transport near the well. You'll find buckcts inside it. Cal will show you where to bring it once it's purified." Al's eyes went wide with realization.

"Wait, you can't be serious," he almost protested. Ryan looked at the boy's stance, and up close he could see the same warrior's quality that had made John so interested in putting him through the training. He raised a single eyebrow in surprise.

"What, can't you do it?" was all he asked. That was more than enough to trigger a response from Al, who immediately got to work. He filled bucket after bucket of water and hauled each one to the tub to be emptied and boiled. It didn't take long for the heat to affect him or his muscles to fatigue. By the time he'd hauled the freshly purified drinking water to a table near the jury-rigged motor pool, he was shocked to realize that this water was not for the operatives.

The line of Waste Raiders extended for a while, and suddenly the chore seemed less menial and more lifesaving. The sight of the people in need, who stood there to receive of the Insurrection's kindness, motivated him to move with more fervor than he'd exhibited before. Their eyes lit up as they watched him, though a few scowls in the line told him that he had moved perhaps a bit too slowly.

"Sorry," Cal called to them with a wry smile meant to placate those Raiders whose trust had not yet been earned. “We got a new guy.” Al approached with the water and once he set it down, it was Cal and Ryan who began to serve the people. It was in that moment that Al saw the true good in these people, and that he felt like he was truly a part of something bigger than himself.

It was a shame that he’d have to tear it all down.

Chapter One

January 5th, 2085, 11:42 a.m.,

In the days since Manny's death, Lukas Bautista refused to allow himself the time to dwell on it. His focus turned to training the next generation of Violet Shadows. Of course, he kept up the appearance of his usual optimistic self during the more academic instruction, but fear struck the hearts of those who had him for combat training. It was as if holding a Reikiken triggered something in him, and a little piece of himself was lost each time. He tried to keep himself afloat and chose to focus on his most positive memories of his father: the one-word stories that adorned his life, the charming smile that brought him comfort in the most terrifying times, the words of encouragement and wisdom that got him through his own training with his Uncles John, Bill and Bryan, the morbid facts that he always somehow made fun.

In the end, though, remembering these things was only accompanied by the fact that he would never hear his father laugh again, or see him taunt an enemy. Manny Bautista would never again voice his pride in his son or hug him. There was so much that he would miss, and the longer Lukas pondered these things, the more aggressive he became until—

"Ow!" One of his students had been caught with a leg sweep and fell to the ground. Lukas stood over them, Reikibo raised in one hand with one of its lit blades angled down towards the young man's chest. His breathing was short, his body trembled, and his own Reikiken rested by his side. Gripped by fear, the boy was too stunned to defend himself further. It was the fear in the trainee's eyes that pulled Lukas out of his own head. It was slow in the coming, but when he realized what he'd done—what he was about to do—he stepped back and lowered his weapon.

"I'm so sorry," he said, not just to his unintended victim but to the whole class. Everyone in this portion of Training Level C watched him, a mix of concern and fear embedded in every one of their faces.

"Master," started one of his students as Lukas' sparring partner regained his legs. Lukas raised a hand and shook his head as his Reikibo switched off. He pulled it apart and stowed the two shortened Reikiken in the twin holsters at either of his sides.

"I think I just need a moment," he told them, then made his way for the exit. The lack of his usual energetic cheer was more than a little concerning for all who had seen him before his loss, but after seeing the increase in his aggression, there wasn't a soul who would broach the subject with him.

****

January 5th, 2085, 4:11 p.m.,

These tunnels are darker, Lukas thought as he trudged along the path of Residential Level G. It took him a while to realize that that wasn't the case, not really. The tunnels seemed darker, true, but between the ongoing reconstruction of the power systems and the recognition of the losses sustained in the bombings, the Insurrection stronghold in the Roan Mountain, the homes that he actively walked by, and he himself, were all but shells of their former selves.

His walk was as aimless as the sum of his thoughts, which were occasionally interrupted by the cries of children still grieving the loss of parents, parents grieving the loss of children, brothers and sisters mourning their siblings, and all in desperate need of a comfort that all of them (no matter their age) knew would likely never come. Lukas was surprised that his heart could still be moved by such things, but quickly realized that this was not a mark of the man he had been before his father was wiped out of his life. It was a result of the relatability of the situation. He had lost so much light in Atlanta, just as the people in his community had in Johnson City in the distance below.

Lukas looked up from the patchy earth-and-steel floor to see Ezekiel McRae holding his young girls, Hope and Aya, in his arms. They cried endlessly, even in their sleep, about the loss of their mother Shonda. In the days since the bombing, helping him take care of them was one of the only things that brought Lukas even an inch closer to reclaiming the person he'd been before. Ezekiel saw him and smiled the best he could, but the cries of his daughters and the sorrow he felt for his wife proved more than a distraction.

"Hey girls," Lukas spoke to them as he bent down to their level. "I went down to the mess and found some candy. From what I saw, it's the last little bit that they had. You want some?" Aya, the younger of the two with vivacious curls in burgundy, the one whose face looked so much like her mother's that it hurt her to look in a mirror, hid herself behind her father's leg.

"No," protested Hope with tears in her chocolate eyes. "We want mommy! Bring her back!" The utterance of the words brought her sister to tears, and Hope herself began to weep in kind. It was enough to break his heart anew, a sharp reminder of how little he could do from a place of his own despair. Ezekiel smiled curtly and took the girls inside, though in his eyes there was as much understanding as there was irritation.

Lukas continued down his path. If he wasn't in his head before, he certainly was now. He knew that today was just a hard day for the girls, for big Zeke, but it was still hard for him to accept that even the thing that brought him back to some semblance of normalcy had failed him. His face, caramel colored and painted pensive, angled at the ground as he stepped slowly through the Residential Level.

"You're just having a day of it today," came the sunny alto of Daxa Yadav, his co-teacher on the Training Level. Lukas groaned mentally, and refused to look in her direction.

"I just need some time," Lukas responded a bit more defensively than he'd intended. He knew she raised an eyebrow, but wondered if she knew how much her never-ending cheer annoyed him. It was an irritation that was compounded by the persistent reminder of his failure to win her heart at the beginning of last year. Ever since then he'd avoided her; just being near her was enough to bring back the memory of striking out. The distance he'd established had worked just fine. That is, until they were approached three days ago by Vanessa Duncan, the Kageryu. Now it was their duty to take on the role of instructor, and Lukas couldn't help but wonder what it was that God held against him so.

“Whatever you wanna tell yourself, Lukas,” Daxa replied with more gravity to her voice. The change of demeanor surprised him enough to look at her. She was just as beautiful as ever, her delicate features encased in smooth, cream-colored skin, her dark eyes framed by straight burnt sienna hair, all brought to life the shaded peach of her lips. She was slender and elegant in her build, gracious in everything that she did, and the way she handled a sword— “Eventually, though, that won’t be good enough.”

“I don’t need you to try and be my therapist, Daxa,” he told her curtly. Her brows moved closer together and she frowned as she crossed her arms.

“I’m not trying to be. I’m trying to be your friend,” she shot back. It was Lukas who had grown flustered now.

“Then as my friend, you’d think you could give me the time I asked for.” She looked at him as if he’d lost his mind and moved closer to him.

“Why, so you can risk hole-punching another careless kid on the Training Level? Or did you want to keep snapping at all the women you like?” She waited for his response, her eyes locked with his, but he said nothing to her. “You’re not the only one who lost someone when the bombs dropped, Lukas, and you’re not the only one who will lose someone later down the road—”

“You weren’t there!” He snapped at her. He knew it was wrong, that it would only make things more awkward and tense between them, but right now he couldn’t care less about all that. “You didn’t hear the explosion echo in the sky. You didn’t see the way his mangled body fell out of the sky or how the twisted metal fell on top of it. And you know what made it suck even more than that?" He paused, his anger as bright as a Reikiken blade. When she didn't answer, he continued. "I want you to imagine this. No, really, take a moment and listen to what I'm telling you. The worst, most unbelievable, most astronomically sucktastic part of what happened was knowing that I would've been powerless to change what happened. It's knowing that I would've just died with him and that the whole reason my father did what he did was to save me if only for a few more moments."

"Grandma Binsa." For a moment, that was all she said to him. It was when the realization hit him that she continued, her voice atremble and her cheeks now slick with fresh tears. "In Johnson City. She was gunned down from above by some of the lower-flying drones during the evacuation. I only heard about it after the fact. Imagine running through evacuees and the officials of another territory, panicking because you can't find the person who raised you. And you know what made it suck even worse than that?" She paused, and he looked down, suddenly ashamed of the way he snapped at her. "I want you to imagine this. No, really, take a moment to listen to what I'm saying to you right now. I was notified during training the day after we started."

"Daxa," Lukas spoke, his voice gentle and soothing like his father's had once been when he was young and scared, "I'm so sorry, I didn't know."

"I don't want your apology, Lukas, I want you to talk to someone about what you're dealing with. If you don't, I'm scared for what'll happen to one of these kids. And for what'll happen to you."

****

January 5th, 2085, 6:32 p.m.,

Darius Hamlin stood proud at the front of the training facility. His initial class of about fifteen had tripled to 45 now, and the number was on the rise. Fortunately, Darius didn't have to teach them on his own. The fifteen that he'd trained before proved to be a challenge for him, especially since the group was largely defined by a rambunctiousness instigated by Lex Ford. The blond-haired brute with a muscular physique and an attitude that raged behind his piercing blue eyes had grown a lot since his first day in class—and his first embarrassment. He had become as easy to deal with as Bobbi Brynarr, who had, for a long time, been thought of as the mother figure of the class.

Bobbi, on the other hand, had become less of the reserved mother figure that she was known for. Her honey-brown hair was styled in a way that seemed as daring as the intensity of her expression. The battle against the Anti-Rebels a few days prior had been a challenge to her, and one that she rather enjoyed. She'd become a lot stronger for all of the trouble of the last few months, and her newfound confidence had its effect on others.

Tony Landry, the androgynous person with golden eyes and black hair, Darius' one-time assailant/covert savior, became a hundred times as bold as they'd been before. Whereas before they fumbled in training, now they logged long hours after practice to push beyond their weaknesses. Darius noted a sharp improvement in each of their moves, and he found the ordeal of teaching them much more…appealing. His hushed fantasies aside, Darius was impressed with the leaps and bounds made within the eleven days since their battle with the Anti-Rebellion faction and brushes with the Scarlet Kingdom. Tony might be able to assist with instruction alongside Lex, Bobbi and Leroy, as reluctant as he was to be responsible for anyone's education.

Leroy Baptiste, a gentleman with black hair, dark eyes, and nigh unreadable expression, had proven to be one of the most valuable assets in the prior conflict. He was laid back, easy to get along with, and fiercely independent in a way that manifested with utmost subtlety. Even so, he took to his new position if only to acknowledge the respect he had for Darius, and to show his respect for his own Master.

Darius and his original underlings had known, even before Vargas had told any of them, that there was a greater need for training and production of level-headed warriors with a mastery of all the techniques that the Yaiba Insurrection were famous for. The Yoroi traps that adorned the grounds surrounding the Grand Canyon would only last for a little while longer, and when that time came, they needed to be ready.

"Don't worry," Darius told Tony as their face twisted from the pain brought by a movement done incorrectly, "you'll get it. Take your time. Breathe. Think about how you can use it practically." Tony took a deep breath, let it out, and adopted a stance that had them tuck one hand behind their back. Their weapon arm lay before them, angled acutely at the ground with the blade of the Reikiken angled upward. They waited a moment and drowned out the sounds around them, then they began. *Inverted inside shoulder block into head strike. Follow up with outside inverted shoulder strike to downward diagonal slash. Transition smoothly*, Tony told themselves, *follow the energy through to a downward stab, then block the shoulder. Flow effortlessly into a midsection swipe and turn to strike shoulder. Switch gears and strike the leg but follow the direction of the move and swing up at the hands. Change the position of the wrist and—* They lost it.

"It feels weird to move my wrist like this," Tony complained. Darius resisted the urge to chuckle. It was the same excuse that he'd given to his father in his youth. Of course, he understood that the Rairyu Form was not for everyone, but they still needed the fundamentals that it taught and the wisdom that it imparted. They wouldn't be long for a battlefield without either.

"Everyone feels that way at first." The look on Tony's face told him that they didn't buy it. "They do! It gets easier once you find your rhythm with it," he said, and took Tony by the hand. Tony was a bit flustered, but did what they could to hide the fact that Darius being so close was getting to them. He guided them through the motions, taught them through the gentle touch of his hand on theirs. There was so much passion in the way he moved, such a deceptive delicacy that almost masked the innate danger of what these moves would mean in combat. He spun them, not in such an awkward manner as what one might expect, but with a grace and elegance that came as unexpected to Tony. For a moment it seemed as some kind of elaborate dance, and between the movements of the Form and the focus on Darius' face, Tony was captivated by it all. "See," he said as he manipulated Tony's wrist. Tony almost dropped the Reikiken, but Darius soothingly moved his fingers down to where theirs were to provide a kind of stability that Tony had never known possible. Darius released them, and watched with pride as Tony completed the maneuver: a sing at the head, followed up by a downward diagonal slash into a straightforward thrust. "You just needed to feel it out a little."

Darius turned to walk away, when Tony spoke up from behind him, "How bad do you think it's going to be?" The question was enough to put a stagger in the Rebel Dragon's step. He tried not to think about that as much as possible, but with what he'd seen from his time in the Clusters and the slower-than-expected distribution of tungsten, he knew that it was probably better to face the situation instead of run from it.

"Frankly, I'm concerned that we have more warriors than we do materials. We'll only be able to fabricate so many Reikiken and kyoketsu-shoge before we have to start thinking of other ideas. Not to mention the Reds are picking at the traps around the Canyon for days now. We've got our work cut out for us. But whatever the case, we'll manage." The reassurance seemed to work for Tony, who nodded with a nervous smile and then went back to practice. Darius only wished that it worked that well for him…

It didn't matter. His job was to train troops and keep morale as high as possible. He clung to the stories of his grandfather Dre on the night of the White Ruins Miracle, how the first showing of the Hanzo Gear proved more than a match for the rudimentary weaponry of the Scarlet Troopers. A smile even curled onto his face when he recalled the story that Levi Taylor had told him of John Hamlin, former Rairyu and current Director of the Yaiba Insurrection, who had walked into the repurposed university and dispatched hundreds of Red soldiers by himself. Somehow, they'd always managed to get through the worst of it by sheer grit alone. *Survive at all costs*, Darius reminded himself.

"Darius," came the urgent huff of one Johannes Thornhill from the training facility doorway, "Ambassador Vargas needs you!" Darius' expression darkened as he turned to face the man.

"What for?" For a moment, Johannes had to catch his breath, and for another he questioned whether or not he should speak. It was the severity of the Rebel Dragon's demeanor that compelled him.

"The Reds have bombed the entire Southeastern region. We haven't had any contact with your father yet..."

****

January 6th, 2085, 1:14 a.m.,

Another explosion rattled the camp from the distance. What was this, the twelfth one in the last week? The intelligence unit that Kyle Crawford commanded was originally numbered at 1,500 operatives, and while they had a reputation for being skilled, Ryan Crawford couldn't help but wonder if it was all just hype. Then again, the expanse of desert around the Grand Canyon had been transformed into a den of traps. The fact that only twelve of them had been triggered in the intel unit's attempts to safely navigate and map the terrain was a sign that they were good at what they did.

It was enough to bring back fond memories from their childhood. Kyle, his older brother, had always been good at sneaking around behind their father's back to accomplish whatever devious little mission his brain could cook up. When he was young, he'd always found a way into the cookies or candy that his mother Ashley had hidden from them. When he became a teenager, the sweets in their parents' room became the money in their wallets. Once, Kyle had thought to steal from Serenity, too. She'd come home from the training academy for Christmas and she'd looked exhausted. Where Ryan had wanted to take care of his big sister, Kyle saw an opportunity to test his abilities. Ryan smiled, because when she'd caught him, she beat him so bad that their father had to get involved. He supposed that that moment was when they all knew that Serenity was best suited for military life.

The smile faded. It didn't make any sense that she would turn traitor. After all that time at the academy, all that hard work, she betrayed everything she knew because of what? Some forbidden love with a fallen prince? The whole thing frustrated him. He got up from the chair that had been his comfort for the last three hours and paced the room, his rifle in hand. The cold metal was a sure reminder for him that if their paths crossed again (and they almost certainly would), he would have to use his weapon on his beloved older sister.

Everything in him wanted to believe that he could do it. He was a hardened warrior, a loyal troop of the Scarlet Kingdom, ace sniper and leader of the 602nd Infantry Battalion. He was the son of the legendary sniper Alan Crawford, and—*When had her eyes grown so sad?* The thought returned to him, and with it, their entire exchange in the moments before she'd fled. It had only been days, but it felt like an eternity ago. He needed it to feel like an eternity ago, because then it would be easier for him to hide away his feelings, to ignore all the times that she'd held him when he was young and afraid, to forget the times that she'd told him stories or wiped his tears from his eyes. She couldn't be his big sister anymore. He couldn't allow it. She was a traitor now, and he had a duty to protect the Kingdom from her and her new allies.

"Sir," came the voice of a young troop from his doorway. "Major Crawford is back from the Capitol. He wishes to see you in his tent immediately."

"Understood," Ryan told him, and dismissed him with the wave of his hand. The soldier swiftly exited the infantry leader's quarters and hastily returned to whatever grunt work he'd been assigned to by his superiors. Ryan looked down at his rifle once again, and with a heavy sigh he set it aside.

****

January 6th, 2085, 1:32 a.m.,

"Finally," Kyle breathed with a tinge of exasperation. He was hard at work, rifling through papers as if to steal all the knowledge that they contained. Ryan wondered if his older brother could separate himself from his work at all. "What have you been doing this whole time?"

"Minding my own business," Ryan quipped with zero hesitation as he folded his arms across his red-clad chest. "You know, you really ought to try that sometime." There was a moment of pause between them as Kyle set his papers down and turned to look at Ryan.

"Really? You're gonna cop an attitude when you couldn't keep Serenity from ditching us for her incompetent Prince?" There was a bite to Kyle's words, but it was cushioned by the fact that he spoke of things he'd not been there to verify.

"See, when you say it like that it just makes you sound jealous of her," Ryan said passively. "Remind me, when was the last time you went out on a date? Or has it just been missions galore since you were a teenager?" Ryan couldn't resist the urge to let his older brother see the corner of his mouth raise into a teasing smirk. Kyle's face flushed as red as his uniform, but his bright blue eyes hid nothing of the irritation he felt. That, of course, was Ryan's goal. He was the little brother, after all, and it wouldn't sit right with him if he allowed Kyle to turn this into some sort of straight-up business meeting. Those things disgusted him.

"Look, we don't have time for this—" Kyle started with a renewed sense of urgency.

"Oh, you have time," Ryan interrupted with an expanded grin, "you just have no game."

"Ryan—"

"Still, you can't let that stop you, bro. We all know that you get awkward around girls, but be confident!" Ryan enjoyed this. It was just the thing he needed to refocus his mind, and even if that didn't work, he at least had a chance to watch his brother squirm a little.

"Captain Crawford—" Kyle's command voice came through. He'd had enough of this game, and needed to get down to business as quickly as possible.

"Ooh, now that was good," Ryan continued with a chuckle. "You know, girls really like it when a man uses a command voice. Too bad that, as per usual, there are no girls around you, brother."

"Four tunnels," was all Kyle said now, and the mocking smile on his younger sibling's face began to fade.

"What?"

"The openings for those tunnels are positioned around the centralized Clusters A, B, and C," Kyle continued, now in a more stoic tone of voice. He hated that his sister wasn't here to fall victim to Ryan's jokes, but she'd made her choice. Now it was time to make her regret it.

"Wait slow down, Kyle," Ryan spoke, his voice somewhere between excited and concern. "Are you saying—"

"We have a way in. We'll have to move carefully since we already know they have Hanzo Gear, but once we're done with the preparations, we'll be able to move in and finally deal a decisive blow against the Yoroi Alliance." Kyle already sounded triumphant, as if he'd already been working on a plan. "We'll be heroes, little brother. Just like Dad."

Ryan swallowed hard. *I wouldn't expect for you to know what it's like to be loved in spite of the blood you've shed rather than because of it!* The shout of his sister haunted him in that moment. He knew she was right, knew that what they were about to do hadn't felt okay in a very long time, but still Ryan resigned himself to answer, "Right..."

****

January 6th, 2085, 9:00 a.m.,

Bryan walked the halls of his new palace, his face expressionless as he took in the sights. The servants bustled about, eager to keep the grounds clean and His Majesty pleased. There was no training grounds on the premises, something that openly annoyed the new King, but that was a small inconvenience. He let his hand rest upon the hilt of his Reikiken as he made for the door. His daughter Lyla had offered to guard him as she had the former King, but he would hear nothing of it. Far be it from him to debase his daughter with the peon title of "bodyguard." She would have a better life, the one that King Bryan had always dreamed of giving her.

Besides, there were rumors of those that thought him unfit to be the King, regardless of what their former leader had declared. He was smart enough to expect that there would be an attempt on his life, and what better time to show off than that? He walked from the palace and strode down the street. The public, generally, feared him too much to look in his direction for too long. Something left over from the reign of his predecessor, and something else for him to overturn with the might of his new rule.

Fear had proven to be an effective tactic for a long while, and it certainly kept the citizens in line, even now. Nevertheless, fear had been rendered useless when dealing with the enemy, and it was Bryan's duty to find a way to make these weak soldiers stronger. The first step in that was bolstering morale.

It felt strange for him to walk through the Scarlet Capitol so freely. Just a month ago he'd been a prisoner of the former King with his own daughter assigned to keep him in check. A few months before that, he'd been an engineer and soldier for the bane of Red existence. Now he was the King of the Reds, free to come and go as he pleased. It made him smile, and the click of his shoes against the pavement beneath him somehow became more confident. Bryan Piccio, King Bryan the Divine Rabbit, had transcended the laws of logic and singlehandedly brought an enemy kingdom to heel. If only Jaden could see him now…

He felt a shift in the crowded street behind him. Someone followed him now, and they weren't alone. *Perfect*, Bryan thought. This was the moment that he'd left the palace for, the moment that would bring him the adoration and loyalty of his subjects. He walked faster to confirm that it was him they followed. With no regard for the others on the street, the pursuers hastened behind him.

The thrill of it was enough to bring a smile to Bryan's face. It had been a while since the last time he was on the battlefield. He'd taken over for Masamune in the Engineering Corps after the old man had been dispatched to Gansu to oversee the production, shipment, and transports of tungsten. He hadn't even realized that he missed screwing up the Reds until now, at this very moment. Bryan turned a corner, and with a glance behind him the smile on his face grew wider. He hadn't expected anyone to take the bait this soon, but he supposed that this was what happened when you became a polarizing public figure.

There was a familiar click in the distance, one that brought Bryan's excitement to a boiling point. There was a brief moment where time seemed to stand still. Bryan's mind considered all the possibilities that lay before him. He slowed his stride now. It wouldn't do for him to move so fast that he would miss all the fun. Moreover, if he sped too far ahead of his assailants, there was a possibility that their shots might miss him. It was hard enough to build morale with the citizens of the Scarlet Kingdom without risking the lives of their people.

The assailant fired, and the loud crack of a bullet flying from the chamber brought the people around him to their knees. Bryan had already removed his Reikiken from its hilt and slashed upward along the bullet's flight path. With the ringing of the ricochet came a sudden burst of power through Bryans bones. He adopted the high stance of the Tsuchiryu Form, bright orange sword high above his head, his face windowed by his powerful arms, his knees bent and his torso toward his attackers. Another blast from the chamber, and Bryan merely changed stances. The way he spun the blade in transition deflected the bullet, and with his open hand extended back and his Reikiken held before him, he returned their hostility.

There were three enemies, each of them now affected by the sweltering heat of the firesword. Bryan's repulsor boots kicked on, and in less than a second he bridged the gap between himself and the first man. Before the man could fire, Bryan had already brought his weapon blazing through the man in diagonal fashion. The second man, mere inches away, lifted his arm to reveal a pistol of his own. Bryan whipped around as if to block an oncoming blade—good technique was indispensable—and as he came to face his second aggressor, he burned his way through his neck. The last of the three would-be assassins turned to run just as Bryan wheeled around to split him down the middle.

The charred bodies of the three lay before the public, and Bryan looked stronger than any King these people had seen in their entire lives. He looked around at the subjects that quaked and cowered against the ground, some of them too scared to move while others watched him through the lenses of their camera phones.

"It's alright," King Bryan spoke with a coolness that sharply contrasted the blade in his hand. He turned it off and placed it back in its sheath at his side, then raised his hands in a placating gesture. "You have nothing to fear from me."

"You just murdered those men!" There was rage and fear in that faceless voice from the crowd, and while the accusation was fair and honest, Bryan saw fit to twist it more to his advantage.

"I defended my life," he responded evenly, then smiled as he added, "and I will defend yours just the same." There was a murmur in the crowd. The "esteemed" citizens of the "glorious" Scarlet Kingdom couldn't merely take the word of some Insurrectionist off the street. Trash beneath a crown was still trash to them, after all. "How many times have you watched as the people who claimed to do what's best for you sent your loved ones to their deaths from the comfort of their penthouses and offices?" A hush began to seize the crowd, and Bryan continued in his warmest, most sympathetic tone of voice. "They told you of the might of your Kingdom but the best they could do was keep your enemies at bay. Now we're in the middle of a war with an enemy that is so much stronger than your former King ever thought possible. I would know. Until recently, I worked with them to create some of the technology that brought battalions to their knees." The crowd erupted in anger. In waves they got to their feet, shouted obscenities at their new King, threatened his life, but still he smiled with his weapon stowed away.

"Why should we believe that you're not working with them now?" There it was, the question that gave him the opening he needed.

"You should believe me," he began, "because just like King Shane and his family mercilessly sacrificed your loved ones, the leader of the Yaiba Insurrection sent my son to his death. I knew, I *knew* I shouldn't have let him go on his mission that day, but I did." He took a breath, and the crowd went silent yet again as they anticipated what was to come next. "When I got the news, it wasn't some personal interaction between our fearless leader and my family. It was in a meeting, delivered as coldly as the first snow in winter. My son was *dead*, and all they could give me was 'We all knew what he signed up for.' How do you suppose I could continue working with people like that?" The King paused as he scanned the crowd with his eyes, brows raised. When no answer came, he continued. "That's why I fixed the Kingdom Drone Network and bombed the Yaiba Insurrection's base." The anger of the crowd had suddenly been assuaged and replaced with not just relief, but elation. "Their field operatives were gunned down, their expansion efforts rendered to ash." The more Bryan described of it all, the more it endeared him to the public, and the more he struggled to keep his composure as the politician. "I know that the KDN won't stop them, and I don't want it to, because that honor belongs to me personally. I will end their reign of terror in this land with their own weapons, and restore peace for all of us who have lost our children, spouses and siblings! None of us will have to live in fear of those insurgents ever again, and Red will cover this continent from one coast to the other!"

Bryan took his leave, the people cheering in his wake. *Things couldn't have gone any more perfectly*, he thought as he continued his walk. *Now to set this plan of mine into motion.*

Chapter Two

January 6th, 2085, 1:55 p.m.,

Leo had finished his chores early, and took the rest of the day to casually stroll around the makeshift Yaiba base. He couldn't help but grin, his eyes alight with a joy he'd not felt since…

He breathed heavily, but quickly righted himself when he saw a trio of lustrous ShadowStalkers adorned in the signature black and purple of the Yaiba Insurrection. The mere sight of them was enough to get his adrenaline pumping through his veins. He'd dreamed about riding a bike like those ever since he first saw the dingy, worn, discolored magazine color he'd found on one of his many adventures as a child. His mother had told him how ridiculous it was to even hope for the chance. The Wastes were no longer such a place where hope was even possible, and yet it never left him.

The sight of them made him want rush from building to tent to building to building until, at last, he found the designated motor pool, and Sora Kaneuji along with it. As gritty and oil-soaked as the bay floor had already become in the short time since the Insurrection's occupation of it, Leo could only see the shimmer of the mechanical array. It was only as he began to salivate that Kaneuji noticed him, and with a wild smile and cunning eyes he sauntered over.

"Well, well, well," Sora cooed with the boyish excitement that he'd always projected in anything close to a lab. He clicked his tongue and out came a brown squirrel from the motor pool that hastily climbed the scientist and took its place perched atop his shoulder. “It looks like we have a straggler, don’t we, Bruno?”

“You…” Leo thought to mention the squirrel, but quickly dispensed with the thought. “Sir, I wanna learn everything about your motorcycles!” Kaneuji laughed.

“The ShadowStalkers? I’m hardly the person to talk to about that,” the engineer replied. “That tech was created by the Kabuto Sanctuary, so aside from a general overview of what they do, I couldn’t tell you much. Blasted Helmets won’t let me take one apart and they certainly won’t let me watch them put one together.”

“Oh…” Kaneuji saw the disappointment in Leo’s expression, which bugged him. He was of the frame of mind that all who had the knack for tech should never feel such disappointment.

“Ah, don’t look so down, uh… what was your name again?” Kaneuji’s question came with a disarming quality, and Leo’s eyes went wide for a moment.

“I’m Leonidus Maximus,” he replied, which brought a quizzical wrinkle to Sora’s brow. “Of course, I go by Leo for short.”

“Well, Leo, I can’t give you any insights to the ShadowStalker, but come with me. I’m sure we can find some other toys for you to play with,” the wily scientist assured him, and with that, Leo lit up like a bright-eyed child on Christmas morning.

****

January 6th, 2085, 3:20 p.m.,

Never before had Leo been so excited. He'd spent the last hour and change talking with Dr. Kaneuji about the functionality of the Hanzo Gear, from the electrically charged kyoketsu-shoge to the heat-responsive repulsor boots, but the thing that excited him the most was that beautiful tungsten firesword. The Reikiken was, in Leo's mind, a work of art. The heating mechanisms in the hilt of each were a stroke of pure genius only matched by the automatic shutoff feature that kept the tungsten blade from overheating and melting in the middle of battle.

He couldn't help but want to play with one. It was cool enough that he'd had a chance to test out the kyoketsu-shoge he'd lifted from a body in the aftermath of the Yorktown Bomb Run, but now he got to see them fresh, and side by side with the full outfit no less.

Leo emerged from the motor pool/makeshift lab with an enormous smile that faded as soon as he saw Cal approach from the other side of the heavily cracked road.

"Hey, man," Cal said with his usual laid-back cheer and a hand raised in greeting. He stopped just in front of Leo, and with an eyebrow raised, looked the newcomer over.

"Hey," Leo replied nervously, "what's up?"

"You," Cal said with a straight face. "You are giant, my guy. But hey, listen. Pops wants you to come with me to the training grounds."

"Training grounds?" The look on Leo's face as he repeated the words reminded Cal of an excited kid. Leo's grin split his jawline in such a way that made his ears raise, a gesture that somehow made him seem…adorable? Cal took a split second to wonder what happened, then got back to the business of why he was there.

"Yeah, he and the Yan-man are waiting for you," Cal explained.

"Bet," was all Leo said in reply before he darted off in the direction Cal had come from.

****

January 6th, 2085, 3:35 p.m.,

"Nice of you to join us, Leo," Al teased with a wry smirk. Leo rolled his eyes as he took his place beside his fellow newcomer.

"Hey, I just got a little sidetracked learning about the Yaiba tech. I didn't even know we had training today," Leo contested.

"That's because nobody could find you," Al elaborated with a chuckle, which made Leo shake his head and toss his hands up.

"Whatever, man. Can we just get started?" He asked the question in earnest excitement, a feeling that only grew once he met the gaze of John Hamlin, Yaiba Director and acting Rairyu, stood from his seated position on the ground a few yards away. Ryan Morrisey, a strong young man of dark skin tone and well-kept black locks that draped over hungry brown eyes, stood with him with a confident smile. It was enough to trigger something in Leo, a yearning for a kind of fun he'd never once known of before this moment, a compulsion to fight with everything in him. He'd had no problem with that idea before, but something about this meeting was…different.

"Today," began John, "is your first day of training. Let me point out that having outsiders like yourselves train with us is unheard of. The only reason I'm allowing this is because of what I saw of you when you fought off that Scarlet transport."

"We won't let you down, sir," Al said with a fervor in his tone that took the Yaiba leader aback. His attitude had completely changed from the way it had been the day before, but it was a welcome change. The corner of John's mouth curved upward.

"You'd better not," he said, "because at the slightest suspicion that you can't hang with my men, you'll be cut from the program and be relegated to maintenance duties exclusively." The two young men swallowed hard, and John gestured with a nod to the warehouse door to his left. "Get into your Hanzo Gear. You have ten minutes, and then we'll begin." Another young man clad in the signature purple and black of the Insurrection approached the Director with haste, and with a whisper and nod the soldier was dismissed. "Cal, Ryan, you're in charge today."

"Bet," Ryan said with an almost sinister expression. John shook his head incredulously before he resumed.

"Run them through the basics. Kageryu Form only. I'll be back to check on their progress this evening."

"Say less, Boss Man," Cal offered with a salute. "You go handle your business. We got the newbies." John nodded at the two of them before he headed away from the training grounds and back towards the abandoned warehouse that served as his office. Leo and Al both looked at each other with an air of caution, then back to the two young men that were designated as the instructors. Cal looked normal enough, but Ryan's face reflected equal parts excitement and devious intent.

"This is gonna be fun," he sang as he pulled his locks back from his face. The boys gulped again, and took to the task of getting dressed.

****

January 6th, 2085, 3:47 p.m.,

John closed the door in haste, an action that proved enough on its own to clear the room. For a moment, he took a moment to consider what that said of his leadership, then let it slide.

"My boy," he all but whispered into the comms unit. It had been less than two weeks since he last heard anything from his baby, but it felt like an eternity. The maintenance and repair crews needed time to reestablish communications after the attack, of course. John wasn't fool enough to think that something that complex could be settled in a matter of hours. Still, it was the first time since Darius had been born that they were forced to deal with a lack of communication. It was not something that John was overly fond of.

"I'm so glad you're okay. I heard about the attack—" Darius started, but paused abruptly at the sound of his father's sigh.

“So you weren’t in it,” John spoke. Darius understood now. John was relieved. For days they couldn’t speak, and with the chaotic reentry to Yaiba territory, John hadn’t been able to focus on the wellbeing of his son until after the damage had already been done. It took everything in him not to crumble from the thought that something had happened to his boy. He took a moment to try and stave off the tears, but he couldn’t. “I was so worried that you’d been hurt.”

“I’m okay, pops,” he assured him. The calm in his voice was surprising to him, given how shaken he was to learn that his home had been bombed by their enemies. The fact that the Yoroi traps were dwindling as they spoke did little to ease his mind. Even so, he chose to focus on the positives. “I’m just glad you’re doing alright yourself. How bad was the damage?”

John hesitated to answer. So many lives had been lost in the attack, many of whom had been fairly close to the boy. Darius had grown up with no shortage of love, no lack of support, and barring the members of his actual family, most of those connections were gone. He took a deep breath and told him about the bombing in detail, the casualties, and the extremely damaging losses of Shonda, Manny, and Vanessa. “We still don’t know where Bill is, but we’re looking.” He waited patiently to hear his son’s reaction, but for a while there was silence.

How was Darius supposed to respond to this information? His heart ached and raced while his mind went numb from the processing. The worry that he’d been consumed by was replaced with a sadness unlike any he’d ever felt, and with tears in his eyes he sniffled. “That’s—that’s a lot to handle, Pops,” he said with a shake to his voice. His register lowered as it typically did when he was overwhelmed. To hear that and not be able to respond was hard for John to handle, but there was no helping it. "Thank you for letting me know."

"How are things going on your end, kid?" The question was genuine, as was John's desire to change the subject from the loss of his friends. Besides, how often did he get to talk to Darius these days? If there was anything to take his mind off of his current situation, it was taking the time to talk to the one person in his family that he'd been separated from for what seemed to be an eternity.

"I won't lie to you, Pops, it could be better." The stutter in the boy's response was enough to convey that. It was more of a problem when he was younger. It was a commonality back then, something that would happen randomly whenever he tried to express himself. It always got worse when he was stressed or anxious or angry or sad, but since John had come back from his survey mission in the Yoroi territory it'd seemed like Darius had gotten better at controlling it. Now, though, all he could hear was the scared little boy that he'd once been so long ago.

"It's okay," John assured him with a steady tone, and for a moment it felt good to step into the role of a father again. "Breathe, my boy. It's me. You know you can tell me anything, no judgment." Darius took a moment to do as he was told and John waited patiently for him to collect himself.

"Okay," Darius told him, "I'm good." It was then that he told John about the Scarlets advancing, how they triggered the traps faster than the demolitions squads could replenish them, how training was slow in the going and only a few of his students were of high enough skill to even consider the more advanced forms. The Hikariryu that they've learned has given them more than enough to defend themselves, but Darius had his doubts that it would be enough to defend the entire Yoroi territory. To make matters worse, the terrain that surrounded the Grand Canyon was flat enough to neutralize any advantage with the Hanzo Gear. It would be like trying to fight the Reds in a straight up fight.

"Not if you take control of their entry points," John told him in that matter-of-factly tone of his. It always made everyone around him feel like they were stupid, but they all knew that wasn't his intention. John just had a mind for these kinds of things, for maximizing the safety of his comrades at the expense of his enemies. "Speak with the Yoroi Council. Have them seal up all points of entry aside from the natural opening of the Canyon itself."

"Why would we do that? Wouldn't that just save the Reds the trouble of fighting us directly and give them a reason to hit us with the KDN?" The fear in Darius' voice was palpable, and the "w's" in his questions carried the bulk of the stutter.

"You don't have to worry about the KDN for the time being," John assured him, and then explained that Cal had uploaded a complex virus to the system that couldn't be so easily undone. The knowledge that the Kingdom's drones had been taken out was enough to take the edge off, until they both realized that a more permanent solution was necessary. "In any case, the tactics they're using are easy to read."

"How do you figure," Darius asked with a little less of a stutter, which made John smile a little.

"They did the same thing at the Fayetteville hideout when the Yaiba commandeered the defunct Fort Bragg base. They scouted the area, found the openings to the hideout, and attacked from all sides. That's why I'm telling you to seal up those openings except for one." John's answer made more sense to Darius now. If the only way in was from above and the tunnels were all sealed, it would be a lot easier to dispatch the waves of enemy troops regardless of what style the Yoroi students were trained in.

"How do you do that?" The question was one that he'd wanted to ask for a long time; his father seemed to know the answer to everything that ailed him, and managed to take on the most complicated circumstances with an ease that the Rebel Dragon hoped to one day achieve. John shrugged through the comms unit, and then felt stupid when he realized that there was no way for Darius to see the gesture. He paused for a moment, then thought to speak.

"Do you remember the two names of the first form in our swordsmanship?" It was such a simple thing, something that every trainee is required to learn upon their entry to the program.

"Sure," Darius replied in an unassuming tone, then answered absent-mindedly with, "Hikariryu and Kageryu."

"Do you know why it has those names?" Darius opened his mouth to answer his father's question, but realized that he didn't know the answer. He confirmed as much aloud. "Sasori-sensei once told the story of a pair of travelers, one in white and one in black, that walked a forest path from Nagano to Kyoto in Japan. They started off as strangers, and entertained idle small talk until they learned that their destination was the same. They resolved to travel the rest of the way together, since it would take three days to complete the journey and both had heard tell of bandits robbing travelers along the route. Hours passed and they talked all the while. When the light of the sun started to fade, the man in black reasoned with the man in white that he would set up camp if the other would go in search of some firewood and cook them a meal upon his companion's return. The man in white was all too happy to oblige, and immediately set out into the forest."

John caught himself in a smile. For a moment, at least, it was like the years of old. He couldn't even remember the last time that he'd told Darius one of the old stories, but just like back then, the boy was silent with attention.

"Well?" Darius' voice brought John back to the present. "What happened next?" The loving father's smile expanded.

"You've always been so impatient when it comes to stories." John took a moment to try and remember where he was, and could hear Darius anxiously tapping his foot on the other end. "The man in white had gone a ways off, and the light of day grew dimmer by the moment. Realizing this, he took to a tree that'd been broken in half, splintered midways up the trunk and pulled as many pieces of the broken wood as he could manage for the fire. He turned around, but before he could return to the path, he stumbled backward out of surprise and fell into the tree. His head smacked against the trunk, and after a few hours and the descent of the sun, the man in black came looking for him."

For a moment, Darius had forgotten all the stress he'd been under, and the problem of the Reds' impending subjugation of the Yoroi seemed more like a faint nagging sensation than the extremely potent focus that it had been until now.

"The man in black found the splintered tree and his companion along with it. His heart sank with his hasty approach, and when he had knelt beside the man in white, he shook him gently to wake him up. The man in white jolted to life without warning, which startled then relieved the man in black. He gripped his head, and silently wondered if what he'd seen was a hallucination or not. Before he could ask the man in black anything about it, his companion pulled him to his feet and helped him back to their camp. They didn't talk much on their way back. The man in black assumed it was from the fatigue of their trip so far and whatever had happened in his search for firewood, so he helped the man in white into his tent and turned to his own." Darius offered a slight hum that told his father that there was a question waiting in the wings.

"So they just decided to go straight to bed from there?" Darius asked the question with such an incredulity that John couldn't help but laugh. "All I'm saying is that if I was going on a three-day trip, the last thing I'd wanna do is skip a meal."

"Must you focus on the smallest details," John replied with a grin still plastered along his lower jaw. "Anyway, the next day the two men woke up, packed their things, and set out to continue their journey. They'd made it quite a ways, and it looked as if they would make good time until the man in white had to take a breather. He was exhausted and his head had begun to throb from the bump to his head from the previous night. The man in black remembered a river that they'd passed not long ago, and told the man in white to wait while he ran back and drew some water. The man in white thanked him warmly and agreed to stay put, and just as the man in black promised, he ran until his injured companion could no longer see him."

John took in the moment. There was one point in his life, particularly during the years he was away surveying the Yoroi territory, that he wondered how much longer his little boy would want his father to tell him stories. He smiled wider now, as he realized that there may never come a time where that stopped.

"The man in white waited," John continued with a quality of mysticism, "and waited, and just when he was going to search for the man in black, the unlikely scout burst through the trees behind him. He breathed hard as he placed a hand on his kneecap and extended a water skin to his friend. 'What happened,' asked the man in white, 'why are you breathing so hard?' His friend smiled at him and told him that as he filled the water skin at the river a dragon with a twisting body, bushy mane, and silver scales appeared to him, as pure as the clouds of the sky. 'You probably think I'm crazy,' said the man in black with a chuckle. The man in white, however, remained unamused. When asked what was wrong, the man in white finally spoke on his mishap in the woods just the night before. As it turns out, he was greeted by a dragon of a similar description, but it was as dark and foreboding as the shadows that surrounded it. The man in black supposed that this was an ill-omen, and for a moment he thought about abandoning his new friend to whatever fate was meant by the shadow dragon's appearance, but luckily he thought better of it."

"Good thing, too," Darius remarked. "Could you imagine if he left the injured man in the woods to get eaten by a dragon?" John rolled his eyes, and somehow through the comms Darius could feel it. "My bad. Continue, Pops."

"Thank you. So, they set out again, watching carefully for the Shadow Dragon while silently asking protection from the Light Dragon. They walked at a hurried pace until the darkness around them made it dangerous to continue. They set up camp, and this time they walked together to collect the firewood and prepared a much-needed dinner. The fear of the Shadow Dragon hastened them through their food and into their tents for the night. And so they slept until the dawn of the third day, when they could hear a cracking of branches and a rustling of trees. They both started awake and peered through the openings of their tents at the dimly-lit forest all around them. The crunch of the underbrush grew louder, and a mysteriously black figure could be seen just beyond the edge of their camp. It grew closer still, its horns and mane now in plain sight. It was the Shadow Dragon that they both so feared. It paused just at the edge of the trees and stared them down, eyes as red as the previous night's fire aglow in the dark. The sun rose higher, and as it did the dragon continued its advance into the travelers' camp. They started to panic until they watched as the darkness of its scales became the stunning silver hue that the man in black had described."

"It was the same dragon all along," Darius realized with pensive tone.

"That they were, my boy. The Shadow Dragon that relied on the cover of darkness and the Light Dragon that openly made itself known were two different aspects of the same beast, and once it appeared this last time before the travelers, it bowed its head and soon retreated into the forest that it once called home. The two travelers, the man in black and the man in white, finished their journey to Kyoto without any more sightings of the dragon. When they reached the inn, the elderly innkeeper asked them how their journey fared. The man in black answered that it was peaceful, and the innkeeper laughed. 'With those bandits out there? Hardly,' she dismissed with a shiver. The man in white smiled at her and told her that while they hadn't seen any bandits, they did meet a dragon that lived in the forest. Her eyes went wide when she realized what he'd just said. 'That dragon is the spirit of the forest. It must've protected you on your journey,' she exclaimed with new energy. She'd supposed that it had been spurred to action by the foul presence of thievery and murder perpetrated by the bandits, and purged them from its home."

"That's a little dark, don't you think?" Darius chuckled a bit as he asked the question, and his father took a second to contemplate the ending.

"Perhaps," John said, "but such is life. The point of that story, and the two different names of our initial Form, is that light and darkness exist in all beings and both sides are appropriate for different situations. The light is direct, difficult to mask, and draws people to it like the man in black was. The darkness, though, is mysterious, imposing, and invokes a deep sense of fear like we saw with the man in white. When you have a hard time facing difficulty with the light, shadow is there to…present the unexpected. Understand?"

For the first time in a long while, Darius felt as if a weight had been lifted from his shoulders. He breathed a sigh of relief as he addressed his father. "Yes, sir. I think I do."

****

January 6th, 2085, 5:40 p.m.,

The sky had gone dark about thirty minutes ago, and now was the time to move. He just wished that it didn't have to be so cold. Nevertheless, he loved what he did and was determined to make a name for himself with the intel he'd collected over the last few days, and a name that rivaled that of the Crawfords. Had this mission been sanctioned by the King or any of the military leaders? Not exactly… but small matters such as who gave the directive didn't bother him. It was, in fact, a quality that had gotten him in trouble often with his mother.

"Patrick Clay Brooks!" The memory of her screaming his full name, while terrifying to this day, was also strangely heartwarming, especially when he considered that it might be taught in Scarlet households as that of a war hero who helped to bring the evil Insurrectionists to justice.

He set out from the dilapidated library in which he took refuge and carefully, stealthily snuck through the Yorktown Ruins. Every step caused his heart to race with anticipation. Not only had he found the kid who'd made off with Project Thunderclap (and in doing so accomplished his actual mission), but they'd led him straight to the Yaiba Director himself! He made it to the northern side of Ballard Creek when he looked back, his stomach aflutter with excitement, and opened his comms.

"Commander Jacobs," Patrick called with a cunning smirk plastered to his face, "this is Feeler One, come in."

"It's about damn time, Feeler One," Jacobs spat into the comms, and Patrick winced apologetically. "What have you been doing the last three days? Did you find the asset?"

"Oh," Patrick said with a devious chuckle that he knew irritated his boss to no end, "I found a lot more than that, Bossman."

****

January 6th, 2085, 6:30 p.m.,

Bill tossed and turned on his ruddy cot. Flashes of light and raucous booms filled his ears. His heart raced as he frantically sprinted and repulsed and grappled across the city. Screams abounded and the cold of winter was replaced by a sweltering heat of fire and explosions. He had a goal, something—no, someone—he wanted to protect but he… He remembered the drones in the sky, that damnable electrical hum that spelled the doom of so many. He could smell the horrid stench of burning buildings and trees and flesh, could see the drones drop payload after payload and then…

He woke in a cold sweat, which was made infinitely worse from the frigid air. He slammed his fist against the stone wall, and imagined what Hank would have to say about that injury later. He could feel that he was close to something important, some key to unlocking a doorway to his past. There was a pull in him to go back to somewhere, but the longer it eluded him the more frustrated he got. He stood up now, grateful that he finally could, and moved to the only little window in his quarters.

"So, I see you're up," Hank said from the doorway. Bill turned to face him and noted the almost pained expression on the man's face. "It's cold as hell in here." Bill gave a half-hearted chortle and turned his attention back to what he saw beyond the window. There were signs of the bombs everywhere, black scorch marks on broken buildings and trees, holes in the pavement and craters beyond them. Bodies were still scattered about, their remnants more preserved than they would've been in the spring or summer.

"I fought in this," Bill spoke softly as the memories started to come back more vividly than before. "I was a part of the Yaiba Insurrection and we were here to…" Bill trailed off again, his head throbbed with pain, and before Hank could properly cross the room to tend to him, he fell with his shoulder to the wall.

"Well," Hank spoke as he helped Bill back to the cot, "it's good that your memories are coming back, and that you can recall who you worked for. But at the same time, you have to give yourself the time to recover. It'll all come back to you."

"It's been two days, already!" Bill didn't mean to snap. Hank knew that as much as he did, but the frustration was getting to him. He might not have known much about his past before this point, but he did know that powerlessness wasn't something he was used to feeling. "I'm sorry, I don't mean to snap at you after all you've done—"

"Kid if I got mad at every patient I had that ever snapped at me I wouldn't be long for practicing medicine. Get your rest like I said. We'll see how you're doing tomorrow." With that, Hank left the room and Bill rested on his back with his eyes to the darkness of the ceiling.

****

January 6th, 2085, 7:00 p.m.,

"You don't say," spoke the King as Commander Marcus Jacobs knelt before him. "Methinks this game has gotten a little more interesting." Behind the Commander paced the still-bloody specter of his little boy, his Jaden, who smiled like hellspawn as he took in the glittering golden molds and the black and white marbled floors as if he'd never seen such decadence of design. One of the things that Bryan had learned of in his "service" to the old king was Emiko Ishikawa's death. That told him all that he needed to know about the current Yaiba leadership and how their forces would be mobilized as a result. John was Director now, and what Bryan had seen in all their years on the same side was the stuff of nightmares. Now they were enemies, which meant that he needed to plan carefully.

"Shall I mobilize a battalion to close off their escape?" Bryan openly laughed at Commander Jacobs' question. He knew the man was serious, but as someone who once took down half a company of Scarlet Troopers on his own some fifteen years ago, he knew there would be no point without someone elite pulling the strings.

"Are you kidding," Bryan asked in a tone of voice that almost betrayed shades of his old, more jovial, more amicable personality. "The Insurrection would demolish at least an entire regiment before they even broke a sweat. No. A job like this requires not only precision but style. Assemble the Scarlet Scourge and have them brought to me. Also," the King paused and took a sheet of paper from his pants pocket and extended it to the Commander, "bring me the people you see here on this list. If we're to stand any chance of taking them down, then we have to do things far more differently than we have in the past. We'll move on them in three days."

"Yes, my lord!" With that, Jacobs was waved out of the room. The door to the audience chamber slammed shut at his exit, and Bryan, left alone with his own mind, came alive with an excitement he'd never known before. He and John Hamlin were not only on different sides of the chess board, they were on a collision course and poised for the fight of a lifetime! Just the idea of it almost made him salivate. No more games on the Training Level. This was winner take all, a fight to the death that only one of them saw coming.

It almost felt like a shame. So, Bryan decided that he would rectify that and show his old friend a little bit of a preview.

Chapter Three

January 7th, 2085, 2:24 p.m.,

It felt strange for Ryan Crawford to be back in the Capitol city when his big sister was somewhere living in the woods and eating berries or whatever it was that the Yaiba did. For a brief moment he contemplated a visit with their father, but how would that go now? Would Alan Crawford, the legendary sole survivor of the White Ruins Massacre, be able to stomach the idea that the little girl he'd taken in as his own had thrown him away along with everything else they held dear? It was almost too much for him to think about, so he chose not to.

Besides, his reason for returning from the western front was much more serious. He'd been summoned by His Majesty the King, and given the change of regime, it struck him as a much wiser move to mentally prepare for that. He'd heard horror stories of the infamous Rabbit of the Divine Wind, a former Yaiba warrior with so much skill with the Hanzo Gear that he could move in three-dimensional patterns on almost any terrain. This was a man who'd come to blows with Prince Nash, the heralded Warrior Prince of the Reds, and not only won, but embarrassed him on more than one occasion. This was a man who relied more on his repulsor boots and those terrifying chains than that blazing sword of his to kill an entire company of soldiers without suffering so much as a scratch.

Now that same monster of a man wanted to meet with him. A plethora of possibilities sped through his mind. Could the king have somehow found out about his failure to capture his sister? Could he have known that it wasn't a mistake but that Ryan had let her go? Captain Crawford had never met this new King and knew nothing of what to expect.

He took a deep breath as he ran through a hundred more possible reasons for this summons, then mocked himself for being so irrational. How could this be about him when there were ongoing military operations being handled on at least two different fronts? Yes, Serenity had defected, but that wasn't automatically incriminating. His best course of action was to treat this with the decorum and sense that his father usually lacked in these most critical moments when dealing with nobility. He thought back to last year when Alan headbutted Marquis West at a war meeting. He wondered if his family would be afforded the same level of impunity for such actions now that the Kingdom was changing.

The transport stopped outside of the Scarlet Palace and one of the public servants, a brown-skinned girl no older than fifteen years old, opened his door. He emerged from the vehicle and looked down at her—she was much shorter than him—with an expression that radiated more sympathy than he'd ever shown to the servants before. For the first time he thought about how their lives would be ended without a second thought if they stepped even one toe out of line. For the first time he thought about how they were subject to all manner of abuse just because of the color of their skin or the status of their birth. Serenity had used the cruelty of the Kingdom as her excuse to leave, and on the battlefield such a concept was easy to overlook. One must do whatever it takes to secure the peace of one's home. But now, looking on this girl in her condition, what purpose did it serve? What was the meaning of this kind of barbarism that was so often taken as a simple fact of life in Scarlet territories?

"Thank you," he told her as he moved for the Palace entrance. She stood there for a moment, utterly dumbfounded that she'd been shown human decency.

Ryan was met with a personal escort, a couple of troops from the King's guard detail, who guided him down the path to the same war room that his family had shared with the late nobles of the old regime. It felt like so long ago, when in actuality it was only roughly six months in the past. The sound of his boots against the black and white marbled floor echoed through the space, and each step closer made his heart pound and stomach churn with fear and expectancy. Before long, the guards stopped before the door, turned to face him with their backs to the wall, and stood at attention.

"His Highness will see you now," said the one on the left. Again Ryan took a deep breath, and without further delay he marched into the room with all the presence of the war hero he was, and knelt before King Bryan out of fear as much as out of custom.

"Greetings, Majesty. It is a great honor to meet you." His tone was as respectful as he could manage, and he did what he could to mask the tremble in it.

"You may rise," replied the King. Ryan looked up from the ground as he stood back to his feet, and when his eyes met those of the King, he found them to be surprisingly…warm. It was almost as if he was looking at his son. "Now that everyone's here, we can begin."

****

January 7th, 2085, 2:40 p.m.,

Bryan Piccio paced the room for a moment in silence, much to the unease of those in attendance. He enjoyed it, that feeling of making his inferiors hold their breath because they couldn't predict what he was going to say or do. More than that, though, was the simple fact that he'd been ill-prepared for Ryan Crawford to enter the room. The young man with a light layer of stubble along his chiseled jaw, muscular body, curly brown hair and bright green eyes looked like an older, alternate universe version of his own son, and had he not known better, he would've hugged the boy out of instinct alone.

"As of yesterday, I've received intel that Director Hamlin of the Yaiba Insurrection and a sizeable number of enemy forces have gathered in Yorktown. Yorktown, as you may or may not know, is where the Insurrection used to get its tungsten shipments for their Reikiken, an operation that was stopped shortly before the KDN bombed it to hell. What you all may not realize is that the Yaiba holding Yorktown and Johnson City means that a perimeter of enemies is forming around the Capitol. Their recent collusion with the Kabuto Sanctuary assures us of this: any openings in their positions should be treated with the utmost care." The warriors in the room showed a mix of reactions to this. Maxwell Cartwright, one of the top intelligence agents under the command of Major Kyle Crawford, bore a stoic expression on his well-groomed face. His black mustache and hair added a certain foreboding to any look he cast, and his strong build was unlike most intelligence agents Bryan had ever known. Still, there was a hunger in those crystal blue eyes of his that affirmed for the King that this man's presence was warranted indeed.

Felix Kilpatrick, the redheaded man in the seat to Cartwright's left, smiled with his green eyes as he slicked back his hair. His skin was pale, almost to the point of being ghostly, and his body was slim but fit. He was a demolitions expert, and perhaps one of the only men in the entire Kingdom that could rival the Yoroi at the craft of making—and dismantling—traps.

Argus Wulfric, though, twitched in his seat on the other side of the war room table. He had long brown hair and eyes to match and was one of the youngest people in the room. He was still strong in appearance despite his clear discomfort and was a brilliant chemist with a penchant for war.

Klaus Oppenheim, a dark-haired man with stern blue eyes and a long scar on his left cheek, folded his arms across his chest with a look of total indifference on his face. Kyle, who had taken his place next to Klaus, seemed to recognize him. Of course, Bryan had chosen this man from among the best infantrymen in the Scarlet Kingdom not associated with the Scarlet Scourge. The King was impressed with his track record, especially since it was he who led the assault on the Midland outpost that killed the King's son. But Bryan was a big enough man to let that go for the time being. Soon all of Prevalence would bend to his wrath, and with that muted reminder the King offered a small smile to Klaus, and then to his younger brother Friedrich, another infantryman of fledgling acclaim, who bore strong resemblance to the elder Oppenheim and sat to Kyle's other side.

The King continued. "Realizing this, I've called you all here to assist me with a very important matter. It is my hope that we can force a break in this developmental perimeter and give our outgoing forces some breathing room."

"Forgive me for the interruption, Majesty," Cartwright spoke boldly, "but how is it that the six of us are supposed to do that?" King Bryan sent him a look that would've melted ice and chilled the blood of a much weaker man, but Cartwright seemed unfazed, much to the delight of the man in charge.

"No harm done," King Bryan said with an air of cruel benevolence that made it clear that interrupting him would not be a habit. "It's good that you all feel so comfortable with speaking freely with one another. To answer your question, you all will be working as a squad from here on, and your efforts will be coordinated with the Scarlet Scourge." The room fell silent in the wake of that statement, and Bryan could see that each man present wanted nothing more than to burst at the seams with a flurry of questions and emotions. "You may speak."

"What do you mean as a squad?" It was Klaus who spoke now, forcefully but duly cautious. He was not fool enough to challenge an order from the King, no matter how great his concerns were. "I doubt all of us here come from the Infantry Division."

"You're right," King Bryan replied with a smile. "Each of you was brought in because you are among the best in your respective fields. I believed that you all would be up to the task of taking your careers to the next level…or was I mistaken?"

"Absolutely not, your Highness," Kilpatrick almost shouted with the excitement of a teenage boy. "I'm always looking for a good excuse to get into trouble."

"I can't say the same," came the shaky voice of Wulfric, the chemist, and Kilpatrick rolled his eyes. "I am curious though," he continued, and his voice became much firmer and more intimidating. "How will working in this squad help me advance in my career?"

"How, indeed. Every person in this room has given their all to the war effort, and your Kingdom thanks you for what you've already done. But what if I told you that you, the six men gathered in this room, *you* could end the war entirely? Three of the best infantrymen in the country sit at this table, along with an expert intelligence operative, a master chemist, and a demolitions craftsman with enough skill to give the entire Yoroi Alliance a run for their money. All this compounded with the fact that we know where our enemy leader is gives us an opening that I, as your Head of State, would be a fool not to exploit, but I can only do it with the gifts that you've so marvelously put on display until now."

"What are you proposing, your Grace?" Captain Crawford asked with more of an even tone than he'd exhibited before, and King Bryan smiled wider.

"Why, chaos of course." The manner in which the King spoke was enough to send a chill down the spines of the newly formed squad, and with their silence came the King's continuance. "I'll be frank. Sending a force of equal size to attack the Insurrection at Yorktown would only result in heavy casualties to our side. It's what the Kingdom has always done to try and do them in, and with minimal results to boot."

"So you expect a group of six men to fair any better?" Friedrich spoke with a voice much deeper than that of his older brother. The King nodded.

"Precisely," he confirmed. "When the Yaiba train their Violet Shadows," he said the name with such disgust that it gave the others in the room another chill, "they spend more time preparing them to work in teams against more tactically advantaged forces. They'll do whatever they can to stay together, because they know that as long as they can do that they'll have an advantage. But that also means that sending in a smaller number of operatives to lay traps and hit the major points of their operation at random, it'll be harder for them to regroup."

"It'll almost be like the attack came out of nowhere," Kilpatrick cooed. "It's starting to feel like the Yoroi Alliance a little bit!" His excitement was palpable, if not infectious, and the others started to like the sound of the King's plan.

"Yes, except instead of waiting around and playing defensively, we'll be a little proactive in our approach. In two days the outer perimeter of their camp will be outfitted with an assortment of mines laid by the Scarlet Scourge. They'll be on their way out later this evening once Mr. Kilpatrick and Mr. Wulfric have completed a…collaboration exercise that I have planned. Once the mines have been planted, the Scourge will switch out of their uniforms to the same kind of tattered garbage that the Waste Raiders in the South have been wearing for years

While they're hiding among them, you six will get into position in the field to fulfill your roles."

"I'm assuming you want us to take up sniping positions," Klaus spoke, and the King nodded.

"But only one of you will act as a sniper. The other two infantrymen will hide among the rabble like the Scarlet Scourge. Legs on the ground will be all-important if the rest of the plan is to go off without a hitch," Bryan supplied. Wulfric raised an eyebrow.

"What would you have me do in the field, my liege?" The scientist's inquiry was more than enough to push Bryan into his warmest dad voice as he paced the room and clapped the wary chemist on the back.

"It is my understanding, Mr. Wulfric, that you've been working on improving the flammability of CS gas. Have you perfected the dispersal mechanism?" The King's question felt like a violation of privacy. They had all known that he'd seen their files, but there was a difference between that and being watched. Nevertheless, there was a massive risk to trying to set boundaries with an autocratic King.

"Just about," Wulfric responded begrudgingly. "It should be ready by the time we set out for the mission."

"That is exactly what I'd hoped you'd say," Bryan smiled, and walked away from the chemist. "Mr. Kilpatrick will help you set up dispensaries of the CS gas at strategic positions around Yorktown. When the Shadows attempt to escape and defend themselves from our advances, they'll be on fire." There was a moment of silence before everyone in the room realized why that plan wouldn't exactly work. Even so, it did little to dampen the King's mood.

"Sir?" Ryan spoke the word with all the caution in the world and attracted the monarch's gaze. Even now, Bryan was unsure how to deal with him. The resemblance to his own son was uncanny, and enough to spur to life a part of the King's heart that he so desperately tried to kill.

"I know what you're thinking," King Bryan spoke with unintended firmness, then corrected himself and offered a warm smile to put their minds at ease. "The heat-treating of the Hanzo Gear would keep their soldiers from igniting and you're right about that. But just because they're safe doesn't mean the civilians in the area are." There was a sinister bite to his words now, something that unnerved some in the room more than others. "Mr. Cartwright, you'll be the one to feed the enemy information. I'm sending you as an envoy to the Yaiba Director ahead of the others with the message that a large enemy force is set to advance on their position should they not cease all operations and vacate immediately." The gentlemanly Cartwright merely nodded his head in agreement, and with a final glance around the room, King Bryan made for the door.

Ryan looked around at the others as they now stood from their seats and took to the position of attention. He followed suit out of simple observance of custom, but couldn't keep his face from adopting the look of a disappointed boy on Christmas morning. The King, of course, noticed this change in his expression, and remembered that he'd forgotten to tell this clone of his son what his role would be in the upcoming mission.

"Oh, and Captain Crawford," the King started with an almost paternal gentleness, "as the only member of this new squad that's worked with the Scourge, you'll be leading our efforts on this mission." Ryan couldn't mask his elation at this news than the King himself could keep his heart from running over with affection misplaced and painful nostalgia. He turned from the boy and his new teammates. "Good luck."

****

January 7th, 2085, 4:00 p.m.,

Training had been over for at least 45 minutes, and still Lukas occupied his place in Training Level C buried in his menpo mask with his Reikiken alight. Looking back, this was the place where some of his happiest memories were formed. Cal and Darius were often at his side, and his father Manny watched him confidently from the sidelines. Now, though, the only eyes on him were those of the Scarlet Troopers generated by the simulation booth. They stood there for a moment. Lukas knew they weren't real, but it didn't stop him from feeling a very jolting pain in his gut.

His palms sweat not from the heat, but from the emotional storm he'd struggled with for days now. His heart pounded, and the longer he looked at these abominations all around him, the more his rage consumed him. How dare they take his father from him? How *dare* they stand there so smugly, as though taking his life was as easy as taking a breath of air? How *dare* they breathe Lukas' air when Manny lay in some charred heap in

Atlanta, indistinguishable from all the other charred debris of the once proud city?

Lukas took a deep breath as his Reikiken came to life in the palm of his hand. Without warning he lunged for them, aura sword alive with every ounce of fury the dragonling could channel into it. Three of the projections met their demise instantly with a single horizontal slash. Lukas turned as the glorified dummies raised their guns and prepared to fire. His Reikiken was enough to distort the trajectory of several bullets, and with a violent thrust of his kyoketsu-shoge the young warrior managed to skewer several of his opponents. He pulled back on the chain, and as it returned to him it brought with it three bodies awkwardly lined up before him. A swift motion of his weapon hand and massive fiery gash appeared in the body of the first. The second one, lifeless as it was, appeared to beg for its imaginary life in the seconds before Lukas decapitated it. The third barely had time to open its mouth before Lukas rammed his firesword through it.

The enraged soldier brought the blade down through the fake soldier's body and rocketed through the carnage to take on more of the somewhat startled illusions. A diagonal slash led to a devastating flourish of the blade into a hard shot at the shoulders. The chains deployed again and rattled with all the foreboding and power of blackened tornado winds. He spun his body as he did the firesword over his head, and the chain that now receded into the brace on his wrist whipped around to slay yet more of his opponents.

They fired on him all the more but between the Reikiken and the shock-absorbent cloak he wore, he was impossible to hit. Lukas blasted from the middle of the formation to its leftmost flank, and unleashed a flurry of shallow jabs and swift strikes that crinkled his enemies like paper.

He moved through them all in a matter of moments, his blade and chains working in tandem with each other to bring the image of the high and mighty Kingdom crashing to the ground. There was about a two-minute pause before the vanquished bodies of the Red projections vanished into thin air, and as Lukas looked at the unbridled carnage of the training session, his anguish reached its peak. He let out a scream that carried so much pain with it that the technician believed him to have sustained injury.

"I won't lie," came the always calm voice of Callan Rouge from the front row of the stands, "that was hard to watch." Lukas was in tears when he rapidly spun to see his uncle there, and the look on the young man's face was enough to melt Callan's heart as if he were just a little kid again. The quiver of Lukas' lip, the scrunched-up face, all of it took him back to a time long ago, when Manny had scolded him for his reckless behavior. It was enough to remind him of how much he missed Manny, too.

"I—" Lukas started to explain, but Callan lifted his hand to stop him. He didn't need an explanation to figure out what was happening.

"I miss him, too," Callan told him with a kind of gravity that coaxed more tears from his nephew. Callan jumped the safety barricade that stood between the stands and the training floor, walked up to Lukas, and pulled him into a hug. For a while there was silence, save for the sound of Lukas' quiet sobs against his uncle's chest. It'd been so long since he'd felt that kind of comfort, the kind of freedom to be open about what he felt. “It’s okay,” Callan told him, “take as long as you need.”

“I just never thought I’d lose him,” Lukas all but whispered, his voice shaky from the crying. “He was so strong it felt like he’d always be with me.”

“He was,” Callan agreed. “Strong, dedicated, so optimistic and strangely morbid that it was easy to love him, even if you were never all that close with him. That’s how he lived, and I’d imagine that that’s how he died as well. He fought with that same optimism, not that he would walk away from that battle, but that you would survive to bring the kind of freedom to our people that he’d always tried to.” The boy—and that’s what he was in this moment, not a warrior, not the young man that he’d grown into, but a boy—felt the rush of tears to his eyes again, and pulled away from his uncle to wipe them.

“I know,” he said with all the sorrow in the world, “but knowing that doesn’t make me feel any less alone.” It was enough to break Callan’s heart a thousand times over, and for just a moment it made him question his reason for finding him in the first place. *I need to follow through,* Callan told himself before he could chicken out, and looked the boy over for a moment.

“Hmm…” It was all that Callan said before he turned away from Lukas and repulsed himself back over the barricade. He paused for a moment with his back turned to his ever-observant nephew, bent down and picked something up that Lukas couldn’t make out. Again the Water Dragon took a moment to collect himself as he eyed whatever it was in his hands, then he finally turned. What he held were the two [illegible] that [illegible] up his father’s

Reikibo. They were a bit singed and the blade of one was completely shattered, but Lukas knew what they were. "They're a little banged up, but they'll still work if you swap out a blade for the broken one."

Lukas fell dumbstruck as the Suiryu placed the weapons at his feet. It was a lot to take in, a lot to process. "How did—"

"A scavenger team was put together to make the run through Atlanta." His answer was brief, pained as was his expression, and that told Lukas all that he needed to know. After the bombing, they needed anyone brave enough to venture out on recovery detail. It made sense. Lukas waited for Callan to say more, but he didn't. The dragonling picked up the broken pieces of his father's swords and inspected them.

"This one's no good," Lukas told his uncle. "The base of the blade is fused with the hilt. The coupler seems fine though, so any other Reikiken should fit." Callan offered little response; just the small upturn of the corner of his mouth at the sight of a boy so much like his father it was as heartbreaking as it was heartwarming. Lukas set down the broken aura sword and attached his own to that of his father. His heart swelled, because for just a moment he felt as if Manny had brushed his hand with his own. Both sides ignited with a furious blaze, and as the dragonling spun the newly fashioned Reikibo by the compound hilt, the sudden heatwave dried what remained of the boy's tears. "Whoa," was all he could manage to say as he played around with it a bit more. The series of strikes he unleashed made him, in Callan's mind, the spitting image of his father.

“Looks like you’ll have a little piece of him to carry with you wherever you go.” There was a warmth to Callan’s voice now, and for the first time since his father had passed away, Lukas smiled a genuine smile.

“Yeah,” he confirmed. “Looks like it.”

****

January 7th, 2085, 4:30 p.m.,

Johannes Thornhill had barely had time to mourn the loss of his beloved Ina before he was brought before the Council and promoted to one of their number. His role as envoy to the other territories would be handled by someone else from here on out. That is, when it became safe to once again leave the Clusters. For now, Johannes’ duty to his people was not to facilitate peaceful negotiations between the factions. It was to keep them from falling into the hands of those scavenging Reds that so desperately scoured the surrounding area for a way in. In only a few days since his rescue, the Scarlet Troopers stationed just beyond their demolitions array had already triggered a third of the traps that served as the Yoroi’s defenses, and even now they were starting to discover the various entryways that made for safe passage.

This was the subject of deliberation among the other Councilors, most of whom were reluctant to even talk to their colleagues due to the drama with the Anti-Rebels that had only just been resolved within the span of the last two weeks. There were many casualties of that conflict, and Johannes had to thank his lucky stars that the KDN bombing failed to reach their location. Given that the bulk of the Clusters was exposed to the open sky, they would've had no way to defend themselves and evacuation would've been impossible.

"Councilors, please," Ezequiel Vargas pleaded. "We are running out of time. The Kingdom never ceases to try and break down our door while we waste our energy bickering amongst ourselves."

"Do you really believe that we don't understand what's at stake here, Ezequiel?" It was the posh Isabella Mariposa that asked the question as she moved her vivacious dark hair out of her amber-colored eyes. She had smooth, brown sugar skin that radiated in whatever light graced her form, and she wore a brilliant blue dress with white accents in intricate designs. "We cannot decide what to do lightly. Or are you really so eager for more dissention among our people?"

"Enough," came the stern voice of Kanza Paddock, a middle aged man of strong composition and hair as black as night. His skin was oaken and his eyes matched in kind, but bore a tremendous power behind them. It was as if he could see into a person's soul. His voice carried a lot of weight in this Council, since he was one of the few within the Yoroi who could trace their heritage to the first peoples who occupied this land. "Focus too much on the past and you lose sight of the present. I agree with Vargas. How much longer must we argue about a plan when our enemy has almost breached our territory?"

"Well then what do you propose," asked Iliya Abernathy, an elderly woman adorned in wisteria dress and an array of gold and silver jewelry. She fancied herself something of a queen. She was the only one. "Are we to consistently beg the Yaiba for more troops or the Kabuto for their technology? Have any of you bothered to think about what awaits us after our alliance with these people runs out? The very aid they send could be our undoing!"

"The Yaiba Insurrection is not so cowardly that we would resort to the use of sleeper agents," Darius said as he walked into the conference chamber. It was nothing like that of the Roan Mountain base. It was lively with color. The purples and blues and greens and yellows in the hanging tapestries played boldly yet delicately with the natural brown of the walls. Images of lakes and flowers and trees gave vivacity to an otherwise bereft environment, and that life that was so present in imagery seemed to complement the storm of emotions that ripped through their conversation.

"Darius," Johannes uttered with more shock and awe than the sudden burst of joy he felt at the sight of him. At first he wanted to embrace the man who'd given so much for him, but then the reality of his station caught up to him, and he knew he needed to maintain the professional façade. "I'm sorry, but you can't be here. This meeting is for the Yoroi Council only—"

"I'm aware," Darius stated with mild irritation. His eyes shifted between the Councilors as he spoke again. "That's precisely why I'm here. Councilors, when I was brought out here, it was under the premise that I would be training a sizeable military force to actively combat the Scarlet Kingdom. For months the most I've had to work with is 45 people. Explain." His tone was forceful, as though he was in charge of the meeting, and Councilors Abernathy and Paddock looked on him with disgust.

"We owe you no such explanation," Paddock growled, "and you have no right to speak in this Council." Darius raised his eyebrows.

"Considering I've done more than my fair share of cleaning up the messes made by your indecision, you do, and I've earned a say in whatever stretch of this territory that my feet wander into." It was clear from their jolted reactions that the Councilors hadn't prepared for such sharp rebuke from such a young man, and before they had the opportunity to justify their actions or spew whatever excuses they could fabricate, he continued. "Do you know why America failed to prevent the Scarlet Kingdom from taking all power?" He paused a moment, but there was no answer. "The House and the Senate kept arguing over what to do about the then-President's overstepping. Those who shared his party were content to let him assume all power. Those who sided with the people that the President oppressed wanted to take a stand. While they spent all their time deliberating, the President galvanized a private army to execute all of them and take control. America fell, and reality as we know it was formed."

"We know the story, Mr. Hamlin," Ambassador Vargas choked. "Some of us are old enough to remember the day with clarity."

"Then you all should also know that the only thing you'll accomplish by this endless bickering is the destruction of your own people. A third of the traps are gone and the demolitions crews can't replace them fast enough to maintain our defenses. Your people are getting more and more restless by the day. Meanwhile, you waste what may very well remain of their lives with indecisive arguments." Darius was harsh, but his assessment as an outsider looking in was exactly what the Council needed to hear.

"Present a solution or be gone," Councilor Mariposa demanded. Darius rolled his eyes and exhaled sharply.

"I've already told you what needs to happen. Give. Me. My. Troops." The agitation in his tone seemed to escalate with every word, and fear began to resonate from Isabella's eyes.

"Even if we could, our military strength is largely focused on demolitions more than anything else," Abernathy answered with a stern chill to her voice. "What good would they do you on the front lines?"

"A lot of good, actually," Darius shot back with no hesitation, which drew visible ire from the purple-clad councilor. "They know the terrain, and have ways to get around the Grand Canyon territory without being seen or heard for the most part. That'll come in handy when they learn to use the Hanzo Gear. My first few students should be more than capable of teaching them the swordsmanship, and with that being the main focus of our training it should go by relatively quickly. That is, assuming you don't waste any more of my time." He waited a moment for the Yoroi leaders to respond. They glanced at each other and glared at him, all except Johannes, who merely sat in awe of the young dragonling that so clearly embodied John Hamlin.

"Our defenses will last for a month and a half," Johannes said, which marked the first time he'd spoken in this meeting. "What can you do in that amount of time that'll make a difference?" The question, genuine as it was, sounded harsher than Councilor Thornhill had intended. Nevertheless, Darius smiled.

"First, I'll have the troops set proximity mines at all entrances and exits leading from the outside to the Clusters. That'll leave the Reds the sole option of an aerial assault," the Rebel Dragon explained. The Councilors, save for Vargas and Thornhill, were outraged at the very idea of self-sabotage.

"You'd so eagerly consign us to our tombs?" Iliya's shrill voice was enough to make Darius slam his fist against the table. Instantly they all fell silent.

"I'm doing no such thing. The KDN has been incapacitated so they wouldn't be able to address their roadblock with bombardment. If you seal all of their possible entry points, you'll force them to push straight through the remainder of the traps and lower their numbers in the process. Even they wouldn't be crazy enough to do that as a first resort, so it should buy us at least another month of training, but more than likely it'll give us more time than that. You tell me how you think it'll go when the Reds grapple down into a canyon with only too many surfaces for our forces to springboard off of."

"It'd be like striking a lineup of Scarlet pinatas," Councilor Mariposa mused. "But there's no guarantee that this—"

"I move to divert half of our military strength to the command of Master Hamlin of the Yaiba Insurrection," Johannes motioned, much to the alarm of the other Councilors.

"Half?" It was Paddock who spat out the question. "Have you gone mad?" Johannes instantly cut a glare his way.

“If you’d taken action to quell the Anti-Rebellion faction before they formed their weird cult, we wouldn’t have lost so much in an unnecessary battle.” All in the room knew that Johannes spoke of Ina, and so sat with a sting of regret deeper than they’d felt before. “If he’s got a plan to prevent us from losing even more, I say we do it.”

“I second,” came the voice of Ambassador Vargas. With his backing, there was little room for resistance, and so the other Councilors voted in favor as well. Darius smiled.

“Have my troops report to the training center first thing in the morning,” he told them. “We have work to do.”

Chapter Four

January 8th, 2085, 1:14 a.m.,

A sharp, icy wind blew through the wall of trees around Johnson City, and fresh snow blanketed everything from the branches and treetops to the bushes and mud below. Scraps of singed, twisted metal still stuck up from the ground here and there, and the fires that raged in the aftermath of the bombing proved far from a distant thought, as new paths were emblazoned onto the forest floor. The broken bark and burned vegetation wouldn't heal for a long time, and Johnson City itself was in equally terrible condition.

Buildings were broken even before the Kingdom Drone Network ravaged it with payload after payload. Now, in the aftermath, several buildings had been reduced to mounds of ash and rubble. Blood and charred remains still littered the cracked streets, and Scarlet patrols passed through freely from time to time due to a lack of Kabuto or Yaiba presence. They felt secure, as if the threat of the multifaction coalition had subsided and they were on their way to tend to business as usual.

That newfound sense of security, however, would be their undoing. Another harsh howl of the frigid wind ripped through the forest, and the faint crunch of supply transports in the snow could be heard a little ways off. It was almost time. Soon the transports came into view, six in all, alongside a well-armed platoon of 50 men and women. Before long they'd be snared and all their wares ripe for the picking.

"You seeing this," asked Aaron Stone incredulously. He was an optimistic and bizarrely talented 17-year-old kid who'd joined the war effort recently. He was startlingly good at stealth and sabotage, and his hand-to-hand combat skills were even better than some of the grown men and women that filled the Kabuto ranks. "Right into the traps? Really? Ugh, and what is that formation? It is such a mess—"

"Radio silence," answered Senior Agent Kincaid through the comms and gritted teeth, "means being as quiet as possible so as not to give away our position or intentions, Stone." The enemies were closer now, and still on the move. The Kabuto agents, perched upon tree branches that loomed over the main road, watched the advance of the convoy with calm expectation. Esau Tillman, the short and unimposing man of brown hair, slim build and a usually alabaster complexion that threatened the deepest red from the cold, made eye contact with their leader. Kincaid held up a hand as the convoy passed directly below them. The central transport was beneath him now, and at the wave of his hand his team sprang into action.

Esau and Aaron swiped their index fingers on the ovular screens at their wrists and a creak of metal on the move pulled the Red convoy to a halt. A series of heavy-duty magnets appeared below the platoon and pulled their firearms from their hands at the same time that the Shock Pads sent pulse after pulse through their bodies. The transport drivers panicked as their comrades crumpled to the ground, but before they were able to flee they were met with the unceremonious thud of localized electromagnetic pulse devices on the hoods of their vehicles. Suddenly, all their ambitions for mobility were brought to ruin. The Scarlet Troopers inside the transports emerged, and were less-than-pleasantly surprised that their weapons were pulled from their hands.

"What the—" one of them began as Erik Kincaid, Esau Tillman and Aaron Stone descended from the canopy, but the unfortunate Trooper was cut off by Levi Taylor's well-timed electro-shuriken. It slashed the Trooper's throat and signaled to Tom Freeman on the other side of the road to launch a volley of his own. The other transports emptied, all with the hope that someone in this convoy would be able to do something against their attackers, but as the Senior Agent and his two subordinates made their way from transport to transport, more electro-shuriken were deployed to deal with the nuisance of Scarlet eyes.

"Excellent work, everyone," Erik called out to his agents as the last of the Scarlet Troopers fell to the ground and choked on the flow of their own blood. "Freeman, signal the salvage team. Everyone else, grab what you can carry and head back to the city."

"Yes sir," the experienced agents replied in unison.

"Yes sir," Aaron Stone replied a bit late. Erik rolled his eyes as he turned away from the boy and let himself smile. Freeman, a shadow-skinned 20-something with sharp features and a buzz cut, pointed his flare gun into the air and fired. Bright red hovered over the forest, and in a matter of moments the salvage team would arrive. Erik made his way to the last transport, with Tom, Levi and Esau each taking one of their own. Aaron, however, got caught up with the haul from the magnetic plates that lined the road in varied intervals. "Hey, Tillman," he called to

Esau, who was already hard at work picking the best spoils from his transport, "you mind helping me release the magnets real quick?"

Wordlessly, Esau ran his fingertips down the screen on his wrist just as Aaron did. The pads demagnetized, and Aaron was free to claim one of the M4 rifles as his own. He took aim, careful to point the muzzle of the gun away from his comrades, and as he felt the cool metal against his palms, his finger slipped and fired shot loud enough to wake the dead. His teammates dropped what they were doing, weapons drawn, poised to strike, and then each exhaled with exasperation when they saw that it was only Aaron goofing around.

"Really, man," Tom asked with a glare that could've melted the snow around them. Aaron winced a little and lifted a hand in a placating gesture.

"My bad," he said, then turned his attention to the fallen Kingdom troops that lay in electrified heaps on the ground. "One of these guys has to have one," Aaron said to himself. He pat down the bodies and searched whatever packs he could find on them. In one such pouch was exactly the thing he'd been looking for: a silencer fitted for the rifle in his hand. Immediately he attached it, and something about the whole thing just felt right. "Oh yeah. I could get used to this."

****

January 8th, 2085, 2:22 a.m.,

Repairs to Johnson City were slow in the coming, but they were coming. The fact that the Yaiba and Yoroi factions labored in equal measure pushed things further along than any single force could've done on their own. This was especially true since the KDN bombing had cost so many lives… It was best for Erik not to think about it. Even now he hoped to salvage what was left of his pacifist nature, to look for peace wherever he found it, but the truth of the matter was that they were in a war. The lives that were already lost wouldn't be the end.

His subordinates dispersed the supplies that the Scarlet transports so kindly brought to their front door while Kincaid himself returned to the underground tunnels that the Kabuto prioritized as their home. It was a safe place for them since the destruction of their former territory in the Northwest region. In another few months it would've been two years since… His feet aimlessly strolled the dimly lit tunnel network, past his living quarters, beyond the audience chamber of the Kabuto Elders. He came to a stop and merely stared at the closed wooden door that, at one point, belonged to Nick Resnick.

He touched the door, and the moment his hand rested against it, he felt a rush of sadness. The memory came back again. The chaotic shouts of Violet Shadows, Kabuto agents, and Scarlet Troopers. The failed attempt to defend the wall around the Bluff City outpost. The hail of bullets and the smoking bodies touched by gunfire and Reikiken. Erik had been in the safety of the Hall of Elders at the time, but less than a day later he was given footage of the battle. He'd made it a third of the way through when he realized that one of the troops felled by enemy gunfire was Nick, who fought alongside the Yaiba on the front lines. At first, he'd been impressed that the typically unmotivated

Agent Resnick met the enemy head-on, and for no other reason than to assist his allies.

"Reliable until the end," was what Erik had muttered at the time as tears welled up in his eyes. He'd inhaled sharply, thanked the agent that brought the report of the fall of Bluff City, and dismissed him promptly so he could mourn his apprentice in private. Little had he realized at that time that the mourning would grow exponentially worse in the span of only a month. The thought of everything they'd lost in this war weighed heavily on his mind, but nothing stung quite like losing one of the kids he'd seen grow up, that he'd trained, and that he'd worked with as an equal. For him, Nick was like family, and his loss would forever feel like losing a child.

Erik balled his fist against the wooden door as anger pulsed through his very blood. His pacifist nature and his blinding rage continued to battle within him, which only added to his sorrow.

"You weren't supposed to die yet, kid," Kincaid whispered to the door. A single tear slid down his cheek and only now did he move his hand. "You were supposed to keep growing, supposed to become a man that could be a better protector for our people than I could ever be. You were supposed to overcome that damned laziness of yours." The more he spoke, the sadder and more frustrated he got. He punched the door. "I swear to you, Nick, your death won't have been for nothing. Every Kabuto agent and civilian will know what you gave up for their future. You have my word." He turned away from the door, wiped his face of the drying tears and marched straight for the Hall of Elders. It was time to pull the Yaiba and Yoroi leaders together with the Kabuto Elders. It was time that they all developed a plan to bring this war to a close.

****

January 8th, 2085, 10:00 a.m.,

Al was happier now than he'd been in the few days since their arrival at the Yaiba camp. The more time he spent with these people, the more he realized that there was a freedom to be himself here. Sure, they had to do chores and the training was grueling, but it was all like some fantasy for him. It was as if he'd been transported from their war-torn world into the peak fiction he so enjoyed.

"Look at you," Leo teased in between grunts. The containers of freshly boiled and cooled water proved to be a lot heavier than he thought they'd be when he volunteered to carry two at the same time. "All smiles and sunshine."

Al rolled his eyes with a half-cocked grin and told him that, "It's just because I like it here." Of course he did. The first time he had been put on water duty he'd recognized that the Yaiba were more than just a band of soldiers fighting for their cause. They were family, and a family that was notorious for giving to the people around them, whether those people belonged to their faction or not. It didn't take them long to make Leo and him feel like they'd always belonged. It was the kind of thing to cause his breath to catch in his throat.

"Makes sense," Leo agreed. "These people make you wonder what you did before they came along to save you." It was a question that Leo thought about often now, but that had more to do with their glorious array of tech than it did their personalities or mannerisms. He couldn't get enough of playing around with the full set of Hanzo Gear. The sword styles they used looked awesome in practice, the way those chain things worked in tandem with the repulsor boots to give the user a unique flight pattern was captivating, and all the extra gadgets that went into each of those suits made it hard to believe that these people were slumming it in the post-Civil War ghettos with the likes of the Waste Raiders.

"Right? It's not like I have any objections, though," Al responded, suddenly pensive enough to cause a concerned raise of eyebrow from Leo. Before the onyx-skinned giant could ask what that was about, Ryan Morrisey gave the Waste Raiders the freedom to collect their rations of food and water for their families. Before long, both of the boys were too busy with their detail to talk, and mostly made pleasant conversation with the people of Yorktown as they approached for service.

Al was starting to learn the names of the people he served, and was far ahead of Leo in terms of matching those names with the faces. There was an ongoing competition between them that started when they were looking for food together only hours after they met three months ago. Leo had no idea where Al had come from or why he'd ended up in Yorktown, and he didn't care. Something about having him around reminded him of when his little sister was… He shook the thought off and glanced in Al's direction, coincidentally at the same time that Al glanced in his.

"There you go, Mrs. Jenkins," spoke the younger of the two boys with so much smugness that Leo couldn't help but grimace. Mrs. Jenkins, a middle-aged, ivory-skinned woman with brown hair and green eyes smiled at him with a slight giggle at the obvious competition between the two. She took her water and moved towards the food stations.

"Happy to help, Mr.…" Leo felt a single bead of sweat drip down the side of his face as he looked at the startlingly thin man with pale skin, dark eyes and shoulder-length brown hair. "Don't tell me, I swear I know it." The man raised a well-humored eyebrow at him and did nothing to mask the smile that had taken root in his sharp jawline. "Mr.…No, Dr. Davis!"

"Good job, kid," Hank Davis commended, and clapped Leo on the shoulder as the boy let out a sigh of relief.

"Still taking care of Amnesia Man," Al asked out of curiosity as much as a need to let Leo know he was still one step ahead with the locals. Leo cut his eyes at him, but the doctor flashed a warm, almost paternal smile.

"Yeah," he confirmed as he gathered his water rations and started to exit the line, "But I told you already, his name's Bill. He's actually in line for the food rations if you want to meet him."

"Uh, yes," Leo assured him with a boyish smirk that detailed his excitement.

"That's really great and all, but you guys are holding up the line," came a feminine voice from behind him. Dr. Davis smiled apologetically and promptly removed himself from the line.

"I'll be right back," he said to the boys. Before he left, he turned back to them quickly and said, "I really admire what you're doing here. We really appreciate it."

Then he left. When he walked away, though, that was when Al noticed the woman that stood behind him. Her clothes were little more than tattered rags, dirt and soot and grime covered her, and her dark brown hair was matted badly on one side. Nobody noticed her just stroll into the Yaiba camp, but Al would recognize that cinnamon complexion and those wild eyes anywhere.

Just like that, Serafina Leyva had killed yet another joy in his life.

****

January 8th, 2085, 10:21 a.m.,

Bill was beyond happy. He was back on his feet, even if things were still a little shaky, and for the first time since he'd woken up, he actually had the strength to move. Dr. Davis had little reservation about putting him to work as soon as he'd regained enough strength to carry some food, but Bill was just happy to be outside of that stuffy room of his. Right now all he did was stand in line and wait his turn to be served, but it was enough. Plus, he reasoned that being around the Yaiba Insurrection's Yorktown-based troops would help jog his memory. At the very least, someone he knew might be there and recognize him.

"There you are," came Hank's voice from beside him. "Oh good, you're next. When you get our food rations come find me. I have a couple of people I'd like you to meet."

"Sure thing," Bill told his temporary caretaker. Hank nodded with a wry smile as the person in front of Bill moved on about their day. Bill turned his head back to the front of the line, and that was when he froze. Before him stood a young man, dark curly hair with a wide but fading smile, faint freckles on his sharp-featured face, one natural brown eye and one mechanical one implanted into his left socket. Immediately Bill recognized this as his nephew, Cal, and suddenly a pulse went through his mind.

"Oh mah gawd," Cal uttered before he was even aware. "Hey, uh, 'Yan Man, can you hold it down for me? I gotta go get my pops."

"Uh, sure," Ryan Morrisey spoke in defeated tone only after Cal had rushed off towards the abandoned warehouse where John usually conducted his business.

****

January 8th, 2085, 10:29 a.m.,

Finally Cal returned with John in tow. The crowd that stood in line at the food rations station was more than a little irritated, and while John's first mind was to quiet their concerns, the reason he'd been summoned proved so much more important. It didn't take him long to spot the man at the front of the line, and the Director couldn't believe what he saw: tall, lean but muscular frame with alabaster skin and brown facial hair that made him seem a lot older than he actually was. It was Bill, Bill Jerrick, the older brother that John had thought was lost to the KDN bombing.

"Bill," was all that managed to stammer out of his mouth. It was soft, but Bill heard it and turned his head to face the Yaiba Commander in Chief. Tears formed in John's eyes despite the stoic look he presented to his soldiers and the Waste Raiders they served. Bill's expression, which had been hardened, pained, even, until now, softened at the sight. He donned a crooked smile.

"Hey, little brother," was all Bill could think to say, and that was enough. John, with no regard for his position as the leader of the Insurrection, rushed to embrace his older brother as the tears finally spilled over. Bill staggered, his strength still in recovery, but returned the hug as tightly as he could've.

"I thought we lost you, too," John choked out. In that moment, in Bill's eyes, John wasn't the Head of State for the Yaiba Insurrection. He wasn't a Lightning Dragon, a husband, a parent or anything else. He'd reverted to being a little boy who was so scared of losing his loving big brother to the horrors of the world. Bill held him tight, and for a while he didn't say anything or try to quiet him down. He just let John vent as best as he knew how, and it took a lot for him to keep his own emotions under control.

"You can't get rid of me that easy," Bill joked, and John laughed as he pulled back. Bill took a second to scan the crowd for Dr. Davis, only to find him just centimeters behind him. "In fact, I've been busy making friends since I've been away."

****

January 8th, 2085, 10:32 a.m.,

Serafina Leyva stood there just as calmly and unassuming as the peasants that surrounded her. She found that she actually enjoyed talking to the tall dark child, Leo, despite the fact that he was so poor she thought he belonged beneath her boot. Leo, of course, failed to recognize her warrior's acumen and merely saw her pretty face. At least he saw something of value beneath the soot and grime that helped to make this disguise.

Every so often, she would throw a knowing glance at Al, the target she'd been sent for, but said nothing as he shakily served water to the other patrons of his line. This was the part of the hunt that thrilled her so. She loved watching their reactions when they realized she'd caught them, and savored every tremble as they searched their feeble brains for some means of escape that would ultimately never come. He looked at her every so often through eyes that begged her to leave him alone, to forego whatever horrors she had planned for him and all the people connected to him.

Serafina simply ignored his silent pleading. For starters, she was under order of the King himself to apprehend the boy and cause as much chaos as she could. Second, things were finally starting to get exciting. Ever since she heard that old man mention his friend "Bill the Amnesia Man," she was curious to know if it'd been the same Bill from the Seven Dragons of the Violet Shadows, and if it was, she would take his head back to the King on a silver platter.

"Your friend the doctor sure is taking his sweet time," she finally said to Al, who squirmed at the sound of her voice. What a delectable sight to behold, prey forced to wait patiently for the strike that would end them. "I'm eager to see if this 'Amnesia Man' you guys talked about is anything worth looking at." She took a moment to scan the crowd of people and spotted Dr. Davis, who stood shaking the hand of John Hamlin, no less.

Serafina was reminded of the brief scuffle they'd had in the tent just outside of Yoroi Territory, how he'd helped that traitorous Serenity Crawford knock her out and how he'd stolen her prey right out from under her. She would pay him back, all in due time. At least, that was what she thought. For a second their eyes met, and when John paid no attention to her she thought nothing of it. Then he looked back at her, and the realization sunk in that they'd met before.

"You okay, miss?" It was Leo who asked the question, but Serafina offered no response. As John became more indignant toward her, she showed no qualms about showing her own animosity. They would clash yet again, right here, and while there were plenty of those annoying Violet Shadows to help him, she knew that she could enjoy the satisfaction of a one-on-one fight. *This is gonna be fun.*

****

January 8th, 2085, 10:44 a.m.,

John kicked off the ground with his repulsor boots and covered the distance in a single bound, blade alight and hungry for Serafina's flesh. He swiped in a downward diagonal, but she leaned just enough out of the way to dodge. He didn't care; the precision of his initial attack allowed John to just trace back toward her in a sweep at her midsection, but with a back handspring she evaded the attack and established distance.

"Why the hell are you here?" John's question rippled through the air like lightning through a cloud, his voice like thunder, warning from the distance of the potential to strike. Serafina giggled, her eyes full of condescension and her face twisted in a look that, barring the filth she was covered in, would've been otherwise taken as seductive.

"Oh silly me," she started with sarcastic intonation, "I thought it was open invite to anyone in the area."

"The only thing I'd invite you to is an execution," John shot back, a grim expression locked into his face. He tucked a hand behind his back, sunk his weight, and extended his ignited Reikiken straight toward that dirt-covered face of hers.

The corner of Serafina's mouth twitched, and she told him, "I'm game. It wouldn't be the first execution of a Yaiba Director I've attended in the last few months." John's entire body tightened, and the heat from his aura sword rose a noticeable degree.

"You were there?" He demanded through clenched teeth. She snickered as she folded her arms proudly across her chest and, with one hand, toyed with her matted dark brown hair.

"Oh, sweetheart," she teased, "I was the one who dropped the axe." The Violet Shadows within earshot gasped and murmured at this revelation, and John himself was mentally bombarded by a plethora of curses and insults that an inferior kind of man would hurl at a woman. Instead, he resolved to treat her as the enemy soldier that she was and snuff her out instantly.

Serafina hardly had the time to laugh at the pained grimace John adopted when he just appeared in front of her again, blade at his shoulder, perfectly wound up for a calculated slice at her neck. The former Rairyu unwound his arm and the blade flowed towards its mark, but the cunning Scourge leader bent away from the blow. John stopped his blade mid-swipe and brought it down towards her head now, but even that strike failed to connect. It didn't matter. The Rairyu Form had a myriad of hyper-fluid and ultra-precise attacks that no amount of dodging or blocking could escape forever. One such example was the sharp upward diagonal swing that, once again, she narrowly sidestepped. It was annoying, but not nearly as annoying as the smile that lined her jaw. She was enjoying this, and that drove John even further up the wall.

The irate Yaiba Director brought his blade back down the path it had just traveled with a downward diagonal slash that once more failed to hit its mark. Serafina's eyes were elated but somehow relaxed. Her face washed with a layer of sweat that broke through whatever else had been there, and as she turned her waist to face her opponent, she was nearly skewered by the straight stab the John executed out of nowhere. Serafina rolled to the side of the weapon and its master, only this time she brandished a handgun and pointed it at his throat. Her eyes narrowed with childish glee as she pulled the trigger.

John leaned out of the way just a second before the bullet to exit the chamber and used a twist of his hips to sling the edge of his firesword into Serafina's firearm and spun out of the way. He was shocked to find that there was no resistance from her when he knocked the gun away from her, but then it made sense. She didn't think the bullet would hit its target, she only needed him to think that so that she could run away. John's eyebrow twitched with a new level of rage

"GET OVER HERE!" He yelled it in a thunderous voice that caused all of his subordinates and the visiting Waste Raiders alike to shrink back, and the sound that followed was that of the snake-like chains of the kyoketsu-shoge as they slithered on the wind. The blade of the extended chain locked into Serafina's shoulder, and with a canine yelp she was slowly pulled back across the dirt, gravel, snow and rubble beneath her. She lost her balance, and when she turned her head the only thing she could see was the bright orange glow of the Reikiken down by its master's side.

The wily Scarlet Scourge member decided that this was perfect, and that she wouldn't fight the pull of the chains. She ran at John now, a hand firmly on the chain that protruded from her shoulder. The snow near him started to melt. She had to be more careful as she approached, otherwise it would all be over. She only had one shot at this, one chance to get away, and something about those odds made her salivate like a dog with a steak in front of it. John swing his sword at her abdomen again with the hope that he'd get the satisfaction of watching her burn in half, but to his surprise, as well as that of the onlookers, she vaulted into the air and flipped over his head. The added twist at the end was enough to sling the slack of the chain around John's neck, and surely the pull he felt come from her end would've been enough to crush his windpipe had he not been smart enough to grab the chain before the constriction.

"Uh-oh," Serafina breathed as she placed her back against Johns and started to bend. "Looks like I touched a nerve. But hey, you wanna know a secret that makes this whole situation a hundred times juicier?" She took a second to collect her breath as John fought back, and felt the tug of the titanium blade in her shoulder as it pulled away from her little by little. She jerked the chain, not to strangle him, but to make him fight harder to get free and, by extension, withdraw his weapon. Serafina scanned the crowd again, and as if on cue, Serenity Crawford walked up to the water station just a little ways behind Bill and Dr. Davis. The Lady Leyva's lips curled into a wild smile that reminded the former Scourge leader just how crazy she was, and then whispered into John's ear, "Your friend Serenity knew all along that I'd killed your dear sweet Emiko. But more on that later." The wave of anger that washed over John was the shock that he needed to pull himself free of Serafina's trap, but when he did so he also pulled the kyoketsu-shoge free of her shoulder.

The Director swiped at her again and again, but even with a massive wound, Serafina was agile enough to dodge. She bolted towards the cracked wall that surrounded the Yaiba camp, and with a final wave to say, "Goodbye," she slipped back into the ruins of the city.

****

January 8th, 2085, 2:47 p.m.,

It took a while to get back to the Scourge, but Serafina managed. In all the time since her little tiff with John, her smile never faded. The search details he'd sent after her were an added delight. It felt like she was playing hide and seek. She won, obviously, and when it was clear to her that the Insurrection had given up the chase, she took her sweet time getting back to her teammates.

She walked through the door of the abandoned restaurant by the pier that once served the Yaiba their tungsten from Gansu. The place was dank, and the putrid smell of a bygone era wafted through the air. Even still, it was a place that nobody would think to look for them during this operation. A few tables remained from when it was a serviceable establishment, and row after row of chairs stood stacked on top of each other against the wall, save for the open spaces where the Scourge members had pulled seats for themselves.

"I'm home, ladies," Serafina shouted into the worn-down building. "I bring you greetings from your former boss!" Kerri Waldheim, the knockout of a brunette with the twin pistols at her hips glanced at her leader for a moment, and in her usual apathy shrugged the comment off and turned away. Cecelia Kant, the voluptuous blonde with blue eyes, full pink lips, and a metal hand, visibly grew disgusted at the mention of the former head of the Scourge. Aria, the woman with the semi-dark skin, black lipstick, and straight black hair, was the only one to approach.

"You look like you had fun," she joked with the full extent of her sarcasm. Her eyes fell to the slightly frosty hole in Serafina's shoulder.

"I certainly did," said the Scourge leader. "More importantly, the mines are set around the Insurrection camp as instructed. I don't see why we were instructed to use those instead of the standard-issue mines we use for everything else."

"We're using those," came the came the voice of a strong, pale-looking man with long brown hair and eyes to match, "because the King gave us orders for a very particular field test."

"Hello, handsome," Serafina said with a suddenly sultry tone. "You must be one of the boys." There was a moment of stillness between them, and her lips curled into the smoothest smile the man had ever seen. Somehow, even with the grime, he was captivated by her.

"Argus Wulfric," he said with gentlemanly intonation, "of the Scarlet Streaks. We came up with the name on the way over. I see that you're more than familiar with what we were going for with that, though." He gestured to her wound, and more accurately the streaks of blood that ran down her arm.

"Funny," she admitted, then placed her hand at the base of his neck and pulled him close. She could feel his muscles tighten as her hand slowly moved from his neck to his chest, then traced his arm until her hand rested gently in his. She met his eyes as invitingly as a seductress, and lowered her voice to a faint whisper. "How exactly are you going to level the playing field against the Hanzo Gear?" She was close now, just centimeters away from his face, and she searched his eyes for any lack of resolve that would've justified her taking his life right then and there. Cartwright, Kilpatrick, Crawford, and the Oppenheim brothers all emerged from the shadows around the room, undoubtedly a flex of their proficiency.

"All in due time," Argus spoke softly as he leaned closer still so only she could hear his response. "I think you'll find that I have a lot of things to show you." She pulled away from him in shocked excitement, and caught his wink as he passed her by.

Chapter Five

January 8th, 2085, 5:37 p.m.,

It'd been hours since his confrontation with that woman from the Scarlet Scourge, and still John felt uneasy. He'd battled them time and time again in the past, and he was wise enough to know that where there was one member of the Kingdom's death squad, there were likely others. Worse still, the Scarlet Scourge had always traveled with anything from a platoon to a brigade of enemy troops if the situation called for it. Cal's assault on the Kingdom Drone Network shortly after they'd gotten it back online was probably enough to cement their status as a threat, and it was possible that their presence in Yorktown was taken not as the search for Bill that it had been, but as an audacious attack after having taken so many casualties. No wonder that Raider came and told him of an impending enemy attack if they don't pack up and leave. The King felt threatened, and that was highly unusual.

He didn't like it. There was too much caution in whatever this was to be the devising of King Shane. Something wasn't right, and John had no way of knowing what it was. That was why he ordered his troops to start shutting down the camp. They were to leave at first light in an attempt to escape whatever battle the Reds were wont to entertain, and it would've been sooner had Bill not brought someone that John just had to meet.

"So," started the Director, which indicated his emergence from his own tumultuous thoughts. Bill and his guest, Dr. Hank Davis, sat before him and Cal Richmond, Ryan Morrisey, and Serenity Crawford stood guard at his back. "I don't think we got to finish our conversation earlier, but Bill tells me that you're the man who saved his life. The entirety of the Yaiba Insurrection is in your debt."

"Perfect," Hank responded with all the bluntness in the world. "Then you wouldn't mind supplying us with a battalion of your best troops." John was taken aback by the straightforwardness of the request. For a moment he thought the man to be joking, but the stern look in the doctor's eyes assured them all that he was all business. He couldn't help but groan. John hated politics with every fiber of his being. *Emiko,* he thought, *I know you're dead and all, but I'm still mad that you left this job to me...*

"Make no mistake, I'm grateful for what you've done for my brother, Dr. Davis, but don't you think this is a conversation better suited for your community leader?" The sincerity of the Director's question was met with a knowing chuckle from the Waste Raider doctor.

"You're looking at him," Hank replied. "Being one of maybe three medical experts in this region tends to carry a lot of sway with the commonfolk. So now that you know my 'secret identity,' shall we get down to business?" John gave him a curt smile as he rested his arms against his seat.

"It would be difficult to oblige your request, you understand," John attempted to reason. It was the truth. The casualties from the bombing were still being accounted for from the Roan Mountain base to Jackson to Atlanta and everywhere in between. Maneuvering a force of 300-1,000 troops from the mountain base to the coast would be a challenge. Dr. Davis merely nodded.

"Difficult doesn't mean impossible," he said frankly. John let out a sigh.

"Alright, then," the Director started up again, "what would it benefit the Insurrection to give you what you ask for? Surely you can't think that patching up one of our members is enough of an exchange."

"Of course not, sir. I'm not stupid. But consider it an invitation for occupation. You gain territory and get to restrict the movements of the Scarlet Kingdom. We get protection, and in exchange we'll give you all the secret workarounds for navigating this part of the Wastes so you'll always have the edge on our enemies."

John's brow perked up. "'Our?' That's news to me, considering that the Waste Raiders haven't wanted any involvement in the fight against the Reds since the end of the Second Civil War."

"Well look around, Mr. Yaiba Director," Davis snapped, a much bigger fire in those staggering dark eyes. "Sixty years ago we raged against a government that abandoned us and got the hell kicked out of us for it."

"We did too—"

"Except you had engineers to give you Hanzo Gear. We had outdated guns they don't even make ammo for anymore. You could continue the fight at your leisure, but we had no choice but to stay out of their way." A hush fell upon the room. John didn't know what to say, and Hank knew he needed to calm down. Rage was hardly welcome at the negotiation table. "As you can see, that didn't work out either. My people are scared. Those that are alive, that is. The ones that can move are doing everything they can to help the others survive but we've got more people wounded than I can shake a stick at."

“I understand.” John was silent for a moment and reflected on all that was said. It would strain his forces a bit, but surely Kincaid and the other Helmets would be happy to fill in the blanks during operations. It might even give them the kind of unpredictability they would need to turn the tide against the Reds, especially once the Yoroi were able to join the fight. “Would three hundred Shadows work for you?”

“Absolutely!” The Doctor was more than happy to take what he could get, and John was relieved that he could get away with giving him all the bodies he could spare.

“Excellent. Then we’ll be concluding our business for the evening. You’ll have your battalion upon our return to base,” John assured him, and the two leaders shook hands.

“Lookin’ forward to it,” said Hank, then left at Ryan’s urging.

“We should finish departure preparations before the temperature drops too much. We’ve got an early morning tomorrow, so the sooner we get this stuff out of the way and head to bed, the better off we’ll be.” The Director stood and made for the exit.

“John, I—” Serenity started, but a single glare from John made her fall silent.

“We will discuss what happened earlier at a later time, Serenity.” There was ice in his tone, and a tremble of fear shot through the former Scourge leader as she watched him leave.

****

January 9th, 2085, 7:08 a.m.,

First light had come, and the improvised base of the Yaiba Insurrection was no more. For the most part, everything had been packed in a transport or was attached to personnel, and all that was left to do was leave. A few of the Waste Raiders opted to see the Yaiba off, and to John's surprise there was much more of a crowd than he thought there would've been. That was part of the reason they wanted to get out of dodge as soon as possible. Nothing good ever came of involving civilians.

As soon as that thought crossed his mind, that was when the screams started. Something had happened just beyond the outskirts of their camp. Immediately he went on the defensive.

"Cal," was all he said, and his adoptive son knew exactly what to do next.

"Looks like some kind of gas," he said, his voice far more serious than John had ever heard it.

"Can you tell what it is?" John felt the hairs on his arms begin to rise even as he asked the question. Cal was slow to answer, but he looked as though he had an idea.

"At first glance it looks like CS gas, but it ain't normal," Cal supplied. "They must've did something to it." It only took John seconds to process his next moves.

He took to the comms unit in his Menpo mask and immediately sought to command his subordinates. "Violet Shadows, fan out. Gather any civilians you can and take them someplace safe. Do not, I repeat, DO NOT use Reikiken and keep all repulsor activity to a minimum. Seems our enemies are finally making their move." All

Insurrection operatives acknowledged the order and got straight to work. "Cal, Ryan, find the boys and get them out. Don't let them inhale too much of the gas."

"Say less," Cal spoke, and together they were off. Serenity and a few others took the transports and rolled into the city beyond their perimeter, while many more Shadows ran into the growing cloud of smoke on foot. Every second that passed made the edges of the camp harder to see, and while under normal circumstances they would've had the geo-sensors to help them keep track of movements, most of them had been taken offline in the KDN attack. Just when John figured things couldn't get any worse, he heard a loud *CRACK.* The sound of sniper fire resounded through the air, and a trail of fire erupted through the cloud that immediately spread through the gas in all directions. A series of smaller explosions erupted just around the perimeter, and a number of the Shadows were caught in the blast. In that moment, the smoke cleared a little, and a mix of Insurrectionists and Waste Raiders lay in charred heaps on the ground. More gunfire echoed through the panicked screams and scrambled steps. John's fists balled at his side as intense fury overtook him. And that was when five small ovular devices emerged from the smoke that they now pushed away.

****

Serenity couldn't believe what she was seeing. Two tones of smoke, one gray and lifeless, the other black and foreboding billowed through the air. The sporadic flashes of gunfire illuminated the streets and woods on all sides, and somewhere, perched atop a building with a very good view, was a sniper happily picking off the Shadows as they saw them.

She refocused on the task at hand. She was tasked to get the Waste Raiders to safety, and though they coughed and wheezed through the blanket haze, they were still overjoyed at the sight of her. It was a strange feeling. Usually people looked at her and fled because of who she had been up until a few weeks ago. Colonel Serenity Crawford, the fearless leader of the Scarlet Scourge. Now, none of that mattered. She was just a woman with the power to save a people she'd previously left to their own forsaken place in the world.

More gunfire. It was getting closer now, and she'd only just begun loading the Raiders into transports alongside three others. They picked up the pace, but with the injured and air-deprived civilians in their charge, they still could only move so fast. A filtered whistle sounded behind her.

"My, how the mighty have fallen," teased a mask-ventilated Serafina. Serenity turned around to see that her successor had fixed her looks before her return to the battlefield. "To think that at one point you were the Terror of Prevalence, a hero to the likes of our kind."

"Oh, sweetie," Serenity cooed as her subordinates continued their work of rescuing what civilians still had a pulse, "looks like your muzzle is defective. Come here and I'll fix it for you." Serafina's taunting expression shifted to a gravity that would've sent a chill down the spines of any other. Serenity was all excitement as she clutched the pistol at her hip. "What's the matter? Is the spoiled little noble girl not used to being told to shut up?"

“You talk pretty big for someone who lost her station, her family and her life,” Serafina shot back. Serenity took her pulse, eyes off in the distance with all of the pensiveness in the world, then looked back at her opponent with a shrug.

“Well would you look at that? I’m still alive,” she said dryly, and though Serafina couldn’t see it through her former commander’s mask, she could feel the witty smirk rise behind it.

“Give it time,” Serafina giggled, and then they both whipped out their firearms and dislodged a bullet from the chamber. The bullets clashed in midair, and while Serenity was as calm as her name suggested, Serafina raised her eyebrows in total bewilderment, then narrowed them in a devious glee. “See, at first I was gonna kill you quickly. I can see now that I’m gonna have to take my time to do this right.”

Serenity laughed a genuine laugh, her first since she’d abandoned everything she’d ever known. “This is why I never took vacations. You step away from the action even a little and people forget who you are.” Her tone darkened, and before Serafina had the chance to register what was happening, Serenity opened fire.

****

Cal and Ryan quickly found Leo and Al rushing haphazardly into the battle towards the gunfire. It was a miracle they’d managed to even get their Hanzo Gear on straight, but obvious that they couldn’t handle it well enough just yet. “We can help,” Leo protested when they were stopped and told they needed to get on a transport for evacuation.

"You saw what we did before," Al added, but the two Shadows would hear nothing of it. Cal clapped him on the shoulder as he and Ryan started walking the boys towards the vehicle.

"It was dope," he admitted, "but this ain't like it was when we found you." Both of the boys adopted the same disappointed scowl.

"Didn't y'all just see a bunch of people literally just get flamed because of this weird smoke," Ryan asked with more energy than anyone should have this early in the morning and after everything that'd already happened. Nevertheless, he was right, and it didn't take the boys a lot of convincing for them to see it for themselves. "We just don't want y'all to end up like…" he gestured to the broader parts of the city ruins behind them. The gunfire closed in from two different directions, then was replaced by hasty footsteps on their position.

Cal audibly groaned when he recognized the first enemy to emerge. She was blonde and voluptuous with blue eyes and a metal hand to replace the one he'd taken from her in their last encounter. Cecelia Kant.

"Yan-man, get them boys outta here," Cal told him. "I'll hold 'em off." Ryan didn't argue. The gravity of Cal's voice was all he needed to hear, and even the boys were less than thrilled to argue. They fled, and a man of dark hair, stern blue eyes, and a muscular build appeared from around the corner opposite Kant.

“They’re getting away,” the brutish man snapped at Kant, who cut him a nasty look that almost made Cal’s blood run cold.

“So go get them,” Cecelia challenged. The man was content to do exactly that if it meant getting away from such a difficult woman, but before he could give chase, a Lightbeam landed in the path between the aggressor and his intended prey.

“Uh, hold on there, partner,” Cal directed at him. “You just gone ignore me like that?” The man merely glared at him, posture strong, rifle in hand, ready to fight him at the drop of a hat. Cecelia fired a round just past Cal’s ear.

“You mean like you’re ignoring me right now,” the angry Scourge member prodded. Cal raised his eyebrows and shook his head in disbelief.

“Lady, that’s different,” he assured her. “Every time I see you we fightin’. Then you came at me last time like you was tryna ‘Hulk Smash’ me and not in a good w—”

“Enough,” shouted the man. “Let’s get this over with.”

****

The transport came into view and Ryan never felt so relieved. Without a second to spare, he loaded the boys onto it and pat the back of the vehicle twice so that its driver knew to take off. The engine started, and the transport suddenly launched itself through the trees it had previously been hidden behind, destined for the Roan Mountain.

"Fire!" The command bellowed from behind him almost as loudly as the crack of gunfire that followed. On instinct, Ryan repulsed himself onto a tree branch only seconds before the hail of bullets could reach him. There were two enemies, one of which he recognized as the bombshell brunette of the Scarlet Scourge, Kerri Waldheim. The other one was a strong man with dark hair and a set of blue eyes that proved more than a little unnerving to Ryan. They tracked him to his position, and as the muscular man shot at the branch Ryan sat on, the energetic neo-ninja fell backwards off his perch toward the ground.

In the second it took for the Scarlet duo to lower their guards, he quickly tossed a pair of balloons at them before he caught himself on the ground. The enemy troopers fired another round through the unlikely projectiles and were splashed with ice-cold water. They exchanged a glance and smiled.

"Did you really think that splashing us with a little water would do anything?" Waldheim asked with condescending disbelief. Ryan returned their smile as they both took a step forward.

"Oh not at all," he beamed. "But that Shock Pad definitely will." The two of them looked down at the ground, but when they saw nothing, they carelessly moved forward out of spite and overconfidence. "Code 1642, engage." Ryan's smile brightened all the more as a ferocious jolt of electricity pulsed through their bodies, and as they lost control of their trigger fingers, a swift swipe of

Ryan's kyoketsu-shoge relieved them of their heads. He was gone before they even hit the ground.

****

Serenity fired a string of bullets at Serafina faster than her wily replacement could respond to. The new Scourge leader ducked behind a line of long-abandoned cars for cover, and fired shots in return when the ex-colonel relented. Serenity ducked behind an old utility vehicle, pulled the tab from a grenade at her hip and rolled it to the other side of the street. Serafina, whose ears still rung faintly from the previous gunfire, only barely caught the sounds of the metal orb against the broken concrete. She jumped aside to duck behind the fragmented remains of a nearby building's face only seconds before detonation. Black smoke filled the air between them, and had it not been for the gas masks that Serafina wore, she might've been totally incapacitated.

Serenity moved in shortly after the explosion, pistol raised and ready to do its work. Slowly she reached the enemy's position, but to her confusion the Lady Leyva had disappeared.

"Don't tell me that was enough to make you turn tail and run," the eldest Crawford taunted loudly as she stalked the ground in search of the conniving adversary. She turned the corner of the massive slab of brick she'd seen Serafina dive behind, only to be met with a sharp upward push and a kick to the gut as her weapon was knocked from her hand. Serafina extended the muzzle of her own gun and placed it right between the eyes of her old boss, but Serenity dodged to the side just a second before a freshly dislodged bullet could punch its way through her skull.

She gripped Serafina's wrist with one hand as the other slammed into her elbow with enough force to cause a knee-jerk reaction. Serafina dropped her weapon. Serenity, in her motion to kick her would-be angel of death in the teeth, knocked the gun across the street. Serafina rebounded from the kick with a back handspring, then launched a wide spinning kick of her own. Serenity dodged beneath it and bridged the distance in a single fluid movement, then caught her former subordinate with a leg sweep. Serafina looked completely taken aback, a sentiment the only deepened when Serenity crashed her leg furiously into the other woman's midsection.

Serafina spat blood into what was left of the snow, then folded into the ground. The Shadows under Serenity's command alerted her that the transports were loaded.

"Excellent work," Serenity said with an absolute calm that made the downed Scourge leader grind her teeth as she got back to her feet. Serenity rolled her eyes as she told the operative, "I'll be right there." Serafina lunged for her, her movements sloppy and loud enough for Serenity to hear. Crawford sidestepped a punch without so much as turning to face her attacker. She did, however, lower her stance and deliver a sharp elbow to the place in Serafina's abdomen that had taken the brunt of her kick. The breath left her opponent, and Serenity pulled hard on Serafina's hair. There was an unceremonious thud as Serafina's face graced the ground with a collision, and Serenity stood with a brand-new sense of relief and satisfaction as she whispered to herself, "I've always wanted to do that."

****

“Man I hate this,” Cal said in an overly exaggerated tone. “How y’all gone just gang up on me like this?” A loud crack echoed through the city as the sniper, some distance away from him, fired on his position. A Lightbeam immediately came to his defense, and Cecelia raised her brow. “Ay, lady, this don’t mean nothing!” Another crack of the sniper fire and a bullet whizzed through the air that only missed the boy by a hair. Cal reciprocated Cecelia’s expression, and she shrugged in indifference.

She punched the ground with her metal hand and the ground beneath them rumbled just as it had when last they fought. Her teammate, the bulky man with steeled azure eyes that sharply contrasted his dark hair, lost his footing against the Lightbeam that occupied his attention. The androids merely locked in place to avoid a similar disruption to their battle pattern, but unfortunately Cal was not so fortunate. While he was off-kilter, Cecelia and the brute fired on Cal. Fortunately the Lightbeam nearest him erected a shield to catch the bullets.

“Okay, that ain’t even fair,” he said flatly. He hurled a hand forward and the kyoketsu-shoge at his wrist lurched for her weapon. Another blast from the distant sniper and the titanium chains shattered. The force of the bullet against Cal’s weapon knocked its blade off trajectory, and before he had time to respond, another bullet shattered the head of the Lightbeam nearest the strong man. “Hey!” The shout was immediately followed by a sudden blaze of bullets that forced Cal to hide behind the shield of his Lightbeam. He grumbled to himself, then shrugged his shoulders as a wide smile took hold of his face. "Kiringan, initiate 'Weave Mode.'" A mechanical whirr emanated from his left eye as the light in it changed from yellow to purple.

Cal grew more excited by the second, but another shot from the mysterious sniper zoomed past him only barely off its mark. They were moving along the distant rooftops, but only in a limited range. The sniper couldn't move too much, otherwise the accuracy of their shots might be skewed even more than it already was, and if they stayed still for too long then it would've been no major feat to track his position based on the flight path of the bullets.

"You can't hide forever, kid," the man shouted over the gunfire. *Oh, I don't intend to,* Cal thought smugly. He pulled the tab on what *looked* like a grenade but was actually a well-disguised smoke bomb. The sniper was too far out of range at the moment to directly engage, but that didn't mean Cal was out of moves. A purple smoke blanketed the area and shielded him from view. The Reds, both of whom had fallen for the ruse, had ducked out of the way and awaited a more lethal kind of detonation. It never came, but fear washed over them as easily as the smoke as they realized they'd lost sight of their target.

Cal laughed loudly as he ran through the smoke. A gunshot echoed through the air, but was promptly met with Cal shouting, "Weave," as he dodged it. It was amazing. His Kiringan could track the movements of the projectiles based on the vibrations in the air. It was a small sensory feature he'd included in the design, but the difference it made in this fight was huge. He let loose the kyoketsu-shoge, and with the rattle of the chain they fired more shots. Each was met with a "Weave," and a laugh that, through the smoke, proved a little creepier than he'd intended.

He slashed with his chain in the direction of the man, and though they shot blindly in the direction of the sound, none of their repetitious blasts met their mark. Cal's projectile, on the other hand, did. The strong man cried out sharply, then he fell to the ground with a thud. The sound jolted his teammate, who reloaded her rifle and shot in the direction of her teammate.

Cecelia hated this. She wasn't the kind of person who was suited to stealthy encounters, and she definitely couldn't stand for an opponent to turn the tables so quickly. She sighed. Whether the loser over there was dead or alive wasn't her problem. She knew when to get out of dodge, and this was it. Cal himself took the opportunity to disengage, and disappeared into the still remaining shadows that surrounded the smoke with another unnerving laugh and the utmost satisfaction.

****

John watched as the egg-shaped devices dispersed the gas and a familiar frame entered his sights. He was of stocky build and garbed in the signature Hanzo Gear of the Yaiba Insurrection, though the deep violet of the tunic had been replaced with a bloody red. The shadows of smoke and morning cleared from the figure's face, and John's heart twisted in pain as he took in the blond hair, blue eyes, and well-trimmed goatee of one of his oldest friends.

"Bryan," was all he could manage, and the signature stoicism that John displayed on the battlefield even now brought a perfectly sinister grin to Bryan's face. Suddenly everything made sense. The Scarlet Kingdom's change of strategy, their caution and the chemical attack on Yorktown, all of it was too crafty to have come from King Shane, or evermore the Scarlet Scourge for that matter. The fact that they'd so easily managed to work around the Hanzo Gear made it a certainty that someone with an intimate knowledge of Yaiba tech was pulling the strings behind this operation. "So, you've turned traitor, then."

"What? You thought you'd never see me again, didn't you?" Bryan's voice was oversaturated with a playfulness that John didn't recognize. "Or if you did, I bet you thought I'd be the broken, pathetic mess that I was when I left."

"I had hope that you'd come to your senses," John retorted, his voice filtered through a low dragonic hum that emulated thunder between lightning strikes. Bryan's eyes narrowed on his former friend, and with a cunning smile he let his hand drift towards his Reikiken.

"So you think I'm without my senses, John?" Bryan was all business now, and the Yaiba Director noted something much darker had come to the surface.

"I think that Sharon misses you," John replied with more kindness and sympathy than Bryan deserved. "She's been in shambles since you left. First she lost the kids, then you walked away. It wasn't fair to her—"

"So you're the expert on what's fair to me and my family now? Enlighten me on how I *should* respond to the loss of my son! One of my best friends sent my son to his death, and the other one expected me to just forget about it because I 'knew what he signed up for!' Just what about that situation was fair, O Great Lightning Dragon? Impart your wisdom that I may better conform to your narrow-minded, insensitive and ignorantly idealistic expectations!" A silence fell between them. John was at a loss for words, because he knew that Bryan's pain was justified. Just as the former Rairyu thought to ask him to come back, Bryan spoke up again. "I left," he said in a much calmer tone, "because all of you just expected me to stay exactly where I was: childless, grieving, and pretending to be okay with being on the losing side of a fight against a system that might not work for you, but cam sure as hell work for me."

John caught himself. His nostrils flared, his hands shook, and his soul yearned for battle.

"So, what," John shouted, "You're selling your services and expertise to the King of the Reds so you can exact vengeance on the people who supposedly wronged you?" John's question was met with a knowing look. Bryan paced back and forth like a wolf before freshly cornered prey, hand casually atop the hilt of his Reikiken.

"I forgot, you didn't know," Bryan teased, and paused just long enough for John to ask for clarity.

"Know what?" The forcefulness of the Director's question only added to Bryan's delight that the moment had finally come.

"I am the King of the Reds." John was completely taken aback, but then Bryan continued. "As for my plan, you're not far off the mark. I have a lot of power now, and I can think of no better use for it than to take everything away from the people who cost me everything. Oh," he exclaimed with a borderline boyish excitement that, in the saddest way, reminded John of Jaden, "I know! I think I'll start by taking Darius away from you." The grave shift in Bryan's words caused something in John to snap, and in an instant his sword was drawn.

Bryan followed suit, and for the time it took for their Reikiken to syphon the heat from their palms and magnify it, they paced the ground, each with his own target in his sights. The snow beneath them started to melt, and the visibility of their breath diminished fully amid the rise of the heat field. Bryan blinked, and already John had repulsed himself across the broken concrete of the former campground. Bryan only narrowly blocked the strike to his head, but quickly rebounded with a sharp pivot beneath the blade of his one-time friend. John spun out, which established enough distance for him to parry the move through and bridge the gap again with a thrust aimed at Bryan's heart.

Bryan slapped the stabbing blade off to the side with so much force that it caught John off-guard, and carried his weapon around his head and into a downward slash. John sidestepped it and attacked Bryan's shoulder, but was quickly met with a hard shot from his enemy's firesword. They clashed, and the impact sent both blades quickly off to the side. Bryan wasted no time, however, as he shot out one of his kyoketsu-shoge in the hopes of catching John off guard. When John dodged, he whipped the chain around in a plethora of directions to see if his old teammate could keep it up.

John proved to be more than up for the challenge. He sidestepped the first swing, then cartwheeled, then dropped into a back bend that turned into a back handspring, then again into a hasty parry with his Reikiken. He scowled. Distance was Bryan's forte since swordsmanship had always been his weakness, and right now John was being pushed further and further back.

Bryan pulled the chain back only to extend it again, the diamond-shaped titanium blade hungry for the blood of its master's enemies. John pushed it off to the side with the Reikiken and grabbed hold of the tether before it could retreat. He pulled Bryan forward, but the Rabbit of the Divine Wind vaulted into the air with a tempestuous burst from his repulsor boots, aura sword raised high above his head. He brought it down with force, but the overall motion of the blade was guided by a gentle push from John's weapon. John struck at the shoulder, but Bryan slammed his blade into that of the former Rairyu and followed up with a wild swipe at John's midsection.

John evaded with a cartwheel and deflected a secondary shot as he flipped. Once upright, he swiped from Bryan's hip to his shoulder but another hard knock to the side hindered any possibility of a connection. Bryan again carried that momentum around his body and struck at John's again, but was guided off course by a gentle push from the spec ops master. John stabbed for Bryan's throat unsuccessfully, then immediately swung to the left shoulder. He failed to connect with anything more than his enemy's sword, then redirected the flow of his weapon down towards Bryan's right leg, then, in anticipation of another block, at his head.

Bryan blocked again, but before he could do anything further John's blade bounced off of Bryan's and swung in reverse, then upwards towards the Rabbit King's abdomen. John was getting faster, more aggressive, and the more Bryan fought him the more he realized he needed far more training before he could fight John on equal terms.

Still, though, he had other tricks to employ. He jumped away from John and threw out three heat-treated kunai with a blue jewel in the hilt. John deflected each one with relative ease.

"That the best you got," taunted the former Lightning Dragon. Bryan smiled as the kunai emitted a pulse of electricity that shot straight through John's body. The King knew that it wouldn't do too much damage. The Hanzo Gear was excellent at insulating a charge. Still, it would be enough to weaken him, and that was all he needed.

John snarled out of a mixture of rage and pain. His body twitched as he dropped to his knees, immobile but fixated on the single biggest threat to the Yaiba Insurrection to date. Bryan stowed his Reikiken as he kneeled down in front of his friend. He grabbed John by the jaw and stared into his eyes.

"First," he began, "I'm gonna take your son from you. Then I'm gonna take your friends. Then, and only after I've made you suffer to the utmost, then I'll take your life. Until then, do your best to stay alive, John Boy. You don't have my permission to die yet." Bryan stood to his feet, then drove one of them into the side of John's face. That was the last thing the Director remembered before he passed out.

Chapter Six

January 9th, 2085, 2:44 p.m.,

John jolted awake, but the sudden throbbing in his head nearly made him black out again. He willed himself to stand, to move forward from the spot he'd lost to Bryan, and then anger boiled hot within him all over again. As much as he wanted to focus on that and let his fury consume him, John recognized the futility in that line of thought and sought a way back to the Insurrection Compound in Roan. He wasted no time to look around for any of his comrades. Those who had survived the encounter with the Reds had already left for the mountain base, which was really the most important thing.

It took all the strength he had just to move to the cold metal wall of his quarters in the now dismantled camp, and it became clear to him that on his own power he wouldn't be able to get back to base in one piece. He looked up to the sky, more than a little annoyed that he had to call command for help.

"Well, well, well," came the sarcastic voice of Vanessa Duncan, the Kageryu that John had left in charge as his proxy alongside his father, "a transmission over frequency 22597! I wonder what this could be about!" Her voice was loud and overly dramatic so that John knew he was being mocked, though he needed none of the extra help in figuring that out.

"Yeah, yeah," John replied, and couldn't help but smirk beneath his menpo mask. "Listen, I may have run into a little bit of a hiccup."

"You don't say," Vanessa supplied in mock astonishment. "Don't tell me that you, John the great and powerful, need help."

"I do, and you can stop with the sarcasm, you've made your point," he told her with a bit more bite than he'd expected.

"Does that mean you acknowledge that your place is here in command?" She needed to ask the question for two reasons. First, because in all the time since the offset of the Second Civil War and the founding of the Insurrection, there had only been one Yaiba Director to take to the battlefield and she'd died only last October. Second, because Vanessa knew her strengths, and would hardly list working with Dre Hamlin on administrative work as one of them.

"Not at all," John admitted, "and you know just as well as I do what my presence in the field means. Besides, we accomplished our mission to find Bill."

"So he really was alive! Ugh that's such a relief. Now I don't have to keep avoiding Bri or abruptly changing the subject when she asks about him…" John was about to speak but then paused. Vanessa offered nothing else for a long while, and awkwardly shuffled her feet loudly enough on the other end for John to hear it in Yorktown. The Yaiba leader folded his arms, exhaled deeply and tapped his foot against the ground as he sucked his teeth in contemplation.

"You avoided her?" He could feel Vanessa wince from the other side of the comms channel. "You could've at least told her that we were working on it, or that we had a plan to bring him home. She's pregnant, for God's sake! Who knows how this might've impacted the baby?"

"Look, it wasn't my proudest moment, okay? I'm not a bereavement counselor. I'm not even fit to be your proxy," she asserted. John disagreed, as she'd done a wonderful job of maintaining the standard of order within the Insurrection while he took to the battlefield. More than that, he understood where she came from. He wasn't prepared to be the Director, and in many ways their feelings mirrored each other.

"I get it," he reassured her, "you're a warrior. But even still, Bri is family. She deserves to know when something happens. Speaking of people who have a need to be in the know, how do you think Aaliyah will feel when she finds out that I'm stranded in Yorktown?"

"Wait, what do you mean?"

"Exactly what I just said, Vanessa. There aren't too many interpretations for the word." She cracked a smile as she rolled her eyes.

"I mean," she stressed to imply a need for clarity, "how did that happen?" Another long pause. "John?"

"You sitting down? If not, you're gonna want to…"

****

January 10th, 2085, 11:17 a.m.

Vanessa took little time in dispatching another transport for John, though it took all her strength to manage that. Even now, hours later, she hadn't recovered. Bryan Piccio was the King of the Reds? It was all she could do not to scream in utter agony at the betrayal, but John had ordered her to tell no-one. She was to keep quiet about it until his arrival, and fortunately for her that would be any moment now.

She made her way through the Level X command center towards the power-lift on the other side, every step steeped in the mire of her thoughts of Bryan's betrayal. She wanted so badly to believe that it wasn't true, even more to believe that she didn't understand why, but there was no running from the truth. She saw the way he looked back then, when Emiko had told him of his son Jaden's death. She knew that there was no coming back from that, even though she didn't have any children of her own.

Vanessa pressed the button of the power-lift and made her way to the Deployment Level, the place where all personnel would enter or exit. The mechanical whir of the mobile platform was almost hypnotic, and on a normal day it would've been enough to make her lose herself to its music. Today, though, their Director was due to return from the battlefield with pertinent information with regard to the war effort. That exact phrasing was how she chose to focus on it.

The power-lift stopped a lot sooner than she was prepared for, and she emerged onto Level A to a cacophony of noises that characterized life in the Insurrection. Supply coordinators issued transports and salvage equipment to dispatched teams as needed, though since the bombing they'd been given clearance to issue repair equipment as well. Johnson City was too valuable a position to sacrifice for a few scorch marks and shattered buildings, after all.

Senior team leaders went over the procedures for their respective missions with their assigned groupings, some as small as squads and others as large as full battalions. Some of those leaders, the personal apprentices of some of the fallen Dragons, did what they could to help boost morale in the wake of their thinned ranks. Vanessa couldn't tell if it was out of sincerity or if it was an attempt to replace their masters. She supposed, at first, that it didn't matter too much, but when she realized that all this was the direct result of Bryan's backstabbing, it brought her rage to the fore.

The Kageryu made her way through the crowd and kept an eye out for Dre. He'd gone on ahead of her and formed a welcome party from the higher-ranking members of those who had returned from Yorktown. After a moment's search she found him, and he wasn't alone. Bill Jerrick, clothed in a tattered black coat and worn boots, stood in the middle of the crowd and brightened the room with his smile as usual. Vanessa's heart almost skipped a beat and the water in her eyes dripped to the floor before she fully processed what she saw.

She immediately pushed through the swarm of Shadows to wrap her hands around him and rest her head against his chest. The relief she felt was almost enough to shatter her entirely. The losses they took in the last couple of weeks weighed heavily on her. Never in her life had she witnessed so many of her friends' deaths. It made Bill's return so much sweeter.

"I was so worried," Vanessa said with a minuscule shutter in her voice. Her embrace became firmer, and a warm smile seamlessly took its place on Bill's face. His eyes softened as he hugged her back.

"I've been getting that a lot lately," Bill joked, and she playfully slapped him with a smile of her own in full bloom. Dre shoved his hands into his pockets and said nothing. It was a genuinely happy moment, and he'd learned a long time ago to cherish them when they came.

Transport wheels screeched to a halt just beyond the Deployment Level's entrance. The two Dragons turned to face the direction of the sound just as the doors slammed and the Director emerged. He was a reasonably tall man with skin of brown velvet and black hair. His eyes were the tone and texture of melted milk chocolate, but the ferocity in them more than hinted at their sharpness. His body, lean but muscular, seemed more tightly wound than usual, and upon closer inspection of his appearance, Bill and Vanessa could see the barely noticeable tremble of a Lightning Dragon's rage.

The others that stood around Bill and neglected their work found their way back to it while the senior team leaders hastily departed for their missions. John Hamlin moved through the crowd and toward the deeper reaches of the compound. Vanessa and Dre met his stride and followed him back towards the power-lift with Bill close at their heels. He didn't speak, nor did he make any eye contact with those around him. Whether that was his choice or not was up in the air. John's skill in combat, whether it be hand to hand or with the Hanzo Gear, was legend amongst the denizens of the Insurrection, and though they knew he would never do anything to intentionally harm them, people with power provoke if not fear, then a healthy respect of their station and abilities.

"Have the remaining Dragons and community leaders meet me on Level D in an hour, then arrange a meeting with Vargas and Kincaid set for an hour beyond that. I want the Engineering Corps looking over that sword that Al brought to our doorstep, and once Leo and Al are set up on the Residency Level, have them report to Lukas on Level C for advanced training." With nothing more, Vanessa and the others scattered to make happen what had been commanded of them.

****

January 10th, 2085, 12:00 p.m.,

Lukas Bautista was less than thrilled to get two new additions to his class, but that didn't mean it had to show up on his face. He was determined to see what these two could do. From what he could see, they were just as eager to show him.

"Alright," he started, and the previously loquacious class of burgeoning warriors ended their conversations. Leo and Al were surprised by the level of respect given to their teacher, who hardly looked to be any older than them. "We have two new students in the class. Your names, gentlemen." His tone was slightly more playful than it had been recently, and for a moment he was hopeful that his prior optimistic personality would come back. He couldn't help but run his thumb over the hilt of his new Reikibo.

"Good afternoon," spoke the tall one with the short curly hair and smooth dark skin. "My name is Leo

Maximus, I like long walks on the beach, dancing under the moonlight, and winning people's hearts with jokes as funny as I am tall." The class chuckled and Lukas smiled against his will. Al rolled his eyes, and the grin that slid across Leo's face expanded. The giant returned to his spot in the formation and the young man with wavy brown hair, alabaster skin and bright green eyes took his place.

"Hey everyone, I'm Al Westershire," he spoke, somehow more and less formally at the same time. "I look forward to learning all that I can from you." There was a degree of sincerity to his words that made Lukas smile authentically. Al took his place next to a still smiling Leo and stuck his tongue out at him. It only made him smile wider. Lukas paced the ground in front of his two new students, his own smile wide as his eyes flit between the two.

"Nice to meet ya," he extended in as formal a greeting as Lukas would give anyone who wasn't the Director. "I heard that Cal and Ryan ran you through some of the basics of Hikariryu." He spun his Reikibo over his head in a glorious blaze and then extended his weapon hand behind him. "Show me what you got, then." Leo's smile vanished as the two youngsters were caught by a sudden ineffable apprehension. They knew that Lukas was only a little older than them, that much they could tell by looking. They could also tell that his battle experience far exceeded the sum of theirs.

Leo shrugged as he pulled out his Reikiken and adopted the Seigan stance he'd been taught. His arms were angled towards the ground, both hands attached to the hilt of his firesword while the tip of the blade was aimed at Lukas' head. He sunk his weight and straightened his back before he gestured for Al to follow suit. The two boys circled their new instructor, who stood frozen like a statue between them.

They both suddenly lunged at him, Leo from the front and Al from behind. Lukas didn't even need to look at them to deflect their shots. He spun and pulled the firestaff close to his body, one blade high enough to shield his shoulder and head from Al while the other sank low to the ground to protect his legs from Leo.

"Not bad," the teacher said with a smile. "But don't think you can win just by size or number advantages."

"Yes, sir," Al replied, and immediately jumped back when he saw that Leo was charging in. The young giant took wild, uncoordinated swings at Lukas' shoulders, and each time was met with one of the two conjoined blades as the instructor stepped away from the neophyte student. With each deflection, Lukas noted that Leo grew stronger with every attack. *Interesting*, he thought. The boy struck again, though this time he applied enough force to knock the Reikibo wholly to the side.

Al leaped in just as it seemed that the instructor had lost control, but Lukas followed his weapon around and parried a well-executed attempt at a head strike with relative ease. The instructor, with a wide smile across his jaw and a glint of humor in his eye, spun his Reikibo off the parry and thrust towards an oncoming Leo. Leo slapped the stab off to the side under the assumption that Lukas would be thrown off, but the established neo-ninja simply turned with the momentum. One of the blades made contact with Al's abdomen as the other slashed across Leo's chest, and while the Hanzo Gear's heat-treated and shock-resistant clothing shielded them from any real harm, they were both knocked off their feet.

"Well, that was underwhelming," Leo joked as he dusted himself off and stood back up. Al held his hip at the point of impact as he hobbled over to his friend.

"Nah, it was impressive," Lukas told them as he disconnected the two Reikiken and stowed them at his hips. "You did a good job of watching the second blade and your teamwork was better than I expected. Your attacks were extremely basic, though, and I could tell you were having a little trouble with managing the weight of your weapons. The good news is, we can fix that with enough practice. The only question is, do you think this is the right path for you?"

The boys exchanged looks of pure joy, and for a moment they forgot that their training was mandated by the Director. The optimistic evaluation of their new teacher was much more than either had expected, let alone the illusion of choice in the matter, and when they turned back to face him, they eagerly said, "I'm in," with unified voice. Lukas, who finally felt like himself again, smiled brightly as he clasped his hands together with a loud clap. They could tell he was satisfied, not just with their response, but with what they had managed to accomplish.

"Then let's get started, shall we?"

****

January 10th, 2085, 12:24 p.m.,

Sora Kaneuji was more than happy to receive the order to analyze the sword. He'd already been in the middle of it when Cal came in to give him a hand.

"So whatcha find out about it," asked the curious young scientist. Kaneuji was hunched over the weapon, a sharp, curved blade attached to a somewhat boxy guard that shielded its otherwise straight metal hilt. Sora took a moment to respond as he scribbled findings into his notepad.

"Oh, so much," the engineer finally offered with such a giddiness in his tone one would think he'd lost his mind. "This thing is two-toned. The back part of the sword is made of titanium and the edge is T10 steel." Cal's eyes went wide with the implications. The titanium alone was enough to pose a match to the Reikiken, since it was essentially heat-resistant up to 3,034°F. Moreover, it was tougher than most other metals so it could take a solid hit or two. The steel, though, was a mystery to him.

"Why put steel on it if you have titanium," Cal had to ask, which made Kaneuji light up all the more.

"At first I wondered the same thing, but look at the hilt," Sora urged. Cal did as asked and moved closer to inspect the handle of the weapon. What he found was a strange green button attached to the back of the cubic guard. He hit it, and the edge of the blade detached from its back to reveal a complex array of wiring that was clearly designed to funnel an electrical current through its edge alone. "Oh my God…"

"You can say that again," Cal said as he snapped the blade back together. With the right kind of charge, a blade like that could mimic the cutting power of a Reikiken with much greater precision. "Where this come from?"

"This lovely piece of craftmanship came to us by way of those delightful kids from Yorktown. Leo's friend. I think Al was his name," Kaneuji supplied with a rueful smile. "It makes you wonder doesn't it?"

"Yeah," Cal answered, "about where he got it from…"

****

January 10th, 2085, 12:25 p.m.,

John waited a moment for the noise in the conference room to die down. He knew that this would happen as soon as he told everyone the truth about Bryan, but that wasn't good enough reason to keep that information from them.

"What the hell is he thinking," Dr. Anna Dominguez demanded to know. It was a rare show of abrasiveness on her part, as she was one of the most even-tempered people John knew.

"He's out of his mind, Anna," Callan huffed. He didn't know how to feel about the matter since he and Bryan Piccio had never been particularly close, but he'd admired his tenacity on the battlefield and his work in the Engineering Corps after his days as a warrior were done. His loss alone was a major sting to the Insurrection, but his sudden and unpredictable ascension to the Scarlet Throne was more than enough to make his former comrades bitter. The only reason Callan could imagine a person would defect to the Reds was if they were crazy or shallow, a combination he recalled as being the hallmarks of Aria Black's personality.

"But he's not," came the timid voice of Micah St. James, one of the Civil Center leaders. He gripped the hand of his wife Sam for support. He was never one to speak out on anything in meetings like these. He and Sam were comfortable to sit quietly unless something impacted the Civil Center's ability to run smoothly.

"He lost his children, John," Sam added sternly. "Are you saying that if Darius or Cal were taken from you, you wouldn't have acted rashly?" The very question hurt John to even consider, especially when Bryan had made it a point to threaten Darius with the intent to kill. He opened his mouth to respond, but was quickly cut off.

"This isn't the result of some rash decision," Vanessa contested. "Bryan's the new King of the Reds. For him to do that with no noble ties and no lengthy history with them, this had to take some planning."

"Do we know what he's planning?" Bill asked the question to lower the tension in the room as much as get the meeting back on track, and John flashed him a curt but appreciative smile.

"As you all may have suspected, he's different from Shane O'Neill. He doesn't want to bring glory to a white supremacist nation. He wants to get revenge on all the parties he deems responsible for the death of his son Jaden," John elaborated with an impressive degree of composure.

"So literally everyone involved in this war, then," Zayvier Peters, the Tsuchiryu, interjected. "What are the odds he can pull that off?"

"He's already orchestrated the KDN bombing that wiped out half our forces and taken over Kingdom Scarlet," John replied as he interlocked his fingers and rested his lowered head against his hands. He looked up at the people that sat around the table. "Moreover, Manny, Raven and Shonda all passed away in the attack and the Seven Dragons of the Yaiba Insurrection are not currently at full strength." The room fell silent at the mention of the fallen Dragons. Each of them had given their lives for their missions, their families, their friends, and it felt wrong to even suggest a replacement of such heroes. But every person at the table recognized what the Dragons had come to represent. They were more than just legendary sword masters or teachers of the next generation. They were the pinnacle of the Insurrection's military might and the heart of the Yaiba's morale. "I think it's time to discuss how to proceed."

"What do you mean," Callan asked with raised eyebrows. John inhaled deeply as the eyes of everyone in the room fell on him, then exhaled with a new sense of calm.

"I think it's time we replenish the Dragons' ranks. It's time we return to our roots with a selection process," he told them. From their assorted stares and dropped jaws, John could tell that simply filling the open positions was less than an acceptable idea to his fellow leaders. In truth, he wasn't crazy about it either. Since the founding of the Insurrection and the establishment of those titles, the Dragons' successors were chosen by the ace warriors themselves. A selection process hadn't even been entertained since the time of the Founders.

"John," Vanessa started with due incredulity, "tell me you're joking." John shook his head, folded his arms across his chest, and sat with a stern look on his face that openly invited a challenge from any at the table who were brave enough to contradict him.

"I'm not. The fact of the matter is that we need the leadership of the Seven Dragons. They're the basis of comfort and security for our people, and stand to be a major contribution to our Alliance with the other territories," John supplied.

"But won't our allies see us as cold if we replace them so soon? I mean, they were our family," Bill protested, and earned a sharp glance from John.

"Our allies," John started, "are oblivious to our relationships within the Insurrection. Moreover, they're more concerned with our ability to provide military support on the battlefield than they are about our independent practices. Besides, you know just as well as I do that Manny, Shonda and Raven would've wanted us to move ahead, especially if it meant moving one step closer to the world we all envisioned." For a moment there was no further discussion. They all knew him to be right, and with that understanding came a sudden resolve that had been missing in the days since the Reds' attack.

"How do we begin," Zayvier asked. John felt a tingle run through his body, the sign that tension had subsided and a small victory had been won for his fallen comrades as much as for the future of their people.

“This matter was always intended to be settled by the Dragons themselves,” John began to explain. “I submit that the remaining members should stand proxy for their fallen colleagues. Callan, Bill, and Vanessa, as the seniors, I’ll ask you to consider the three best candidates for promotion. Zayvier, as the newest member of the Seven Dragons of the Yaiba Insurrection, you will act as an evaluator of their choices.”

“If that’s the case, I already have my candidate in mind,” Vanessa offered. John and the other leaders looked on her with surprise, but with a gesture toward her, the Director invited her to speak her mind. “I nominate Cal Richmond for the position of Kiryu, Wood Dragon of the Violet Shadows.” The room came alive with murmurs as the others discussed the suggestion. Cal was still young, and hadn’t even been a full Shadow for a year yet. One had to wonder if putting someone so inexperienced in that position would lead the allied forces to question the Yaiba’s sanity.

“On what grounds,” the former Lightning Dragon asked with even tone. The whispers of their fellow leaders ceased.

“Three times, now, Cal has come face to face with the Scarlet Scourge and matched them blow for blow. Two of those times were after he’d lost his left eye in the Johnson City Raid. He may be a bit too bold sometimes, but he’s tenacious and cunning. I hate to admit it, but if he hadn’t disobeyed my orders to stay in the compound, the casualties of the KDN airstrike would’ve been much higher,” Vanessa elaborated.

“The Kiringan is impressive,” Dr. Dominguez agreed. “It was his own design, you know. To think that someone with no formal training could come up with such an advanced example of biomedical tech just by asking me a few questions. I’d say that his genius complements his experiences well enough.”

“That’ll be left to Zay to decide,” the Director reminded. “We should take no longer than a month to decide which individuals will take up the mantles left behind by our late friends. For now, we should all continue to do the best we can to address the fallout of the attack within our community. Meeting adjourned.” The leaders rose from their seats around the table and made for the exit while John prepared his mind for the next meeting.

****

January 10th, 2085, 1:30 p.m.,

The meeting with the allied leaders began with a somber status report. Each group, the Yoroi Alliance, Kabuto Sanctuary, and Yaiba Insurrection, shared the number of their losses following the events of the last month as well as their current battle strength. Each faction was wounded in the aftermath of it all, and the structures that once kept them safe proved to be more of a liability these days.

“Our main problem,” spoke Erik Kincaid, “is that we’re so fixed on fortifying our established territory while the Reds run roughshod over the rest of the map.”

“Fortification is necessary,” Ezequiel Vargas spoke up through the projection at the center of the conference room table. "Without it, we may as well surrender to the enemy now."

"I think what Agent Kincaid means is that fortification means nothing if advancement isn't on the table," John clarified. "It's a perspective that I agree more and more with as time marches on."

"The Yoroi have no need for advancing territory. Not since the Kabuto so graciously allowed our expansion into the Northwestern Territories," Vargas replied. "Right now the Kingdom is at our door, limiting our movements as we speak." It was true that their faction was already a massive one, with the Clusters marking something close to a capitol for their people, but the fact remained that they were still underground, hiding in the caves and rock formations of the Grand Canyon with no hope of moving beyond it.

"Even still," Kincaid uttered through a screen of agitation, "my people have been overly reliant on the tunnel network beneath the surface since Prince Nash nuked us almost two years ago. We need the freedom to familiarize ourselves with the terrain aboveground."

"Both of you are correct," John interjected before the conversation between leaders devolved into an argument. "All of our territories need to be fortified, Vargas. The KDN bombing proved that well enough, let alone your current situation. Expanding the territories would give us a bit of breathing room to avoid being so cornered in the future as well. But I would argue that rather than both of those things, right now we need organization." Kincaid and Vargas sat in silence a moment as they pondered the former Lightning Dragon's proposal, the former from a much calmer position than the latter.

"What do you suggest we do," the Senior Agent prodded with his arms folded across his chest. John leaned forward to place his elbows on the conference table, interlaced his fingers and shifted his gaze between his fellow faction heads.

"First, the Violet Shadows of the Yaiba Insurrection and the Black Smoke of the Kabuto Sanctuary should cycle through joint training. A sharing of technology and battle strategies will reinforce this sharing of intel that we've already got going. After that, we should organize commando units to patrol enemy territory and engage in sneak attacks on major transport routes and Scarlet Kingdom points of interest," John offered, but the other faction leaders seemed less than impressed with his plan.

"This sounds like a small start," Vargas said with a dismissive wave of his hand. "After all this, I didn't think—"

"I wasn't finished, Councilor," John interrupted with a bit more bite than the elderly Yoroi big leaguer expected.

"My apologies," Ezequiel conceded, his tone now much more placative than even he had ever heard it. "Please, continue, Director Hamlin."

"While our commando units stir up chaos on one front, it'll give our major forces the chance to come and assist with the trouble at your doorstep without much resistance from the Kingdom forces en masse," John continued to explain with a nod in Vargas' direction

"During this time, secondary forces would be deployed in relief and recruitment efforts in the Southern Wastes."

"The Southern Wastes?" Kincaid wasn't just incredulous, he was nearly irate. "What makes you think they'll want to help us out? They've only ever been about themselves since the Reds turned on them. What makes you think this will benefit us in any way?" John thought carefully about his reply. He recalled the conversation that he'd had with Hank Davis in Yorktown, how his blunt and brash expression did little to mask the desperation underneath it all. The fact was that the factions weren't the only groups of people who were affected by the KDN bombing.

"One of the Waste Raider leaders asked for our help, and promised us an edge over the Kingdom should we give it," John clarified. "They've already lived in a region that's been a war zone between the Insurrection and Kingdom Scarlet since the end of the Second Civil War, and even after 60 years, they're still here. Adding them to our alliance would be a smart move." The other two glanced at each other, uncertain in the tactic but at least certain of John's credibility as a leader. They nodded their agreement with wary looks, and the Director smirked.

"We'll give it a shot," Erik vocalized. "I just hope you know what you're doing, John." The former Lightning Dragon chuckled in a low dragonic hum that made the hairs on Vargas and Kincaid stand at attention.

"Of course I do," he said, then the image of Bryan slipped into his mind and changed his whole demeanor. "It's too risky for me not to."

Chapter Seven

January 27th, 2085, 9:10 a.m.,

Class was in session, and Darius felt a kind of relief he hadn't known since this mission began back in October. Two weeks had passed since the new trainees entered the program, and while it was rocky at the start, the new troops got smoother by the day. Training preexisting military proved to be an easier task than taking on former civilians like Bobbi, Leroy and their classmates. The initial group made it even more effortless, as they took almost instantly to teaching their new junior students and correcting form when necessary.

At this stage, Darius said next to nothing in class, but the present focus on Hikariryu drew to its end all the same. It was enough to lift a bit of the weight from his shoulders, as it was almost time for the students en masse to choose fighting styles to focus on. All this after less than a month.

The Rebel Dragon sat, knees bent and hands folded in front of his face, on the floor near his usual instructional position as he watched his fifteen former students run the several hundred new recruits through the more advanced drills. The clamor of their blades and voices, the rattle of chains mixed with the occasional boom of exterior bombs triggered by Red soldiers swirled together in such a way that made Darius feel…invigorated. He took to his feet and pulled his arms behind his back as he clasped his hands together and took about three steps forward. His teacher assistants were the first to notice his silent change of position, then each group of new recruits followed suit with their eyes on their Sensei.

The Hanran no Ryu smiled at them as his eyes sped from one troop to the next. They wore Hanzo Gear, much like his own, but as per the instructions of the former Yaiba Director Emiko Ishikawa, the color was an earthy brown to better match their surroundings. Darius lowered his mask and cleared his throat, smile still firmly in place, while his subordinates awaited either the approval or rejection of their exhibited form.

"*Kimi-tachi ga Hikariryu no kata wo kanryou shimashita yo*," Darius spoke in a baritone that swam deeper than that of his father, but echoed a similar note of pride. The group looked at him through a plethora of puzzled eyes, and it was then that the boy remembered that they weren't as adept in Japanese as he would've liked. Not yet, anyway. "You all have completed the Hikariryu form," clarified the instructor. He was solidly impressed with them, with their work ethic, but only showed his delight in them enough to hint at more complex tasks later down the road. "As you can hear," he paused for a moment to allow the sudden detonation of an exterior trap a chance to subside, then continued, "our enemies are a little on the persistent side. Now, by all means, take this moment to celebrate your speedy completion of the first form of our Reikiken combatives program, but bear in mind that we've only got enough traps to last us two more months on the outside and there's still a long way for you all to go. Right now, I'll be demonstrating the other forms to you. Think carefully about how your body works and what you'll be able to do, because by end of day tomorrow, your focus will be shifted to the style you choose." Darius took a moment to survey their faces, the fear in their eyes born from their suppositions that the road ahead would be, at least in the minds of the initiates, far more difficult than they could possibly imagine.

He took center stage before his massive student coalition as his Reikiken blazed to life, and it struck him as odd that he would be the one to demonstrate the forms held sacred by his people. He tucked one hand behind his back, and with a flourish of the wrist his firesword snapped into position before his face and then down again into a neutral stance. “This,” he began anew as a slightly devious smirk crept into place, “is the Rairyu or Lightning Dragon Form. Where Hikariryu intends to disarm the opponent with two-handed, wide-swinging arcs at close range, Rairyu is a one-handed fighting style that focuses on a more fluid but precise, distance-based approach to combat.”

Darius, almost overcome with the elegance of his father’s fighting style, breathed out as his blade spun into a downward strike to the head of his imaginary opponent. He followed the energy into the circle that it created as the blade came down; he stepped forward, and his Reikiken struck at the midsection of another phantom to the rear. He spun and blocked his face with his downward pointed sword as he did so, then struck the shoulder of a right-facing specter before a twist to his body and flick of the wrist cut diagonally through the trunk of another ghost to facing left.

A reversing of the aura sword allowed for an effortless change of stance that saw his dominant leg take the rear while his weapon hand rose above his head. The tip of the weapon itself was angled slightly downward, as if at an opponent’s face while his arm stretched out, almost as if to lure the opponent into an elaborate trap. "Next is the Suiryu, the Water Dragon. Whereas the first two styles are balanced in offense and defense, this style prefers to rely exclusively on the latter. It alternates between a one- or two-handed grip depending on what's best in terms of combat, and like the Light Dragon, it enjoys being close to the opponent."

He suspended his speech as he stepped forward, his exposed non-weapon hand now tucked against his body as the blade moved to block an imagined shoulder strike. He flowed even more freely now as the aura sword swung around to protect a now uplifted leg. In a single fluid movement he blocked his head, spun to the right and flourished his blade into a shoulder block that transitioned seamlessly to a leg block and swung around to another before he pulled the Reikiken up to block his face and midsection. He disengaged his plethora of phantomic foes and pulled his weapon into a seeming shoulder guard.

The Rebel Dragon's sword rested by his side with the tip of the blade pointed straight up, his weight mostly on his rear leg, his arms close to the vest and his eyes somehow sharper than they were before. "Now this one," the Yaiba combat trainer continued, "took me a little while to learn this one, and if I'm honest, it's more my brother's specialty than mine. In any case, it's the Kiryu or Wood Dragon Form, an acrobatic fighting style that does more attacking than defending, and works exceptionally well with the kyoketsu-shoge. This is the one we allow rookies to skip because… Well, just watch," he told them as he smiled at the memory of his adopted brother and best friend.

Darius sunk his weight on his back leg, and without warning sprang into the air. His blade swung out in a wide arc that would've taken the head off of an enemy in a heartbeat, then made a complete circle with another explosive swing. He let his body follow the energy of the motion and turned as his feet met the floor of the training hall. As his face came forward, his blade moved to protect it then shift into one of the fluid transitions of the Water Dragon style he'd displayed moments before. From the back end of the sword's spin came a downward slash that seemingly lifted the Rebel Dragon from his feet and into the air in an elegant spiral. His students watched in awe as for a second it seemed that he was suspended. Then he unwound, and another downward slash cut through the air in a searing gust.

As if that wasn't impressive enough, Darius jumped through the air a second time and paused midflight before he unwound in a sideways sweep of his ghostly opponent's hips and took to the sky for the third time at a different angle. His grip, the students noticed, had somehow been reversed, so when he chopped down and burst into the air, his initial swing was closer than the previous attacks he'd exhibited. The swing that followed saw Darius switch the grip back to standard as it came with thunderous force to the ground.

The Rebel Dragon strained to breathe, but fortunately he drifted far enough from his original position and could catch his breath as he walked back. "I doubt I need to explain why we allow you to skip this one," he joked to the sounds of a light chuckle here and there among his pupils. He made it back to his starting point and with a powerful flex of his martial knowledge, adopted a forceful stance that matched the intensity of the heat of the sword. Darius poised the firesword high above his head, his arms bent, and his feet spread wide in the dusty floor of the training grounds. He was low to the ground, focused, and powerful. "This will be the last one that I show you. I don't want to over-complicate things by giving you too much at one time. This last style is the Tsuchiryu or Earth Dragon Form, and is as powerful as it is grounded. It excels in deflecting blades back on their users and cleaving through them in a brutal follow-up. Watch."

The words had only just left his lips when Darius swung down in all power, then in a fluid motion blocked his head and delivered a barbaric upward diagonal slash. He carried the energy into a shoulder attack, then broke the flow to slide back and position his Reikiken parallel to his face. The tip of the sword pointed at the invisible opponent, who apparently attempted a return strike to Darius' shoulder but was repulsed with a strong batting defense. The Hanran no Ryu followed through with a single-handed downward diagonal cut from shoulder to waist, brought the tip back to the front with aggression, plunged it towards his enemy, then spun it over his head only to strike once at the shoulder with a two-handed attack, once at the legs with a single hand, and then down through the body again in another slanted motion. He followed the energy through and repeated the cut with two hands, broke the flow, then spun the blade at his enemy's gut until it was back over his head in reversed two-handed grip.

The students were dumbstruck, completely at a loss for words in the wake of Darius' display of skill and intensity. Here, in this moment, everyone in the room became so distracted by his power that they'd forgotten his young age of 18. His hazel eyes, passed to him through his grandfather's blood, seemed much older, much more intense, as if the boy had practically grown up on the battlefield. He slashed down to his side and stowed his weapon after he switched it off. With a huff and a smile he stretched his arms wide and leaned back to pop his bones before he returned his focus on his students.

"End of day tomorrow," Darius reminded them with a stern tone. "Make it count."

****

January 27th, 2085, 11:17 a.m.,

The metal trees of the training grounds were raised, the air was tense, and Leo stood across the steel forest from Al as the others in their class watched. It'd been almost a month since their arrival at the Yaiba camp in Yorktown, almost a month since the dawn of their training, and now that they'd proven themselves to be the best fighters in the class, Lukas had them square off against each other. Neither of the young warriors backed down from the challenge, although the presence of the Director on Training Level C was more than enough to make them nervous.

Both of the boys put their shakier feelings aside as they met each other's gaze through the thicket of pillars. Their hearts beat wildly, and the excitement of the moment forced a wry smile on either face as they awaited their Sensei's signal. Lukas raised his hand. Here it was, the moment they'd waited for since the beginning of their unofficial rivalry. Both of them could feel their focus intensify, and when Lukas dropped his arm, neither of them wasted any time.

Al ran left into the metal pillars when he saw Leo run right, and after ten feet grappled into the canopy of the training posts with his kyoketsu-shoge. He'd paid attention these last eleven days and knew that his best bet was to use Leo's weaknesses against him. He latched onto one of the poles and waited in silence. He listened to the sound of Leo's footsteps as he ran along the ground. They were faint at first, but their volume grew and grew until finally, the giant emerged from the shadows.

Leo only narrowly blocked Al's falling head strike, and cursed the day that that boy learned to use kyoketsu-shoge. He blocked his leg as he stepped back to try and reclaim some leverage in the fight, then blocked his shoulder. Al was relentless, but pure aggression wouldn't be enough. Al attempted a slice of the hips, but to his surprise Leo parried it and drove his Reikiken towards Al's face. Al had to take a step back to block the move, only to find that Leo had retracted the blade. Leo moved for an upward diagonal slash at extremely close range and smiled as he did so, because any chance that Al would be able to parry it was incredibly small.

Al parried, though he nearly fell to the ground, a mistake that he'd quickly wished Leo hadn't seen. The swarthy giant took a powerful swing at Al's stumbling legs, and though he was blocked, he attacked the hips just as his rival had done a moment ago. There was so much power behind the blow that Al found it easy to push it away from his body, but was almost caught off guard by the strike at his shoulder that followed. There was no time to block or parry the move, and on a combination of instinct and adrenaline, the shiny-eyed combatant jumped away and deployed one of the blades at his wrist to grapple into the canopy. Leo couldn't help but smile. He grappled after Al, and though Al sought to fight back with a swing of the Reikiken, he was ultimately parried and met with a stiff kick to the sternum by Leo. Al rocketed towards the ground, and only seconds before he landed unceremoniously, he kicked on the repulsor boots to slow his fall. Leo landed a few feet away from him with a big smile locked onto his face.

"Guess that means I win," Leo said with his arms spread and his eyes bright. He walked over to Al, who sat on the ground visibly frustrated that he'd lost this fight, but equally determined to win the next one. The giant extended his hand to help his friend off the training floor, and Al graciously accepted.

"Well done," Lukas said in a playful tone that, since his installation as a combat instructor, his students had never heard. It was enough to make everyone in the room except John feel a little weird. "You guys did a great job!" Both of the boys looked up into the stands where the Director stood with his arms folded and a pleased smile on his face, and at the shimmer of pride and expectation in his stare, they knew that their teacher told the truth. Lukas turned to face the other students, all corralled along the front three rows of the stands, and told them all, "This is my expectation for you all. You may not all be as aggressive as these two, and you don't need to try for that, but please hear me when I say that you need to be as quick on your feet as they were. Make use of the enemy's weakness. Take advantage of openings. Adjust your plan when it goes off the rails, and make no mistake," he paused for a second, though whether from his own rather limited experiences or dramatic effect, it was hard to tell, "it will go off the rails."

"Sir," they all replied with fervor as the Director took his leave. Lukas nodded a silent approval, and walked back over to where Al and Leo stood. Al gripped his gut, and Lukas frowned.

"You should probably go get checked out on the Medical Level," he recommended, then realized that both he and Leo were new to the Insurrection in its entirety, not just new to his class. "Do you know where that is?"

"I think I remember it from the tour we got on our first day in the mountain," Al supplied, mostly through clenched teeth. "I think I can find it."

"Then I'll leave you to it," Lukas affirmed. He turned his attention back to the others and motioned for the next two to get on the floor while Al made for the exit. It was only when the young warrior had made it to the power lift that he stopped faking his injury.

****

January 27th, 2085, 11:42 a.m.,

Alphonse Westershire was a child. That was, at least, what most people thought when they saw him. Back home it was more than a little irritating, but here in the Yaiba compound it was a blessing in disguise. He'd presented himself as helpless and helpful, which proved more than enough to win over the Shadows just as his intel suggested. It was a stroke of luck that he'd met Leo in the

Wastes, and a happy coincidence that together they'd encountered the Director, of all people. They took him in, fed him, clothed him, started teaching him their combat techniques, even made him feel like he belonged… He knew that they would watch him, knew that they would be wary of the random child that came to them seemingly out of nowhere, but he also knew that when they saw him as nothing more than a normal kid, he'd be written off as yet another background character in the story of the great Yaiba Insurrection.

If all went well, he'd accomplish his mission and get out before his cover could be blown. Before he could witness the fallout of his breech of their trust. He thought about how Serafina had nearly done just that when they were still encamped at Yorktown. It was bad enough that she was the reason he was even on such a dangerous mission without her threatening to mess it all up. If anything, Al hoped that he would be put on the battlefield and get the chance to surprise her with his new skills. All that paled, though, in comparison to his real prize.

He made it to Level L, the Engineering Level, and noted the substantial lack of personnel on the floor. There were a number of research labs with countless gadgets and schematics strewn across tables and the work floor, and while all of that was of interest to him, nothing quite appealed to him like the weapon he'd brought through the front door nearly a month ago.

Its codename was Project Thunderclap, a secret weapon of Kingdom Scarlet that could withstand the high temperatures of the Reikiken but dish out an electrical charge with every strike. Al had stolen it from the research facility in New York City as a way to get back at Serafina.

It was his prize, and he intended to take it with him once the job was done.

The door to the workshop's office opened, and Al's heart jumped into his throat. He took refuge behind a giant pod of some sort that stood against the stone wall of the room when he heard the power lift just outside the research lab come to a halt. He didn't know what to do. He needed to figure out where his weapon was, and more to the point of the mission, he needed to figure out a way to get the latest Hanzo Gear designs back to the Kingdom. He couldn't afford not to.

What do I do, Al thought over and over again, frantically. His first mind told him to fight, an instinct he'd developed from his time in the Southern Wastes, but the second the thought crossed his mind was the second that the fight left him for the first time in a while. He truly had come to think of the Yaiba as a kind people. They only wanted to help him, and his means of repayment was treachery. Didn't they deserve better than that?

Al shook the idea out of his head. This was no place, no time to think about something like that. His mind needed to be focused on getting his weapon, getting the intel, and getting out. Sentimentality would get him killed, and realistically, there wasn't enough sentiment built up between him and the Insurrection or him and Leo, for that matter.

"Is someone there," called the wary voice of Sora Kaneuji, who struck everyone he met as something of a mad scientist. His brilliance couldn't be denied, though, which could turn out to be a massive hiccup in Al's mission. The door to the lab began to open, and Al just thought it best to reveal himself.

"It's just me," he said with a hint of nervousness in his tone. "I didn't have anywhere else to go after my checkup, so I thought I'd come in here and look around. Sorry if I bothered you."

"Not at all, my boy," Kaneuji exclaimed with hands spread in pure manic joy. "It warms my heart that a boy your age would take such an interest in our technology! Is there anything in particular that brings you my way or are you looking for a more in-depth tour than what you got before?" Al opened his mouth to speak but was promptly cut off by yet another sudden exclamation from the wily scientist. "Cal! So happy to have you back!" Al turned to see the strong Violet Shadow. It impressed Al that despite all the work that Cal had clearly done in the Insurrection in only the last six months, he was still the tall, thinly built person that he'd been when he started. The artificial left eye added an extra layer of intimidation that he usually undermined with the easygoing personality of a jokester.

"Just wanted to work on the Apollo's Star some more," he replied, his tone as breezy as it always was. His eyes, however, betrayed his sense of suspicion.

"That's one of your Lightbeams, right," Al had to ask, partly because it was of interest and partly because it diverted attention from his actual intentions. "I've been hearing about those things since I got here and I've been curious about how they work."

"Is that right?" Cal's response was unusually short, almost to point of irritation? Al couldn't quite put his finger on the projected emotion. "That's gone have to be some other time. Work comes first, conversations later."

"I can fill you in," Sora interjected. "Who knows? You might get the itch to come and fiddle around with tech yourself." The suggestion made Al's ears perk up.

"Would that really be okay?" The shock in his voice was genuine. He'd thought about deepening his relationships within the Insurrection, even forming new ones with some of their key leaders. Their inherent kindness, though, made him wary of such a manipulative tactic. He liked them, and even though he knew that he was doomed to hurt them, he wanted to avoid twisting the knife any further.

Kaneuji smiled as he clapped the boy on the back. "Of course! And don't worry about experience with Yaiba tech. I'll teach you anything you need to know." Sora ushered Al deeper into the lab, and while the boy felt a great relief wash over him, Cal still couldn't shake the feeling that something was off with him.

****

January 27th, 2085, 1:04 p.m.,

Ryan Morrisey couldn't stop shaking. He'd spent the last two weeks and change working with Callan Rouge and Esau Tillman to strengthen the coordination efforts of the Yaiba and Yoroi. It was an enlightening experience, and on top of giving him new perspective on old Reikiken techniques, it also gave him a front-row seat to the technology of their allies. The stealth tech was so cool to him, and filled him with all kinds of fun ideas for the battlefield. The excitement that he felt after the debut of the Nightshroud Filter, a plate-like fixture to the Hanzo Gear and the Kabuto's shinobi-adjacent attire that mimicked the ShadowStalker tech in more versatile ways, paled in comparison to what was about to take place. After Ryan spent the last few months learning the ways of stealth and further refining his combat strategy on the battlefield, he felt that this moment was long overdue.

He looked around at the crew that journeyed with him on the transport. To his left was Isaiah Parkman, a tall, skinny, fresh graduate of the Violet Shadows training program with an even temper that would serve him well on the battlefield. His brown eyes, brighter than his chestnut colored hair, mirrored the sense of anticipation that Ryan himself found difficult to suppress. He was a strong kid, one with a lot of power and a whole lot to prove.

At Ryan's right side was Tez Johnson, a young man of chocolate complexion, dark hair, and deep brown eyes. His build was lean but strong, not unlike the others on this excursion, and while his height made him more imposing than he knew, his laid-back attitude towards life made all in his company more than comfortable with him. The reason he was on the team, though, was that he exhibited an unusually high proclivity for combat, especially since he was of the formerly pacifistic Kabuto faction.

Directly across from him were Hector Rubio and Diego Cruz. The former was a Kabuto rookie just below 5'2" and had a nasty combat ability that hardly matched his kind nature. He was, at least in Ryan's mind, the best example of the model Kabuto. The latter, though, was one of Ryan's best friends from his training days, someone he hadn't seen since the morning he was selected to assist

Callan Rouge at the Bluff City Outpost. Cruz was a markedly handsome young man with brown sugar skin that matched Hector's, deep brown eyes, a strong build, naturally inquisitive expression, and slick black hair that rested flawlessly on top of his head. While the one was nervous about what this endeavor would entail, the other treated it as any other day.

At the wheel was the excitable Kabuto rookie Aaron Stone, someone with as much skill as any warrior that Ryan had ever seen, but (thankfully) was so unorthodox that he could distract anyone from the task at hand. Even as one of his feet manned the pedals of the transport as it rolled down the long-abandoned roads, the other tapped away as a sign of his energy boiling over from expectation.

Ryan rubbed his hands together as his mouth took the shape of a big smile. They were the first commando squad of the new coalition, and as they drew nearer to Penn State, each of them thought about what the Kabuto Sanctuary had done just a few months ago. They'd incapacitated the sum of Scarlet troops stationed at the former college, sabotaged an array of advanced technology, and uploaded a complex virus to the Kingdom Drone Network. The job of the commando squad, though, was to survey the current patterns of the Reds' movements.

The transport came to a stop at the back of a building labeled, "Alde Mmons." It was, at one point, an abandoned apartment complex that rested just a little beyond the old college campus. Now it stood as a safehouse for the commando squad, a makeshift base of operations while they spied on the Reds from right under their noses. They hastily disembarked the vehicle and entered through the rear door of the building, each man carrying what supplies they could. Not a word was exchanged until they were safely tucked away. The handheld generators were deployed along the walls, and once their equipment was solidly charged and ready to go, Ryan rehashed the plan while his squad got to work. He took a deep breath as the nerves slowly started to fade away. This was going to be a lot of fun.

****

January 27th, 2085, 2:22 p.m.,

"Understood," John spoke into his comms unit. With the first commando team in place, there was a little less that the Director had to be concerned about. The second team was due to deploy in three days, and just as in the days of old, it would be spearheaded by himself. The next encampment was set for Fayetteville, a medium-sized town along the old Interstate 95 that once served as the largest military hub in the United States. It'd been a long time since John got to lead a covert mission in that area of Prevalence, and it made him overwhelmingly excited to step out onto the battlefield as the soldier that he was.

"You got a minute?" Bill had found his way into John's office, a grave expression on his face. John nodded as his eyes shifted back to his comms unit.

"Proceed as planned. Make sure to report back to Vanessa," he ordered, and Ryan on the other end was more than happy to offer his assurance. John ended the call and exhaled, but before he could part his lips to smile or speak or anything else, Bill sat with authority in the chair across from him.

"What are you doing, little brother?" The question was more forceful than he'd intended, but it didn't matter. It echoed the truth of how he felt. John was more than curious now, but only a little cautious.

"What do you mean," he asked of his longtime friend, though he had a good idea of what Bill would say. It wasn't that long ago that John had lost a fight to Bryan in Yorktown, or that Bill was an amnesiac patient in the Southern Wastes. Two weeks wouldn't be enough to assuage his concerns, especially in the wake of Masamune's death.

"Are you really heading back to the battlefield," Bill inquired in an even tone. It was accusatory, menacing, uncomfortable, and John didn't know how he liked knowing that Bill could still make him feel so… young.

"There isn't much of a choice," John replied hurriedly. "That's assuming we actually want to win this war." Bill clenched his fist as his face fell into a kind of darkness that, in all respects, seemed alien to them both.

"There's always a choice, John," Bill argued, his voice as dragonic as his name. "We've raised a number of exceptional warriors—"

"Half of which have already been taken out by the KDN bombing," John rebutted sharply. Bill's eyes narrowed on his brother as his anger reached a boiling point, but he did what he could to calm himself. He knew better than most how frustrating it could be to deal with John Hamlin, but he also knew that responding from frustration would only come back to bite him.

"Even so, there are more than enough that are left over who can manage the simple task of running an operation." John gave an exasperated sigh as he folded his hands together in front of his face.

"You know that it's a lot more complicated than that, big brother," he said just as calmly. "We're not fighting arbitrary skirmishes anymore; we're fighting a full-scale war. The things we used to do to survive won't be enough to cut it, especially since Bryan is running the Kingdom now. If we're to stand any chance of winning, we have to hit them as hard as we can as strategically as we can."

"But you still have the help of the Kabuto and Yoroi for that!" Bill couldn't resist the urge to yell, and John was forced to close his eyes for a moment, lest he react to the sound of pure desperation in Bill's voice. "Why is it necessary for you to be at the center of this?"

"I'm the one who worked with Bryan the most, brother, and you know that already. I know how he thinks better than anybody in the Insurrection, and even besides that, I'm the best fighter we've got," John attempted to explain, but Bill shook his head.

"Don't forget, that you lost to him just a couple of weeks ago, Mr. Best Fighter," Bill shot, and John sat in his chair, his hands dropped back to his desk and his eyes as sharp as a hawk on the hunt. The intensity of his glare compelled Bill to apologize, and then told his brother, "I just want you safe, little bro. I lost my dad," he choked on the words, "and I don't think I could handle losing you, too."

"You won't," John assured him with the softest understanding in his voice. "But you have to understand that I also have to do this. This isn't like it was before where the leaders of the factions could sit things out and let their subordinates take the brunt of the enemy forces. To make matters worse, Bryan is targeting Darius specifically because he knows it'll break me." The shock broke through the anger and sadness that previously made his face sink, and then a rage overtook him that John had never seen before.

"Well that won't happen," Bill growled as every muscle in his arms, back and chest tensed. John was a little more than wary of his brother's current state. "I'll see to the boy myself. Give me a battalion and I'll head out first thing in the morning." John couldn't disguise the mix of concern and fear that washed over him.

"Now hold on," he told his elder brother, "I already have a plan. Don't forget that Darius has more than proven himself capable in both battle and strategy."

"You know that doesn't matter to me, John. That's my nephew. Besides that, Bryan was one of few warriors from the Yaiba Insurrection that could rival the Dragons. I think it'd be best if I was there to watch his back." Bill was, perhaps for the first time ever, completely devoid of the laid-back, pleasant demeanor that he always exhibited. Regardless of how he came off right now, John understood his seriousness. It took everything in him not to head to the Clusters himself. But his presence was more necessary on the front lines, and while he hated to admit it, Bill was better utilized as the spearhead of the Yoroi liberation. The Director sat in silence for a moment as he thought it over. There was still a good two months left before he predicted the Reds would make their move, and Darius could more than handle the Scarlet threat on his own. Still, with his limited numbers it was a massive inconvenience to have a prolonged battle against an enemy that, despite the Yaiba leader's earlier point, collectively had more battle experience than his beloved dragonling.

"You're right," John was forced to agree. Bill cocked a half-smile that radiated something between smugness and lethal intent. "You'll be the one to lead a battalion of troops to the Yoroi's front door, but only after the Reds have kicked it down."

"Wait a minute," Bill said as the smug smirk dropped at the furrow of his brow, "by the time that happens he could be dead—"

"You'll deploy in two months from today," John continued in a pensive calm that sent Bill even further over the edge.

"John, are you listening to me?"

"I heard you loud and clear, big brother," John replied. "I already told you that I have a plan. All you need to do is take this time to relax with Bri. Recover, and make sure you keep a close eye on what goes on around here. You'll be picking your troops yourself." Without another word, John walked away.

Chapter Eight

February 3rd, 2085, 6:46 a.m.,

Ryan Crawford sat quietly on the sofa in the red and black living room of his childhood home as he pondered what he might say. His father, the long-retired Sergeant Alan Crawford, entered the room in more surprise than joy. In truth, the sight of his youngest child startled him, because of course the boy would just enter without announcing himself.

"You kids really need to learn to knock," he told his son in a gruff, barely awake voice. "Thought I taught you better." Ryan offered a sheepish smile that did nothing to break the seriousness of his father. "Any news from your sister?"

That one question shook Ryan with more emotion than he came in with. He knew she'd defected. More than that, he knew that she now worked alongside the Yaiba Insurrection to take down the system that would keep her from her happiness. How, though, was the young sniper to tell his aging father that his little girl had betrayed everything that they'd known? What would Alan's reaction be? Would he have a heart attack? Would he go into a rage? It was too big a risk to tell him, and yet it felt like the weight of a solar system to keep him in the dark. He fixed his mouth to speak, but no words would come out.

Alan sharpened his eyes on his son, but at the quiver in the boy's hand, he let it go with a shake of the head.

"That girl," he said. "I wish she would keep better contact." He went into the kitchen to put on a pot of coffee. "You want a cup?"

"No thanks, dad," he called back to the elder man. Ryan clasped his hands together and sank into the depths of his own thoughts. He didn't like where he was in life. It'd been nearly a month since his promotion to Commander of the Scarlet Streaks, and in that time the Streaks had lost the Oppenheim brothers. Their capacity for infantry had been reduced in its entirety with him as the only dedicated shooter left on the squad. Despite his failures, King Bryan dismissed any notion of his resignation and refused to void Ryan's position as the leader of the new death squad. The whole situation made him uneasy, as if he was being watched for some reason.

"She's gone, isn't she?" The solemnity of Alan's voice dragged Ryan back into the present. The elderly sniper came back into the living room with two cups of coffee despite his son's earlier protestations, and set them down on the table between them. Ryan picked his up, not to drink, but to have something in his hands to fiddle with. He thought about what he would say, but the painful drum of his heartbeat kept him quiet. "I knew it," Alan continued. "There's only so long you can fight a war before you either get sent home or torn apart…"

"She's not dead," Ryan spoke. It was like an out of body experience; his mouth just moved on its own despite the resistance of his mind and the sudden strain in his chest. "She defected to the Yaiba Insurrection with Prince James." He finished speaking, and the panic that he felt only escalated as his father's silence permeated the room. His hands shook, his body had grown numb, and while he was worried about what would happen to his father in this moment, he was equally concerned with what would happen to him. But then, something truly unusual happened. Alan Crawford smiled a warm, wistful smile.

"That's my girl," he spoke to himself in the loving tones of a proud parent. Ryan sat in confusion.

"Dad, didn't you hear me? She's a deserter!" All of the anger that he'd felt before drowned in a sudden whirlpool of rage. Alan's eyes became as sharp as ever, more serious than the boy had ever seen them, and he knew that beneath the façade of retirement the expert sniper remained.

"And you knew about it," he stated calmly with a single uplifted eyebrow. "Tell me, my boy, how long has it been since she left the Kingdom?"

Ryan hesitated to give his answer, but finally told him, "She's been gone since the end of December." Alan's smile grew wider in a way that made his son grow in his discomfort.

"That's my boy," he said with authority as he pulled his son into a tight hug. The confusion was back, and Ryan had a hard time processing the fact that this was the attitude of one of the most celebrated war heroes since the United States reorganized as Kingdom Scarlet.

"How are you okay with this," Ryan demanded as he pushed his father back. "You always taught us the dangers of the Kingdom. Hell, you *showed* us the footage of the public execution you witnessed when you got back from the front lines!"

"So you could know what you're up against, son, never so you could bow your head," the old man stated flatly. Ryan couldn't speak. He didn't have the words. What his father said was preposterous. It was almost as if he *wanted* his children to rebel. Alan noticed the look of incredulity on his boy's face. "This place is corrupt beyond compare; a breeding ground for monsters—"

"Stop," Ryan begged, but his father continued.

"I didn't notice how bad it was until after my life was spared by the one they called 'Rairyu.'" Ryan shot to his feet at his father's admission, his eyes aflicker between cold and distraught.

"You—" the nervous shake in his voice was enough to pierce the old man's heart and shock the boy into something less telling of his uncertainty. "You realize that I could report you right? For all of this?"

Alan sighed and, for just a moment, closed his eyes to collect his thoughts. "You could," he said, "but you won't do that. If you were really the kind of person to turn on your family like you're suggesting, then you'd have already ratted out Serenity and she'd be dead." Ryan hated that it was the truth. He sat down. "Now," the veteran sniper continued, "do you want me to tell the story of that night or not?" Ryan sat there, confronted with the truth of the White Ruins Massacre, unsure of whether or not it would forever damage his view of the man who raised him, the man he sought to model his life after. He chided himself for being so loyal, because even in the moments after the revelation of his father's treachery, he refused to shut him out. The boy clasped his hands together, stared Alan in the face, and prepared himself to hear the tale

****

February 3rd, 2085, 8:15 a.m.,

"You seeing this," Callan Rouge spoke into the comms unit. Ryan Morrisey and Vanessa Duncan were each on the call, with the former surveying his own territory in the Penn State area and the latter still on Command Center X in the Yaiba compound.

"Just a second," Vanessa responded in a tone of voice that bid him be patient, "I have to get the screen up and… Oh, my God!"

"So it's the same for you, too, then," Ryan commented. The other listeners were dumbfounded.

"You mean to say that there's an entire division at both your locations?" Vanessa was chilled to the bone. "Now we know what happened to all those troops that pulled out of the Southern Wastes."

"It's likely that we'll be seeing this at random," Callan theorized. "The Penn State area was already targeted so it makes sense that they'd up the security, but they had no way of knowing we'd be in Fayetteville. That is, unless they knew we'd deploy commando squads." The level of accusation in Callan's voice was enough to make Vanessa and Ryan shift where they sat. Neither wanted to believe that there was a mole within their coalition, but at this stage in the warfare game, it wasn't something that could easily be overlooked. Regardless, they all knew it was best to keep their minds on the mission at hand.

"For now, continue surveillance," Vanessa ordered as she started to run geo-sensor diagnostics. "Anything else would be foolish at the moment. We'll monitor the situation on this end, see if we can find you some kind of opening to engage."

"Roger that," Ryan told her, then signed off of the comms channel. Vanessa was next to go, while Callan just switched to local comms.

"What'd they tell you," asked an unusually optimistic Serenity Crawford once she'd received notice that Callan was back on the line. It made Callan feel strange when she used that tone of voice. Little more than a month ago they were enemies, and she was the reason he'd been held captive. Now it seemed like she wanted to befriend him.

"Our job is to survey, not to engage. The Command Center is monitoring the situation with the geo-sensors." He offered no warmth in his tone, and Serenity's heart fell along with the conversation. Moments passed as they kept up their watch, and Callan couldn't help but feel bad. Despite all that she'd done, he knew that it was for the sake of her mission. It excused nothing, but it did at least let him know that there might be something redeemable about the former Scourge leader. Besides that, she'd lost everything only a little over a month ago, and it made sense that she would seek some form of connection. He heaved an exasperated sigh as his hand came down his face. "What do you want?"

"Excuse me?" Serenity was more than a little offended by the phrasing. It was hard for Callan to find the right words to use when talking to his former captor, especially when they nearly killed each other not that long ago. Even so, he regretted his decision. "What exactly do you mean by that?"

"It's just that you're so…" he took a moment to consider his words more carefully, "warm towards me these days. You're not the kind of person to just change their attitude regarding someone unless something's in it for you. I want to know what that is."

"Wow, Mr. Rouge, you certainly have a way with words," Serenity remarked with sarcastic incredulity. Still, what was she supposed to say, here? Was she supposed to tell the man that they were long-lost cousins whose parents were embroiled in the bitterest shape that family turmoil could take, or was she supposed to find some other means of engaging with him?

"Really? And here I thought I was being as short as possible. I should probably fix that, shouldn't I?" Callan's own biting sarcasm relayed to her his anger. He never was one to take the chiding of outsiders kindly, especially when there was so much trauma associated with one. What was John thinking when he chose them for the same recon mission?

"Look," she said, and broke his train of thought, "let's just address the elephant in the room."

"And what would that be, exactly? The torture? The insults? Perhaps it's your multiple attempts on my life over the years?" She was silent, which upset Callan more than rehashing all of his encounters with the former Colonel. "Oh wait," he continued with venom behind his every word, "are you talking about that time where you said you'd leave my nephews alone if I went with you and then tried to kill them anyway?"

"I'm sorry," she said, finally. He snorted in disbelief. After all, she'd proven herself an expert liar before. "I know what I've done is more than an apology can make up for, but I am so sorry for what I've done."

"Of course you are," Callan told her coldly. He crossed his arms as if she could see him in the shadows of his position across town near the old Fayetteville State campus. "I'm sure that being abandoned by your people will do that to you." He knew that it was a low blow, that it wasn't fair, but with his former kidnapper he felt that the last thing he needed to be was fair. Another pause arose between them as Serenity processed the emotions that he spurred in her.

"My decision to defect to the Yaiba might've been inspired in part by the Kingdom turning on James and me, but I was also confronted with the horrible things I'd done in the name of accomplishing my mission. I don't need you to tell me about all the things I've done or what I don't deserve, and I respect your anger. Hell, I even respect the doubt you cast on my motives because in a different time I would've tried something like this. But I'll be damned if I let you trivialize my growth because you can't see what effort I'm putting in." The entire time she spoke, her voice was even and calm but stern all the same. It was more than enough to teach Callan that she meant every word that she said, which came as a legitimate shock to him. He opened his mouth to speak when a chain of explosions erupted along the All American Freeway that ran through the heart of town.

Smoke billowed into the air, and the two members of the commando squad's scouting cell could only hit the deck as two more blasts scorched and churned the earth near their respective positions. Groggily they returned to their feet, only to see the city dark and ablaze. The Scarlet Troopers that remained in the area were thrown into confusion as a good number of their brethren were mowed down with an odd array of Kingdom-issue tanks, now colored in gold and each with the symbol of a crown with a single line through the center emblazoned on their hulls.

A war cry echoed into the air as the foot soldiers, each one in a golden attire that matched the armed transports that led their charge, sprinted into combat with their red-clad adversaries. Callan and Serenity fought against the ringing sensation in their ears and the disorientation it caused. Years on the battlefield for both and neither had enough experience to get used to that.

"Serenity," Callan called wearily through the comms unit. There was no answer, and he cursed his luck that that other explosion went off near enough to her location to deafen her. He thought to try again before any attempt at a rendezvous. "Serenity, come in."

"I'm here," she said shakily. It struck Callan as surprising that he felt any kind of relief when it came to her, but he did. "We need to regroup with the others."

"You took the words right out of my mouth," he said with more amiability in his voice than he intended to convey. "Stay where you are and I'll come to you." Just as he breathed the words, Serenity caught sight of something—rather, someone—that she never thought she'd see.

It was then that Nash O'Neill, former Prince of Kingdom Scarlet and brother to James, looked up at her and smiled.

****

February 3rd, 2085, 9:03 a.m.,

"All units, advance on Serenity's position," John commanded. The Command Center advised that this was the best time to attack just as Serenity delivered the news of Nash's assault. The Director was already on his way, Reikiken ablaze and the rest of his team in tow.

"Gotcha," came the relatively laid back response of Don Jackson, a man of the same dusky complexion as the former Rairyu and all the fight and soul of black freedom fighters of generations past. He was a calming presence, no matter the situation, but with his muscular build and deeply focused eyes, he proved a massive intimidation for their enemies. Despite his tranquil nature, his heart pounded with the possibility of combat. This was everything that he'd been waiting for, a tipping point in the never-ending war for civil rights on this God-forsaken mass of land.

"I'm on my way, sir," added Latrell McBeth, a thinner, lighter-skinned black man with a relatively gentle nature. John liked and even admired him, because his tenacity when it came to protecting and providing for his family reminded him of Shonda. In a different time, he could've been a Dragon, but his duty as a father outweighed his desire to function as a soldier. Nobody could blame him. When he decided to come back into the fold, though, he quickly reminded everyone that despite his kindness, he's a much bigger threat than the enemy would expect and with half the recognition.

"Gotcha, gotcha," spoke the relaxed but excited tenor of Teddy Grant, a Shadow of a thicker muscular build than most, brown well-kept hair, trimmed goatee, and amber eyes that shimmered in bright conjunction with his vanilla skin. He was the historian of the group, a man who had spent hours in between his combat training learning the full history of Prevalence, from the founding of the United States to the rise of the Scarlet Kingdom, right down to the reason that Kingdom calls the continent Providence while everyone else calls it Prevalence. He was a wealth of knowledge with academics and battle, and he was more than determined to add to the history of the land through his own efforts.

Each of them grappled through the plentiful trees that now overshadowed the Fayetteville roads as they rushed to the Re Stone auto care facility that overlooked All American, the subordinates a little ways behind the Yaiba leader. The air was thick with smoke and the glint of gold sparkled across the fresh battlefield in the morning sun. Serenity stood on the rooftop of the long-defunct mechanic's building as she watched the many foot soldiers and tanks forced the Reds in the area into a full retreat. Callan stood behind her, his back tense from the presence of a force that had yet to be revealed as friend or foe. Given that it was Nash O'Neill who led these warriors, it was more than a little likely that they would be the latter.

"Nash," was all John said to get their attention. Serenity pointed to the ground below.

"He's still down there," she offered, "commanding his forces remotely." The others in the commando squad finally caught up, and in a move to leave the protection of Serenity and Callan to them, John dove from the roof of the building and softened his landing with a burst from his repulsors.

"John Hamlin," the former Prince sang with a degree of amused irritation. He spread his arms wide as he asked, "Strange, us being in the same place and all."

"A lot stranger to see you fighting against the Kingdom," John retorted. Nash shrugged with a dismissive expression, but then sharpened his soul-piercing stardust-gray eyes in an instant.

"I figure that it's well-deserved," the former Prince admitted, "given its treatment of my brother and me. Speaking of which…" John blinked, and in the instant he opened his eyes he found that Nash had not only closed the distance between them, but held the Legendary Shadow in place with a pair of golden sai. The fact that he pointed the sharp tip of one at the Director's throat was surprising enough, but John was more impressed with the one that gripped his Reikiken and didn't distort from the astronomical temperature. Nash continued, his voice hard like the tungsten of the firesword in John's hand. "Where is my brother?"

"Safe," was the only thing that John contributed, which exasperated Nash to the point of pressing the Sai at John's throat a little bit closer.

"Safe *where*," he demanded. John, who recognized the sudden leverage he had over his one-time adversary, snapped the fingers of his free hand to summon Callan,

Teddy, Latrell and Don from the rooftop above. Their Reikiken were drawn, and before Nash could move against their leader, the Shadow subordinates were careful to place their blades in a diamond loosely around his neck. John removed himself from Nash's range without a care, because they all knew that if Nash forgot his place, that diamond necklace of his would become a fiery noose.

John dusted himself off as his eyes locked on the fresh captive. "You seem to be a bit confused here, Nash, but then again, what else is new?"

"Says the leader of a commando squad that so obviously wants to know why I'm here. You're aware that I can withhold all of my intel until you tell me where you're holding my brother, yes?"

"Are you aware that I can order my subordinates to take you out now and therefore rob you of the chance to see your brother on this side of the ethereal plane?" John's voice was hard, yet dismissive. He didn't yell, nor did he have to. It was simply understood that the former Rairyu, despite his change in position, was still the most powerful wherever he deigned to tread.

The air was tense as the two leaders stared each other down, deep and mysterious brown eyes locked with the soul-wounding stardust-grays, the heat and orange light of the Reikiken a fiery glimmer about the scene. The Vulcan glow in their eyes added to the intensity of their nonverbal standoff, and as the group of Yaiba subordinates began to perspire, Callan and Serenity bounded to the ground themselves. Nash was stunned to see her, no longer in the scarlet bodysuit that she was known for, but in the same violet tunic, black trousers and black hooded cloak sported by the Yaiba Insurrection. His eyes, no longer narrowed with determination but wide with surprise, shifted back to the Director.

"You should probably tell us why you're here, Nash," she said with an irritated tone. Truthfully she hadn't put aside her earlier spat with Callan, and the presence of a known simpleton like Nash gave her no reason to be anything other than absolutely annoyed. "And please, be quick about it. We have a schedule to keep."

Suddenly he was irate, and spat at the ground before her as he barked, "You dare address me in such an undignified way? I am—"

"A former prince with less sense than God gave a cabbage," Serenity finished. "You might've had some tactical successes in the past, but it doesn't change the fact that the only thing that kept you in power was your daddy's fearsome rule. You, as a person, have always been an afterthought who could never fully escape your father's shadow and never quite had your brother's charms with the public. Now I'll tell you," she continued with a drop to her tone and the raising of her signature pistol, "I've thought about killing you myself a great many times over the years, and the only thing that kept you alive was the fact that I didn't want your father chasing me to the ends of the earth. Now you have a choice. You can either tell us what you're doing here attacking your own men, or I can reunite you with your dearly departed father right here, right now."

John did nothing to even try to control her. He respected her as a leader in her own right, and more than that, he knew just as well as Nash did what she was like when she was angry. Callan, who now stood behind the

Director, watched with a reluctant respect as she cocked the gun in her hand and narrowed her eyes. Nash held his hands up in a placative gesture.

"Fine," he said through gritted teeth. He turned his gaze to the Yaiba leader and continued, "I was ousted by the Kingdom once your friend Bryan took power. A number of Kingdom citizens opted to come with me out of loyalty to the true inheritor of the throne."

"So this is your attempt at getting the throne back," Teddy asked excitedly. He felt a stirring of historical events on the horizon that would give this presently unsightly rock the kind of rich stories that nations the world over enjoyed.

"At first, that's what it was," Nash was forced to admit, but there was a sudden wistfulness to him that was easily supplanted by a renewed rage. "But then I thought about how abusive my father was. Colonel Crawford was right, no matter what I did, it wasn't good enough for that man, and it gave me a slight insight into why you all fight." John, Latrell and Don all narrowed their eyes.

"Did it, now?" The question emerged from John's lips as a dragonic hum, and for a moment Nash could've sworn he saw John's pupils turn from round to slits. An illusion to be sure, but he could hardly deny that the man's body count was nothing short of monstrous.

"All of you have fought to be seen as worthy, as equal to the person standing next to you, and more than that to simply be left alone to live your lives in peace. I believe that there comes a point where one's upbringing can no longer excuse the actions of a person. They either overcome the wrong that they were taught, or blindly follow in those teachings until they, themselves, are overcome." Nash spoke with a lot more intelligence than any of those present had ever believed him capable of.

"So then I ask again," John spoke with near serenity, "why are you here?" Nash took a moment to look around. Each member of the commando squad stared at him with suspicion and a thinly veiled threat, but neither he nor they could deny that the Insurrectionists were curious to hear his answer.

"I want to destroy what my father and his predecessors built. Everything that led your people to break away, everything that led James and I down the path of gaining the affection of a man sworn never to give it, I want to see it all burn," Nash explained with such a degree of resentment and quiet fury that it was hard for their suspicions to remain. The only member of the neo-ninja entourage that maintained their reluctance to readily join with yet another former enemy. Again the suspense of the moment weighed on them all, and all eyes shifted to the leader of the pack. John smiled as he nodded once, and the four members of the squad pulled their burning blades away from the captive former prince.

"Your brother," John began, much to everyone's utter shock, "is currently helping out at the Civic Center in the Roan Mountain. If you can clear us a path to Fort Bragg, I'll allow you to see him." John could see the shift in his expression, the seriousness he adopted at the suggestion of a reunion with his brother, as well as the shift of internal deliberation in his eyes.

"What do you intend to do with Bragg," Nash inquired with heavy doubt in his voice. "They've got the best security systems of any Kingdom outpost. Besides even if you managed to get past the outer defenses, it'd take a lot more than a six-man squad to bring down the whole base." John knew he was right. Years ago, back when he was still the head of Black Ops, John was sent by his predecessor Emiko Ishikawa to investigate its weak points. It nearly got him killed, but he knew that of all the former US military installations that were decommissioned, this one was left largely intact. He suspected that the Kingdom would have plans for what was, at one point, the largest base in the old United States, but now that years-old suspicion was confirmed through the former noble.

"Oh, I know," John confirmed as a sly smirk slid across his jaw. He approached Nash and placed a firm hand on the ex-prince's shoulder that made him feel like Hell had truly frozen over. "Lucky for us, a massive allied force just fell into our lap."

"Oh you don't mean—" Nash couldn't stop the beginnings of his grumble, which only made John smile wider as he continued a thought nobody ever thought he would voice.

"Do you want to build a siege effort?"

****

February 3rd, 2085, 10:57 a.m.,

Captain Nicodemus Iannuzzi checked his rosters. The gates to Ft. Bragg had been closed on all sides and for the last hour the remaining troopers in their division stood in formation, shielded by the extensive defenses of the base. Iannuzzi ran a hand through his thick jet-black hair as a confident smile crossed his lips. For the first time since his reassignment in December, he was firmly in control of a situation that would make others cower in fear. A part of him was nervous, he had to admit. The question of the gold-clad warriors that disrupted the division's expansion to the greater Fayetteville area was a pertinent one. But the Captain hardly expected them to last too long. Apparently they were led by someone dumb enough to stage a debut of their military near enough to a base that could make their performance a one-act, and knowing that made Nicodemus giddy with anticipation.

The first explosion rocked the grounds of the base. Nicodemus adopted the utmost smugness as he walked through the door of the old US Army Forces Command Headquarters building. He made his way to a room up the stairs and to the right, one filled with the hologram projectors and monitors that already surveyed the chaos at the gates. Red waves battled against shimmering gold at the Yadkin, Honeycutt, and Bragg Boulevard gates. Bombs went off, soldiers died left and right in brilliant flashes, and while at first it looked as though the Scarlet Troopers were pulling ahead, the red color on the battlefield was only scarcely dotted with metallic yellow.

"What's the status," Captain Iannuzzi demanded as his heart pounded in his chest. Myriad questions swirled about in his mind. How many soldiers currently knocked on their door? What kind of weaponry and armor did they have that allowed them to withstand the force of the shock cannons that lined the fences? What was their objective beyond getting into the base?

The response of a subordinate broke the Captain's train of thought. "The enemy is close to overwhelming three of our Defensive Fighting Positions. We can hold them back but not for long at our current power output."

"Cut power to the western defenses," Nicodemus ordered. "Order all available personnel to exit the base by Reilly Road and strike our enemy from behind."

"Sir," came the voice of the subordinate. Within moments the order blasted throughout the base and the sudden rhythmic thud of about 5,000 Scarlet Troopers added to the tremors from the bombs.

Iannuzzi breathed a sigh of relief, then said under his breath as his crooked smile returned to his pale face and his emerald eyes fixed upon the screen at his enemies, "Your move."

****

February 3rd, 2085, 11:28 a.m.,

The problem with maintaining a base that the public thinks has been decommissioned is that unless the powers that be want things to change, everything stays exactly where it is. John couldn't help but smile about it as he and his team swiftly assassinated the defenders of the Reilly Road DFP and made for the Special Operations Command Center. Under normal circumstances, the building would be well guarded by man and machine alike and nobody without top secret security clearance would be able to make it past the front door, but today they had a clear exception to the rule.

It didn't take them long to realize that the power to the defenses at their entrance to the base had been cut, and it didn't take them long after that to go about their mission. They opened the doors to the Spec Ops command, and though they were met with slight resistance, it was little match for Serenity and her gun.

"Alright, let's get the information we came for and get out of dodge before they realize what we're up to," John ordered. If there was one place where he could find a secret, it was usually in the house of the people known for creating, keeping, and killing over them. Serenity and Teddy started work on the computer terminals on hand. Both of them inserted the USB drives given to them by Erik Kincaid before their departure and watched as the virus began its work. If all went well, they'd have most of the files on any and all death squads, spec ops activity, secret research and vehicle specifications in a matter of minutes. What the couldn't find through the Kingdom's digital files would likely be kept as hard copies somewhere in the present facility. Don and Latrell were already on that.

John and Callan kept watch at the main entrance, and both of them couldn't help but feel a wave of nostalgia hit them. They worked together often in their younger days, and it was the combination of Callan, Bryan and Bill that helped John work through much of the distress he felt surrounding his father. Now one member of the old team had committed a betrayal that stung more than that of his own father, and the two present on this mission had a hard time turning their minds away from it.

"How much longer," John called to the others at the consoles behind him. He asked the question more forcefully than intended, but there was little time to apologize.

"It'll be about a minute more," Teddy called back with as respectful a tone as he could manage. It wasn't that he tried to be disrespectful, but he'd long been told that his voice sounded like that of a snarky dad who'd been woken up from a nap: all sarcasm and shade. "By the way," he continued as Dom and Latrell reentered the room, "have you thought about what we're gonna name this operation when we document it for the future historians?" John turned to look at Teddy, who felt a chill shoot through his spine. "Got it, time and place."

Just before John could turn his attention back to the road beyond their position, Don spoke. "Hey, Boss," he spoke with apprehension, "I thought you ought to take a look at this." Don, who had many files in his hands, extended a manilla folder to the Director. John took it, opened it, and then scowled at the picture at the upper lefthand corner. On the page, just beneath the image, the former Rairyu read the words:

ALPHONSE WESTERSHIRE

CODENAME: TROJAN HORSE

MISSION OBJECTIVE: YAIBA INFILTRATION AND TECHNOLOGICAL THEFT.

John snapped the file shut, and marveled at the ferocity of his heart in his chest. "We're all set," Serenity confirmed. John gave the file back to Don and pressed a small receiver on his wrist that Nash had given him.

"Good," the Yaiba leader said with a gravity that concerned each person in the room. "We need to get home."

Chapter Nine

February 3rd, 2085, 12:33 p.m.,

Aaron Stone was bored. When he was told about this surveillance mission, he thought it would be full of action. He grew up hearing about the wild things that the Yaiba Insurrection did whenever they met up with the Reds, and everything in him wanted to be a part of the legend. Now that he was, he sat alone atop the "Alde Mmons" as the rest of his team fanned out over the city. The comms unit at his wrist projected a phase-vision map of State College, and it was his job to monitor the enemy's movements while everyone else was off being more hands-on.

He huffed in disappointment before he spoke like, again, he knew he shouldn't, "Master Morrisey, I'm bored."

"Bruh," Tez Johnson said with a smile beneath his black mask. He lifted his wrist comms to his mouth and said with a thinly-veiled incredulity, "You never could just be quiet, man." Tez camped out in the ceiling of the former chemical and biomedical engineering building that, in the days since Kingdom Scarlet's rise, had been converted to an expansive research facility/hangar for the latest weapons developments. "Got eyes on some kind of strange sword thing. Looks like that thing that that kid Al brought with him to the camp in Yorktown."

"Wait, so why is he here then," asked Isaiah Parkman with a wry smile, a reference to the earlier conversation. Stone scowled through the comms, and while

Isaiah couldn't see the look on his comrade's face, he still smiled wider. Parkman sat atop the remains of the health services building and watched as a few Scarlet transports filtered into the Eisenhower Parking Deck. At first glance it looked like an ordinary parking structure, but there was something strange that Isaiah was loath to put his finger on. "Moving in on the deck," he nonchalantly alerted his teammates.

"Remember," said Ryan Morrisey, the team leader, "this is an observation only mission. If at all possible, do not engage."

"Understood, *Taichou*," Parkman replied, and then stealthily descended through the shattered glass and broken brick of the health building. Like Ryan, one of the other Shadows on this mission, loved stealthing about even before the joint training sessions with the Kabuto. It was always such a thrill to move with the shadows from which the Yaiba took their name, and it was weird to him that more people didn't enjoy it. Granted, the Hanzo Gear did make it a bit difficult to keep a low profile.

"I'm here," Aaron started with an almost comical degree of sass, "because my skills are highly valued by Senior Agent Kincaid and the other members of the top brass."

"Yeah, that's a fancy way of saying that you're a handful and they needed you to go somewhere else so they could focus on the more important problems," Hector retorted. Unlike his comrades, Hector Rubio was at ground level, nestled behind a semi-destroyed library wall to the southwest of the other points of interest. From there he watched the enemy troops in their formations, did what he could to commit them to memory as well as record them through the phase-vision tech in his comms device. Every so often the soldiers would change their pattern. Over the course of the last week, they demonstrated six different formations for their foot soldiers, seven different formations for their transports, and all of their formations resembled more than just security patterns. These were the machinations of war made manifest; training drills rooted in the paranoia of the Scarlet elites were now intermingled with a level of defensive capability that made Hector think of Insurrectionist flavor. “Got another one,” he whispered into the comms.

Ryan was pleased. He and Diego slipped through the new weapons depot at the White Building Gym with perfect silence under the cloak of the Nightshroud Filter, and hastily stuck miniature electro-thermal detonators onto crate after crate of brand-new weapons.

“*Taichou*, come in,” Johnson whispered.

“Proceed,” Ryan acknowledged in an equally hushed tone.

“You and Diego may want to get out of dodge. These blades that the enemy is stockpiling are pretty hardcore,” the young Kabuto informed. There was a nervousness to his voice as he watched a test. The hilt, outfitted with the same external power generator that they’d all seen on Al’s sword from the intel shared by the Yaiba, emitted two small spherical drones. This was an extended trial of sorts that Tez had wandered into, and while one of the drones moved for a hidden location behind the user, the other drone followed the every wave of the seemingly electrically charged sword. “That’s interesting,” Tez said to himself when the user slowed the wave of the weapon. They pointed the tip of the sword at a wooden barrel across the facility, and in a brilliant burst of light the barrel ceased to exist.

"What was that," Diego all but demanded when the ground beneath their feet quaked. He'd almost dropped one of the detonators, which would've fried his equipment and him along with it.

"We gotta get out of here," Tez spoke with heightened urgency.

Ryan opened his mouth to inquire further, but was promptly interrupted by the sudden blaring of an intruder alarm. Now there was no time for questions. It was time to get out of dodge.

****

February 3rd, 2085, 12:46 p.m.,

"What did you do," Aaron asked Parkman with more excitement in his voice than he wanted to seep through. Parkman rolled his eyes, which Stone could see in total clarity thanks to the zoom-in feature in the phase-vision map. Isaiah was slightly embarrassed and declined to answer. He knew that it was Stone's job to keep track of their movements and watch the city overall, so he had no pressing desire to inform him of the fact that he touched the forcefield around the parking structure and triggered the alarm. It wasn't like it was important, anyway. For now, the team's goal was to make it back to the Commons and get out as efficiently as they could.

"That doesn't matter," Isaiah spoke as he ran along what few rooftops remained in State College, "at least not as much as what I found out."

"Come on," Stone said incredulously. "It can't be that impressive."

"Well, that depends on whether or not you think a secret chemical lab with enough bombs to take out the three other factions combined is impressive," Isaiah elucidated in such a nonchalance that it chilled Aaron to the core.

"No, that's not possible," the watchman whispered out of fear, then frantically checked the scans of the city, the phase vision maps, and anything else he could think of that he'd monitored the whole time they were there, but there was no evidence of chemicals or bombs or anything that would pose so much of a threat. "No," he said again, "I would've picked up something like that on the daily scans at the very least—"

"It doesn't matter," Ryan's voice chimed in on the comms. "Parkman, I need you to give me a rundown on everything that's happening."

"I had enemies in pursuit at first—"

"What do you mean," Ryan asked with a depth to his voice that made his subordinates on the comms glitch out.

"The Reds put up some kind of barrier around the parking garage. It shorted out my suit when I touched it—"

"You touched it?!" Ryan couldn't help but make an exclamation of it, and his hysteria was more than enough to make Aaron snicker on the other side

“The Nightshroud came back on a few minutes after,” Parkman replied defensively. There was a moment of silence on the line. Isaiah thought to speak again before Captain Morrisey spoke again.

“Take the long way back to the hideout and we’ll run interference,” Diego told him with way more excitement than any had previously thought possible. He looked over to Ryan, who shrugged and donned a childlike smile of his own.

“There’s something else, *Taichou*,” Isaiah reluctantly continued. He could feel the roll of Ryan’s eyes and the brim of Stone’s laughter. “The moment I triggered the alarm, the transports in the parking deck took off.”

****

February 3rd, 2085, 1:44 p.m.,

“How many detonators do you have left,” Diego called to his best friend and momentary supervisor. It’d been a while since they were teamed together. The last six months had seen their hasty graduation from the Yaiba training program, a slue of battles that were far above their paygrade, and a massive shift in the chain of command that necessitated their rise to leadership. They were, after all, briefed on all the protocols of the Yaiba Insurrection. They just had to give the orders rather than follow them and pray that they wouldn’t cost anyone their lives.

“About seventeen,” Ryan replied, more seriously than Diego was used to hearing him. “You?” Diego ran his hands through the utility pouch that rested at the small of his back.

"Twelve," he said with an air of disappointment.

"I don't think it'll be enough to take those transports off the street," Ryan said. The initial pattern of the transports was a scattered mess that was far too much of a challenge for the two Yaiba operatives to subdue. Already they'd taken down four, but between that and their earlier task to target the weapons depot, most of their payload had already been spent. It didn't take long for the transports to make their goal known: the old Interstate 99. From there, the Reds had any number of paths into Johnson City, and from there it would only take a moment and a flash to cut off the combined Yaiba and Kabuto presence there and swiftly make for the Grand Canyon to snuff out the last of the resistance forces.

"We can still take a couple more out," Diego urged, despite the knowledge that the transports had already made it onto the highway. Even with the full force of the repulsors at his heels and the kyoketsu-shoge at his wrists, he wouldn't be able to catch up, much less do any damage.

"No," Ryan instructed through the channel. "All units regroup at the rendezvous point and prepare for departure. Stone, dispatch an emergency message to command immediately."

"Sir," they all responded together, and when he switched the comms off, Captain Morrisey cursed beneath his breath.

****

February 3rd, 2085, 6:34 p.m.,

Vanessa and Dre did everything they could to round up the necessary forces to fend off this new threat. When they learned that the hidden defenses around Johnson City might not be enough to put a dent in the enemy's operation, they both racked their brains with all the possible combinations of soldiers they could send. With Senior Agent Kincaid on the line, they went back and forth about what could be done to minimize casualties first and foremost. The KDN bombing was still only fresh in the rearview, and neither the Yaiba nor the Kabuto could so easily hide the gaping hole in their ranks left by their fallen soldiers.

It'd already been roughly five hours since the emergency transmission came in and rigorous debate was as far as they'd gotten. John wasn't back yet, and for some reason nobody could patch through to his comms. It was enough to make them wonder if something had happened in his mission, but the worry they'd initially felt would have to wait until they somehow managed to deal with the more immediate threat.

It was scary for Vanessa to think that while the Yaiba and Kabuto sought to expand and gather intel through the two commando squads, the enemy planned a rapid dominance strategy that could so easily put to bed all of the coalition's machinations. If what Ryan said was accurate, then it would be prudent to eliminate the presence of allied troops as much as possible. If that was the case, then surely Cal and his Lightbeams would be able to handle the executioner of this mission. Then again, the Lightbeams were a valuable new asset to the alliance and according to Cal, their inventor, they weren't so easy to manufacture.

That was even with the plentiful scrap they'd salvaged once the Kingdom's drones had been taken offline.

Kincaid suggested that they at least try their luck with the defenses that were already in place, but deep down he knew they would need more. What munitions they'd procured in the Reds' recent attempts to give aid to their western-stationed unit were insufficient as well, and while his faction were excessively talented saboteurs, there was no guarantee of the chance to do what they did best.

Dre simply griped that if the Yoroi had been more proactive in their fight for freedom, they might've been able to lend a hand in keeping the Reds at bay. The others mostly just tuned him out. Right now, they were on the verge of a ground assault at their front door that had a potential to do just as much damage as the KDN bombing, if not more. The Yaiba Ballistics Company could probably do some good here, but not with half of them still with Zahara Boyd as they secured and provided aid to Jackson.

Vanessa looked at the clock on the wall of the command center. With every tick of the clock she grew mad with impatience. Then, she had an idea.

"Cal," she called through the comm link in her Menpo mask. At first there was no response, so she called his name again. There was a crackle from the comms, a loud metal clang, and a slue of profanities and laughter in the background. He was on Engineering Level again.

"A-yerrr," Cal called back as he dusted himself off and coughed through the cloud of dust particles. Vanessa was frustrated with the address, but she didn't have time to correct him. She decided to come right out with what was on her mind.

"What are the capabilities of your Lightbeams?" Cal froze on the other end of the line, a luxury that they did not have. "Spit it out, boy!"

"Okay, chill," he all but pleaded, but the urgency in her tone inspired a haste in him. "Those bad boys are outfitted with the same heat-treating that we give all our Hanzo Gear, along with the same Reikiken, kyoketsu-shoge, and repulsors. They have a tri-weave tri-titanium inlay that allows them to be flexible and hard to break. On top of all that, I gave each one a unique combat ability so it'd be harder for the enemy to figure 'em out. I thought you knew all this already. I sent you the schematics a long time ago." That was true, as was the fact that she knew she should've committed those plans to memory in case she needed to refer back to them at a time like this. Unfortunately the moment had passed and they were in crisis, so the best thing for her to do was pick the brain that birthed the blasted things.

"We don't have time for this," she groaned with peak exasperation as her hands slid down her face. "Do you have some mechanism where they can attract metal objects?"

"Oh yeah," Cal spoke with a complete lack of urgency that irked Vanessa to no end. "That feature is still experimental though. See what I'd envisioned was having the Lightbeams attract and repel the same kind of metal that was in those drones. I mean, plus a few others that the Kingdom is known to use."

"Excellent," said the Kageryu. "You'll be leaving for the eastern border of Johnson City within the hour. Do NOT delay."

"Yes, ma'am," Cal replied in all seriousness."

****

February 3rd, 2085, 9:19 p.m.,

A sharp, icy wind blew through the wall of trees that surrounded Johnson City. The snow wasn't quite as fresh now, and started to melt more and more the closer it got to spring. The heaps of twisted and scorched metal had been scattered throughout the road in such a way that would make it difficult for any inbound transports to make their way safely over the town line, and other obstacles were placed at other potential entrances and exits to deter the Scarlets from further attempts to traverse the territory.

In the distance, the sound of engines and tires could be heard, no doubt a herald of the arrival of the Scarlet Kingdom's latest group of assailants. Shadows moved along the ground in the moonlight, a rustle of the canopy of the trees betrayed the wind, and tension prowled the earth like a hungry beast ready to pounce.

"They're here," Erik Kincaid whispered through the comms. John half-smiled from his branch high above the ground. He was still in a hurry to get back to the Roan Mountain base, to confront Alphonse about his deception and infiltration and whatever else he had planned for his little visit to the Yaiba, but this matter momentarily outweighed that meeting. As always, John had to put first things first.

"I see them. Everybody get ready. We'll be following Cal's lead, but as soon as they see any part of us they'll scatter. We need to do what we can and take out as many as we can. Do NOT allow them to breach the city until the bombs have been extracted."

"Sir," everyone called back. The second commando unit made it back before Ryan's team, and after being briefed on the situation they fell in line with the operation without hesitance. Ryan's squad would add pressure from behind while John's force would engage directly and Cal's Lightbeams would strike from above. It didn't take long for the Director to coordinate with Senior Agent Kincaid on the matter and figure out a way to scatter the enemy to the wind. Now they waited. Now they watched. Now, there were mere seconds for the troops on the line to get their minds right before…

"Now!" John's shout into the artificial calm spurred the shadows to strike. Teddy Grant, Don Jackson and Latrell McBeth pounced on the second transport in the driving formation. The driver screamed at the hooded figures that appeared from the darkness and swerved with everything he had in his efforts to knock them off. Teddy waved with a glint of childishness in his eyes as they grappled up into the tree branches above. The electro-thermal detonator went off, as did the other bombs in the back of the now defunct transport.

The explosion rocked the surrounding area and the destroyed vehicle vaulted into the air, only to land in fiery glory atop a second. Another explosion felt, another car in their convoy gone, but that still left nine more that needed to be stopped.

A bullet broke through the windshield on one of the three that led the pack. The driver, overcome with shock, fear, and a momentary muscle spasm, turned the steering wheel so hard that he flipped the transport and another ran into it. Their respective doors were ripped open and their payloads extracted by two overhead Lightbeams, but before the fresh projectiles could be deployed anew, the Scarlet enemies started to branch off.

“They’re branching off!” This was the loudest that anyone had ever heard Erik get, and the sense of urgency in his voice generated one in everyone on the battlefield right then.

“On it,” John assured him. “Cal, divert a couple of your Lightbeams towards Austin Springs Road. Teddy, Don, Latrell, follow suit on the ShadowStalkers. Callan, you’re with me. We’re gonna do what we can to stick on Highway 19.”

“Say less,” Cal confirmed, and the two Lightbeams with enemy payloads rushed to engage. The ShadowStalkers got on the move shortly after, and in seconds there were two more massive explosions that blew the snow off the trees on the other road.

“Erik, engage the external defenses,” John ordered.

“What do you mean?” The question was more worried than anything, but he did as he was asked.

“A couple of transports managed to slip through our formation,” Callan clarified. Just then they got a tap through the comms channel.

“Mind if we join the party,” inquired Diego Cruz in such a manner that almost convinced the others that the battle was exactly as festive as he indicated. Without confirmation, Ryan, Tez and Hector jumped from the sides of their own transport. Isaiah kept it steady enough for them to move seamlessly to the enemy vehicle before he pulled back all the way and swerved around. The back of their transport now faced the rest of the battle. It opened, and out of it came two ShadowStalkers upon which sat Diego and Aaron.

"We'll handle the two in the front," Stone volunteered. There was too much going on and not enough time to stop them from reaching the edge of town, so nobody argued. Aaron motioned for Cruz to get on a private comm channel. He did, and that was when the youngest warrior on the field beamed with delight. "We should hit them with a pincer maneuver." The suggestion was almost cute to Diego.

"Pincers usually work with more than just two men against armored cars," Cruz replied with a poor show of energy. Clearly he wasn't convinced that it would work.

"You got any better ideas," Stone asked in mild exasperation. The truth of it was that Diego didn't see another way to go about it. Another explosion emanated from behind them, and a glance back confirmed that their comrades on the team were safe.

"I'll take point," Cruz all but groaned. "I do have more experience after all." Stone shrugged with a boyish smile, giddy that his idea had finally made it to the battlefield.

"No argument from me, *Mon Capitan*," Aaron joked. "Lead the way." As Stone's speed reduced, Diego used the boosters on his ShadowStalker to glide between the two vehicles and vault the debris that lay in the road. The chill in his face was otherworldly, as was the look of abject terror on the faces of the enemy drivers. Stone reached into the utility pouch on his uniform and retrieved two of the disc-like detonators from his prior mission. He threw them with the skill of a shinobi of old, then peeled off to the side. Diego pulled out two of his own, tossed them onto the windshields of the bomber cars, but just before he was about to blow the charges, one of the drivers sped up in pursuit of him.

"Diego, get out of there," Ryan ordered. There was something in his voice that Cruz had never heard before. It was more than urgency, more than worry. It was an emotion so primal and forceful that it was only ever seen on the battlefield and between siblings in arms just before something unspeakable happens. The enemy transport rammed into the back of the ShadowStalker and Cruz almost lost his balance. What was worse was the fact that they were less than a minute's distance from the edge of Johnson City. "Cruz, that's an order!"

"I can't," Diego spoke solemnly. "Ryan, listen…" there was a rattle to his voice, the kind where he knew exactly what he needed to do but didn't know if he had the strength to go through with it. "I'm glad we got to work together one more time before it all ended."

"No," Captain Morrisey shouted through the comms line with a fury that very few had ever seen, "don't you dare start talking like that."

"See the fight through to the end, bud." Two more explosions, screeching tires, and a strong man's wail into the night.

****

February 3rd, 2085, 10:00 p.m.,

King Bryan sat, hands clasped in front of his face, from a rather comfortable black chair in the central office of the central research facility of the Kingdom's Capitol. Zachary Smithfield sat across from him, a wide smile plastered to his face as the Public Servants from the curb outside brought the two their coffee. Whatever Bryan felt about the Kingdom before had started to subside. Sure, the idea of white supremacy was deplorable. Sure, he still needed to make this accursed nation pay the price for his son's life. But a change had started upon his arrival. It was easy for him to believe that once he'd taken down the Yaiba and their ridiculous alliance with the other factions, he'd be able to fully remake the Scarlet Kingdom in his image.

"I hope it's to your liking, Majesty," Smithfield said in a calm, gruff tone that almost sounded authoritative. Fortunately for the Kingdom's chief engineer, Bryan knew the man's habits and was more than aware of the fact that he would never speak to the reigning monarch so carelessly. The King took a sip and found that the coffee was brewed to perfection. Not too bitter, not too sweet. It was balanced, as all things should be.

"It is," he assured his host, "but as I'm sure you're aware, I didn't come here for coffee and idle conversation. There's something much more important that I was hoping to discuss, something that Serafina actually brought to my attention after the Scourge and the Streaks returned from their last mission." Zachary looked upon his ruler with a deepened curiosity.

“What is it that she could possibly know about me,” he asked with a bit of an attitude. It was no secret that since their initial meeting at the audience with the King, Smithfield had come to despise the Lady Leyva. Something about her unnerved him, and the idea that she was snooping around in his life without his consent made him feel a kind of filthy for which there was no cure.

“The break-in at your facility a couple of months ago,” Bryan elaborated. “To bypass the security measures that I, with all my technical know-how, couldn’t during my stint as a provisional citizen is an impressive feat. Imagine my surprise upon the discovery that it was done by a mere boy of sixteen.” Zachary’s face distorted with the news. “Tell me again. What did he take, exactly?” Initially, Zachary thought to hold his tongue, but the stern gaze of the King was enough reminder that the man would have it removed without a prompt and honest answer.

“It was a prototype weapon designated ‘Project Thunderclap,’ Majesty,” Smithfield offered with a combined fear and, admittedly, uncharacteristic humility. “It’s functionality is akin to a sword, firearm, and a drone all in one. It has an electrically charged heat-treated blade that can withstand the high temperatures of the enemy weapons. Initially it was set to go with the Scarlet Scourge to be tested in the field of battle, but the thief—the boy, rather—broke in and stole it before any field data could be collected. Even without that, I was able to recreate the initial formula and modify it as needed with a bit more durability or flexibility depending on the intended users. I just wish I knew where the original model was.”

Bryan smiled as he took a sip of his coffee, then said with inviting confidence, “Oh, I do.” The simplicity of the statement was what struck the engineer so. "As it happens, both the boy and the blade are in the custody of the Yaiba Insurrection." The scientist frowned.

"That's horrible—"

"It would be," Bryan interrupted with a devilish gleam in his eyes, "had the boy not been instructed to infiltrate the Insurrection in the first place."

"I'm confused," Zachary admitted. "The boy committed a crime against the King's military and only pretends to defect?"

"All an elaborate ruse," Bryan confirmed with a smug lifting of the head. "Apparently two years ago his parents subjected him to the black ops training division where he excelled in combat and espionage. He was gifted, even among such an elite class of warriors that would give the average Shadow decent trouble. He was sacrificed on the altar of Old American Values and somehow managed to rise from the ashes of his own burnt offering. Truly impressive, to say the least."

"Why are we talking about this?" The curiosity in the engineer's voice and expression filled Bryan with such joy. There was nothing that he loved more than a willing student in a moment of revelation.

"The leader of the Insurrection is an old friend of mine, one with a knack for uncovering the deepest secrets of his enemies even under the nastiest circumstances. If I know him like I know I do, then he's probably already stumbled upon our young agent's file. You might get that field data after all." He watched as the scientist lit with a joy that could only be understood by a fellow engineer. He raised his coffee cup in toast to the King, and wordlessly the King reciprocated the gesture. They took a sip, and then the King's eyebrows raised. "I am curious, though."

"Hmm," Smithfield prodded with a pleasantly unassuming upward inflection. The King set his coffee beside him on the floor, leaned forward to place his elbows on his knees and clasp his hands in front of his face again. His eyes were trained on his subject as though he were prey, and a chill ran down Zachary's spine. There was something monstrous about the King, something that both terrorized the loyal engineer and exhilarated him all the same.

"Where have you sent the other Thunderclap weapons that you so diligently worked on?" There was a darkness to his voice, a sharpness to his eyes, and a tension in his grip that all worked together to tell the chief engineer that there was, in fact, a right answer to the question. All of his muscles tensed and, against his will, he hesitated to give the King an immediate and definitive answer.

"I—I sent them t-to the i-intelligence unit in the western territory…" The conclusion of his sentence, at least in his own mind, should've brought about some kind of end to the suspense of this moment. He was wrong. Bryan lowered his hands to reveal a frown as if something was terribly wrong, stared deep into the eyes—into the soul—of the man before him, and again tilted his head back with the cool confidence, not of a monarch, but of a warrior with years of battle experience. For Smithfield, it was hard to assess a man with that many layers, with a military bearing that proved not only impenetrable, but capable of instilling terror in whoever looked in his direction. For someone of common birth, Bryan Piccio was suited for royal life.

“I see,” said the King as he lifted from his chair. On instinct, Zachary stood as well. “This is a most interesting development indeed. Do our enemies know?” The engineer contemplated a sigh of relief but ultimately decided against. Again, he knew that there was a right answer to this question, and he also knew that the answer he provided would reflect it. He beamed with the pride of a good and faithful servant.

“Absolutely not, Sire,” the servant replied. “They know that the technology exists. A lone Kabuto signature was detected at Penn State earlier today, but only at one of the many decoy facilities. The main weapons facility was untouched, and the shipment deployed without fail.” Bryan took a moment to admire his subject. The level of craftiness that went into the day to day operations of a distant research facility, the preemptive measures in place to deal with their extensive list of foes, the fact that Smithfield had apparently expected just this meeting, all pleased him greatly.

“Perfect,” Bryan told him, that devilish expression on full display. The King made his way to the door as he said, “Then let the games begin.”

Chapter Ten

February 4th, 2085, 1:05 p.m.,

Darius stood upon the training floor, sweat-soaked and fatigued in all his muscles, but he knew that to stop now was to bite the dust. He couldn't help but smile as he flicked his firesword down at his side and held up his free hand in a pointed two-finger gesture. It'd been ages since the last time he'd encountered a challenge to this extreme, and he was proud of the fact that it was his own doing.

The rattle of chains echoed behind him as a pair of kyoketsu-shoge shot towards his back. Darius spun on the balls of his feet and with the slightest pull of his wrist, he knocked the projectile blades into each other and off their initial trajectory. He spun his Reikiken behind him to block the aura sword assault to his new blind spot, then spun his body to face the assailant and slam his own weapon into their face. The orange glow illuminated the cheery expression of the Rebel Dragon, who promptly disengaged from his current opponent with a repulsor-assisted leap to the rear. Almost instantly he found himself flanked by two more attackers.

Their earthy brown Hanzo Gear variants paid homage to the sands and sediments that ran throughout their home, and in this particular moment gave Darius the impression that they'd emerged from the very walls. They struck at him at random intervals from either side but were deflected by the fluid defenses of the Hanran no Ryu. A kick met the midsection of one of the attackers while the other was controlled by the meeting of their blades and a stream of parries that forced them back. The four other opponents managed to regain their bearings and charge in, but Darius was more than apt to welcome the challenge.

"So you know," the young neo-ninja spoke with a surprisingly even tone for someone under so much pressure, "the minimum number of opponents that a Yaiba operative is expected to be able to take on is eight. The five of you have more than your work cut out for you." He deflected a shot at his legs with a low parry that seamlessly transitioned into a casual block to his head, then with the flick of his wrist he blocked his back in the same manner as before. One of the assailants took the time to stab directly for him, but in an almost playful manner, Darius guided the enemy Reikiken away from the mark as he spun into a back-to-back position with the unlucky brown brute.

When the Yoroi warrior moved, so did the Yaiba at his back. The other four warriors were more than a little hesitant to continue their attack, because they knew that if Darius read their movements enough he could evade, and it would mean the effective end of their teammate.

"Sensei," Lex Ford growled, his back still connected to that of his teacher, "this isn't fair and you know it." Darius couldn't help but snicker.

"It's not supposed to be," the Rebel Dragon replied. "Battles usually aren't. You may be used to fighting against an enemy using demolitions and deception, but it's a whole different ballgame when you're standing face to face with independent thinkers." He thought back to his first assignment, the salvage mission in Johnson City that ended in his Uncle Callan being taken hostage by the Scarlet Scourge. The all-female death squad fought dirty, and added plenty of insult to the wounded heart of a boy who had lost his grandmother only a couple weeks before. “That’s enough,” he called, and the other students under his charge switched off their fireswords and returned to the formation.

“Sir,” they shouted in unison, “we await instruction.” Darius took stock of his soldiers, now numbered 150,000 and more than the usual training hall could contain. They stood at the bottom of the Canyon, shielded by the shade offered by the rocky chasm. Each soldier, man, woman or nonbinary, all looked to him and his original 45 as their definitive leaders. The discipline that they showed far outweighed the initial playfulness of his class, and for good reason. The time drew close where Red uniforms would swarm everything that they loved. The Yoroi Alliance had hardly had any chance to recover from the discord sown by the Anti-Rebel Faction in the latter months of 2084, and the only thing that kept them safe this long was the now dwindled demolitions that were at one point scheduled to replace the ones in the terrain beyond the Cluster entrances.

“As many of you may have assumed,” Darius began as he stowed his Reikiken in its holster and clasped his hands behind his back, “our outer defenses are on their last leg. The unit of enemy troops that’s been outside our walls for the last few months has already gone down by half, but even then there’s a thousand troops with superior firepower that we’ll have to fight.” Darius half expected them to have something to say on the subject, but there wasn’t so much as a shudder in any of the new trainees. It made him feel better about his odds, though he knew that it was unwise to expect the battle to be won with numbers alone. “In order to drive them off, you’re going to have to be more than soldiers following orders. Your intuition, your experience, and your motivations for fighting are invaluable assets on the battlefield. Use them. Rely on them. Do what needs to be done." As Darius spoke to his troops, Johannes Thornhill, the former emissary and newest among the Yoroi's Councilors, now approached the young general with an entourage of three men of impressive physique.

Each of the new entrants, sans the man who led the way, carried metal crates on their backs that were as impressive as the visible strength exerted to set them down as gently as they did. Darius raised an eyebrow, as did the others that watched their arrival.

"In preparation of the upcoming festivities," Johannes spoke in a deeply diplomatic voice that contrasted the image of the sweat-covered soldiers that now stood in earshot, "our demolitions department fashioned some new toys that truly capture the nature of the Yoroi Alliance. Leaders, I implore you to take a look." There was a certain flair about Thornhill's tone that hadn't been there in so long. It was rare to see a smile on his face in the months since Ina died, which told Darius that he was either in better spirits or what he brought with him really stood a chance at making a difference.

Bobbi Brynarr and Leroy Baptiste were the first of the 45 to look into the crates, and when they were shown to be stunned to silence, others started to wander up to the silver toy chests dropped in front of them. Johannes folded his arms across his chest as he took a place next to the fledgling commander. Both of them smiled from ear to ear, and while they said nothing to each other, both of them took a great deal of pride in the sudden childlike excitement that bewitched their troops.

****

February 4th, 2085 4:26 p.m.,

Major Kyle Crawford watched as the three-dimensional projection of an area map circled over the command center table. He had to marvel at the wisdom of the Yoroi, to place the heart of their meager civilization between the Red Canyon to the east and Hance Canyon to the west. The clusters numbered as many as the letters of the alphabet, but the only priority targets were Clusters A, B, and C. They were the brain of the entire faction, and once they fell then everything else would fall, too.

Kyle shook his head with a sigh of agitation. Ever since the change of leadership, nothing had felt quite right. The King seemed to be on their side, but there was something disquieting about him. Bryan Piccio, a man who had previously dedicated his life to ending the Scarlet Kingdom, suddenly turned on his former comrades at the death of his son. It was the kind of thing that would leave a normal man broken and distraught, and yet here he sat, this foreigner, as the current King of the Reds. It was his calm demeanor, his calculative, procedural, methodical mannerisms that gave Kyle more than a little reason to fear a man known as the Rabbit of the Divine Wind.

If he was honest, things hadn't felt right for him since Serenity left. Every time he tried to think about what must've crossed her mind to make her abandon the Kingdom—to make her abandon him—he grew furious. A part of him wanted to track her down and tell her off, to vent his anger and confusion, to remind her that she still had him and Ryan and parents who, even now, worried for her safety and—no.

His focus, as always, should be and *would* be on his mission. Right now that meant mapping out a route into the Yoroi for the bulk of his forces while the others attacked the main entrances on the banks of the Colorado River. The problem, though, was getting down there without being noticed. It was true that the majority of the traps laid throughout the terrain were gone, but so was a substantial portion of the intelligence unit. The 602nd Infantry Battalion had taken losses as well, but in much smaller scale. Together, the force that at one time numbered roughly 3,000 now totaled at about 1,000. Without the requested reinforcements it would be a challenge, but there was something in the works from the engineering department. At least, that's what he'd been told by his former subordinate Maxwell Cartwright.

There was the crackle of transport tires on the sandy rock outside the Major's tent, but his focus remained on the map of the enemy territory. There was shouting, something about being careful with the crates, and all of a sudden Kyle was confident that Cartwright's intel was as true as ever. Good thing, too. If the goods that apparently just came in were as good as Maxwell implied, then they may be the difference maker in the assault and conquest of the Yoroi Alliance.

The tent entrance flew open, and piqued the irritation of the commanding officer. Still he pored over the hologram of the map, and while there was no change to his posture or even the expression on his face, the man who disturbed him could feel a shift in the atmosphere around him.

"I would hope that you have a very good reason to disturb my planning," Major Crawford all but growled. As an intelligence specialist, it was imperative that Kyle have time to evaluate all the intel. His ability to do so was tantamount to the Kingdom's ability to find a way forward, not just in the conquest of the Yoroi Alliance, but in bringing all of Providence to heel. It was, in the Major's eyes, his sacred duty to his nation, and one that scorned all interruption.

"That depends on if you think a special delivery of Project Thunderclap weapons is worth looking up from your maps, Major." Kyle resisted the urge to groan as he noted the voice of one Felix Kilpatrick, who undoubtedly smiled brightly through his mystical green eyes. He turned to face his less-than-welcome guest with an expression of hollow pleasantry.

"So it's ready for use, then?" The question was pointed and warned of his immediate demise should his answer prove less than satisfactory. He might not have chosen the path of an infantryman, but Kyle Crawford was still the son of a legendary sniper and had a marksman title in his own right.

"Ready and waiting, sir," Felix sang with an impish delight. Crawford eyed the map again, careful to take stock of every confirmed location of the Yoroi's damned traps, and sighed an agitated sigh.

"Show me," he commanded, and Felix ushered him out of the tent.

****

February 4th, 2085 8:45 p.m.,

Al Westershire relished in his extracurricular activities as a workman in Sora Kaneuji's lab on Engineering Level L. He was there to steal the secrets of Yaiba technology, namely the Lightbeams that stopped the KDN in its tracks, and though Cal was more than reluctant to let him anywhere near his mechanical babies, at least Kaneuji was indifferent in the return of Al's weapon.

"Analysis is done," he'd said with an excited glint in his eye as his hands fidgeted at his sides. "There's no real reason why I would keep it." There wasn't anything particularly noticeable about Project Thunderclap. Not unless one knew how its secret mechanisms worked. Handing it back over to Al was effectively the dumbest thing that Sora had done.

Now he sat at a work bench, his electric sword at his side, and worked on the assembly of some Hanzo Gear while his spy drone got to work. He knew that Cal's workstation was nearby, and that soon enough he would leave the lab—and his precious Lightbeams—behind. All Al had to do was let his drone hover in the shadows above his senior student, and it would be a simple matter to probe the androids for the data he came for. His hands worked diligently to solder the thermal amplifier mechanism, his eyes focused on the sparks about the wires and metal, and once completed, he carefully slid the fork-like gadget into a straight metal hilt that was heat-treated like everything else around the Roan Mountain.

Al felt a buzz at his hip, and a smile of excitement and relief briefly took to his face before he returned to his focused expression. He looked up to see Cal head for the lab's exit, and with a subtle tap to the box-guard of the Thunderclap, the drone went in to do its work.

****

February 4th, 2085, 8:57 p.m.,

"Yeah, he in there," Cal spoke quietly into his comms. He knew that Al had watched him work on the Lightbeams, and had to admit that if he'd still had his original left eye, he wouldn't have noticed. The skill level on this kid was a lot higher than any of the Yaiba had expected. "I can see his drone buzzing around my Lightbeams looking for details. You want me to take it out?"

"No," John responded sternly. "Sit tight. I have a plan in place already. I just need you to keep an eye on him for me."

"Say less," Cal submitted. He was less than excited to have some Scarlet spy skulk over his things, but he trusted John's tactical mind, even more so after that assault on Johnson City last October. It made it much easier for the young warrior to look forward to the plan's execution with excitement.

****

February 4th, 2085, 10:13 p.m.,

Al wiped the sweat from his brow in a moment of relief. It'd taken an hour and some change to get enough data on the Lightbeams to report on. Even then, it was clear to Al that it wasn't all the secrets they held. He could've taken them apart, but there was hardly enough time for a full analysis, much less for reassembly. He knew going in that he'd have to get all the intel he could without making it obvious, which is why he watched Cal through the drone from the moment he deployed it.

They were connected to him through that artificial eye of his, the Kiringan. Each Lightbeam had an individual function, but there were some programming nuances shared between them. One of them was to hack and disable, another to deflect bullets, but that was all that could be gathered aside from their shared vision with the Kiringan. Mix that with the fact that each one had its own Reikiken and built-in kyoketsu-shoge and it wouldn't be hard for anyone to believe that Cal could handle full-scale military operations with twice the efficiency and a fraction of the force of the others in the Insurrection. It wasn't much to go on, Al already knew, but it was more than what the Kingdom had before and enough for them to figure out a countermeasure to Cal's little gadget gang. Though for added insurance, he could always take the Kiringan out of Cal's head and bring that along.

Al breathed in deeply, then out with a shudder. He wasn't strong enough to take Cal on, even with all the training he got from the Kingdom and Insurrection combined. He'd only just started to get the hang of the Kiryu style and Cal was nearly a master at it. If he was going to take the eye, he had to do it when Cal least expected it, otherwise it would be Al's head on the chopping block.

The drone returned to him and quickly returned to its place in the Thunderclap's box-guard. *That's enough for today,* Al reasoned. It was partly fatigue but mostly confidence. He'd accomplished his mission without causing any unnecessary harm to the people of the Insurrection. He knew it was wrong for him to want that. They were the enemy, but some things he couldn't help. After all, they'd been nothing but good to him since his arrival with Leo.

Al got up from his work station and made for the exit. He tried to focus on the accomplishment that he felt more than the discomfort at his preplanned betrayal. He tried not to think about how Leo would feel when he walked out without a word, something that proved next to impossible when he saw his friend approach in a light jog from down the hall. Al flipped the switch inside his head and flashed a warm smile despite the sudden flurry of emotions behind it.

"You're here late," Leo huffed. He was out of breath, but not as much as he would've been before. He was getting used to moving around with the Hanzo Gear on his person. He stood straight up, pat Al on the shoulder and asked, "What have you been up to?"

"Just helping Mr. Kaneuji out with some more projects," Al said evenly. He took a moment to size up his friend. The longer they stood out in the open on Level L, the more it put him at risk. He didn't want a fight, but if he was caught now, he might not have a choice but to go toe to toe with a 6'8" monster in addition to whatever reinforcements spawned in the meantime. Al donned a look of spontaneous memory as he gestured to his hip. "He gave me my sword back as a reward." Not entirely true, but Leo didn't need to know that. Leo smiled incredulously.

"There's no way Lukas-sensei is gonna allow you to use that in training, you know," warned the giant, but Al rolled his eyes as he moved towards the power-lift and Leo walked beside him.

"I wasn't thinking about that," the spy uttered with a bit more thoughtfulness in his expression. Leo opened his mouth to ask about the sudden change in demeanor, but Al quickly cut him off at the pass. "What about you? Any reason you're up right now?" Leo smiled.

"Oh, y'know, I'm just passing you up even more." Al knew that the child in distress taken in by the Yaiba act was just a cover. He knew that his presence at training and all the work he did was just a ploy to help him blend in with the locals, but he still couldn't stand that Leo was so much better at it than he was. Where Al had made it all the way to Kiryu, Leo had already made it to Tsuchiryu, the strong form that he made look effortless. His imposing stature contributed to his ability to make it look even more intimidating than it already was, and it was enough to make Al want to stop holding back as much and finally let his instincts blend with the new training. He'd always been the competitive type, and that didn't change while on a mission.

"You won't be ahead of me for too much longer," Al challenged with a wry grin. Leo shrugged as they boarded the power-lift.

"We'll see about that," he said as his confident smile grew wider. The loud clang of the lift's elevation mechanism overpowered their ears, and both young men knew it would be pointless to try and continue their conversation while they rode. It would only take a few moments to get to Level G and return to their quarters, but the road to the exit on Level A would be a much more difficult journey. Al had already taken the time in the last few days to map out the route. In case things got messy, he'd also taken the liberty to plant some of the microbombs he'd been issued the day he got this mission.

The power-lift came to a stop, and the moment Al faced forward, he was met with the bright orange glow of a Reikiken. Leo was stunned as he watched his friend raise his hands. *Well, that's not good,* Al thought. *I've been made.*

"You're coming with us, kid," said the first of eight Shadows. Al didn't recognize them, which put his mind at ease for the moment. He didn't bother to glance at the Thunderclap. He knew that the moment he had the thought to go for it, it would be the last one he would ever take. He needed to play this casually.

"All this just for me," Al taunted with an impressed whistle. "Seems like you finally figured it out."

"Figured what out," Leo demanded. His voice was harder than he expected, but there was no way that he, in his state of astonishment, would be able to regulate himself. "What's going on?" Leo took a step forward as if to stand between them, but froze under the gaze of a fighter much more experienced than him.

"Get back," the leader of the apprehension squad ordered. "This doesn't concern you. Alphonse Westershire, under the order of Director John Hamlin, you're to be brought to Level D immediately." The moment seemed suspended in time, Leo too afraid to breathe and Al far too comfortable in the tension wrought by the gaze of the leading Shadow.

"I understand," Al spoke in his most defeated tone. He extended his hands forward as the rearmost agent in the squad's formation approached him with a pair of cuffs. "Lead the way." The moment those words left Al's mouth, the receiver on his wrist flashed off and on, and a wall of explosions erupted from behind the apprehension squad. They were blown from their feet, Leo with them, and Al took no time in his pursuit of the Deployment Level.

Leo grunted, coughed on the smoke and dust mixture in his lungs, and pushed himself off the ground. He tried to yell, but the sudden reintroduction of the smoke to his faculties made him choke. He hobbled to the nearest wall and crouched down on one knee. He looked around as he applied his menpo mask and caught his breath. The members of the squad of Violet Shadows were still faced down, firmly planted from the blast that rocked them. Eight people were dispatched by the Director to come get Al for a reason that Leo couldn't comprehend. Now, those eight men and women were face-down in the dirt and Leo needed answers. Every inch of his body screamed with pain, but regardless of that, he sprinted through the corridors after the person he thought was his friend.

****

February 4th, 2085, 10:27 p.m.,

John and Cal monitored the situation from Level D through the holoprojectors. From the moment Al and Leo emerged from the power-lift, Cal positioned two

Lightbeams at Deployment Level A. He didn't know if he should expect Al to make it that far at first, and even went so far as to believe that John's use of eight soldiers was a bit excessive for just one Kingdom spy. Then the bombs went off in the tunnels. They weren't strong enough to force a cave-in, but they were still a lot stronger than expected for their imperceptible size.

"He's clever, I'll give him that," John was forced to admit. Together they watched as Leo, the furthest away from the detonation, got back up and sprinted in full Hanzo Gear after the person he thought was his friend. "That's interesting…"

"You want me to intercept?" Cal's question brought a smirk to John's face as he folded his hands in front of his face with his elbows on the desk before him.

"No, not yet. Let's let this play out," John returned, much to Cal's surprise. The younger Shadow looked at his Director with marked disbelief.

"Whatchu mean 'not yet,' Pops? You want him to blow something else up?" John couldn't help but smile. Apparently even now there wasn't anything too serious for Cal's sense of humor.

"It's not that," the Director assured him, "but if the friendship between Al and Leo has any kind of truth to it, we might be able to use it to our advantage."

"Sure, man," Cal replied with an upward change in octave. John knew it to mean that the Dragon prospect had his reservations about the plan. John rolled his eyes.

"Rendezvous with your Lightbeams on Level A. I'll have Vanessa to order our apprehension teams to light pursuit so they can steer him in your direction with a bit more haste," informed the Director. "As far as Leo is concerned, let's leave him to his own devices. I'm sure he can come up with a much more agreeable solution to the matter than we could at the moment."

****

February 4th, 2085, 10:39 p.m.,

Each level of the Roan Mountain base had three to four power-lifts, and Al took care to memorize all of their locations. He knew better than to take one straight up to the Deployment Level. No doubt Director Hamlin and anyone else he saw fit to rouse would've seen that coming by now. If he stood any chance of getting to the other side of this unharmed, he would have to segment the path through a few of the other levels.

His sprint through the Residence Level was, thankfully, a bit lengthy, and the presence of the majority of Yaiba civilians throughout the hall was enough to make his pursuers think twice about another involuntary detonation. He banked east. The power-lift was visible at the end of the hall. It seemed as if he would make it, but then he heard the rattle of chains.

A pair of kyoketsu-shoge swiped at him, one at his head and the other at his legs, but Al already twisted through the air in the space between them. The two Shadows that coordinated the attack, who stood on either side of the hall and watched Al tuck and roll out of his airborne spiral with more grace than befit a rookie, watched awestruck as he bounded for the lift. He turned around, flashed a smile, waved, and then dropped his cocky expression when he noticed Leo come up behind his would-be captors.

“Sorry,” he told his friend only a moment before the lift pulled him up towards Education Level E.

****

February 4th, 2085, 11:04 p.m.,

Leo clenched his teeth, his breath harder with every step, but still he couldn’t allow himself to give in. The weight of the Hanzo Gear on his body made him wonder how the more experienced Shadows fought wars in this stuff. He grew increasingly frustrated with the sluggishness that it brought him, and the more he felt his body slow down, the more he willed himself to go faster. Fatigue be damned, miscoordination be damned. Right now his friend was in trouble with the Yaiba Insurrection and he was determined to knock the crap out of him and find out what he did.

Sorry, he heard Al repeat in his mind. What the hell did he mean by that? What was he sorry for? Keeping Leo in the dark? Trying to run away without a word of clarity? Bombing homes with women and children in them? And then he thought about it. There was only one way in and out of the compound and after an attack like this, Al wouldn’t be able to get out in any kind of straight line. Now that he’d risked the lives of so many civilians on Level G, Leo realized that Al would be a fool not to do it again.

Leo ran to the northern lift as quickly as he could, and set his destination to the one he imagined Al would go to next: Education Level E.

****

February 4th, 2085, 11:27 p.m.,

"Alphonse!" The fury of Leo's voice sent a tremble through Al's spine. The fugitive stopped in his tracks, just a couple of feet away from the next power-lift. "Tell me what's going on!" There was a tremble in the execution of Leo's demand that betrayed feelings of pain and confusion and immeasurable anger. Al stood there, eyes on the lift as he caught his breath, and realized that his hands were clenched into painfully tight fists. "Oh, so you're not gonna face me? After all we've been through, you're just gonna blow me up and run away? Turn around!" Al did, and where Leo half expected some kind of remorseful expression, there was none, just a level of warning that he'd only seen directed at their enemies.

"Back off, Leo," Al ordered, and Leo's brow furrowed in confusion as he tried to figure out who this kid was talking to. "This has nothing to do with you." The arrogance of that statement made Leo's eyes widen with irritation.

"You almost killed me!" Leo didn't care enough to restrain himself at this point. "We watched each other's backs in the Wastes, fought side by side and protected each other and after all that I'm just some collateral damage in your fight with the Yaiba Insurrection, huh?" He took a few steps forward, his eyes locked with Al's.

Al, meanwhile, struggled to maintain his stoic military bearing. He wanted to explain what his mission was. He wanted to tell Leo that he still wanted to have his back, that he was the first person to make him feel like he had a family. He wanted to say that the bombs were more to stun than to kill because despite his orders, he couldn't bring himself to hurt these people. Instead, his training as a spy took hold, and he uttered in all seriousness, "I told you to back the hell off."

Leo pulled out his Reikiken, which came to life in a brilliant orange blaze as he challenged, "And what if I don't?" He didn't know what happened in the span of the last 24 hours, but he resolved to find out even if that meant he had to force it out of Al.

"It's not gonna end well for you," Al replied as he drew his own aura sword and pointed its luminous blade straight into the air. The temperature rose with the tension as Leo took a grounded stance. He pulled his arms close to his chest and held his weapon parallel to the ground with both hands.

With the full power of the repulsor boots, Al leaped forward and slashed through the air. Leo instinctively parried him through with enough power to force his landing, but before he could respond with a cut of his own, Al followed the energy through with a spin on his grounded leg and almost instantly swung at Leo's head. The giant brought his hands up as he carried his downward pointed blade to meet the blow and blocked with enough force to bat the enemy weapon away and send a shockwave through Al's arms. In the spy's moment of surprise, an enraged Leo quickly rolled his aura sword into position for a head strike.

Al bounded away. This wasn't how Leo fought in training at all. His movements were stronger by far, and it would take him a moment to regain enough feeling in his arms to keep up the battle. Before he could think of his next move, Leo had taken a massive step forward and went for an upward diagonal slash that Al only narrowly parried. Leo whipped his Reikiken back around for a shoulder strike born of all the speed that his rival fed him, and Al had no choice but to block. The force of the blow sent another shockwave through him, but when Leo went for the legs, Al had no choice but to open himself up to more punishment.

From the leg block, Al somehow found the will to leap into the air for a close range Falling Leaf, but when it looked like his blade would crash down on Leo's head, the gargantuan warrior did something that neither of them had expected: he parried the Falling Leaf. Al was knocked off his trajectory and hit the ground hard but still somehow managed to roll back to his feet. Leo spun, and with one hand he executed a wild horizontal slash. Al narrowly parried it, but with the level of stress his arms were under it was sloppy work. The enemy blade only lightly tapped his wrist, but that was all it took to shatter the receiver for the other bombs scattered around the compound. Leo, who saw that his opponent was off-balance, closed the distance with another spin, but this time with a strong upward diagonal slash.

It was more than enough to knock Al's Reikiken away, and when Leo saw that it was all the boy could do to hold onto it, he brought his own sword down towards Al's head in a mighty swing. Al had to fall to the ground completely to feed any kind of stability into his hasty block, and even then realized it might not be enough. Not only was Leo tall, but he was heavier than his lean physique could possibly betray. Now, he had leverage over Al, power and weight fueled by rage and confusion. The blades, interlocked with no chance of disconnection, inched closer to Al's face.

"Leo," Al called, but the ferocity in Leo's eyes remained. "Leo, stop!" Al was frantic now. He shouldn't have stopped. He should've just run, but his pride and his hope that there was some way he could just brush Leo off wouldn't have it. Another inch. Another rapid increase in a heat that was already so strong he sweat bullets. Another. The bright orange cross was now only centimeters away from Al's face. Leo leaned his head back just slightly, and suddenly Al could no longer see his friend in those eyes. All he saw was darkness faintly pierced by luminescent orange.

Al turned his head to the side as the distance between the swords and his face, but it was pointless. In a matter of seconds, the side of Al's face was met with a searing pain. His lungs emptied themselves of all air as his voice ripped through the halls of Level E. Leo ripped his sword away from his downed opponent's face, the skin of his cheek burnt onto it, and before he could even take a moment to admire his handiwork, a shock shot through his body that brought him to his knees. In a matter of seconds, both boys were out like a light.

Chapter Eleven

February 7th, 2085, 9:55 a.m.,

John sat at his desk on Conference Level D, his eyes focused on the holoprojector in front of him. Vanessa sent it over to him with the report that a sufficient number of the damaged geo sensors had been restored to working order, which proved to be some much-needed good news. Now it would be easier to track the enemy's movements throughout the Wastes and figure out their most prominently used routes now that Johnson City has been taken. The commando units should also be easier to deploy now without putting them in so much danger. A knock came at the glass door.

John looked up to see Dr. Dominguez, and he couldn't help but smile. It was a compulsory response that happened every time he saw her, regardless of his mood. She'd been like a second mother to him for his entire life, told him stories of her life as a little girl in the early days of the Insurrection, before Hanzo Gear training or the Roan Mountain base. She watched him play when he was little, held his hand with his mother May when she couldn't convince him to go to school and make friends, scolded him when he broke things or played too close to a battlefield. She liked to joke that it was no wonder he was as good a warrior as he was, because he always found a way to get into trouble.

Anna flashed a quick smile, but her expression was one of exhaustion and her face soon became as stern as he'd ever seen it in his youth.

"How's he doing," John asked with more sympathy than he intended. He knew that Al was a spy, that he should maintain some kind of hostility towards him for his deception (which he did), but he also couldn't bring himself to hate a child, much less wish him harm. It was enough to soften Dr. Dominguez's seriousness for a moment.

"He's recovering nicely from the surgery," she told him. "He's gonna have a nasty scar, though."

John shrugged as he rose to his feet. "He's lucky, then. Deceiving us is one thing, but betraying someone he was in the trenches with? Considering Leo hardly knows his own strength, I'd say that could've been a lot worse."

"It still can," said Anna as she escorted the Director from his office and out to the power-lift. She set the destination for Medical Level I. "From the intel you shared with the Insurrection's leaders, he's a top spy of the Scarlet Kingdom. Hard to believe that a boy that young could be such a threat."

"You remember how I was, don't you," he asked as a rueful smirk crept across his jaw. "High energy, passionate, quick-witted—"

"Reckless, impulsive, hard-headed," she continued with a slick smirk of her own. He wanted to challenge it but he knew she was right. A part of him missed how he was back then.

"You didn't have to say all that," John told her, which made Anna chuckle. "Anyway, my point was that he has a lot of similarities with me. It shouldn't be all that surprising that he's as dangerous as he is."

"But conscripting a child, John," Dr. Dominguez replied with a sense of anger and worry in her slightly shaken voice. "It makes you wonder how much of a choice he had in the 'serving of his country,' doesn't it?" John took a moment in silence as the mechanical whirs and clangs of the power-lift resounded throughout the compound in its descent.

"It doesn't matter," he said, and was met with an appalled look. He raised his hands placatively and told her, "At least not right now it doesn't. Al Westershire infiltrated our home, attempted to steal our technology for enemy use, and jeopardized our people by setting off bombs near our residences. I understand wanting to extend every sympathy to the child, but our desire for kindness doesn't change the fact that he's been hostile towards us since day one and we couldn't see it."

"I love that you've grown up into a brilliant leader and a strong warrior, but I hate it sometimes, too." Anna started, then groaned. Still, she was proud of him. He'd done a lot of good for the Insurrection since he joined the Violet Shadows at 18, and then she remembered. It'd been four days since his birthday. "How old are you now, John?"

The question caught him off guard, and to embellish his surprise he had to think about it. Somehow his birthday had flown past him without his notice. "I'm 39 now, as of the 3rd. Can't believe I'm almost 40."

"It is a milestone. Not many of our people make it that far," she reminded him solemnly. "Hopefully we can fix that and increase our life expectancy a bit." There was a pensiveness there that told the Director that she had a plan to do just that, but before he could even open his mouth to ask a question, she donned an aura of unmitigated focus. "We're here. He's in isolation, so you won't be disturbed while you question him."

"Thank you, Anna," he said earnestly. She smiled and squeezed his shoulder.

"Anytime," she replied. She exited the power-lift and returned to her work. John, hardened his expression, and proceeded through the Medical Level to do the same.

****

February 7th, 10:22 a.m.,

Al woke up in a bed on the Medical Level, groggy from the pain. It took him a moment to figure out where he was, but in an instant his mind flashed with the events of the night prior. His mission had nearly been completed, he was nearly out, but then Leo had to come and ruin it all. He felt the right side of his face, ran his fingers along the scar that now stretched from the corner of his mouth to just below his right ear, and was overtaken by a heavy mixture of emotion. He was horrified that his face was mangled and furious at Leo for what he'd done. He was sorry that he'd hurt him when he wanted nothing more than a clean escape, and he was disgusted with his failure to accomplish any of his goals. Most of all, though, he was worried. His parents were the only thing on his mind…until the Director cleared his throat and commanded Al's attention.

"Alphonse Westershire," read the Yaiba leader from an aged and stained manilla folder in his hands. He sat in the chair beside the bed, his expression cool as he eyed the page. "Born to Louisa and—heh—John Westershire in

New York City, whom you lived with from birth until your fourteenth birthday, where they remanded you into the custody of the Kingdom for espionage training where you proved to be head and shoulders above your peers and a fair amount of your superiors." John looked up from the folder with an intensity in his eyes that made the young spy want to flinch. "And now you infiltrate the Yaiba for the second time."

"That's ridiculous," he protested. It was pointless, they both knew, because his cover had been blown and his file now sat in the lap of a man who could—and if approached carelessly, would—end him without so much of a strain of his muscles. Even still, he didn't want to admit anything and give the Director the satisfaction of being right.

"Really? You're going to pretend that I'm not looking at your entire record right now?" Al said nothing in response, so John continued with an all too knowing smile. "It says here that about a year in, you caught the eye of one Major Kyle Crawford and were taken into the Scarlet Intelligence Corps as active personnel six months ahead of schedule. It also says that the mission that earned you your spot took place around the same time that my son and his friends went on their first scavenging mission." John remembered it well. Callan was captured by the Scourge and held for days, Darius was a wreck, and the Kabuto were dispatched by Emiko to bring back their lost Dragon.

"Big deal," Al answered as he folded his arms. "It's purely coincidental."

"Except for the fact that it isn't," John countered with gravity to his voice that warned the young soldier that if he dared to insist on having an attitude, it would be met with a much greater one. "Your report is in here from that mission. Here, let me read it for you. 'I selected August 28th for mission start and placed a micro-comm on the hostage, here listed as Callan Rouge, Water Dragon of the Yaiba Insurrection. Target accessed through meal deliveries between interrogation sessions.' I have to say, it's a clever plan. Micro-comms are difficult to find even by trained intelligence operatives like myself, so it's no wonder we missed it." Al turned his head away from him, but then remembered that it was exactly that that resulted in the delivery of his hideous scar. He returned his attention to the Director, who asked, "How long do those things last, by the way? Three, maybe four days before the batteries go kaput?"

"What do you want, Director Hamlin?" The glare of the former Lightning Dragon made Al realize that there was far too much of an edge to his voice. The instantaneous fear made John deescalate.

"For now, I want to review the facts so I know I'm up to speed. Your comms device ran through a channel that went straight back to Major Crawford, who ran the leaked intel—most likely from our last meeting with Director Ishikawa—to the Infantry Division. That about right?" Al didn't know what to say, and again John spoke in his place. "You knew that we would be preparing for an attack on Johnson City, so just before we were ready, your superiors launched an assault on the Roan compound and had our previous leader executed." Al's eyes sharpened on the man before him as a cold sweat ran from the top of his head down to his scar. "You might not have directly infiltrated our home before, but you still managed to get past our defenses twice without our notice."

"And whose fault is that," Al erupted. "You know how weird it is for you guys to just take in a couple of kids you found wandering around in the Wastes? And then you subject them to this oversaturation of affection that has no place in a military organization! You have some great tech and some amazing fighting skills, but you're too soft where it counts. That's why I got in and that's why I almost got out just as easily."

"Spoken like a frightened child whose parents failed him," John retorted coldly. "What would you know of normalcy when you were raised in the cult of the Scarlet Kingdom? How can you decide that what we're doing is wrong or wasteful or weird when your parents fattened you like a calf and left you on the altar of the State? Let me ask you, do you think you're being a good son by sticking to your training and going behind enemy lines?"

"That's exactly what I'm doing," Al shouted back, fists full of the blankets draped over his hospital bed. Even here, John never raised his voice or resorted to more than that stern, threatening, judgmental glare.

"I got news for you, kid," John said with a degree of directness that gave Al pause. "They didn't raise you to be a son. They raised you to be a projection of their own miserable lives."

"You're wrong," Al whispered, distraught. Even though the words left his lips, he knew that a part of him recognized what John said as true.

"In their minds, you don't exist to be loved or respected. They showed you that when they turned you over for military training at the age of fourteen. You exist to live up to the fanatical ideals of people who can't delineate their own personalities from the conflicts of their homeland. For them, dragging you into a bloodbath is their idea of love."

"And how the hell are you any different," Al demanded, tears in his eyes. John's previously rock-hard expression fell soft.

"We're different," he said softly, "because we don't fight for the glory of our home or the punishment of those who disagree with us. Our purpose now is the same as it was with the Civil Rights Movement of the 1960s: we fight so that one day our children won't have to. You asked me what I wanted before. *That's* all I want. Did it ever occur to you to ask Leo about what he's had to go through before you met him?" The question shot right through Al's heart. After all this time, he regarded Leo as something of a brother, but where was the validity of that when all he knew was what he saw? "Director Ishikawa was the kind of person who would help anyone who needed it. Sure, she presented herself as a hardline leader, and she could be from time to time. Ultimately, though, she was a kind soul who just wanted to set things right on this battered wasteland of a continent. That's why, even after knowing everything that you've done, even after you just ridiculed her approach to life and war, I'm going to extend that same kind of kindness to you. You can try to break out again with our intel, fight our soldiers again, probably end up getting yourself killed in the process just as was your original plan, or you could help us put a stop to all this once and for all."

Al was quiet. His eyes flickered back and forth across the blankets spread over him as he contemplated his life, his mission, and more than all that, his next steps. He took a deep breath, closed his eyes, and unclenched his fists. "What do I have to do," he asked the Director. John clapped him on the shoulder and simply smiled.

****

February 10th, 2085 3:25 p.m.,

Major Kyle Crawford was decently impressed. The Thunderclap weapon was an intelligence operative's dream. It was a lightweight sword that could fend off the Yaiba's Reikiken for a few minutes if the battle got heated, but it also came with surveillance and ionic pulse drones that could assist in expert information gathering or a speedy escape. He'd taken the last six days to figure out for himself whether or not they would be good for his men, and as much as he wanted to deny Felix's input, he would be a fool to do so. There were only enough for a small battalion, but the multifaceted functionality of the weapon struck Major Crawford as enough.

Kyle walked the makeshift training grounds at the center of the camp, Scarlet Swordsmen—a term he'd never thought he'd even consider for the Kingdom, let alone his ranks—busy with a strict regiment of wide swings and calculated defenses. He couldn't help but smile, and to his chagrin Fitzpatrick noticed.

“I see that the Thunderclap has lived up to your expectations, Major,” the excitable redhead smiled as he jogged into a confident stride beside the intelligence agent. Kyle resisted the urge to roll his eyes as they continued to pace.

“Strange of you to speak so highly of something that doesn’t explode, Lieutenant,” Major Crawford commented. “Speaking of, how goes teaming with my little brother?” He couldn’t help but worry about him. He’d been so shaken when Serenity left, and Kyle could tell that Ryan’s head wasn’t where it needed to be. It frustrated him when he was stationed at the Western Camp, but now that he’d been called back east it was hard to keep an eye on him.

“Ah, but the Thunderclap can make things explode,” Felix elaborated as the corners of his mouth lifted higher. “But it’s fine. Ryan is a good man, excellent sniper, even better leader from the single operation we’ve been on. I see a lot of accolades coming for Seargeant Crawford if he keeps down this road.” Kyle hummed, partly out of suspicion but mostly out of reassurance.

“Let’s hope he does, then,” the Major spoke thoughtfully. Before Felix could tease him, Kyle walked away from him, fixated on the nagging idea that his brother may just go astray.

****

February 12th, 2085, 7:45 a.m.,

Within the span of a month and a half, Bryan had become a beloved ruler. The people, still beholden to the disgusting philosophies of Kingdom Scarlet, were at least able to see that his changes to their society had helped them. He had, single-handedly, retooled the Scarlet Training program with the techniques he'd taken from the Insurrection. He'd covered the recent gaps in the Scarlet Scourge with the formation of the Scarlet Streaks. Even though a couple of them died in their first op, they were a more than capable group worthy of the title of "death squad." Everything that he did made the Kingdom stronger, something he promised he'd do when he destroyed the fool who attacked him on the street. The Crown was secure, as were the borders, and despite Nash's recent attempts to tear it all asunder, the former prince was left to roam outside Scarlet territory.

King Piccio felt a degree of security that he'd never experienced during his time with the Yaiba Insurrection, and he understood why his daughter Lyla never went back. The air was fresh, not the artificial breezes from the vents of a hollowed out mountain. There was no expectation of war during days where he wanted to sit in his palace and look down upon his subjects. He could detach here, like he's wanted to from the moment he was old enough to recognize what he'd been born into.

He was loved. He was powerful. He had a right to decide his next move with no Director to order his steps, and with a twisted smile he resolved once again to avenge his son. He sat on his throne, the ghost of his child Jaden right beside him, and patiently waited for the guest he invited. It had been something he'd meant to do for a while, but until now his schedule did not permit.

The door opened, and the ghostly Jaden smiled with dubious intent as he sauntered to meet the man escorted in by the guards. He was an older gentleman with unkempt brown hair with streaks of gray and skeptical green eyes that scanned the chambers of the King's Court, though none of the chosen members had been invited to this little meeting. The man's body was lean but still fit, as if he halfway expected that his time on the battlefield wasn't over just yet, despite the fact that he'd been retired for years.

"Ah, Mr. Crawford," Bryan said with an immense pleasure. He'd hoped that it would alleviate a bit of the tension that Alan Crawford had brought in with him, but when it didn't, the King simply moved on. "I've been meaning to reach out to you for quite some time." He paused for a moment, as if with expectation, but there was no bow or other gesture of honorific ascribed to His Majesty.

"Apologies, my King," Alan offered in as earnest a tone as he could. "If I bent my knee to you now, I wouldn't be able to get back up again." Bryan narrowed his eyes. It was an obvious lie, but he chose to overlook it so as not to sour his mood.

"I see," said Bryan with a disappointed sigh. Jaden stuck out his tongue at the old man. "Well, I wouldn't want you to hurt yourself on my account. Shall we?" The king gestured to the side door as he stepped down from the throne. Though it was perfectly natural to assume that a man who sat most of his time would want to get out of his chair every once in a while, the fact that King Piccio offered to walk alongside him took him aback.

"It would be an honor, Your Grace," Alan remarked. It was a lie, of course. He'd always hated the noble class, especially the ones that only recently had the courtesy to die, and there was nothing about the wily Rabbit that would inspire a change of feelings. Nevertheless, they walked together through the side door and towards an elevator. "So," the former Sergeant Crawford started, "to what do I owe the pleasure of His Majesty's summons?"

"You can drop the formality," Bryan assured him with a half smile. Jaden strolled out of the elevator ahead of his father, and the King happily trailed after the shade of his son. They were on the floor of the Empire State Palace that had been converted into a botanical garden of sorts. It was lush with an array of greens and purples and yellows, each one a vibrant gift of the assorted flowers that lined the walkway. "I can tell that you're not a fan of the ruling class. In all honesty, I'm not either."

"That makes sense," Alan replied with considerable apprehension. He wasn't fearful, but he knew better than to trust his kind. "You were Yaiba before you took the throne, right? I wouldn't be surprised if you're the reason why the former King and all his Court mysteriously died within a week of each other."

"Well, I am," Bryan admitted without a shred of concern. The ghost boy that walked before them clapped in praise of his dad. "They were partly to blame for the untimely death of my son, but my reasons for taking them out run a little bit deeper."

"And what other reasons could you have for killing a king and his associates," Alan asked with a degree of foreboding brought on by thoughts of his own renegade daughter. He would kill the new King right now if it meant she'd be safe, but after what Ryan told him, the chances of that were unlikely. Even if he were to die, the Kingdom was too loyal to Bryan, too enraptured by his cause to wipe out the other factions rather than subjugate them. The best way to ensure that Serenity remained safe was to bide his time and wait for the opportunity to strike against the madman.

"My main reason to kill that bastard Shane was that he raped my mother in front of my father. It took her years to get over that, and she was reminded of it every time she looked at me, right up until the day she died." The King Rabbit's tone was wistful, twisted into a knot of pain at the memory and the admission of his history to a stranger that his uncle probably should've killed. Alan's brows raised in genuine surprise.

"Wait, you don't mean—" he asked, and the King glanced over his shoulder at the old sniper and smiled a knowing smile.

"The most common dispute of my claim to the throne was that I wasn't nobility, and that the honor of ruling the Kingdom should've gone to one of Shane's actual descendants. Even he didn't realize that in naming me the new heir to the throne, he gave me the inheritance I never thought to stake claim to." There was a brief pause of reflection on Bryan's part, but Alan didn't know if it was in thoughtfulness or some kind of sick admiration of his work. Here, the new King had just confessed to the murder of his own father, and no matter how justified the killing was, Alan couldn't help but feel that a man who would kill his own father was unpredictable in the best of cases. "Anyway," the Mad Rabbit continued as Jaden, wholly invisible to their guest, skipped in circles around them like he would've when he was little, "none of that is why I summoned you to me."

Alan again raised his eyebrows, then asked in what he believed to be reasonable caution, "How can I be of service, Your Grace?" The sudden return to honorifics told Bryan that Alan was duly afraid, and the King resisted the urge to let the corner of his mouth tip upward.

"I wanted to ask you how you survived," the King asked with a kind of knowing inflection.

"Survived…" Alan trailed off, as if he didn't know what the King insinuated, but he knew it was hardly enough to convince either of them.

"Within the Yaiba Insurrection, the report of the White Ruins Miracle—although I understand that you in the Kingdom have called it the White Ruins Massacre all this time—say that there were no enemy survivors upon the debut of the Hanzo Gear. Of course, the report of the incident comes from the only survivor from the Field Test team, Dre Hamlin," Bryan informed him with dubious tone of voice. Alan could hardly stifle the surprise. *So* that *was his name,* he thought. For years he'd only known that man as the one who had spared his life—the one who had opened his eyes to the truth of Kingdom Scarlet.

"Fascinating," Alan whispered, and unwittingly drew the full attention of the King. Bryan turned to face him, eyes as fierce as his predecessor's but more jovial, more excited at Alan's moment of realization.

"It is indeed," the King assured him. "My uncle wasn't known for his mercy in his missions, but the fact that you went head to head with him and still draw breath implies that his ruthlessness might've been exaggerated. So, what happened?" Alan was reluctant to continue the discussion, unwilling to offer an answer to his King, but knew the potential dangers of refusal.

"To tell you the truth, I have no idea. He let me go on a whim, I guess," Alan elucidated to a wild smile from the King.

"Marvelous," spoke the Rabbit. He turned away and continued his stroll through the botanical gardens. "You're dismissed." Alan bowed his head, then turned back the way they came with little hesitation.

****

February 12th, 2085, 11:11 a.m.,

Zayvier Peters sat on the bleachers on Training Level C, and carefully watched the current cycle of students. They ran varied drills of the full range of styles, and the Bautista-sensei moved between them to correct form. Lukas had become a surprisingly good teacher since Callan gave him the remains of Manny's Reikibo. There was a freedom in his expression of movement that told Zay that it was safe to finally move forward on the third commando squad. He knew that Lukas was Bill's candidate for Kazeryu, and intended to use the upcoming mission as a measure of his abilities with that weapon. The Wind Dragon Candidate glanced over to the Tsuchiryu, and a confident smirk took its place along his jaw.

"Alright," Lukas called out to his students, "keep working independently, remember the corrections I gave you. I'll be back in a minute." He disassembled the Reikibo and stowed its two halves in twin holsters at his side as he approached the man on the bleachers. Zayvier couldn't help but smile.

"You lookin' good out there, man," the Tsuchiryu complimented. "Come a long way since you were in their shoes." Zay and Lukas were about three or so years apart in their training experience, with Lukas starting just a month before Zay graduated the program, but the senior fighter always knew that that rookie was worth the watch.

"Thanks, man," Lukas said with a smile and a complete dismissal of formality. "It means a lot coming from Uncle Bill's replacement. What brings you down here?" The change of subject was abrupt, yet smooth, as was typical for Lukas and his late father. There was an optimistic tinge in his voice, as if he knew to expect something to appear from beyond the horizon.

"A mission," Master Peters informed him with a slick expression. "I've been tapped by Director Hamlin and Senior Agent Kincaid to head up a commando squad."

"Wait, are you here to ask if I wanna be on the team?" The excitement he projected was palpable, and it made Zayvier chuckle despite the fact that he knew Lukas to be a powerhouse of a warrior. For a moment, the optimistic look in Lukas' face, that disposition that he'd understandably neglected since the death of his father, almost moved Zay to tell him of his underlying assignment.

"More or less, yeah," was what he went with. "You, Daxa, and me are supposed to head to Johnson City in the next hour. We gotta rendezvous with the Helmets' side of the team."

“Where are we going,” Lukas asked with practical stars in his eyes. “What’s the mission?” Zayvier stood to his feet and clapped the young instructor on the shoulder.

“I’ll brief you when we get there,” said the Earth Dragon. He turned towards the exit and started on his way as he said, “I’mma let you get back to your class, though. I’ll see you.” Then he was gone, and Lukas was on pins and needles with anticipation.

****

February 12th, 2085, 2:20 p.m.,

It had been a little over a month since Serafina had started seeing Argus Wulfric. It’d been a long time since she’d been this excited, and for a moment it felt like they might actually have a future together that didn’t involve guns and fireswords. Serafina Leyva was the self-serving type, the kind of woman who would do anything to advance herself and prove herself invaluable to the cause. She not only braved the battlefield, but looked forward to it almost as much as Argus did the testing of his chemical weapons. But when she looked into those chocolate eyes of his and ran her fingers through his oaken hair, it made her think she could actually leave all that behind.

So here she was, back at the shooting range now that her wounds had had a chance to heal up. Each round she discharged from the chamber gave just enough of a recoil to send a stinging shockwave through her formerly injured shoulder. It reminded her that she was alive, and more importantly, that she had a job to do. Serafina was hardly the kind of person to buy into that patriotic nonsense that most of the other Scourge members did. She wasn't white, so the inherent superiority that those girls felt didn't apply to her, or for Aria Black, for that matter. She simply believed herself to be superior, and from the time she joined the military she resolved to prove it.

The first stage in that plan was to destroy the legacy of Serenity Crawford, a stage at which she'd only just begun to work. As long as the former leader of the Scourge drew breath, Serafina would continue to live in her shadow. That was just something she wouldn't tolerate. Once Serenity was out of the way for good, she'd have no problem with stage two: the destruction of the Yaiba Insurrection. It was harder than she made it sound in her head, but with her darling little spy about to report back at any moment, she had a feeling she could kill two birds with one bullet. Maybe after that she could give some more thought to a future with Mr. Wulfric.

Serafina discharged her last round, and in the moment it took to reload, Aria walked through the door behind her. The Scourge leader knew who it was without a single glance to the rear. The footsteps were lighter than Cecelia's, and with Kerri lost at the Battle of Yorktown, it didn't take much more brainpower than that to deduce the identity of her visitor.

"If you're interrupting me, Aria, I hope you have some good news," Serafina sang in the wildness she was known for. Aria opened her mouth to speak, but then realized what stood against the targets in Serafina's sights. There, bound by the hands with a look of sheer terror plastered to their otherwise gagged faces, were John and Louisa Westershire. Bullet holes adorned the paper around their heads and arms and legs, and while they shook with fear they knew better than to move. The horrific display was only enough to make Aria shake her head, and that was what struck her as truly terrifying.

Aria was Yaiba by birth, and only defected from the Insurrection after she'd burned every bridge she'd had. It was her every intention to help solve the problem of Kingdom Supremacy from the inside, but all that had happened was she got used to the Scarlets' cruelty. She breathed a heavy sigh and put aside the sudden urge to reach out to her former allies for extraction. She had a report to give.

"As it turns out, I do," Aria finally said. The look on Serafina's face changed from an intense focus to that unusually disturbing Cheshire Cat grin she'd made herself known for. She stowed her weapon, much to the relief of her captives, and turned to face her subordinate. Aria donned a cautious smile as she continued. "Westershire has made contact. He's got the intel we were after and is about to make his way home."

"For the sake of dear ol' Ma and Pa, here, I hope he's got the Thunderclap with him," Serafina said with a shiver of delight. "Otherwise I'll have to aim for the center of my targets!" She shouted it over her shoulder just to see her captives squirm.

"No need to worry," Aria confirmed. "He assured me that everything will be as it should be once he's back in Kingdom Territory."

"Excellent," Serafina cooed with delight. She pulled out her pistol again and exchanged the empty clip for a fresh one. She took aim at the space just beside John's head and shouted, “You hear that? Mama’s baby is coming home!”

“There’s one more thing,” Aria urged before the Scourge leader could pull the trigger. Serafina licked her lips as if to savor the fear of her would-be victims.

“What’s that,” she asked in a girlish tone that truly emphasized her madness. She massaged the trigger with her finger in a carefree manner that could only be described as “Serafina.”

“The kid was able to get us information on our enemy’s next move. They mean to take Charlotte and decrease our range of motion,” Aria explained, and Serafina shot a round just past John’s ear.

“Do they, now?” The question was laced with excitement.

“There’s more,” Aria told her.

“Out with it, already,” the Lady Leyva demanded. “You know I can’t stand those suspenseful waiting games you like to play.”

“Serenity is the one they’ve chosen to lead the charge.” Aria’s tone was nonchalant and reeked of a lack of concern for what might happen. Serafina shot again, but this time the shot connected with John’s leg. As a pool of red quickly spread along the floor, the wily gunwoman smiled with disturbing ferocity.

“Excellent,” she said, and pat a freshly stunned Aria on the shoulder as she walked out of the range.

Chapter Twelve

February 14th, 2085, 3:26 a.m.,

Serenity awoke to the gentle but irritating beep of her comms unit, and for a moment she mulled over the options before her. She could just stay in place, ignore the call and go back to sleep, or she could take a moment to wake up and see what Director Hamlin wanted now. She chose the latter. She reasoned that it was a testament to her strength on the battlefield that they called her so often, and that it was a matter of personal obligation that she answer. The denizens of the Insurrection had been kind to her, as if she hadn't been an enemy to them a little over two months ago, and welcomed her as the refugee she was. There were no snide remarks (aside from Callan), no calls for her head, only a kind of sympathy she never would've been shown in the Kingdom. These were people who understood what it meant to be displaced, and every time she thought on the subject, Serenity realized how badly she'd been led to misjudge them.

She crossed the room to answer the call with a sense of urgency that reflected her military history, and while she expected the voice of her new leader or one of the Dragons, the voice on the other end was enough to bring her to tears.

"Rise and shine, kiddo," came the voice of her father, Alan Crawford, with a warmth she'd missed more than anything in the world, "we got a lot to discuss." Serenity sat stunned with the only sound between them a soft cry. Alan gave her the time to process. It was, he knew, the first time he'd gone through this encrypted channel to contact her, and she didn't know about it.

"How are you—" the former Scourge Leader felt the question catch in her throat, but before she had a chance to ask it in full, Alan answered.

"It's how we tracked the enemy's movements on July 19th." She knew instantly to what he referred: the night of the White Ruins Massacre. "We tagged the most frequently used channels of the Yaiba Insurrection and listened in on their comms. I'm honestly surprised it's still in use."

"Isn't that dangerous," Serenity blurted out in a cautious whisper. Alan smiled on the other end of the line. She was the fugitive, but she was overly concerned with his condition.

"Not really. Anybody else who knows about this is dead, including the King who ordered us to do it," Alan explained. He took a breath, then got right to the root of what he wanted to discuss. "Speaking of Kings, the current one knows a secret that could end me in the Kingdom."

Serenity's eyes narrowed as she asked her father, "What kind of secret?" She could hear the fatigue in his sigh, a weariness that spoke of his foreknowledge of this exact circumstance.

"I was spared," Alan told her with a directness that she hardly expected. "On the night of the White Ruins Massacre, an enemy soldier by the name of Dre Hamlin had the chance to off me right then and there, but let me go." He took the time to recount the events of that night, of how he thought he had them dead to rights with his skills as an expert sniper. Of how he was proven wrong almost instantaneously. Then he explained to her how if it got out in the Kingdom, he'd be seen as a coward and killed by the people he once tried to protect.

Serenity was silent. Alan, in the comfort of his home office, paced back and forth as he awaited his daughter's response.

"Alright," the former Scourge leader finally uttered. "That's a lot to take in." She tried not to think about her biological father's death, to focus on the conversation at hand, but the tear that slid down her cheek reminded her of how hard that was to do.

"About Owen," Alan spoke with hesitation, but the mention of the late Lieutenant Kluger made her eyes sting with a sadness she'd thought herself long over.

"It's alright," Serenity interrupted. "I'm sure there's nothing you could've done. But getting back to the matter at hand, what do you plan to do about this secret?" There was silence now. Alan mulled over whether or not he should involve his daughter in his plan, but then resolved that it would likely fail if he didn't.

"I'm going to destabilize the Kingdom," he told her.

"Dad, you can't be serious," Serenity responded with due incredulity in her tone. Alan, unbothered, continued.

"And then I'm taking Ash, Ryan and Kyle and we're getting out of dodge while we still have the chance." Even without a visual of her, he could see that her disbelief and worry had grown so much that it could almost be its own person. They both knew that King Bryan was unstable, and while the father thought it a reason to take him down swiftly, the daughter thought it was a reason for her father to keep his head down.

"Why are you telling me this," Serenity demanded in a command voice that almost brought her old man to attention. He couldn't help but crack a proud half-smile.

"It's because I need you to do something for me."

"And what's that?" As soon as she asked the question, Alan heard the words of his former enemy echo in his mind as clearly as if they'd been said to him yesterday: *If you come looking for us again, I'll kill you before you can speak a word.* His smile remained, but there was unease behind his eyes.

"If he's alive, I need you to get me a line with Dre Hamlin."

****

February 14th, 2085, 8:27 a.m.,

Callan rolled his eyes as soon as Serenity entered the Command Center on Level X. The meeting to discuss next steps would commence in the next three minutes, and Serenity was supposed to be there as a consultant on all things Scarlet, but Callan couldn't shake the feeling that it was wrong to include her in anything. He knew that she'd apologized for her role in his capture and torture six months prior, and in the true spirit of the Yaiba, they took her in. He also knew that her remorse and her neediness in the moment weren't enough to erase the sins of her past.

He had to wonder how many of his friends or students she'd killed in the name of doing her job. The sight of her made him grit his teeth and clench his hands in a nearly uncontrollable rage. It was understandable to anyone who knew of his capture back in August, but not so much that he could forget his place. The Yaiba Insurrection had always taken in refugees since the night of the White Ruins Miracle, regardless of their former affiliation. Nothing about his anger would change that.

Serenity took a seat at the conference table, and while Callan had expected her to assume the position to his right or left, she sat on the other side of the table near his Uncle Dre. His eyebrows raised, then narrowed in a suspicion that was as old as the animosity between the Yaiba and the Reds. James walked into the room, and for a moment Serenity looked up, but then promptly ignored him with a cold expression on her face. Callan took notice, and smiled a bit.

"James," Callan called to him, which was more than enough to elicit a nervous and slightly desperate smile from the banished Prince, "pull up a chair." The Suiryu relished in the reluctance that radiated off of his one-time captor, and watched with joy as the now-consultant took his place beside the cunning Dragon.

"Callan what an...unexpected surprise," James was forced to admit, and while he gave the image of cordiality with his voice, his eyes never left Serenity. Callan didn't mind. It meant that it was easier to appeal to his sensibilities.

"She still icing you out, huh," he asked. He'd noted the tension as soon as they were brought into the Insurrection, but more than anything he noticed the annoying persistence with which the former Scourge leader attempted to make friends with him.

"She is," James replied with a disheartened sigh. His stardust-gray eyes had lost some of their shimmer in the last couple of months, and while he volunteered himself to work in the Civic Center and operate as an occasional consultant to the cause, nobody—James included—could tell if it was because he wanted to help, or because he wanted to distract himself from his romantic problems. "I don't even know how to fix it." The tone that he used was almost enough to spark a feeling of sympathy, but in that moment he was reminded of their conversation in Johnson City, and how the horrible conditions to which he was subjected were on James' order.

"What'd you do," Callan asked in somber tone that conveyed a care that was decidedly absent. "If you don't mind me asking, that is." For just a moment, James thought about telling him. Why wouldn't he? This was the first time in his life that he'd been made to suffer without the care of the public, without the default praise that was befitting a Prince of the Scarlet Kingdom, and, at least since he had met her, without a single loving expression from Serenity Crawford. In this moment, Callan appeared to express more concern for him than anyone else, and though he knew that the Water Dragon still likely harbored a grudge against him for his role in the Johnson City affair, the former prince couldn't bring himself to fully mistrust his intentions.

"I kept something from her that, in hindsight, could've brought her a sense of closure and of hope, then used it as a bargaining chip for our safe passage into the Insurrection," James explained with such an inflection that conveyed every ounce of pain and regret the action had brought him. It made sense to Callan that he would have something up his sleeve. A prince of the Kingdom hardly had the kind of sway with leaders of the Yaiba, especially given the harrowing clashes between them in the past. Still, there was a newfound curiosity that welled up within the Suiryu that drew him further beyond his desire for pettiness and a bit of revenge.

"What was it," Callan felt compelled to ask, but then immediately felt ashamed of his nosiness. "I'm sure it wasn't that bad." James grew quiet again, contemplative to the point that Callan had grown a bit restless in his seat.

"Callan," James started in a voice so suddenly stern that it reflected his history as a leader of his people, "I don't know if I should be the one to divulge that kind of information—"

"I can only help you," Callan interrupted, "if you let me. You already lost your father, your home, and every luxury you've ever known. Are you willing to take a chance on losing Serenity as well?" James sighed.

"I don't deny that I need help, Mr. Rouge," he said, "that much is apparent. I just wonder about how much help I'll get if I share with you the reason for our little disconnect."

"Okay, now you have to tell me," Callan spoke with more amiability than even he thought himself capable of in the moment.

"Fine, then. A few months ago I learned that her father was the late Lieutenant Owen Kluger, one of the officers in charge on the night of the White Ruins Incident," James explained, and Callan's eyes widened with genuine shock. Suddenly it all made sense to him. She must've learned of her father's role in his father's death and wanted to somehow make amends for it now that the Kingdom didn't want her.

"Ah," Callan said with more understanding than the former Red heir had expected. Then again, he knew the Water Dragon to be remarkably composed in high-stress situations. "Is that why she keeps trying to get close to me?"

"Yes and no," James answered, then huffed out of his nostrils with a strange determination that, at the moment, Callan couldn't quite grasp. "You might assume that since her father had a direct hand in the death of yours, she feels some guilt there." Callan could hardly hide his discomfort that James repeated the same thoughts from deep within the Insurrectionist's mind. "Tell me, Callan, do you know why Carson and Owen clashed that night?"

Callan was the quiet one now, and tapped his foot with anticipation. John entered the meeting room and a hush fell over it. He began to divulge the long-awaited details of the next few operations. Bill had been given charge to head west with a full battalion of troops ahead of schedule. Something about recent intel suggesting that the Reds would strike against the Yoroi a lot sooner than expected and they need to be ready. Serenity, who jolted at the mention of her name, was to lead a joint company to Charlotte as part of a trap for the remaining members of the Scarlet Scourge.

"I know that they hated each other," Callan whispered, which prompted a strained smile from the former monarch. John continued to delegate roles in the coming proceedings in the background.

"That's only a part of it. Do you know the reason?" It had never occurred to Callan to ask for a reason, or that there was a reason much deeper than where they aligned. James, whose eyes never left the Director as he expounded on plans to expand to the east and west, picked up on Callan's sudden burst of confusion. "And so we reach the reason that Serenity can't stand to look at me now. Your father wasn't originally of the Insurrection." As soon as the words spilled from James' mouth, Callan could tell where he intended to go. "He was Owen's rival, initially in the training academy and then ultimately in the Scarlet Military. It was friendly at first, but at some point in the middle of their time in service they began to hate each other's guts."

"I—" Callan was at such a loss for words that he couldn't finish. He wanted to say something, to defend his father's honor, to say that there was no way that he could have ever been some Scarlet Dog, but what reason did James, who was more fixed on his imploded romance, have to lie to him?

"I understand," James continued with a soft kindness in his voice, "that this must be difficult for you to take in, but please understand that that was not the part that Serenity continues to exercise her anger over." The simplicity of that revelation was enough to make Callan's breath catch in his throat. "They hated each other so much that their efforts to undermine each other transformed into a determined sabotage of each other's operations. My father gave them the choice to either separate or be executed for shaming the Kingdom. Even still, that distance wasn't enough to kill their animosity. At least, not entirely."

"What do you mean by that?" Callan asked the question before he realized, and a little louder than expected.

"It means," John offered with a stern glare that only a Lightning Dragon could give, "that Zahara Boyd has shown her mettle as a new recruit for our cause and has more than earned her right to head up the restoration of Jackson. I know your issues with the Scarlet Kingdom run deep, Callan, and I don't blame you, but at least try to remember that she's on our side now once you go with her to advance talks with the Waste Raiders. I'll give you the details of that plan at a later date. Now, once our missions in Charlotte and the Grand Canyon have been handled…" The Director continued to elaborate to the other leaders while the Suiryu returned all attention to the Prince, who sat with a smirk on his face that told the seasoned neo-ninja that he was poised to respond.

"To answer your question, your father was ready to let it go. Serenity's, on the other hand, was not."

"I still don't understand," Callan interrupted, a bit quieter this time. He loved a good story, that much he had to admit, but this was not the time. There was something that James withheld here, something that pertained to his family history, and Callan needed to know now. Whether James procrastinated the heart of the matter due to fear or some other reservation was irrelevant to him.

"A few weeks before the order was given for Carson and Owen to disengage, right after Owen assaulted him for his promotion to the rank of Captain, your father fell in love with Owen's sister, Rosaline." The moment he heard her name, Callan had a suspicion about her. His eyes widened at the mention and his heart beat faster by the second. "They managed to keep their relationship a secret from Owen for a long while, and even got married in secret. It wasn't until she got pregnant that he started to make plans for an abrupt evacuation of his family." Callan's heart nearly stopped. *So, it was her*, he thought. This was the first time in his entire life that he'd heard anything about his mother. He wanted to think deeper on the subject, but in his stunned state the only thing that he could think was her name. He finally knew his mother's name. "Around the time your family was supposed to escape from the Scarlet Kingdom, you had just been born, by my understanding of the report, and it was only a few days after that Scarlet Troopers busted down the door to your first home." The shock was amplified at this, and Callan snapped back to reality.

"What…" Still nothing beyond the single-word response. At this point, Callan wasn't even sure he wanted to ask anything. All he wanted now was to hear what really happened to his mother and father, and finally understand why he grew up an orphan raised by the Yaiba Insurrection.

"Rosaline threw herself in the way of the Troopers and attacked a couple with a kitchen knife. She managed to put them in the hospital before another soldier shot her in the leg, and she urged Carson to take you and go without her. Your father didn't want to at first, but knew that he had to—"

"So he did," Callan finished with a shake in his voice. A single tear slipped down the side of his face, and James's brows took to a sign of sympathy.

"Yes," he confirmed. "He ran to the Insurrection with you in his arms. From my understanding, he'd always intended to come back for your mother, but by the time he was ready, she'd already been executed by firing squad for crimes against the Kingdom. It was her brother Owen who took the first shot." A flame birthed in Callan's eyes, and the fury of a thousand storm-tossed oceans bubbled to the surface of his face. He mourned her, James realized, even though he'd never had the chance to even know her. "That night of the White Ruins Incident came a year later. Kluger made it a point to try and kill as many Yaiba as he could just so he could hunt down you and your father. He intended to kill you both to make up for what he thought to be his sister's greatest sin. But they both died that night, leaving you and Serenity without your parents, or the understanding that you two were family. That was the secret I used to buy our safe passage into the Insurrection. That was the thing that made Serenity stop speaking to me."

For a long while, Callan said nothing. When he engaged James in conversation, it was with all intentions to get Serenity to leave him alone. Now he had more in common with her than he realized. More than that, he understood why she was so nice to him all of a sudden, and had had a change of attitude towards him and the rest of the Yaiba since the night they traded blows in the Clusters of the Yoroi Alliance. He glanced at her, then back at James, but ultimately he decided that his best option would be to just sit and digest the meeting.

****

February 15th, 2085, 12:53 p.m.,

Bill could feel his blood pump with a ferocity that he hadn't felt in a long time. On a normal day, under the usual conditions, Bill Jerrick was a mild-mannered kind of person. He was a gentle soul full of love and had a fierce determination to care for everyone. Since even Emiko's ascension to the Directorate, Bill was almost singlehandedly responsible for bringing in hurt or disadvantaged people from the outside, and made it a point to move them out of the way of the battlefield wherever it would spring up.

He was indeed a deeply compassionate person, one who split his free time between taking odd missions that put him in the path of those unfortunate enough to be in the Kingdom's path, and teaching students in the Civic Center or on the Training Level. With every person he encountered, he found something about them to love, and it was precisely that love that made him so dangerous.

Devin Dross, one of his former students, ran through the details of the operation with the rest of the command team while a designated leader did the same in each of the other transports in their egregiously large convoy. The enemy, they knew, was positioned in the space between Sheba and Solomon Temple, protected by the jagged landscape of the general Grand Canyon Area and poised to observe—when willing—the border to Yoroi Territory. They also knew that the enemy continued to search for a way into the Clusters embedded in the rock of the Coronado Butte. The main forces would take positions on the eastern side of the Red Canyon while the command team would rendezvous with the Yoroi Council through a secret entrance known only to allies.

The path was not without its own dangers, but the wide array of traps would only be a problem for anyone not aware of their existence, location, absolute number, or the passage needed to get around them. Bill knew all of that, and had passed that intel along to the others in his charge so that they could get to his nephew in as much haste as he could manage. His first order of business would be to coordinate with the Yoroi forces that Darius had been sent to train. They would wait until the Reds broke through the last of the defenses, and while they served as a vanguard, the rest of the reinforcements would catch them from behind in a pincer attack.

They were almost there, and with every second that passed, Bill could feel his heart pound and his blood rush. To the core of his being he was excited to brave the battlefield as before, even more so since this was his first time in a fight since the KDN bombing. But there was another feeling it was intermingled with. Someone had threatened his beloved nephew. That, to the persistently loving and expansively protective Neo-Lightning Dragon, was exceptionally unforgivable. The transport stopped moving, which meant the others had already branched off into their respective places. Soon it would be time to unleash every ounce of fury on his enemies and let them know that his family was never to be crossed.

****

February 16th, 2085, 2:30 p.m.,

There was a calm about Kyle Crawford that exuded the confidence that most of his subordinates vocalized. It hadn't taken them long to get used to handling the

Thunderclaps, and understanding their close- and long-ranged effectiveness only added to the sense of wonder they all shared. Kyle strode through the camp with a smug smirk on his face. *This was what it looked like to be favored by the King*, he thought. He figured that after their victory he would be lavished with it and given the same kind of treatment as his father Alan. He would be heralded as a hero, and an unsurpassable one at that, for there had been none before him that could ever push the Yoroi this close to the brink, and not a soul after him would be able to match the accomplishment.

"What's the status," Kyle asked Felix, who seemed to be in the process of packing his things.

"The preparations have been set and the entrances marked," the fire-haired demolitions expert assured him. "I have to hand it to you, your intelligence corps are worth every bit of the praise given to them by the King—past or present." The Major smiled. Kilpatrick hadn't said anything that Kyle didn't already know. Kyle had done an extensive mapping of the Grand Canyon himself based on a satellite map updated just after the KDN was revived. He ran teams on occasion, practically to the enemy's front door, to acquire as much information as he could to use against his targets. With all that he'd learned over the last few months, Kyle knew that his invasion plan would, in almost explicit certainty, spell out the end of the Yoroi. Kyle also knew that with Felix at his disposal for the time being, the traps would be a simple matter to dispose of.

"I trust that that means a path has been cleared to their door, then?" Kyle asked the question with more cool in his voice than he felt in his entire body. It was the centerpiece of his entire operation. A modified pincer, where his main forces would swarm the main entrances to their compound and a secondary force with the Thunderclaps would descend into their depths like angels of death.

"Of course," Kilpatrick said with an air of exasperation. He hated to be micromanaged, and was glad to get the summons back to the Scarlet Streaks for their next operation. "Main entrances on the north, east, west, and south are ready for your descent. Honestly I don't know how it is that nobody's disabled those traps before. It was less than child's play for anyone with half a wit in bombwork." Felix closed his rucksack and tossed it over his shoulder. He turned to face Major Crawford with the kind of look that almost sang his relief to be done with the grueling work that only he could do for the operation.

"Well," Kyle said with a measured tone that almost told his intention to skip over the numerous factors that once worked in favor of the Yoroi in the past, "I appreciate the work that you've done, Warrant Officer." Felix raised his eyebrows with nearly genuine surprise.

"Gratitude. I have to say, I wasn't expecting that." Major Crawford smirked at the comment and shrugged more or less indifferently.

"I didn't expect you to be useful, but here we are," he stated as if it was simply a fact that the Warrant Officer should expect. "In any case, I believe in showing honor to whom it is due, and for your services you've proven to be the lynchpin of my entire operation. I'm in your debt." The fire-haired demo-tech shook his head and yielded to the urge to smile.

"I'll take what I can get, honestly," he returned. "Besides, I answer directly to the whims of the new King. I hardly need your approval at this point." The smile on the Major's face became a bit more genuine.

"Then why follow my orders?" Kyle's question was sincere, as the two had never had much in the way of love for each other, though they were far from a sense of mutual hatred. What they shared, at its purest form, was a singular desire to steer clear of each other as much as possible, so from that angle Felix could understand that the question was valid.

"I recognize that your plan could work—"

"*Will* work," Crawford corrected with a fold of the arms. "Surely you don't expect that our combined efforts to come to naught." Kilpatrick shrugged as he made for the entrance to his tent. He stopped just in front of Kyle and looked him over for a moment.

"There's always that possibility, Major Crawford. Be careful not to operate in overconfidence." He continued on his way as Kyle watched on. The expert intelligence officer took a moment to mull over what was said.

"Don't worry," he muttered, firmly of the belief that his plans were beyond the likelihood of disruption, "I'm just confident enough."

****

February 17th, 2085, 3:05 p.m.,

Callan looked out over the expansive forest below. It was warmer than it had been in weeks, and for the first time since the KDN bombing, bird songs filled the air. There was still a chill, and the remnants of snow still glistened in the distance under the afternoon light of the sun, and it would have been a truly relaxing picture for the Water Dragon if he had been alone. Serenity Crawford, the former leader of the Scarlet Scourge, an unlikely ally in the war against Kingdom Scarlet, and, as he'd learned only days ago, his long-lost cousin, stood only a few feet away with her back turned to the scenery and her eyes focused on the machinations of the Yaiba.

He had called her here, and quickly she had come, but now that she stood so close to him he had no idea what to say. She was so different from him, but he understood now that it wasn't her fault. She'd been raised in an environment that saw people of color as tools to be used or nuisances to be dealt with, and even though she viciously defended their ideals, she worked to unlearn all of that. It was still so hard to trust her, to be open with someone he knew could turn and kill what friends he had that she hadn't tried to already. But still, knowing that they were family and that they were screwed out of that connection by the Kingdom made him want to try and forge a new one.

"Look," they said at the same time as their eyes met awkwardly, unsure of whether to show hostility, reservation or open emotion. They looked away from each other, and Callan said, "I'm sorry I've been so hard on you." Serenity's head snapped back to face him, a look of relieved incredulity emergent in her countenance. "You've been with us for months and you've fought hard against people you've probably known your entire life just to prove yourself to the Yaiba. Even so, I've only judged you by what you've done in the past."

“I can understand that,” Serenity said sheepishly and without any control. “I played a part in torturing you, killing your friends, fighting to wipe you out of existence because of what I’d been taught growing up. I know I don’t deserve your forgiveness,” she assured him with the kind of resolve befitting her former station, “but I owe it to you all to express my remorse for all the horrible things I’ve led others to do to all of you.” Callan stood for a moment in awe of her. He never thought he’d see the day where Serenity Crawford, the Bladebreaker herself, would express remorse for her actions and take accountability. There was a shudder in her breathing as she visibly prepared to say something else, and Callan knew what it was. “I learned something a few months ago that I’ve been meaning to tell you, but I don’t know where to begin.”

Callan brandished a smile. “I figure it might be hard to tell a former enemy that you’re cousins whose parents killed each other thirty-something years ago.” He watched her jaw tick open in surprise as her eyes blinked rapidly. “James told me.” Instantly she showed a flicker of her temper, and Callan almost reacted with his Reikiken out of habit.

“Of course he did,” she all but growled, then turned away from the entrance to the Deployment Level as if it was the man himself.

“Why are you mad at him,” Callan had to ask. He’d thought about the situation since James first told him, and it seemed rational. “He did what he could to protect you from the Kingdom—”

“I never asked for that,” she interrupted through clenched teeth. “I was the best of the best in the Scarlet

Kingdom and even with my defection there's not a single Trooper, man or woman, who could hold a candle to me. I would've been fine going my own way."

"Ah," Callan said knowingly. "So that's why." She cut her eyes at him, and sauntered closer to him than he would've liked. Still, he couldn't keep the smile off his face.

"What do you mean," she demanded, and folded her arms across her chest.

"You still sound like the leader of the Scarlet Scourge," he informed her. "Military life is who you are, which makes sense, but you lost all of that for James. He chose to use our family history for leverage because he knew it was the only way to get through to John and give you something to live for in the middle of a life or death crisis." She was silent. She hadn't considered that as a possible motive. "How much of a change have you seen in your day to day?" The question cut through her thoughts like a sword.

"Aside from who I fight, there hasn't been much of a change," she was forced to admit, her voice a little stronger now, like her usual self. Callan nodded.

"That's my point," the Suiryu assured her. "Besides, have you seen the guy since you stopped talking to him? He's friggin' sad." She laughed in a girlish way that sent a chill through him. It was like he saw her as a person for the first time. In this moment, she wasn't a warrior, a former enemy, or the thorn in his side that he thought she was when she'd first arrived. She was a woman with thoughts and feelings and a desire to live her life as best she could in the face of (and sometimes in spite of) the people around her.

"He is that," she agreed with a chuckle. They both caught sight of Cal Richmond, one of the members of Serenity's team as he approached, a sure signal that it was time to head out. "I'll have to talk to him after my mission."

"Hey, one last thing," Callan said as she turned to join her team. "What was up with you and Uncle Dre in the war meeting a few days ago?"

Serenity looked over her shoulder at her cousin with a smirk and an excited look in her eye as she said, "Wouldn't you like to know?"

Chapter Thirteen

February 17th, 2085, 10:25 p.m.,

The training ground, for the first time since October, stood in a state of unusual silence, like the fleeting moments before the detonation of a bomb. Darius stood somewhere between expert confidence and childish nervousness, all because of the success of the one major operation that he'd endured since his arrival. For all the experience it gave him, he was still new to all of this. Being set as the head of a massive experimental military force was an honor to be sure, but it did more to highlight the lack of experience that he or any of the Yaiba had in this situation since the inception of the Hanzo Gear.

Even still, all he needed to do was look beside him to his Uncle Bill for the confidence to outweigh the nerves. He'd come in only a few hours ago, and after a long-awaited and much-needed hug, the senior soldier brought him up to speed on the plan. The current Rairyu was content to operate on a support-only basis and defer to the plan that his nephew enacted. A ping came over the shared comms network and the visor of Darius' cloak at the same time. The geo-sensors, installed a couple of years ago during John's prior deployment, registered the movement of multiple forces at the surrounding main entrances to the Yoroi Clusters.

"The enemy's on the move," came the voice of Devin Dross. "It's about that time. Following your lead, Master Darius." The acknowledgement of his station was nothing new, and in the time that he'd spent amongst the Yoroi, Darius had gotten quite used to the honorific of

"Master." Still, it was a completely different matter altogether for someone of notable accomplishment within the Insurrection to do the same. The nerves that he'd struggled with from the outset of his mission up to this point were gone, and all that was left in its place was an unrelenting resolve.

"Yaiba forces, abandon Strat Alpha and move to Beta. This pincer move just got a whole lot broader. Yoroi forces, maintain your positions in Clusters A, B, and C. Keep your eyes on all entrances and the opening above." There was silent compliance, and a near certainty that they would pull out a win. Bill clapped his nephew on the shoulder and let a mischievous smile slither across his jaw. Darius didn't turn to look at him now, but knew that he'd made Bill proud all the same.

****

February 17th, 2085, 10:40 p.m.,

Fifteen minutes. That was all it took for the bombs to go off at the south, west and east entrances. Scores of Red troops had been taken out in the blasts, all because the threat of a thousand Yaiba troops dispersed to cover every point of interest was enough to inspire an error in judgment. Before long, the screams and booms that surrounded the core Clusters were replaced with echoes of battle cries and gunshots. For all the commotion at the other entrances, the front door was startlingly quiet. Darius watched it from the shadows with a knot in his throat as the whirlwind of lethality swirled around on every side.

"What should we do," asked Lex Ford, who stood ready as always to enter the fray. Lex was assigned to secure the main entrance, and with his platoon he stood behind a makeshift barrier that faced the darkened and bomb-filled tunnel. Darius heaved a sigh, then responded.

"Sit tight," Darius ordered. "We don't make a move until the outside force drives the enemy into position above us."

"Roger that," Lex replied with a degree of sincerity that Darius hadn't expected. The Rebel Dragon couldn't help but smirk with satisfaction at the sheer growth of Lex's character. There was a shout overhead, not far from the opening to the Clusters, that told the warriors scattered throughout that the enemy would drop in at any moment.

"Everyone brace," Darius ordered, "enemies inbound."

****

February 17th, 2085, 10:55 p.m.,

"So that's their plan," Kyle muttered to himself as he looked at the screen on his Thunderclap. It was, the Major thought, a remarkable piece of technology, and the drones were only the beginning of it. He gently fingered the trigger just below the box that served as the guard on the hilt, then decided to press it fully. A second drone deployed from the Thunderclap and shot around to the western entrance to blast along the ground. It left an indiscriminate trail of bodies, though Major Crawford was satisfied that it was mostly the enemy that was taken out. The surviving Yaiba quickly bounded up to the side of the Butte.

Crawford summoned the small orb, a devilish smirk on his face. He reasoned that if the other entrances were loaded with bombs, the main one should have been prepared in a similar fashion. It was enough to prompt him to test the power of the Thunderclap when pitted against that of the Yoroi's legendary traps. He pointed the blade of his new prized weapon forward and the newly recalled drone blasted through the tunnel in a brilliant flash of red. Bombs detonated before the eyes of the three-hundred men and women that stood at his back, much to their shock and awe.

"Shall we proceed," one of his subordinates asked. Kyle's eyes brightened with ambition and an almost manic desire for the chaos of war.

"By all means, Lieutenant Stevens," spoke the Major with a theatric gesture towards the still-smoking tunnel. "After you." The war cry came shortly thereafter, and while the three-hundred soldiers marched into the darkness with their new weapons ready at their sides, Kyle Crawford relished in the history he had just made and thought of how the entirety of the Kingdom would sing his praises as the man who came to a head with the greatest pitfalls of the Yoroi Alliance and dismantled them all with the greatest of ease.

****

February 17th, 2085, 11:17 p.m.,

The bright red flash came without warning and launched the entirety of the ground platoon across the center of Cluster B. A few of them were able to regain their legs before the enemy flooded in, but those that weren't, some twelve Yoroi trainees, were either shot or run through with the blades of the Thunderclaps. Before long, the sound of metal on metal broke through the low rumbles of the still-situating rubble. Then, *he* entered. Darius and Bill watched as an imposing man of pale skin, sharp blue eyes, and a muscled physique that was the mother of intimidation.

"That's not good," Bill muttered, which made Darius' heart pound as hard as the eardrums of the survivors of the ground platoon.

"Can you handle him, Uncle Bill?" Darius's question was so stern that Bill had to take a second look at him to make sure it wasn't John that sat beside him. He looked into his nephew's eyes to see that there was still fear there, yes, but there was a determination to make the plan work. Even now, there was nothing about this situation that ran contrary to their expectations. Bill nodded in affirmation, then rose to his feet. Before he could take the leap to the ground below, Darius caught him by the arm and looked him square in the eye, no doubt in reflection of all the other mentors and adopted family that literally went up in smoke on Christmas. "Be careful," he urged his uncle.

"Don't worry, kiddo," Bill replied with a gentle tone that reminded the Rebel Dragon of visits in his childhood. "I'm a lot tougher than I look, even now." Darius drew in a sharp breath as he thought back on Bill's absence for weeks in the wake of the KDN bombing. He hadn't realized that he was worried about his uncle's recovery, nor did he think about Bri, pregnant with their third and—by far—youngest child at home, but in this moment everything hit him all at once. Nevertheless, this was a man that Darius' own father opted to replace him as

Rairyu and lead the Violet Shadows into battle. Darius reprimanded himself for his doubts.

"I trust you," the Rebel Dragon told him, and with a loving smile, Bill clapped him on the shoulder and made his descent. "Swing Units, hold your positions. Nobody moves until the enemy grapples in. Ground Units, how are you holding up?"

"Not bad," Leroy Baptiste chimed in through harrowed grunts and audibly gritted teeth. "All things considered—whoa!" The line went static for a moment after the exclamation. Darius caught sight of another red flash, much stronger than the one from before. "Sorry about that, boss," Leroy told him with a slight embarrassment in his voice. "Looks like the Reds have some brand new tech. Swords that can more than hold their own against our Reikiken."

Darius' eyes narrowed as he took a moment to survey the battlefield. "That's not good," Darius said with a bit of a pause in the middle. His strategic mind raced for a way to swiftly deal with the forces on the ground but with their formalized military training and close combat weapons, it could create a bit more of a challenge. Another brilliant red flash shot along the ground of Cluster B and swept up through the air and three buildings. *How are they doing that,* he thought. The Hanran no Ryu scanned for the origin point of the burst, only to find the small orb just above the battlefield. Above it were many more, each one only barely visible under the shine of the moonlight.

"What do we do," Lex asked as he dodged yet another flash. Between the ground troopers and the drones overhead, it was hard for them to find their footing. For a moment, Darius contemplated a solution.

“Kibaku-shuriken,” said the young Dragon, but offered nothing in the way of an explanation. Instead he watched the battlefield with those dragonic eyes he’d inherited from his father John, in hasty search of something—anything—that he could use to his advantage. Then he saw it: there was a five-second cooldown window on the drones before they could fire again. What was even better was the fact that while the Reds proved to be moderately competent swordsmen, they were far from capable of the kind of multitasking that the strange sword-drone configuration demanded. “Everybody listen up. Those blasts are coming from the drones hidden in the dark above your heads. Half of you coordinate in a diamond formation while the other half engages with the enemy head on. They aren’t coordinated enough to manage fighting you off and controlling the remotes. Use that to your advantage.”

“Roger that,” Lex responded, and before long the thirty men and women on the B-Cluster Ground Unit lit into their opposition.

****

February 17th, 2085, 11:49 p.m.,

Bill Jerrick watched from a distance for a moment as the strong man calmly marched through the battlefield. He donned the same scarlet bodysuit that came standard with the Reds, but over it he wore a black cloak with silver trim, one that seemed impervious to the ash, smoke and blood of its surroundings. The pale warrior had a look of near therapeutic release about his face as he listened to the shouts and screams of the war-ravaged Cluster, and that was Bill's invitation to finally emerge from the dark.

"You seem weirdly happy with all this carnage," spoke the Lightning Dragon as he brandished his Reikiken. Within seconds the temperature escalated, which solicited a condescending smirk from the enemy.

"It hardly has to do with the bloodshed," he said in a tone that radiated privilege and higher society. It was almost unfit to belong to a soldier, but then again, the Kingdom spared no effort in trying to assert their superiority over the other Factions. "You're looking at the first person to have ever breeched the traps and explosives of the Yoroi Alliance."

"Hmmm…" Bill hummed as he tucked a hand behind his back and pointed the tip of his blade at his opponent. "A rich white man proud of knocking down the defenses of the poor and disenfranchised. I have to hand it to you, you sound about as historical as they come. Why don't I help you out with that and erase you from the present?" The Scarlet enemy raised his eyebrows with a greater sense of delight as he readied his box-hilted blade and pointed it to the ground. Bill could actually appreciate the bravado in his stance.

"Why not," shrugged the enemy. "I suppose I could add taking down one of the Seven Dragons to the list." Bill gave the man a curt smile.

"Ya mama," he said, and braced for the man's attack.

****

February 17th, 2085, 11:55 a.m.,

Bobbi Brynarr jumped out of the way of the oncoming blast, rolled along the ground and came out of it on her feet. From her grounded position, she tossed the Kibaku-shuriken that, at some point amid the initial vault, she'd pulled from the pack at her waist. The four-pronged metal stars soared through the air near the small remote from which the explosion came, and just before the projectile blade could make contact, Bobbi clicked the switch on her wrist and triggered a detonation of her own. Fire and metal permeated the air to take out four of the destructive drones, but before the smoke could fully disperse, another bright red burst erupted from the cloud, aimed at the Yoroi troops below.

Another dodge, and Bobbi was surrounded by four Scarlet Troopers, two with their M4s and two with Thunderclaps. The honey-haired Yoroi took only a moment to survey the situation before she bounded into the air with the full force of her repulsor boots. The sudden burst against the ground blanketed the hostiles with a cloud of dust so thick that even the orange blade of Bobbi's Reikiken was masked within it. She flipped forward, just behind one of the M4-armed Troopers. With a single swing of her arm, she decapitated him with the firesword as she shot her kyoketsu-shoge into the chest of the woman beside her initial victim.

The dust cloud faded, and while the other two Troopers saw their attacker, they were powerless to stop her. Bobbi spun along the ground, and in a bright orange flash the remaining Scarlets lost their legs. As they fell to the ground, the Yoroi Spearhead slashed them across the abdomen with twin kyoketsu-shoge and, after taking one of the Thunderclaps for herself, bounded deeper into the battlefield.

****

February 18th, 2085, 12:04 a.m.,

Scarlet Troopers descended from the height of the Coronado Butte and brought with them a swarm of the little drones. Darius, who felt a continued string of explosions ripple through the ground even on his perch, watched the enemy troops as they dangled from suspension cables. He rose to his feet from his previously crouched position and, with the ignition of his Reikiken, ushered in a wave of Yaiba and Yoroi soldiers. It was Toni's team that lead the charge into the airborne battle, and like bats spat out from Hell itself, they swarmed and spiraled about the near helpless enemies. A few of the Scarlets managed to fire off a blast from their drones, and though a few of the airborne aggressors were caught in the brilliant red burst, more emerged from the shadows to storm the cables and the living meat bound to their ends.

Another blast rocketed seemingly out of nowhere and all but atomized Darius' position. Had he not jumped, there would've been one less Hamlin in the world. He used his repulsor boots to kick himself higher and higher into the air, almost as if he walked in the sky, and with a staggering level of stability, he pulled four Kibaku-shuriken from the pouch at his lower back and hurled them along four paths before him. He didn't get the chance to detonate them, because another drone handled that for him with yet another shockwave of red-hot energy. Darius dove backwards down into the Cluster to narrowly avoid the compound explosion that took place, and skillfully used his kyoketsu-shoge and repulsors to safely grapple to the side of the Canyon wall.

Bodies fell from above, scorch marks along the whole ones and burns all over the charred remains, but still more Scarlet Troopers flooded the opening to the Cluster. Of course, Darius knew, they had no choice. Their entire strategy was to push them into the pit and dissect them before they touched down. Another blast, and another wave of Yoroi blown away. The drones of the Thunderclaps proved to be an equalizer with more than enough potential to be deadly in the grander scheme of things. Darius moved back towards the upper stratum of the battle, firesword in hand and ready to cut down the would-be invaders.

He noticed that Toni was already there, a look of absolute ferocity on their face. They beat through a cloud of drones to throw a wave of Kibaku-shuriken. In a flash, Toni and their entire squad dove a few feet down to avoid the blast, but quickly grappled to the wall. Detonation and an eruption of screams. More Reds arrived as the smoke billowed up and to their surprise, largely before their drones could even be deployed, Darius and a detachment of Yaiba operatives emerged from the black cloud, only intelligible because of the orange of their swords. The Reds thought for a moment to call for help, or perhaps to tell their comrades to cease their advance and fight their way back down the sides of the Butte, but each was burned away before they could act on their feelings.

The warriors of Yoroi and Yaiba retreated to the shadows with all eyes on the opening and the Kibaku-shuriken that lined it, in eager anticipation of the next wave.

****

February 18th, 2085, 12:13 a.m.,

Bill Jerrick stood in his signature stance: his feet adjusted to a wide stance, knees were bent, back was straight, shoulders squared, and the hands in which his Reikiken rested stood arched over his head. Major Crawford raised an eyebrow as he watched his opponent take comfort in the stance.

"I thought the Lightning Dragon was supposed to use the Rairyu Form," he prodded with a smugness that Bill couldn't stand. "Don't tell me that you're intimidated by me, Master Jerrick." Bill narrowed his eyes and tossed a Kibaku-shuriken to his rear. It collided with the glass lens of the volatile drone that Kyle assumed would take him by surprise. When the Major's expression soured, Bill smiled as cheerily as the day he saw his nephew take his first steps.

"Don't flatter yourself," Bill warned. "I know the kind of underhanded tricks you intelligence agents'll use if you get caught in a fight. My little brother was nice enough to teach me what to watch for at a basic level, so your little drones won't do you much good with me."

"Hm," Kyle frowned, "it looks like I'll just have to put you in your place the old-fashioned way." The Major pointed his Thunderclap at the Dragon with his free hand raised above his head. "*En Garde*!" The Scarlet elite opened with a thrust that was easily smashed downward by Bill's powerful swing. Crawford carried the energy of the blow around his body before the Thunderclap touched the earth, and parried the Rairyu, whose blade had moved into a more sideways angle parallel to the ground and now swung up as if to go across his enemy's chest. Bill flowed to the side with the parry, and though Kyle attempted a blow to the back, the new Lightning Dragon blocked it with such force that his enemy's sword was pushed back with a crackle of electricity on the burning tungsten.

Jerrick swept with absurd force at his adversary's shoulder, was parried, continued the flow with double the force, and struck at the same shoulder in a move that forced Major Crawford to block. The Scarlet leader only narrowly managed it, and was pushed back a few inches. He took the chance to spin out of the way of the cut at his abdomen and rested in a stance that showed both hands on the Thunderclap's hilt, weight sunken, and the blade pointed at the enemy as it rested parallel to its master's face. Bill smiled.

"You're a lot better at this than I thought you'd be," the Yaiba general was forced to admit.

"All the details of your swordsmanship were fed to us from the inside. From there it was child's play to reconstruct it," Major Crawford said haughtily, which only made the Insurrectionist smile wider.

"I meant strategy," said the neo-ninja with a mildly taunting tone. "Attacking all the entrances at once, blasting through the traps to stroll in with the confidence of a king.

We didn't have any idea where you were coming from when we first got here."

"And yet," Kyle returned with a scowl, "you knew how to strike at us anyway. It's almost as if you had someone on the inside as well."

"Oh, not at all, bud. I just did what we've been doing for years: exploiting your overconfidence as a major weakness," Master Jerrick openly taunted. It was true, that was the typical tactic of the Yaiba forces against the Kingdom. How else could they have survived so long against an opponent that outmatched them in number and in military might? Even after nearly 39 years, they hadn't learned. Bill smirked as he bent his knees and lowered his body. His blade rested in his hands parallel to the ground and pointed out passed his leg at his opponent. He didn't move, but blew a kiss at the Major with a bit of boyish charm that was rarely seen by his opponents. Kyle lunged for him with a ferocity that almost reminded Bill of an advanced student throwing a temper tantrum. He was confident in his skills of replication, but he was still far below the level of a Dragon.

Major Crawford swung his Thunderclap at Bill's head, but the former Tsuchiryu pivoted out of the way and let his blade whip around. The Red leader narrowly avoided being split in half with a well-timed parry. Bill, still with a smile plastered to his face, and with a spin of the blade its tip now moved for a reverse thrust hidden in the shadow of the Thunderclap. When Kyle deflected it, he had to turn his entire body to avoid a trick shot at his gut. He tried to retaliate with a thrust of his own, but by the time the move was executed, the Master Dragon had already spun away from the would-be conqueror of the Yoroi.

Bill stood with his Reikiken in a reverse grip and held away from his opponent, while his free hand taunted Kyle with its extension. The neophyte swordsman took the bait, and with a degree of elegance, alarming speed and otherworldly power, Bill spun on his back leg and swatted the Thunderclap away, then returned to a standard grip as he turned and swung upward in a hard diagonal. Somehow, Kyle's defense was good enough to barely protect him against the Dragonic beating, and even his offense wasn't so bad. Bill felt like he stood opposite a student with a remarkable amount of potential.

Kyle's blade, off the upward diagonal strike, dragged the Scarlet warrior's arm into the air, and again just barely moved into place in time enough to provide a sturdy shield against the continued onslaught. The shock of the Thunderclap and repulsed the firesword, but Bill brought it back down again and again, until Major Crawford had no choice but to kneel. Bill pressed down harder with the next blow and, in the split second before Kyle could be crushed beneath the weight of the tungsten and the heat that it brought with it, Bill drove his knee into the enemy officer's face. It was enough force to send Crawford across the ground. He rolled and skidded on his feet as he braced with his free hand, his sword to the rear.

"You implied," Bill said as he returned to the stance he'd had before his flurry of attacks, the tip of his blade pointed back at his opponent, "that I was intimidated by you because of my Tsuchiryu style. Nah. I use it because it's comfortable for me, and since you walked in here trying to kill my nephew, I didn't see a reason to hold anything back." Kyle rushed his enemy, his movements a bit more shaken, and struck at his side, but with a simple roll of the Reikiken, the strike proved pointless. Three more movements, a blow to the head, to the leg, to the other shoulder, each one blocked effortlessly and with such fluidity that it became clear to the middle Crawford sibling that he never truly had a leg to stand on in this fight. The entire time that Bill exhibited such brutality, such cunning, he was playing.

Kyle watched as his troops surrounded the Dragon and jumped away. He commanded them to fire, and instantly Bill was taken back to the moment he was shot in Yorktown. He listened to their footsteps, past and present, as they formed up, heard the click of their guns as they took aim, and with a gentle press to his wrist, he heard the detonation of every Kibaku-shuriken he'd spread across the battlefield. The enemy troops were engulfed in a now inextinguishable wall of fire that only Bill could escape and Kyle, the overconfident leader of the Scarlet Intelligence Corps, stood steeped in confusion as he asked the only question that registered in his mind to ask: "When did you even do that?" He took stock of Bill's now grim expression. There was no playfulness left in him as he stood straight to his feet and, in the shadow of the fire, glared into the soul of the Major.

"Every time I turned, I threw another one. You were so preoccupied with keeping yourself alive that you never picked up on it, and now I have you all to myself." Bill's words sent a chill down Kyle's spine, and though there was no way out, the second Crawford child frantically surveyed the terrain for even the possibility of an opening in the flames. "Now," Bill continued, "I'll show you what you get for threatening my family." Before Kyle could plead with him, Bill launched his kyoketsu-shoge into the Major's chest, pulled him by the chain across the broken earth, and stabbed him in the throat with the Reikiken. There was another explosion in the distance, and Bill knew that things were wrapping up.

****

February 18th, 2085, 12:36 a.m.,

Hundreds of Kibaku-shuriken detonated just as the next wave of enemies grappled down into the cavern on their suspension cables. The sound nearly deafened the joint forces of Yaiba and Yoroi, who sat in the safety of the shadows and watched as the cables were blasted from the rock. The screams of the unsuspecting Scarlet Troopers echoed throughout Cluster B as they plummeted hundreds of feet down towards the battered buildings and broken streets below.

****

February 18th, 2085, 12:36 a.m.,

The explosion rocked the entirety of the compound, but only added force to Lex's swing at an enemy's midsection. The man burned in half and fell to the ground, and just as another three ran to take their place, a large stone broken from the mouth of the canyon landed between them. For just a moment, Lex allowed himself a smile, then darted into the darkness and away from the rocks.

"All troops fall back," Darius ordered over the comms unit. "This battle is ours." All around Lex there were victory shouts as the other Yoroi, clad in their earthy brown Hanzo Gear, retreated into the myriad tunnels from which the Faction had been built. For the first time since its formation, Yoroi was free to move as it wished.

****

February 18th, 2085, 1:44 a.m.,

It was a little more than an hour before the dust settled and what was left of Darius' force to come back together. The strategy worked better than expected, all because of the sudden emergence of the Yaiba reinforcements led by the new Rairyu. In a whirlwind of conversations, Darius dispatched the joint force to survey the Clusters and take stock of the damage. He charged them to finish off any Red survivors while he, Bobbi, Leroy, and Lex would head to the bunkers and deliver the news to the Council of Elders that after all these years, they were no longer beholden to the whims of the Reds.

Before long, all of the troops under his command went about their assignments, and while his personal squad trailed behind him, Bill Jerrick hastily caught up with him on the way to the emergency crater carts. The loving uncle tousled his nephew's curly black hair, and while on a normal occasion it would be taboo to touch a black person's hair without permission, Darius was so happy to have won a major battle alongside his uncle that he didn't care.

"Thanks again for the assist," the Rebel Dragon told him with a boyish smile he was glad his students couldn't see. "You guys coming out here and covering our blind spots kept any deviations to the plan firmly under control."

"Well, that and your quick wit, kiddo," Bill shrugged with a smile. "You were amazing out there, the way you kept your cool and assessed the situation in real time."

"It wasn't enough to keep everyone safe, though," Darius replied solemnly. Even now, he couldn't help but think back to his first bout with the Scourge in Johnson City when his Uncle Callan was taken hostage to keep him from dying. Ever since, he wanted nothing more than to afford all of his comrades safe passage to a normal life. He knew it was an unrealistic goal in war, but after everything that had happened with Callan, with Johannes and Ina, with the Anti-Rebellion faction, he felt all the more determined to force it if he had to.

Bill noticed the boy's tightened fists, his grim look of grit and determination, and decided to stop walking and pull him into a hug. "I understand," he told him, "but you still did everything you could to minimize the casualties. I know that it's hard to lose people you trust, even harder to lose people you taught, but never forget that more of your students have survived from your teachings and your decisions than have fallen. I guarantee that every single one of them is grateful for the work you've done." It was a lot for Darius to take in, but he found his uncle's wisdom to be more than soothing.

"Thanks," he responded sheepishly as Bill pulled away to look at the boy. "I needed that." Bill shrugged again as they started to walk again.

"We all need to be brought back to reality every once in a while. For as much potential as we're all born with, we all have our limitations, too." There was a brief pause. "That said, I think we've focused on the limits a little more than we needed to, so I want to let you in on a little secret that I'm not supposed to tell anyone about." Darius smiled against his will.

"You sure you wanna do that? The last time you did, you—"

"Yeah, yeah, I know," Bill cut him off, fully aware of the punishment for running his mouth the last time. He let slip what John and Aaliyah had gotten Darius for his birthday, and when they found out about it, John waited until the night of his party to put Bill on the spot as the evening's entertainment. Bill, never one to back down from any sort of a challenge, mustered all the fortitude that he could, and sang his heart out despite the fact that it was nearly enough to make his own ears bleed. There was a wave of embarrassment after, both from John for choosing that moment for revenge, and from Bill who was verbally ripped apart by his extremely judgmental audience. "But all things considered, I feel as though this situation calls for it." In all truth, there was no way that he would get in trouble for it, since this was more his homework from the last meeting.

"I mean," Darius began again, his smile a lot wider than it had been, "if you want to take that chance, you go right ahead." Bill returned his smile, and for a moment it felt like a normal day, like war was the farthest thing from them.

"Eh, I think you're worth that risk," Bill told him with a faux contemplative tone. "There've been some conversations happening at the Roan base about the next recruits to the Seven Dragons." Just the mention of such a thing was enough for Darius to stop dead in his tracks. He eyed his uncle, who took a few steps forward and then stopped himself, more for dramatic effect than anything.

"Uncle Bill," Darius started with a hard swallow, "why are you telling me this?" Bill Jerrick turned around with a wily smile on his face as he pointed his Reikiken at his nephew in as dramatic a fashion as it was comical.

"You're a Dragon, Dari," he said in his best attempt at a cockney British accent, and while he thought it was a great joke, Darius stood stunned to silence.

Chapter Fourteen

February 23rd, 2085, 5:45 a.m.,

Lukas was jolted out of his sleep. It was hard for him to sleep in Johnson City. Or maybe it was simply the fact that he had trouble with the stillness of the city. It was too bright, too open, too…vulnerable, and even though he slept in a guarded barrack outfitted with some of the deadliest weapons conjured by the minds of the Yaiba and Kabuto engineers, there had already been a large-scale attack on their territories in a moment of peace. Even now he could hear his reaction to it in the back of his mind, that sky-ripping scream that burst from his belly when he witnessed his father's demise.

He breathed a distrustful sigh and wiped the sweat from his bare torso. Just as he was about to get up, he jumped at the sight of a smiling Daxa, who sat in a chair just a foot away. When she saw his startled expression shift to mild irritation, she smiled with all the joy of an innocent child.

"Oh my God," Lukas exhaled with a pointed scowl, "what are you doing?" Daxa declined to give a straight answer and shrugged.

"You know, you're kind of cute when you're sleeping," she told him. He rolled his eyes and got out of bed. His barracks room was dark, but he'd already committed the layout to memory. It was a homely shack of gray brick walls and broken tile floor. The windows were of an opaque, incredibly thick glass that looked as bulletproof as it was supposed to be. The bed was a twin size, covered in beige blankets that were little more than linen kindling for a fire, and the chair in which Daxa sat was built of oak. It was fitted with a faded royal blue cushion that contrasted the depressing hues of the room in a way that could only be described as military design. The room itself was cramped, and the furniture only offered so much room to maneuver. Thankfully, Daxa had moved the chair at some point before he woke up, and Lukas could move as a result, which meant that there was nothing for him to stub his toe on at the moment.

"I don't know if you'd call what that was 'sleeping,' Dax." He watched her peach-colored lips adapt a subtle frown and her dark eyes grow a bit hazy. Suddenly he realized that she'd had trouble sleeping too, and his irritation faded. "Well, we might as well go on a walk since neither of us can get any rest." She blinked at him, stunned at how easily he read her all of a sudden, but nodded in agreement.

They left the humble room and walked down a dark hallway with patchy brown carpet, cinder block walls painted in stark white, and wooden doorframes painted the same faded royal blue as the chair cushion. They were silent, even after they came down the creaky stairs and into the main lobby of the barrack.

It was when they opened the door to the chilled night air that Daxa spoke again. "You seem to be handling yourself better these days," she acknowledged, careful not to force open the healing wounds left in the wake of Manny's death. "You seem stronger, somehow. Almost happy again." Lukas thought about it for a moment and carefully considered his answer. He knew that the loss of his father was still a weight on his shoulders, but he couldn't deny that it had become a bit easier a burden to bear. He held up his twin Reikiken, one with a standard straight hilt with an intricately designed tsuba to guard his hands, and the other one straight and smooth save for the grooves that ran down its sides. He looked at them thoughtfully, and Daxa found that she did too.

"This one," he said as he lowered the standard, "belonged to him. Uncle Callan brought it to me after it'd been recovered. Somehow it had been spared in the bombing of Atlanta." There was a pause, a moment of contemplation for him that evoked a deep sadness in her. "Having it makes me feel like he's still here."

"I understand," Daxa replied as she pulled the moon-shaped necklace from beneath the collar of her uniform. She looked it over for a moment, felt the sharp points at the ends of the crescent form and, as if for the first time, saw it as the mesmerizing moonstone masterpiece that it was. Her sudden pensiveness was enough to bring Lukas back to the present moment, and create a new sadness in him at the recollection of Grandma Binsa. Before he could offer his condolences in a much more sincere manner than when Daxa first brought it up, she continued. "She really loved this necklace, you know. She got it from her mother the day she married my grandfather. She would tell me that her mother told her it was shaped like the moon to keep her eyes company. She'd always said that Grandma Binsa's eyes looked like they were too heavenly to be on Earth." Lukas' heart panged with a mixture of feelings. Joy at the realization that such kindness had always existed in the lives of those within the Insurrection, but a sadness that Daxa would never hear sweet stories from her family's past again.

“How have you been holding up,” Lukas asked with the most earnest look on his face. Daxa looked at him, and though she thought to joke about his regained ability to show sympathy, she couldn’t. Something about the way he spoke to her struck her internally, a strange feeling of connection that was only augmented by the look in his eyes. She shuddered in a way she thought impossible with Lukas Bautista, of all people. But he truly cared for her, and she could see it as clearly as her grandmother’s reflection in the moonstone necklace.

“It’s been hard,” she admitted, “but I’ve been working through it. The training helps. Giving other people motivation for self-improvement helps me to find it for myself.” He smiled at that, and then his smile grew wider. She grew serious for a moment as she tried to puzzle out what it was that made him so happy to look at her.

“You’re blushing,” he teased, a clear sign that the old Lukas had come back to the fore. She was surprised to find that she’d missed him in his absence. “I’m happy to hear you’ve found a way to grow beyond the pain, though. I’m pretty much the same, you know? I’m still struggling with the loss,” he explained with a quake in his voice, but then, as if he remembered something at the last minute, said, “but I’m doing better. The spare sword helps me focus more on what my dad taught me instead of the fact that he’s not here anymore.” This time she smiled at him, then fixed her eyes back on the road before them as they walked through the cold dark with only their company to provide them warmth. It was nice, they realized, being in each other’s presence. For all the time they spent ignoring each other or getting into arguments in the past, the moment had shown them that they had more in common than they realized, from the battlefield to their sense of humor.

Footsteps approached from around the corner, and instantly the niceties of the moment had passed. Lukas and Daxa turned in the direction of the sound and, Lukas in front, moved to cover the corner of the nearest building, hands on the hilts of their Reikiken. Seconds ticked by in slow motion while their heartbeats accelerated to light speed. The footsteps grew louder as they crunched in the still-present icy aftermath of the winter's snow, which told them both that whomever it was that they heard had little concern for their safety.

Over the last few months there'd been so much conflict surrounding Johnson City because of its importance in trade between the Kingdom and the Alliance, and even with the dissolution of the Flagstaff Ceasefire, it was still a valued outpost for simple expansion. It would have surprised neither Lukas nor Daxa if the current peaceful state of the city would dissolve in this exact moment. The footsteps grew closer still, and in moments were only a few inches off. That was when the two emerged from their counter-corner stance and brandished their trademark fireswords at any would-be aggressors.

It was Zayvier Peters, the Earth Dragon, surrounded by a team of two Kabuto warriors and someone unfamiliar to say the least. The soldiers behind him held their hands up in a placative gesture to appease the apparently angry Yaiba warriors, while Zay just looked at them with a smile that stretched from ear to ear.

"I see you two are having a good morning," he joked. They stowed their weapons and bowed their heads out of respect. It was not lost on them that they were only a few years younger than him, but he had the rank to demand such courtesy. "Lemme get the intros out the way: Tareena Hendricks," he said with a gesture to a lovely woman with skin the color of night that glistened under the light of the moon. Her hair was in locs and her deep brown eyes showed a playful seriousness that gave her onlookers an uncertainty of how to handle interacting with her. She smiled a slick smile and nodded to Lukas and Daxa. "Jake Parrish," the Tsuchiryu continued with a nod to a man with the skin tone of fresh snow, auburn hair and piercing blue eyes. He beamed at them with a quiet kindness that spoke of his determination to befriend those around him. His gentle soul seemed to pour out of him in a way that reminded Lukas of his Uncle Bill. "And finally, Aiden Moore, from the Yoroi Alliance."

"From the where," Daxa asked incredulously. "I thought they couldn't mobilize yet." Zayvier shook his head.

"Not in large forces, no, but they've deployed some of their best demo experts to several points of interest." It was always jarring when Zay switched from his usual vernacular to military jargon, but nothing was as jarring as the person that stood before them as he told them, "Just like this guy." Aiden Moor was about a year or so younger than Lukas, and stood with a slim-muscular build wrapped in light caramel skin. His face showed the sharpness of an adult mixed with the delicacy of a child's, though it was clear that he was closer to the former than the latter. His bright brown eyes showed a curiosity, but not of anything someone of that age would usually be concerned with. There was a quiet madness behind them which bore a kinship to the experimental insanity and morbid fascination found in Sora Kaneuji and the late Manny Bautista respectively.

"Wow, we're so diverse," Lukas pointed out. "Lot of minorities on this mission." He laughed in the whimsical way that he had before the KDN rained Hell from the skies, and his surprisingly upbeat attitude mixed well enough with his comments to elicit a chuckle from everyone present. "So what's the mission, boss?"

"Oh that's easy," Zay supplied. "We breakin' into the capitol."

For a moment, everyone was stunned to silence, but when he saw that nobody else was going to, Aiden took a deep breath, cleared his throat, and when the Earth Dragon looked at him, asked in as deadpan a way as he could, "What?"

****

February 23rd, 2085, 10:20 a.m.,

Serenity had waited long enough. It had been nearly a week since her arrival, and all the preparations were set. Ryan Morrisey and his commando team of Hector Rubio, Isaiah Parkman, Tez Johnson and Aaron Stone had already done the necessary recon to verify that the Westershire boy's intel was good. Now all that needed to be done was to take the city in quick and orderly fashion. She had more than a thousand troops under her command, which felt strange since Callan wasn't here to supervise her, but she would make it work here as she had during her time as a leader in the Red Military.

She broke down her battalion into smaller squads and stationed them around key points of Uptown Charlotte, where the enemy had most of their forces concentrated. The report of the Battle of Yoroi provided intel of Scarlet Troopers in use of the Thunderclaps, those same swords that Al had brought to their doorstep and used to nearly blast a hole through the Roan base. By the looks of things, though, his was a prototype, and the ones that they would encounter were the genuine article.

Even still, she would succeed. The nature of war was as much adaptability as it was the ability to plan an operation, and in her years as a soldier for the enemy, she had mastered the art of both. Moreover, a change of protocol happened a lot faster in the Yaiba Insurrection than in the Scarlet Kingdom, so she could count on the fact that she had an overwhelming advantage in the battle to come.

"In position," came Tez over the comms, "awaiting orders." It made her happy to hear. In the short amount of time that she'd had with the Yaiba so far, she couldn't help but notices a surprising degree of competence in each operative that only seemed to escalate as they grew in their craft. No wonder they'd proven to be such a threat to the Kingdom. If given the right resources, they could easily rule all of Providence…Prevalence. She had to catch herself in her address of their home-turned-battlefield. What was Providence to the Kingdom, an ultimate expression of their might and fortune, was Prevalence to all others. It was a glimpse of everything they'd survived, partially at Serenity's hands. It was the least she could do to respect the difference in terminology.

"Wow," remarked Aaron Stone, dumbfounded at the various ruins that once might have been attractions to the now desolate city. "There's so much cool stuff around here. Hey, Boss Lady, what do you think you'd have done in the old days where people actually lived in Charlotte?"

"Not important," Serenity said with the same kind of grit in her voice that turned the Scourge into the death squad it was known to be. She suppressed a smile. "Are you in position or not?"

Stone looked around from his perch atop an old hotel building, which gave him a clear view of the city's Fourth Ward (along with the stadium in the Third and the caved-in roof of the convention center in the Second). He focused on the instructions sent through his Menpo and realized he was in the right place. "I guess I am," he said with a tinge of satisfied incredulity.

"Then maintain radio silence until you receive further instructions," Serenity commanded, then as soon as she ended comms with Stone, Hector patched in from inside the First Ward Apartments. The roof showed a considerable age, the walls and windows were cracked or crumbled under the slightest touch, and yet a squad of twelve managed to make it work as a base of covert operation.

"Uh, Master Crawford," he hailed, though it felt weird for him to refer to her as anything other than her former title of Major, "enemies inbound from the northeast."

"What route are they taking?" Serenity asked briskly. There was a flutter of excitement in her heart, then a raging calm washed over her. For her, the battlefield had become as much a home as the luxury penthouse she'd lived in back in New York, and there was a pleasantness about it that she couldn't shake.

"North Davidson," Rubio attested. Serenity checked the geo-sensor readouts, and surely enough there was an increase of activity moving along that road. She couldn't help but smile. The enemy knew they were there. For a week, this game of chicken had gone on and both sides were hesitant to strike first. Now, though, now the Reds moved into position, clearly awaiting a force of over a thousand. Serenity wouldn't be intimidated. In fact, it was the trap that she'd set from the very beginning.

"Orbit Units, begin enclosure," she commanded. She stood atop the Ank of Eri building, the tallest point in the city, and listened as the first shots were fired. She watched as waves of enemies, a scattered assortment placed around central Charlotte, were forced little by little to retreat. Explosions erupted in a couple of places, and it struck Serenity as a chord of blissful music. The traps they'd stolen from Scarlet convoys that passed near Johnson City in the last few months had proven their worth, and it was poetic, because why would the Reds expect their own weapons to be used against them to such a degree? Within the next few moments, what was left of the auxiliary supports of the Scarlet Kingdom in Charlotte were forced to rejoin the main force, and the Orbit Units faded into the shadows of the broken city like a pack of wolves in a forest.

****

February 23rd, 2085, 11:39 a.m.,

Serafina ran so contrary in this moment that it surprised Aria. She was a picture of calm, reserved as she called out orders over the comms to the main force. So what if the auxiliary support was gone? They were only there to flush the enemy out of hiding. The Yaiba weren't up for a direct fight, but that didn't make them weak by any means. They would keep to the shadows and try to pick off Scarlet Troopers little by little until their forces were naught but a few quaking cowards.

It was interesting for Serafina to face Serenity in this arena. Now they would know beyond a shadow of a doubt which of them was the better strategist.

"Aria," said the Scourge leader with a coldness to her voice that she'd never exhibited in Aria's hearing, "it's time. Tell Ryan to move into position and start picking off any Insurrectionists he sees. Do you know what to do?"

"If you're talking about my role in the battle, then you know I do," Aria said with more of a tone than she'd intended. Serafina turned her head with a snap, and for a moment Black believed that it would be the end of her. She resolved to defend herself, and reached for the dagger stowed in a holster at her lower back. There was a ferocity in the Lady Leyva's eyes as she now strode towards the former Yaiba. Aria thought to jump back, to lunge forward, to do whatever she could to protect herself or run, but her body wouldn't listen to her. She was frozen to her spot, incapable of little more than shaking with every thump of her heart.

Serafina placed a gentle but firm hand on Aria's shoulder and smiled a wily smile that betrayed the Scarlet Usurper's true insanity. It was a miracle that Aria didn't drop to her knees. "Better get going then," Serafina said with a devious inflection. She continued to the door, then through it to the darkened halls of the battered Mint Museum while Aria crumbled to the floor.

****

February 23rd, 2085, 12:24 p.m.,

Ryan Crawford thought there would be more. More tears, more screaming, more of a desire to just stay at home and do nothing, but the only thing that he felt more of was a resentment towards those damned rebel factions. First they took his sister, now his brother, and the only thing that he had left was a father who had already turned traitor. He knew that he could never do anything to hurt him. He knew he could never turn him in and definitely could never hurt him, but he was angry with him nonetheless. He needed to vent, about all of it, but the people who were his usual confidants were the same deserter and deceased he wanted to talk about. He thought there would be more emptiness in him. That was what all the books and songs of old always talked about when loss occurred, but all he felt was a seething anger that festered in him like a thousand sores.

He grappled up the side of the Ank of Eri building, straight for the broken spires at its top that made up its shattered crown. Thunder burst through the air and he could feel the electricity charge in the dark clouds above. The sound of rain filled his ears, and it amused him that the sky could shed tears that he could no longer muster. He reached the top, and before he could silently thank the King for breaking down the Hanzo Gear formula for the engineering department, he saw her.

There, at the edge of the broken crown dressed in black and purple, stood his beloved older sister, the treasonous Serenity Crawford. She turned to face him when she heard his boots hit the concrete of the rooftop, and he watched as her hard military bearing washed away in the rain.

"Ryan," was all she could manage before he cut her off.

"So you actually showed up." He shook with anger at the sight of her. "I doubt that you'd just surrender and make something easy for me for once."

"Ryan—" he raised his pistol to her, and she stopped in her tracks. What she saw in his eyes wasn't the playfulness that he was known for or the poise that he showed everyone outside of their family. What she saw there was a brokenness that all but ripped her soul in two.

"Stop," he demanded. "I don't want to hear anything you have to say, you shortsighted traitor!" With every word, he grew louder. His scream was visceral, and the shaking of his pistol made her nervous at first, then calm. Ryan hadn't decided if he would fire yet.

"Ryan, put the gun down," she said firmly, evenly, "and tell me what's wrong." He could hear the sincerity in her voice, which crashed down on his anguish like a hammer on a nail and his eyes flickered between a hardened glare and a shaky wince.

"Oh, you mean to tell me you don't know?" His tone was sarcastic and incredulous. "It's almost like you were disconnected from everyone or everything! I never would've imagined that your pure selfishness would have caused problems for our family!"

"Alright, that's enough," Serenity snapped. "First, I don't owe you any explanation beyond what I've already told you. I won't apologize for choosing myself over the tyranny of the Kingdom—"

"Oh, now it's 'tyranny,' sis?" Ryan's offense was clear, but Serenity didn't care.

"Yes! There are people that live in *caves* because of the never-ending bloodshed that our people are responsible for—"

"And some of those cave-dwellers are the reason why Kyle is lying in the morgue with a stab wounds to the chest and throat!" Serenity immediately remembered the operation on the Yoroi territory, where Bill and his forces had been dispatched. Her heart sank as she vehemently shook her head in fervent denial. Now it made sense, why he looked the way he did, why Ryan was so angry. He, the baby of the family, had lost his two older siblings in two different ways. He was alone, but before Serenity could give Ryan a response, he continued in a rage. "If you hadn't chosen your 'happiness' then he would still be alive!"

"You don't know that, Ryan," she argued, and he raised his eyebrows at her, unable to believe the utter nonsense of that statement.

"You said it yourself, right? The last time we were together? You're amazing, you set the tone for me and Kyle, and you basically told me that you were better than us in every way. Sure sounds like someone we needed in our corner." Suddenly, Serenity felt guilty for all of that. She wanted to crumble to the ground, but she had no idea what her little brother would do to her if she did. Instead she steeled herself for what she knew would come.

"What are you doing here, Ryan?"

"Taking out as many of the enemy as I can from the highest vantage point in Charlotte… starting with you." She gave a startled blink and ducked on instinct as the first shot rang through the air. Adrenaline ran through her veins as she darted for her brother. She ran in an erratic fashion as fast as she could, but it almost wasn't enough. Ryan was a good enough shot to predict her path towards him, but she had been through enough battles to know how to avoid it. She bridged the gap and only narrowly sidestepped a point-blank shot to the face. Ryan fired a couple more rounds into the air now, as Serenity pushed his hand up and gripped his wrist tightly.

It always amazed Ryan how much brutish strength she had, but she was as she told him months ago: an excellent warrior who had trained non-stop. It was no surprise that even after she changed sides, she was still very much a beast.

He drove his knee into her abdomen so hard that she hunched over out of compulsion. Ryan's weapon hand slipped free of her tight grip, and in that instant he brought the muzzle of his pistol down to burn the back of her neck. Click. The shot fired off course. Serentiy had shifted her bodyweight to push him off balance, which saved her for the moment. He spun out of the predicament and pointed the gun back at his sister. Lightning flashed and thunder roared over the sound of the gunshot, but to his surprise, she brushed his hand and weapon off to the side. He spun to the other side in an instant, fired two more rounds directly at her face, but she ducked and slipped behind him.

Ryan, spurred in his anger by the sudden clap of thunder, revolved with an extended fist. She blocked the blow and stepped off the center line. He didn't understand how Serenity could intuit the attack as a feint to better position himself for a shot at her stomach, but she did just before he could pull the trigger. She kicked the gun out of his hand and took a deep breath as it slid across the Ank of Eri rooftop.

Cold rain continued to fall, and she was grateful, because Serenity Crawford had never let her youngest brother see her cry, and she wouldn't start now. Lightning and thunder after. A harsh burst of wind that whipped her long black hair out in front of her. Everything in her hated this. She watched him seethe with a fury that was so unlike him, and she knew that he blamed her for everything that had happened. It pained her that he was so undeniably brainwashed by the Kingdom's propaganda that he wasn't able to see why she had done what she'd done, and even more so because he was driven to the point where he'd try to kill his own sister.

"Fight back, damn you!" Ryan's bark seemed strong enough to summon the thunder that burst loudly against their eardrums. Serenity stood there in silence, her sullen eyes still locked on a hateful little brother that she loved more than anything in the world. He released a frustrated yell as he charged for her again. He punched at her, was pushed aside, then punched again with all his strength. She side-stepped him and watched him stagger.

Serenity knew that it was the perfect chance to strike back, kill him even. But she couldn't bring herself to fight him. He turned back to her and moved for a roundhouse kick that she promptly ducked. She took a step in and lifted her shoulder into the bend of her brother's knee. Ryan almost couldn't keep his balance, so she let his leg down easy.

"Stop this," she begged, "and let's talk." There was a break in her voice when the words came out, which only seemed to anger him more.

"Talk? What do you wanna say, sis? What could you possibly tell me to make the pain go away?" She had no answer. "What?!" His impatience had reached the breaking point, and his tone startled her more than she realized it could. He started for her again, but she held up her hand and he stopped, much to her surprise.

"I'm trying to end this," she told him earnestly. "To the best of my ability I'm trying to put a stop to this endless fighting—"

"By raging against your own people—"

"By realizing what we were doing was wrong!" It was her irritation that broke through this time and singed the air. "Do you know how many people have died because of our fixation on status and property? Have you ever thought for once about the kids who lose their parents to satisfy our bloodlust, or the parents who are forced to outlive the children they were powerless to protect? And for what?"

“For what? For unity, Serenity! Ever since the Dawn King took public office, those people you betrayed us for haven’t been happy with the way the world works—”

“Because who the hell wants to be unified with their abuser? Who decided that that’s how the world works? Who woke up and made the damn decision that if you aren’t rich enough or don’t have light enough skin then you’re expendable?”

“I didn’t hear any complaints from you for all your years of service. For the longest time you were the one to tell us how we should act according to the glorious vision of our Kingdom!”

“And I’m telling you that I was wrong!” Her breathing was heavy, and the threat of tears was a distant memory at this point. “Do you really think that murdering entire communities is some glorious pursuit? Was maintaining the Kingdom’s ideals worth Kyle’s life?” He grew silent, and for a moment Serenity didn’t know what went through her little brother’s mind. The wind blew between them and around them, and every drop that seeped into their uniforms did so with an absurd lucidity.

“You know,” he broke, tears visible in his eyes even amid the rain spattered on his face, “you know I don’t know how to answer that. The Kingdom—”

“Is what you’re talking about most right now,” Serenity interrupted coolly, “not Kyle. You learned of his death, and while it bothers you, you’re clearly more concerned with the Kingdom.” His eyes widened with realization that that was, at his heart, his main focus. He’d shown up to work. He hit the battlefield. He tried his hardest to fight his sister. Every ounce of sorrow he felt, he turned into anger and funneled it into the war effort he'd been given, because the burden of his own emotions was just too much.

Before he realized it, she caught him in an embrace on the rooftop. They cried together.

****

February 23rd, 2085, 1:40 p.m.,

Flashes of red exploded throughout the city. The Scarlet Troopers that made up the enemy's primary force had finally been forced to spread out when the Yaiba and Kabuto launched their offensive, and while they fought in back and forth manner to either maintain or gain control of Central Charlotte, Serenity limped as fast as she could through the warring mob. She knew that her brother watched her, and every so often she would hear the crack of sniper fire as it ripped through the screams and blasts that filled the long-ruined city.

Each of Ryan's shots found its way into and then through a target, and Serenity knew that she couldn't keep this up for too long. She expected his aim to be thrown off, or for the trajectory of his shots to be distorted by the storm, but there was no such luck. What was worse was that he was still up there on top of the Ank of Eri, and there was little she could do to bridge the gap.

The former Scourge leader still reeled from their fight, from the tears, from the news of Kyles death. Serenity, however, was never the type to lose sight of her mission, and she knew better than to give into the wealth of emotions that welled up inside her.

She used the overgrown trees on Tryon Street for cover, then ventured off the path and into the old Tryon Plaza. It was more than enough to quickly obstruct Ryan's vision and buy Serenity a moment to catch her breath. Her body crashed against the wall of the Plaza building against her will as she gasped for air. It had been a long time since she was put on the defensive this much, but she relished the challenge. She was determined to show her old nation exactly who was the backbone of the Scarlet Scourge.

Just as she glanced back up in the direction of the Ank of Eri, she heard the faint croaking of her name from a strained albeit familiar voice. Her head whipped around and her pistol almost magically found its way into her hand. Just as her index finger caressed the trigger, she realized that the person she almost shot was Aria Black, her old subordinate. Alarm took her, and she quickly tucked the gun back in its holster as the Scourge member fell unceremoniously to the ground. Serenity rushed to her and noted the tattered state of her clothes, drenched in dirt and sweat and the scattered particles of debris that continued to waft through the air with every blast from those confounded Thunderclaps.

"Oh my God, Aria," Serenity breathed. She rolled her former teammate over, hopeful that if she was alright, she could prove to be a useful ally.

"So…tired…" Aria wheezed. "Need a…minute…" Serenity shook her head with a smile. Aria Black was suited for espionage and interrogation. She had fighting skills, but she had very little in the way of stamina. It seemed like she fought her way into this corner and finally reached her limit.

"I always told you to pace yourself," Serenity said with a sympathy that she'd thought no longer applied to anyone from her old life in the military. "You'll be alright." The former leader of the Scourge moved to dump her former teammate to the ground as she had in the days of old when Black gripped the former Colonel's wrist with desperate force.

"Was attacked…betrayed…" Black told her with a deeper sense of urgency that gave Serenity pause. "Help me." Serenity glanced up in the direction of the tower from which her brother looked down. She knew that in her present condition, she could barely help herself. Aria, though, was one of her squad, and she couldn't in good conscience just leave her to die in the streets of a dilapidated Charlotte. She was short on supplies, and frantically surveyed the area for anything that might help her to help Aria. She noticed an old restaurant across the Plaza.

"Hold on," Serenity told her as she regained her shaky legs and staggered out a step towards the restaurant. "I'm going to get you some water, and then you can tell me what happened." Aria merely nodded, and Serenity hobbled her way across the broken concrete.

Once Serenity was out of hearing range, Aria, who remained in the same supine position, tapped the switch of a microcommunicator tucked behind her ear and beneath her hair.

"Have you found her," Serafina asked from the other end. Aria gulped, somehow wracked with guilt at having moved against a woman she saw as a protector and friend.

"Yeah," she replied. "Transmitting location to you now. I'll do what I can to keep her here until you arrive." She ended the call, and continued her act as Serenity came back none the wiser.

Chapter Fifteen

February 23rd, 2085, 2:00 p.m.,

Callan was an unusual cool as he walked with Zahara and Hank Davis through the surprisingly pristine shelves of the H.T. Sampson Library. Books on top of books were stored in the aged hall of tomes, and the quiet of the space was more than enough to relax them all. Before they'd entered, while they climbed the brown and gray staircase beyond the solid white statue in the foyer, Zahara had told Callan that the Waste Raider leader, the most prominent voice in the Old American South, was a hard woman who struggled to be diplomatic. She only understood strength, and that was a quality that her predecessors had shown. Already Callan could tell that he would like her.

Hank cosigned Zahara's description, and added that for as hard as she was, the legendary Raider leader was also a well-educated woman with a penchant for reading the literature of Old America. That was why her base of operations was on the worn campus of Jackson State University, and why her domain stood within the halls of its historic library. Callan could feel the tension in the air with every step, and the white brick walls, which shone yellow under the light of the afternoon sun, somehow amplified his feelings. Each brick was a blank canvas ready to take on the image of every feeling and expectation that ran through his mind.

The trio came to a stop just in front of a wooden door. Zahara smiled as she watched Callan blow out a nervous breath and wring his hands before he shook them at his sides to loosen up. Even Hank raised an eyebrow, since it was unheard of for a Dragon to get so nervous about a simple meeting. They all knew, however, that Callan was right to be cautious and to prepare himself, because this was no ordinary meeting.

"Are you ready," Zahara asked, a bit of teasing to her tone. Callan looked at her and raised his eyebrow.

"About as ready as you are to get back together with Dross," he jibed, to which her jaw dropped as her lips curled into a smile she desperately tried to resist.

"If you two are done," Hank cut in before Zahara could respond with a joke of her own, "I don't think it's wise to keep the lady waiting. You earned this meeting with that battalion of troops you sent to Yorktown. Best not to blow it by being late." They both grew as serious as the aged wooden accents that girded the ceiling and railings throughout the library.

"You're right," Callan spoke with another nervous huff. Zahara steeled herself, because this could be the moment that decided the war. The Suiryu reached his hand out and opened the door to find two women of alabaster skin, brown hair, and devious smiles at a circular table.

"Well finally," said the older one, who wore glasses and her hair in simple ponytail. "I thought you were gonna leave me waiting here until I died of old age." Callan and Zahara were stunned at the complete lack of decorum. They looked her over and were underwhelmed by what they saw. To them, she looked like an ordinary woman with no training of any kind. It was hard for them to believe that she was the legendary Queen Raider that they'd heard so much about. They looked at the other woman, younger and more in shape, but the spitting image of the older one. They deduced her to be the Queen Raider's daughter, and then she opened her mouth and removed all doubt.

"You losers gonna take a seat at the table or are you gonna keep standing in the doorway gawking like idiots?" She was just as gruff.

"Of course," Zahara started as she moved for the chair across from the younger one. "Might I say, we appreciate your willingness to have this mee—"

"Yeah, that's enough of that," said the Queen. "We're not here for the schmooze, Princess, we're here for business. So bring your tuches over here and sit down so we can get to it." Without another word, Zahara sat down and Callan sat next to her. Hank merely stood at the back of their back and acted as their enforcer. "So, what brings you to my door?"

Callan gave the question a moment of thought, but after an impatient flare of the eyebrows on the part of the Queen's daughter, he decided to just come out with it. "We wanted to enter an agreement with you and your people."

"Hell no," she said without skipping a beat. "I know what you people are like, man, and I don't want any part of it."

"What do you think you know?" The question was enough to make the Queen's jaw drop in a mixture of irritation and shock.

"Oh, so you think that because I'm a woman from the Southern Wastes I don't know what's what?" Callan immediately pulled his hands into a placating gesture in response.

"I didn't mean to insinuate—" he started, but was cut off.

"Let me tell you something, bucko," the Queen continued in her fury, "I know that it's you guys' fault that those bombs got dropped on our heads. Always running around and getting your supplies, stirring up trouble wherever you go. Now you're losing ground in the fight you picked and you have the nerve to come ask us for help."

"Who said we're losing," Callan asked, now a little humored himself. The Queen opened her mouth to speak, to tear him a new one just as she'd done this entire time, but her curiosity was piqued and she wanted to know more.

"What's that now?" The Queen's tone was lighter now, more girlish, and less like the fearsome and somewhat brutal Queen Raider that the rumors conveyed.

"We managed to cripple the Kingdom's movements with the help of the Kabuto Sanctuary and have taken back the West by teaming with the Yoroi Alliance. The Kingdom is still strong, but they've suffered heavy losses—"

"More losses than we have?" The question came from the girl beside the Queen. Her eyes were narrowed just like her mother's, and Callan noted a wisdom behind them. She couldn't have been any older than 17, but she'd clearly seen a rougher life than she should have. "I watched friends of mine go up in smoke right before my eyes. I smelled burning flesh in my own clothes for weeks after the bombing. My childhood vanished in an instant. So please, answer my question. Have they suffered more losses than we have?"

"It's not the time for that, Mikki," said the Queen, which earned a scornful look from the girl. The Queen returned with one of her own and quieted her daughter in an instant. "I do wanna know what kind of losses are we talking about?"

"The Scarlet Scourge is down to its final three members and we've managed to sway its previous leader to our side. One of the heirs to the throne came with her," Zahara explained, and watched the Queen's eyes widen with intrigue. "On top of that, one of Director Hamlin's sons took down the Kingdom Drone Network by himself, so they have to fight us on our terms. We also have it on good authority that the other Prince of the Reds has been ousted from the Kingdom, and seeks to destroy what his predecessors have built."

"Sounds like you're doing pretty well for yourselves," said the Queen. "So what do you need with us?" Callan clasped his hands together in front of his face as he leaned forward on the table.

"Honestly, we want you to help us add pressure to the Kingdom from the outside," Zahara spoke up. "If the Southern Wastes join our coalition, it'll nearly be the entire continent against the Reds in a relentless onslaught of specialties."

"There's more you're not telling me," the Queen deduced after a moment of silence. "I wanna know what it is." Zahara and Callan exchanged looks, and each let out a sigh.

"You're right," Callan admitted. "Do you happen to know why the princes have been banished?" The Queen adjusted in her seat.

“Why don’t you go ahead and fill me in,” she urged.

“One of our best warriors and greatest technical minds betrayed us and took over the Kingdom,” Callan explained. “We don’t know how he did it, but he managed to kill the Scarlet nobles and seize power for himself.”

“So you’re saying that this man who knows all your strategies and how your ‘legendary’ weapons work is the one you’re up against? Yeah, that sounds like a winning battle,” the Queen joked and crossed her arms before her chest. “I figure you wouldn’t be here if that weren’t true, though. So, what’s the plan?” The question made Zahara smile.

“Actually, it’s a little bit like the one I used to liberate Jackson a few months ago—”

“Whoa, hold on. What?” The Queen and her daughter both sat with their mouths agape at that intel. “I thought it was that one broad. Which one was she,” the Queen Raider pondered aloud, then snapped her fingers. “Wait, she was the Wood Dragon, right? The one that always called herself the Light Dragon?” Zahara nodded, but before she could continue her thought, she was interrupted again by the Queen. “Why did she do that anyway? It was confusing as all crap.”

“She was like a sister to the Kageryu, our Shadow Dragon, to the point of being inseparable. We started calling her the Light Dragon because wherever there’s light there’s shadow. It just kind of stuck,” Callan explained.

“Oh…” The explanation seemed less appealing to the Queen Raider than she’d originally thought. She shrugged, and turned her attention back to Zahara as she said, “So you were the brains behind me getting my favorite spot back, huh? How’d you manage to pull that off?”

“It was easier than you would’ve thought,” Zahara answered, “since I was an ace sniper in the Scarlet Army. I just used my status with the Kingdom to get into the Jackson fortress and sabotage it while Raven and her forces attacked from the outside.” There was a moment of silence as the Queen Raider stewed on the story.

“So that’s your plan?” The Queen didn’t sound impressed, just as Zahara knew she wouldn’t. “You’re going to use us to apply pressure while you slip into another fortress?”

“In a manner of speaking,” Callan offered in assurance. The Queen burst out laughing.

“Oh, that’s rich. It’s not like it’ll work twice, you know. Tell me, Mr. Water Dragon, what’s your target even gonna be this time?” It was when she asked the question that Callan smiled back at her with such a deviousness that it gave even the Queen Raider pause.

“Nothing too, major,” Callan told her, “just New York.” The Queen didn’t say anything, and for a moment they didn’t know if she was quiet because she thought them fools or because she considered them brave. Then she smiled a wild-woman’s smile at them as excitement burst out of her like fireworks.

“You guys are friggin’ crazy,” she said with a giddy tone. “I like you.”

“Does that mean you’ll help us,” Zahara asked a little too earnestly for Callan’s liking, but he knew she wasn't exactly a politician. It still impressed him that she'd done as well as she had up until now.

"Well, that depends. If you can get us more materials like food, medicine, and a larger defensive force, I might be inclined to say yes—"

"Done," Callan promised, and everyone in the room was taken by surprise. "I received a call before we came in today. We happen to have an acquaintance who needs a larger fighting force. If you don't mind having some of your people train to fight, I think he'll be more than happy to supply defensive measures to your territories."

"Hmmm..." suspicion crept back into the voice of the Queen as she considered her options. "Who's the acquaintance?" Zahara thought to open her mouth and explain, but she had no chance to do so. A door slammed on one of the lower levels with a sound that should have been more muted than it was, and suddenly the meeting had grown quiet. Footsteps could be heard as they approached from the stairwell and the outer hall. All eyes trained on the knob of the door as it twisted slowly and ramped up the suspense of the engagement. The door opened, and Callan's lips split into an excited smile while the Queen and her daughter sat stunned.

"Nash O'Neill," the Suiryu started, "meet Claire Sommerfield, Queen Raider of the Southern Wastes."

****

February 23rd, 2085, 2:05 p.m.,

When Serenity reemerged from the building with a glass of water in her hand, she was stunned by the eerie silence that had taken the city. There was no sniper fire to hide from, no explosions or red light in the distance that threatened to bring down every structure in Charlotte. There was nothing but the smoke and fire left in the battle's wake. The former Scourge leader dropped the glass and immediately went for the comms.

"Hector, come in," she demanded with more concern in her voice than had ever been displayed by her on the battlefield. "I need an immediate update. What's going on?" The second that followed her inquiry felt like an eternity, and in that instant she contemplated more worst-case scenarios than she felt comfortable with admitting. She didn't know if something had happened to her little brother, or if something had happened to her troops, but she was determined to get an answer.

"We're good," Hector assured her from the other end. He sounded out of breath but relieved all the same. "The enemy sounded a retreat before the good fighting got started. Still managed to take a few with us, though." There was excitement in his tone, but it was his relief that was contagious.

"That's good to hear. Hold your position," she ordered. "Keep your guard up just in case they circle back."

"Understood," the young Helmet responded, and then the whistling came. It echoed through the shadowy alley from the end that, just a few minutes ago, had invited Serenity in. It was eerie in the silence of the battlefield, poignantly augmented by the fall of rain and the clap of thunder that railed against the foundations of Charlotte, then it gave way to a hushed singing that disturbed Serenity to her core.

"It's raining, it's pouring, the old man is snoring…" It was a woman that approached, and chanted the tune with an obvious sick delight in her voice. Serenity turned to face the origins of the song, who stood as a confident figure shrouded in the darkness of the old walkway. The figure continued to sing. "He went to bed and bumped his head, and couldn't get up in the morning." It was Serafina Leyva who emerged from the shadows. She licked her lips with dark intentions as she prowled the ground. Aria shrunk back from her out of pure wisdom, even if it did betray the falseness of her prior shown weakness. Serafina smiled. "Looks like you fell for the trap."

Serenity reached for her pistol on instinct and pointed its muzzle directly at her replacement's face. The Lady Leyva smirked devilishly still as a bright red beam struck it from her intended victim's hand. Serenity watched it fly, scorched to black, across the alley and land near the spot that Aria had moved from. She had to focus, but the former Scourge leader noticed the small red-eyed orb that hovered above the dark passage.

"I see you got some new toys while I was away," Serenity quipped with a sly smirk as she shook her hand, still warm from the sting of the focused blast. "I guess you had to fill the void I left behind in some way, right?"

"Cute that you think it was that big a void in the first place," Serafina clapped back. "How's fugitive life, Hun? Still galivanting around with your little terrorist pals to the disgrace of your friends and family?"

"I can't complain," Serenity said with a shrug. "It's a lot better than being a slave to the Kingdom, I'll tell you that. But hey, as the King's premiere lapdog you seem to like how the collar fits, so I guess you don't have many complaints either, huh?"

"Wow," Serafina gawked in a faux sense of wonder, "so your gun gets knocked out of your hand and all you can do is talk trash and call names? I knew you'd fallen far, Ms. Crawford, but I didn't know exactly how far. Well," she brandished her Thunderclap and smiled as a bright spark flashed along its edge, "at least this will be easy for me." Serenity reached over her shoulder and grabbed a dark metal hilt. She pulled it out, and from under an opening in her Hanzo Gear cloak there came a sharp-tipped tungsten blade. She whipped it through the air and down by her side as she tilted her head the other way with a mocking smile.

"Sorry, all I heard you say was 'bark, bark.' Think you could repeat that?" Before another word could be said, Serenity noticed the drone move to one side as Serafina flanked to the other. A burst of red much stronger than the previous blast burst from the tiny orb and set the entire stretch of the wall ablaze. Serenity spun out of the range of the beam and into Serafina's line of attack. Serafina went for a swift decapitation under the assumption that her predecessor knew nothing of how to use a Reikiken, but she was alarmed to find truth in the contrary. Serenity parried the horizontal attack and followed up with an intended slash across the chest of her old subordinate.

Serafina parried the move out of the way, but when she sliced at Serenity's midsection, the veteran warrior had already spun around. Her blade revolved around her body in time enough to knock the oncoming Thunderclap away, and with the newly established distance, Serenity stepped in for a midsection cut of her own. The sudden burst of the move caught Serafina off-guard, and the current boss of the Scarlet Scourge only narrowly managed the parry. Serenity smiled as she compounded the fresh flow of energy with her own, and changed her sideways swing into a downward-flowing head strike.

It took all that Serafina had to bring her Thunderclap up in time enough to meet the powerful Reikiken in a block. She angled the blade so that Serenity slid off, but before she could retaliate, the former Head Red followed the energy into another downward strike. Serafina had no choice but to disengage if she wanted to live, and just as the did so, another red burst came from the small levitated orb. Serenity rolled along the ground to get out of the range of the blast and quickly returned to her feet. There was a ferocity in her eyes as she stood there, just a few feet away from Serafina and gradually closed the gap. The incumbent Scourge leader failed to notice the change of grip that came along with Serenity's change of stance. All she saw was the exposed stomach, and was compelled to take the bait.

The moment Serafina plunged the tip of the Thunderclap forward, Serenity jumped as she spun away, then stepped in with a reverse-grip cut at the noble's stomach. Serafina batted the Reikiken away and went for a head strike, but failed to connect. Serenity had already moved to push it out of the way the moment their swords connected. The fresh neo-ninja spun again, but this time made a move to plunge her weapon's sharpened tip into the exposed underbelly of her enemy. Serafina jumped back again, and this time the bright red beam shot at Serenity's head. She ducked and rolled forward, though this time she took a stance that brought her arms down almost to the ground and left her sword pointed straight at her enemy's knees.

"Okay," Serafina groaned, unable to take any pleasure in this fight, "I'll admit it. You're better with that thing than I thought you'd be." She took a stance with her hand behind her back and her weapon brought up to eye-level. Serenity stood in shock. For as much as Serafina undermined her, she thought it was impossible that her replacement would even deign to give a compliment.

"Well, woof-woof," was all Serenity could manage, and just like that, the fight resumed. Serenity stepped forward as if to stab her adversary in the face, but Serenity stepped off the center line with a wide swing of her sword and slashed quickly enough at Serafina's face to make her stumble backwards. *There*, Serenity thought. Like a shark at the scent of blood, she was on the attack. She rolled into an overhead strike, then when she was deflected, carried the energy sideways into an attack at the hips. Serafina parried so sloppily that the only thing that dulled the speed and power of the Reikiken was the narrow cut that ripped through her scarlet uniform.

Still, Serenity didn't feel it. She pressed the attack, this time aimed at the leg, and was met with a loud clang from the opponent's weapon. Serafina pushed with all her force her arms could muster just to keep Serenity's blade from getting through, and while she thought she would use this block to regain her standing, Serenity smiled as calmly as her name would suggest. A wave of pain shot through Serafina's arm as her mind recognized the burns. The cut had been so fast that she had a delayed reaction and the only thing her mouth could produce was a single question: "How?"

Serenity watched as her opponent dropped her guard and backed away like a frightened child would from the monster of their worst nightmares. She stepped forward. Serafina stepped back. The whole thing only deepened the smile of the once-unofficial princess of the Scarlet Kingdom as she answered. "You forget, Ms. Leyva," Serenity uttered with the utmost contempt, masqueraded as angelic benevolence, "that I carried the Scourge before they could even fight properly. I trained every day since I was a little girl to live up to the legacy of my parents. I put the entire Scarlet military on my back and I marched them forward. If you're wondering where my strength comes from, it comes from the fact that I did everything in my power to be excellent. I didn't have to manipulate my way into power, honey, I took it by force." Serafina fell back, and from a seated position continued to push away from the one person who she felt was the ultimate evil. "If you'd been a woman, I would've told you that a real one always does what she needs to in broad daylight and holds the standard high enough that everyone has to strive after her for something. But you're not a woman." Thunder cracked as Serenity's eyes grew cold and unforgiving. "You're just a rabid dog, and it's long past time that I put you down."

Serenity slowly approached her as Serafina quickly slid away, spitting and cursing as she went.

"You think you're walking away from all this?" Serafina sounded mad now, madder than even the perceptions of any that encountered her. "After the way you treated me, you think I'll just let you live? Fire!" She screamed it with a vengeful might that rang through the atmosphere and reached the tiny orb loud and clear. Its red eye lit up as it charged for the shot, and in another second it released the biggest flash of red that it had thus far. At the same moment, Serenity felt the double boot of a dropkick plant squarely in her back. She was launched forward, toward the downed Serafina in fact, who saw her moment and seized it with near demonic glee.

The Thunderclap pierced Serenity Crawford as thunder clapped overhead, and Serafina let loose a joyous screech as her enemy fell to her knees. Serenity looked behind her as she gripped the blade that had gone into her abdomen. She hissed out a breath and felt the fresh chill break through the heat of her still-lit Reikiken, partly from the blood loss and partly from the realization. Aria Black rested in a heap of charred flesh and fabric beneath the rubble of a freshly collapsed part of the alley. She'd been caught in the blast, and when Serenity knew this, she also knew that her old sister in arms had sacrificed herself to save her.

The former Major Crawford looked down at the wound. It was deep, and if left without medical treatment, it could be problematic. All things considered, it was a bit too low and too far left to be fatal. She smiled, though, because it was clear that Serafina didn't know that. The current Scourge leader continued to gloat with shameless intensity, and with an erratic spin that accentuated her mania, turned back to face Serenity to gloat to her face. Before she could open her mouth, though, the word "No!" rang out over even the storm, and then the sound of sniper fire echoed even the more.

Serafina Leyva fell dead right in front of Serenity, who noted that while the front of her skull had splattered with her brains, her jaw still curled into that twisted smile that so adorned her life. Serenity, now relieved that the threat had passed, pulled the sword out of her lower abdomen and, with it, collapsed to the ground. It took a moment for her to completely fade, but her body couldn't handle any more. She laid there on the ground, rain descendant from the heavens above, and the approach of loud footsteps to lull her to sleep.

****

February 23rd, 2085, 4:32 p.m.,

"A-yerrr!" Cal's typical greeting was a welcome sound to Darius' ears as he arrived.

"Bro," Darius said as he clasped Cal's hand and pulled him into a hug. It was the first time he'd been home since October, and already there was a flood of emotions over everything that had happened in the last four months. "I dig the eye." Cal smiled wider at his brother, pleased that he'd recognized the cybernetic advancement of Cal's own design.

"I mean…" Cal let his voice trail off in genuine modesty, and then an expression of sudden realization hit him. "Hey man, I'd love to tell ya more, but I'm actually supposed to tell you. We have been summoned by the Director himself." The playfulness Cal exhibited when he spoke had been sorely missed, but then Darius realized what had been said.

"What do you mean," the Rebel Dragon asked, to which Cal only shrugged and turned back towards the entrance to the Roan Mountain base.

"Follow me!" With the infectious energy of an explorative ten-year-old, they were off.

****

February 23rd, 2085, 5:00 p.m.,

Cal and Darius arrived on the Conference Level to the complete absence of light. It was a lifeless shell of its former self, and the quietness of the dark cave made them both tense up. Darius, whose eyes had grown as stern and focused as his father's, took the lead. Cal, on the other hand, refused to move until his Kiringan took effect.

"Night Vision Mode," he whispered, reluctant to make any loud noises in the event that someone lurked in the darkness. The view of the Kiringan shifted from black to a ghostly pastel green, and though it increased the creepiness of Level D, it gave him back some modicum of sight. "Hey D, be careful." Cal's call to his brother was, perhaps, more serious than Darius had heard, but before he could comment on it, a fist stuck him in the jaw. Darius staggered backwards, but kept himself upright.

A second assailant came from a different direction, but Darius was ready for them. Just as another punch hurdled toward him, the Rebel Dragon ducked and drove his elbow into his unknown enemy's gut. The person, a man, exhaled heavily as he stumbled back. Cal, who flew through the air, kicked him in the head and knocked him into another would-be attacker.

"How many do we have," Darius asked with a confidence in his tone that had never been there before the

Yoroi mission. It was more than enough to make Cal hesitate in his answer.

"We got about four right here," he informed, "and there seems to be a few others down the path. Ain't lookin' like we gone get through so easy." There was a mix of amused exasperation in his words, then the sharp crunch of another person's chest as he drove his boot into its center. They hit the ground with a thud just as Darius made a similar sound on another person's head.

"It looks like we have two options," Darius said as he swept another enemy's leg. He punched them in the throat just hard enough to incapacitate them. "We could fight here—"

"Or," Cal grunted as he held one of his attackers in a perfect sleeper hold, "we could make a run for it." Darius heard footsteps approach from the distance and his smile grew wider as he ran to meet them. He jumped into the air and planted a foot in the face of one of his attackers, then used him as the launchpad to springboard a knee into another's chest. Both hit the ground unceremoniously, and for a moment Darius turned in Cal's direction.

"I don't think we'll be able to make a run for it," he said with a little too much joy in his voice. Cal sprinted towards him and then hit a baseball slide at Darius' legs. The Liberator of Yoroi jumped over his brother, who took out the person behind him. As soon as Darius landed, he dropped backwards with an extended elbow and drove it into the downed assailant's upper back. They let out a pained cry, and then went silent. "How many more?"

"One," Cal told him with a slick smile, "but wait for it." They stood there, amid the broken warriors that had fallen before them, as the final champion ran at them from the other end of the corridor. The ground started to shake, and Cal watched with greatest humor as Darius tried to silently work out what was happening. Darius took a fighting stance, but quickly realized it to be pointless, as a golden flash rocketed through the wall and derailed the course of the attacker. "Shall we?"

Darius blinked, but followed Cal down the hall with an unbothered and unhurried pace.

****

February 23rd, 2085, 5:15 p.m.,

The two young warriors entered a room at the end of the hall to the sight of two Dragons on either side of the room with the Director at its center. Behind him sat two teenage boys, one with free hands and the other in shackles. Darius noted a momentary flicker in Cal's calm demeanor at the sight of the skinnier of the two. Still, the presence of their father commanded a level of respect that restricted their tongues and their actions.

"To the center," John told them sternly. They walked deeper into the room and took notice the kanji inscribed above the marked out positions on the floor, with Kage, Ki, and Hi on the left and Tsuchi, Kaze, and Sui. In the center of them all was that of Rai. Without all of the positions filled it was hard for either of them to determine their purpose here. Darius assumed it was for the Dragonic Ascension that Bill had told him about, but he'd never heard of such a proceeding happening with so few of the core members. "State your names and ranks."

“Darius Michael Hamlin,” spoke the Rebel Dragon, “Master of the Violet Shadows.”

“Cal Marcus Richmond,” spoke the Kiringan, “Master of the Violet Shadows.” Suddenly, both of them were nervous and it was abundantly clear what this was.

“Recite the code,” spoke the former Rairyu.

“‘Refine the mind through art, history, and culture, for it is impossible to live in a world one does not understand. Protect the weak, for it is the responsibility of the strong to do so. The community is a lifeline, and is only as well off as the least of its citizens. Live in peace with allies, rain terror on enemies. Lead fearlessly. Survive at all costs.’” The two young men spoke in unison. A pleased spark appeared for only a breath in John’s eye before he nodded.

“The three pillars of the Yaiba. Go,” he commanded. Again, the two warriors prepared to speak in unison. Both of them felt as though they were boys again, being tested on the lessons that their father had taught them. Then again, this moment came with a brand-new sensation. The things of which they spoke had grown beyond the mere recital that they’d learned. Cal had fought against the Scourge multiple times and had become an unofficial right hand to the Director. Darius had liberated an entire faction from the oppression of the Reds and trained a military force on his own.

“Honesty, Battle, Liberation,” they said with a pensiveness that spoke to their experiences.

“Honesty with self and one’s surroundings, with one’s circumstances and companions. It is essential if one is to defeat delusion," Darius spoke before he was prompted.

"Excellent," John said quickly when he saw the sudden realization and then fear on his son's face. "Cal, explain the nature of battle."

"We battle for honesty's sake, against delusion and what it might bring into this world, and against all kinds of tyranny," Cal supplied. Both of them breathed a little easier.

"And liberation?" The Director asked it as a question, and his boys responded together again.

"Liberation is the end goal of the Yaiba. We do not fight solely for ourselves, but for the rights of all people to live without fear." The former Lightning Dragon looked to the Dragons on either side of him, who the boys recognized to be Vanessa and Bill. Both of them nodded, and John continued.

"Well done, my boys," John told them with fatherly warmth that nearly brought Darius to tears. "You are now members of the Seven Dragons of the Yaiba Insurrection. Cal, take your place as the Kiryu, the Wood Dragon. Darius, take yours as the Hiryu. The Fire Dragon." The boys took their places on the left side of the room under their kanji, only a few feet apart. From there, they smiled at each other and looked at the two boys that sat on the floor behind their father. One was tall with a shadowy complexion and gentle brown eyes that knew far too much of betrayal. The other, the one in chains, was shorter than the first but still tall. He was of a milky complexion with short brown hair, but whereas the taller one met their gaze head on, this one watched the floor as intently as if it talked to him.

"Director," Darius asked, cautious not to seem overly familiar, "if I may ask, who are they and why are they here?" John smiled at them, more with that tactician's flair for which he was known.

"I'm glad you asked. These young men are Leo and Al," he informed as he gestured to them both. "They're here because they're in need of a master, and you two an apprentice."

Chapter Sixteen

March 6th, 2085, 8:00 a.m.,

Lyla Ortiz stood in the former Court Chambers silently behind her father. Together, they listened to Cecelia Kant report the deaths of her Scarlet Scourge teammates. She was the only one left. Lyla couldn't help but feel some sense of sympathy for her. Cecelia had lost so much in this war already. Her sister died at Bluff City. Her friends died between Yorktown and Charlotte. She was alone, just as Lyla had been before her adopted father came back into her life, and yet the King sat upon his throne with nothing but cold contempt in his eyes.

"Ms. Kant," he spoke with a mildly exasperated sigh, "do you have anything useful to report?" The gall of the question was more shocking to Cecelia than the harsh delivery. Even Zachary Smithfield, who stood to the other side of the King, raised a curious eyebrow. "You come to me with the news of your comrades' deaths like this isn't what you all signed up for when you joined the military, but let me remind you that it is. You were soldiers, a death squad, in fact. You mean to tell me that you never assumed that death was a possibility?"

For a moment there was silence, and Lyla suddenly questioned where the kindness in her father's voice went. It was so unlike him to be this cold. Then she wondered if that was true. Cecelia gritted her teeth and forced herself to stop shaking. She knew, just as Lyla did, that it wasn't that long ago that this man was an enemy of the State. He sat here as King only as a result of opportunity and dumb luck.

Nevertheless, she answered him with the respect due a King of the Reds. “Charlotte was taken.”

“Again,” King Bryan spoke with measured irritation, “you tell me what I already know.” There was such an apathy to his demeanor that, for some reason, made Lyla’s heart race. It was as if the man who raised her to cherish all life suddenly couldn’t stand the sight of it. “If that’s all you’ve come to say, then you may leave.” He dismissed her with a careless flick of the wrist, but she remained.

“The hell do you think you are,” Cecelia burst, unable to endure his indifference for a moment longer. “I just told you that the last of our bases has been taken by the enemy. That means that moving around will be a lot harder for our forces! Not to mention we’ve lost our head of intelligence along with several top-ranking military officials. I may not be a tactical expert like Serenity was, but I damn sure know when we’re on the brink of losing!” A shot rang out over the room and suddenly Cecelia gripped her bloodstained shoulder.

“Watch your tone,” Bryan demanded with a sudden bite to his coldness. Bryan stood from his throne and pushed past his daughter without so much as a glance, and to Lyla it was as if the frost had permeated the air. He approached Cecelia, his pistol in his hand. He crouched down, and while he looked directly into her face, she couldn’t help but look down at the barrel. “You know, you might not think I have a legitimate claim to the throne but I do. You see, my mother was raped by that bastard Shane. In front of my father, no less.” His indifference only magnified the weight of what he said. Cecelia breathed heavily through clenched teeth as she endured the burn in her shoulder from the fresh bullet wound. "Not long after that, she discovered she was pregnant with me. So regardless of how you feel about it, I am the King of the Reds, which means that all authority in this place is firmly within my hands. Nod if you understand." She did as instructed. "Good girl. Now, what you're gonna do is get the hell outta my face so I can work out a suitable strategy, and you're gonna be thankful that I decided to spare your life instead of counting against you all the friends I lost to you and your Scourge sisters."

He turned away from her and returned to his throne. Cecelia, the bloodthirsty woman that she was, thought him bold to expose his back to her. Everything in her craved his death by her hand, every cell in her body urged her to stand to her feet, grab him by the throat with her prosthetic hand, and crush his windpipe as she watched the light drain from his eyes. What stopped her, though, was the bleeding reminder in her own flesh as to what this man would do to someone who defied him. Instead, Cecelia did as she was told, but resolved to wait for a moment to strike. She was a member of the Scarlet Scourge, and no neophyte king was going to rob her of her worth.

"Dad," Lyla started incredulously, "what was that?"

"It doesn't matter," Bryan said briskly. He turned his attention to Smithfield and spoke as evenly as if nothing had happened. Cecelia was an afterthought to him, much to the horror of his daughter. "Zachary, prepare a studio for me. We need to address our people."

"Right away, Sire," Smithfield supplied obediently. He bowed his head and swiftly left the Court Chamber. The

King sat and watched as the door closed, then smiled a rueful smile.

"What are you planning," Lyla asked cautiously after a moment of silence. He looked at her, as if wounded by the question. After all, there was such distrust in her voice.

"What do you mean, Lyla?" The sincerity in his voice did nothing to fool her. She couldn't recognize the man that sat on the throne. Part of her wanted to believe that this was just the effect that power had on him, but another part of her, a part that she wanted more than anything to suppress, whispered to her that it was just who he had always been beneath the surface. "I understand your concern, but know that I have a responsibility to the people of our nation to keep their morale high."

"And yet you shot Cecelia in the shoulder for having concerns just as valid as my own," Lyla argued, and watched the genteel expression of her father shift to a darker look.

"That was different," the King explained a bit sharper than he intended, though he thought little of changing it. "Cecelia Kant has murdered more of my friends than I could number at this point. She's the kind of person that would only ever see me as an enemy, and so she needs to be controlled. Kindness is a luxury that I cannot afford in that situation."

"It doesn't change the fact that she was right," Lyla exclaimed with a sorrowful shake to her voice. "What's your plan to pull ahead in all this? Is it to be as calloused as you were with her?" To this, Bryan flickered back to his usual compassionate demeanor. He stood from his seat, walked across the room, and placed a gentle hand upon his adoptive daughter's shoulder as he smiled what seemed to be an honest smile at her. Lyla felt as if she could almost trust it—trust him—but there was something wrong with all of this.

"I assure you, my dear," he told her sweetly, "I'll do everything I can to protect these people, and I'll start by summoning back all of our remaining forces. As much as I hate to admit it, Cecelia's right. Unless we do something to defend the Capitol at this point, we'll lose this war. Would you do me the favor of rounding up the Scarlet Streaks? I'll be needing them for a special task going forward." There was another moment of silence between them as Lyla did her best to determine the King's sincerity.

"I'll do what I can," she said reluctantly, and hastily left the room. King Bryan, on the other hand, simply took to his throne again and watched the door as a maniacal smile brimmed from ear to ear.

****

March 6th, 2085, 9:23 a.m.,

Ryan Crawford lay on his father's couch a disheveled man bereft of any joy. For the past eleven days, he'd hardly said a word to anyone. First, he was steeped in shock at his own actions. He not only had the lack of sense to follow his sister's plan, but he shot and killed one of the leading officers in the Scarlet Kingdom. The thing that got to him was that he didn't even know why he did it. He knew that she was a fugitive, that he should've shot and killed her on sight, but she was his sister even after all that she'd done. As much as he wanted to kill his heart, there was no way for him to pull the trigger.

He thought about Serafina, the daughter of the late Viscount Ronaldo Leyva. She was a noble, an heir, and now a corpse because of a round that Ryan fired into her skull without thinking, all because he couldn't do what a soldier was supposed to and set aside his sentimentality. He'd wondered for days about how long it would take for the government to trace the bullet back to his gun. He sat up for the first time in hours, and the sudden movement made him painfully aware of his ripened scent. He needed a bath.

"Oh, you're up," came the voice of his father Alan. It startled Ryan, who clearly suffered from the anxiety born of the wait. The young sniper faced the older, at first ready to snap from the fear, but he relented. The look of deep concern in Alan's expression was enough inspiration for a more muted response.

"Yes," Ryan hissed between clenched teeth, "your criminal son is finally off your couch—"

"Hey, you know what you did was right, don't you?" Alan attempted to reassure him as he walked from the kitchen into the living room. He placed a tender hand on his son's shoulder and eased him back to the couch. "You protected your sister. If you could've pulled the trigger on her without any kind of remorse, I don't know if I could still call you my son." Ryan couldn't help but laugh. Of course he felt that way. He was a criminal in his own right, a conspirator against the Kingdom who also needed to be brought down.

“Funny that a fraud of a war hero would be proud of his rebel children,” Ryan chided as he looked through the glass top of the black and red coffee table at the center of the room. The old man raised an eyebrow as his grip tightened on the young sniper’s shoulder.

“So you really wanted to be the only one left, then,” Alan remarked with a dark look in his eye. Ryan turned his head back to his father, an incredulous look plastered onto his face.

“Says the man who hasn’t shed a tear over Kyle’s death,” snapped the boy. “He died, and there hasn’t been a shred of emotion on your part—”

“Not that you’ve been around to see it, kid,” Alan retorted evenly. “You wouldn’t know how much I’ve cried over Kyle. Or Serenity, for that matter. The only thing you seem to know is loyalty to a government that would murder you in cold blood the moment you proved to be inconvenient.”

“I’m loyal to the people that keep us safe—”

“Ask Kyle how safe he feels right now, Ryan,” Alan ordered. Ryan bit back his tears. “Go ahead, ask him!”

“You know I can’t!” Ryan could no longer restrain the wild mix of emotions that had tormented him since the news arrived.

“You might be loyal to this country,” Alan started with a much calmer tone of voice, “but from the moment I married your mother right down to the day you were born, my loyalty has always been to this family and others like us.”

"But, Dad, you're betraying everything you've ever known," Ryan pleaded. In that moment it was clear to Alan what his son felt. He felt that he was alone, and that he was trying his best to hold together a world that was destined to fall to pieces long before he came along. He offered a smile that echoed as much concern as it did genuine goodwill.

"Son, I'm protecting everything I know and love. Would you be able to forgive me if I chose what I'm familiar with over your safety?" Ryan couldn't answer. He knew what his duty as a soldier was, and though his father retired years ago, he knew that Alan was aware of it just as well. Realistically, though, he couldn't fathom his father not being in his corner. "As long as I'm alive, making sure that you know you're never alone takes precedence over any duty anyone else might think I have." Ryan felt his body respond before his mind could. Somehow, his father knew exactly what he needed to hear, some reassurance that he was cared for outside of the scope of his duty to the Kingdom.

"How is it so easy for you to say that," the boy asked. The veteran sniper smiled as he cupped his son's face in the palm of his hand.

"It was never a difficult thing for me to choose you. The Kingdom is devoid of anything close to authentic love. People are fed propaganda from the moment they learn to walk. Reading and writing skills are only taught to military families so they can better follow the instruction of their betters. Men and women are either conscripted or coerced into military service and promised a chance at glory when their true purpose is cannon fodder. Why would I make my family second to the machine that would kill them without remorse?"

The more Ryan listened, the more he understood. He'd never been afforded the chance to think about what true horrors the Kingdom presented to its people. He was the son of a war hero, who had access to the best education and privileges in the nation while others were merely pacified with their screens and the flashy messages of their government. They were little more than cattle being fattened for a feast, and the King and his Court stood as both the butchers and the beneficiaries of their collective demise. All the talk about wanting good for the nation sounded hollow next to the cannon fire that was the news of Kyle's death. Suddenly his sorrow subsided and red-hot anger took its place. He met his father's gaze with a determination that the old sniper immediately recognized, because after the night of the White Ruins Massacre, it was a determination that he modeled himself. Before the young soldier could open his mouth to address it, though, his comms channel lit up with a message from Lyla Ortiz, the King's Right Hand. He looked to his father, who smiled a proud smile through soft eyes and gentle expression.

"Go ahead, tend to your duties," Alan urged with a sincerity that caught Ryan off guard. "We can talk later. I have to go out and run an errand anyway. Just…" his voice caught, and he had to take a second to calm himself. "Be careful, alright?"

"Will do," Ryan assured him sternly. The old man pat the boy on the knee as he rose from his seat and paced towards the door with a smile that stretched across his face. Finally, after all this time, he was ready to put his plan into motion.

****

March 6th, 2085, 11:53 a.m.,

Lukas stood on the left of Zayvier with his back to Daxa. They kept their eyes on the park, Lukas to the north and Daxa to the south, prepared to warn the other members of their commando squad if they had a fight on their hands. They didn't expect to be noticed, though. The cloaking tech of the Kabuto Sanctuary was more than just a little effective, and even more so with Jake and Tareena monitoring its status from the centermost point of their formation beneath the trees. Aiden watched the waters of the Hudson River, and strongly resisted the near overpowering urge to lay traps along the edge of the shore.

Zavier, who had previously been engaged in comms chatter, finally turned to address his squad. "Our contact should be here soon. While we wait, we need to go over a few things that weren't in the initial mission brief." The rest of the team rightly understood this as an invitation to pause in their current responsibilities and approach their commander. "Our contact goes by the name of Alan Crawford, a legendary sniper and only Scarlet survivor of the White Ruins Miracle." The two Kabuto and the single Yoroi among them didn't bat an eye at the news, because in truth they wouldn't have known either which way. The Yaiba, though, were stunned.

"Wait, what?" Daxa was visibly confused, and rightly so. Until now, everyone in the Yaiba Insurrection had been led to believe that Dre Hamlin was the only survivor of that ordeal. To hear that there was someone else, or to hear that the vicious Thunderclap of the White

Ruins spared a life, was to all but violently upset everything that they knew to be truth.

"We not gone get into why we didn't know beforehand," Zay continued, more in his natural manner of speaking. "This the man who'll bring us in. Because of him, we have no recon to do outside of the palace itself. He'll give us the key points to target once we get in. After that, we spend time as ghosts, planting the bombs our friend from the Yoroi can whip up."

"So we'll be the first strike against the Kingdom, then," Lukas said with a near childlike wonder. Zayvier shook his head.

"Naw," he told him. "It's deeper than that. We have to be the gateway for the other forces, and Lukas, you got point on the mission."

"Hold on, what?" That was all that Lukas could think to say. Zayvier smiled as he pat the young warrior twice against the cheek in total amiability.

"It's only natural for the newest Dragon to take charge," was the Tsuchiryu's response. Footsteps sounded in the melting snow and fallen leaves of the park. "Time to go."

"Good to see you're all here and ready," Alan Crawford said with a ring of excitement. "Time to go. The troops are in a scramble right now preparing for the King's address. It's the perfect time to get you in unnoticed but we have to move now."

"Roger that," Lukas said, still stunned at the news but excited nonetheless. They were off.

****

March 6th, 2085, 12:00 p.m.,

"Gamma Team has infiltrated the Capitol," Vanessa verified from the conference room on Level D. The Yaiba leaders were all present either physically or via holo-projection. The Elders of the Kabuto and the Yoroi Council were also on the call, and heard the historic news. For the first time since the Fall of America, the Capitol had been breached. It was at this that John prepared to speak, only to be interrupted by the physical arrival of Claire Sommerfield, the leader of the Waste Raiders and Nash O'Neill, former Prince of the Scarlet Kingdom. James looked up in shock, and resisted the urge to shed a tear. John smiled.

"Welcome, everyone, to the first full meeting of our Senshi Coalition. I know that in the past we've all been at odds, but because of our combined efforts, we've not only managed to survive in this war against Kingdom Scarlet, we stand a chance at winning. Here at present, we have leaders from the Yoroi, the Kabuto, the Southern Wastes, and the Yaiba Insurrection, and it brings me great joy to stand together with you all in this fight." The other leaders clapped at the gracious introduction. None objected to the name that John had given their union, and many were thankful that the Yaiba leader had taken such initiative in naming it. "As it stands, our joint commando unit has breached the enemy capitol and will work over the course of the next few weeks to locate key targets and prepare a covert assault on Scarlet resources."

"And what will we do in the meantime," asked the Queen Raider, Claire with her arms folded.

"First, we need to take inventory of our resources and split whatever we have among our allies. That's pooling all the technology and weapons we've made and keeping production as high as possible for the foreseeable future," John explained. "Moreover, we need to give our people time enough to learn how to fight efficiently as a unit."

"I believe that our people have learned quite a bit of that from your son, Darius," Johannes Thornhill stated with a deep satisfaction. Of course, Darius took pride in the comment. He had trained the Yoroi well, he knew, but it was nice to see that his hard work hadn't gone without notice. "The Anti-Rebellion Diffusion and our faction's liberation speak well enough of that."

"Agreed," came the cool tenor of Erik Kincaid, "but there's still a lot to do. None of us have had experience fighting alongside the Waste Raiders, and while our people have worked closely with the Yaiba since the Scarlet Occupation of Johnson City, the primary interactions between our factions, Mr. Thornhill, have been centered around territory negotiations."

"Yeah, about us 'fighting…'" Claire interjected again with a wry smile on her face. "We don't have much in the way of a formalized military and our resources boil down to a lot of family heirlooms, prized possessions, and jury-rigged mechanisms that are meant for pure chaos more than any battle plans."

"Good," Vanessa chimed in. "We still intend to give you the same training as everyone else, but we encourage you to make use of anything you've used to keep you alive until now."

"Nice," Sommerfield beamed.

"The same goes for all parties represented in this meeting," John continued. "When the time comes, the area surrounding the Capitol should have more than the expected amount of Yoroi mines and other demolitions. We should have them cloaked with ShadowStalker tech, as well as a sizeable force made up of all of us."

"How long would we need to coordinate something like this?" The question came from Mercutio Forza, a man with black hair and a graying goatee whose dark eyes promised unforgiveness should they all fail.

"I anticipate that it should take no longer than two weeks to familiarize ourselves with the tactics of our allies and coordinate combat styles. As far as swordsmanship goes, all of what we know stems from Sasori-Sensei and the other Founders. We should spend time syncing our tech rather than focusing on swordplay."

"Agreed," they all answered. The unity of voices from all the leaders across Prevalence gave John chills. Never in his wildest dreams did he envision this as a possible future.

"Excellent," he said with the calm, rational tones of a Yaiba Director. He couldn't help but think about Emiko, and how gracefully she'd handled proceedings just like this. He hoped he did her proud. "The deployment of our forces to each other's territories has already been handled to some extent but we'll continue to shift people as needed over the coming weeks. As we move forward," the former

Lightning Dragon spoke with a greater degree of seriousness, "I want you to think about the people that you've lost. Take care to consider what they meant to you in the past, what they mean to you now, and what their loss has meant for you as you've tried to move forward. What we do now, we do for them, and for those of us who are still alive so that they don't suffer as we have." The room had grown quiet with pensive understanding. "Let's adjourn for today. We'll reconvene in two weeks when we've had time to take the next steps discussed."

The others agreed, and in waves returned to their respective territories.

****

March 6th, 2085, 1:26 p.m.,

Darius and Cal approached the Director shortly after the meeting had concluded. Most of the other leaders hadn't even left before those two, who smiled like idiots, began to ask their father what their upcoming assignments were.

"That's easy," John told them. He motioned for the table and the boys took the hint to sit down. "Cal, you and Leo are going to lead an aerial assault on the Kingdom using the Lightbeams. By the end of the initial assault, there shouldn't be any bombing targets that you'll need to be on the lookout for, but once we make our presence known we'll need a diversion for all the troops that are sure to come after us."

"Whoa now, hold on there, partner," Cal said with his hands raised. "You mean I gotta take a rookie into my first solo op? Bro ain't even been out in the field yet—"

"Then I suggest you commit some serious time to training him for his big battlefield debut." John watched the blood vessel in Cal's head throb with irritation and resisted the urge to snicker like he wanted to. "Darius, while Cal and Leo create chaos in the sky, you and Al will lead the ground forces with a team of your choosing."

"Yeah, Pops," Darius started apprehensively, "I don't know how much I can trust that kid."

"Oh, you can't trust him at all," John verified with all bluntness, and watched the hysteria creep onto Darius' face. "Just do what you can to get through to him. He's a 17-year-old boy who's only known life as a soldier. If I'm honest, it feels wrong to let him anywhere near this operation, and more for his sake than ours."

"Then why do it," Darius asked in a tone that made his father raise his eyebrows. Darius quieted. He might have been a Dragon, but he wasn't Dragon enough to match John Hamlin. Still, though, there was something strange about this situation. After all, Al had initially been brought to Darius in cuffs. After the situation had been explained and Al returned to the cell that he called home on the Holding Level, it struck him as quite the wild machination for the clear Scarlet spy to be made an Apprentice in the Yaiba Insurrection and placed in the care of one of the newest of the Seven Dragons.

"His knowledge of the Kingdom and its protocols is the freshest," John answered frankly. "He's offered to help us, but that was just to avoid death. I don't think he believed me when I explained to him that we weren't in the business of killing children, so I need you to show him what we're about."

"Understood," Darius said. Cal shook his head beside him.

"All that work and we still babysitting," he said. The Director, who again resisted the urge to smile, waved them off.

"Get to work," he ordered, and when they were gone, he rested his head against the back of his chair.

****

March 6th, 2085, 2:20 p.m.,

Cal and Darius watched as the guards brought Al to their spot on Training Level C and removed his cuffs. He was already equipped with the Hanzo Gear that was the expectation for the upcoming battle, and that meant that it would be a lot easier to move this training session down the path that the two young Dragons wanted to take.

"Good," Darius began, "you're finally here."

"Here for what, though," Al responded with a degree of attitude that made both Cal and Darius make a high-pitched "Hmm!" sound. Leo appeared behind him and smacked him on the back of the head.

"Show some damn respect," he growled, and sent a shiver down Al's spine. Neither of them had forgotten what their last encounter was like, and though Al wanted more than anything in this moment to ask Leo's forgiveness, the

Dark Giant made it abundantly clear that such a thing wouldn't come without a fight.

"Both of y'all chill out," Cal said with more force in his voice than Darius thought him capable of, and immediately the two boys snapped to attention. "Y'all know why ya here?" They shook their heads, nervous to open their mouths again.

"We decided that the best way to get you prepared for the field is to get some joint training in," Darius said with a devilish smirk. Al's face shifted to horror as Leo beamed a bright smile.

"Oh, yeah," said the giant as he ran a hand through his thick curls. "Tell me we're pairing up as master and apprentice!" The question was more than enough to raise Darius' eyebrows.

"Funny that you think this is supposed to be a fair fight," Darius joked, and Cal snickered.

"Yeah, naw," Cal told the trainees. "Y'all gotta team up to fight us." Immediately Darius and Cal brandished their fireswords and ignited them. Darius raised his weapon over his head as he extended his free hand. Cal pulled his to his right side and placed all of his weight on his back leg. Their charges verbally objected, but the masters would hear none of it.

"You might want to take a stance," Darius instructed. "Otherwise this is going to hurt." With eager anticipation, Leo shrugged with a smile as he lowered his weight and lifted his blade to shoulder height and pointed the tip straight ahead. His eyes were locked on Cal, since he and Al both practiced the Kiryu form and Leo wanted to know every weakness it presented. Al, on the other hand, did his best to ignore the two of them and instead focused on Darius alone. He adopted a more open stance than Cal did, one where his weapon hand was pointed behind him and his free hand was in front. The two rookies took their time as they inched closer to their masters, and were duly alarmed when the metal forest of the training grounds erected to the ceiling.

"Let the games begin," Leo whispered. Before long, the rattle of chains echoed even above the noise of the other training locations on the level. There was an eeriness to it that unsettled Al but excited Leo. Al resolved to grapple through the thicket himself, because the worst thing he could do against anyone from the Insurrection was make himself a sitting duck. He headed for where Darius had been, and when he saw that his master stood exactly as before, Al swooped in.

Darius watched as the boy swooped in and used the repulsors to add a little flair to his spin. He came in with a wide swing at the midsection that would have certainly proved impossible to block given the ridiculous amount of force behind the cut. Unfortunately for the overzealous apprentice, Darius lowered the tip of his weapon and gently guided the move off of its trajectory. Al spun out of control for a second but found his legs again, and quickly sprung off the ground as he lunged for Darius and stabbed through the air. Darius with an effortless flick of the wrist brushed the attack away, but before the boy's foot touched the ground, he stabbed again.

Darius smirked, but still he knocked the move off course as his opponent flew past him. Al had only just turned back to face his master when he realized that Darius was now on the offensive. Darius swung at the midsection, a movement that Al only narrowly blocked, and just as Al jumped and spun away with his own blade extended, Darius blocked the initial strike and returned to his starting stance. Al wisely took up the closed stance that Cal modeled in the beginning and waited more patiently for his opponent to do something.

After he realized that Darius wouldn't move unless given a reason, Al dove back into the battle just as Leo deflected Cal's flawless Falling Leaf maneuver. Cal smiled, as it took a considerable amount of skill for someone to deflect a move that saw the user spin like a mechanical saw blade towards an opponent, and this kid had done exactly that. For a Kiryu user of average skill, that would've given them pause and they would've had to disengage. Cal, though, was too fast. Before Leo could even follow the energy of his deflection, Cal slid along the ground under the blade of his apprentice and swiped at his legs with a vengeance. Leo spun away with the blade extended to keep Cal away, and immediately realized his mistake the moment his Reikiken came to rest in reverse grip high above his head.

Cal, like a master craftsman, followed the energy straight through as was his nature, and landed with his back to the boy. Just as the thought crossed Leo's mind to step forward and clash with a power move, Cal executed a one-handed back hand spring with the tip of his aura sword aimed for Leo's chest. The boy deflected as he stepped off the center line, but his attempt at evasion only put him back in Cal's line of sight. He swung now, a brutal downward diagonal motion that would've torn another man apart, but again, Cal was too fast. He parried it on entry and cut down, a move that Leo blocked only barely successfully. Cal disconnected the swords abruptly and spun to the rear in a move that nearly cut the gargantuan legs from under the giant boy.

Leo jumped back and met stiff resistance from Al, who'd been pressured by his own opponent.

"You doing alright," Al asked with a sarcastic bite. He felt Leo shrug behind him.

"Not really getting anywhere with him," Leo said curtly. "What about you?" Al shook at the question.

"I can't hit him at all," he said, and for the first time he genuinely sounded like the innocent boy that he pretended to be. "And what's worse is, he keeps coming close to hitting me." The two teachers circled their students now, and the students circled to keep watch over their teachers. Leo grumbled under his breath, then let out a sigh.

"Follow my lead," he said, "I have a plan." Al nodded, and with a cocky smirk, Cal flew at him. Leo took Al by the arm and threw him at Cal to disrupt his flow while he himself went for Darius. Al, who was alarmed at first, executed a Falling Leaf of his own that was parried out of the way. Al cut at Cal's legs, but Cal spiraled in the air to evade the strike, only to nearly get caught with a shoulder attack from the opposite direction. Cal blocked and attempted a strike at Al's head, but the wily newcomer rolled to his left and took a stance behind him.

Leo, meanwhile spun with all the force he could generate and crashed his blade into Darius'. The Rebel Dragon blocked, something he almost never did against [illegible] to the other side. He moved in, but Leo pulled his front leg to the rear and sank his weight as he slammed his Reikiken in the space in front of him. Darius was forced to take a step back. They found themselves locked in a stalemate, and at that point Darius smiled.

"Good," he said as he stowed his blade and Cal followed suit. "Next time we'll start you off with the teamwork and see how that goes." Without another word, Cal and Darius walked off the training field and left Leo and Al to stare at each other in awkward silence.

Chapter Seventeen

March 6th, 2085, 4:41 p.m.,

Ryan stood perfectly still as he listened to the King. The engineering staff was hard at work, outfitting the World Trade Center as a colossal workshop with a plethora of bombs at various intervals. Scientists checked them for stability, disguisability, and projected impact. The streaks were assured that they would be perfectly safe if used at the perimeter of the Capitol, but it was the giant one that stood behind King Bryan that gave Ryan pause. Surely this was madness, and he couldn't expect anyone to be dumb enough to go along with it. The loud mechanical whirring ate at him as his comrades on the Scarlet Streaks began to cheer the nationalist ideology spewed by the King. *Wiz*. For the glory of the Kingdom. *Rattle*. Down with the terrorist. *Bang*. An ultimate sacrifice too high to come back from. Ryan had to ask if that was even a part of the plan. Sure, he conspired against the Kingdom, but this…

A clap to the back from Maxwell Cartwright abruptly stirred him from his innermost thoughts. "What's the matter, Crawford? You seem a little unenthusiastic." There was a chill to his voice, and while the others would never have known, there were certain things that Ryan couldn't be fooled on and the actions and attitudes of an intelligence operative were at the top of that list. His thoughtful expression must've been betrayed by his face, otherwise Cartwright wouldn't have known about his apprehension.

"I'm just in awe," Ryan responded with a slight rattle to his voice that sold the stunned look on his face.

"He's willing to go so far to keep the enemy from taking the Kingdom." The answer seemed to appeal to Maxwell, whose thick black moustache spread gently as his lips curled into a deeper smile. Something about it horrified the sniper, but he resisted the urge to show it.

"Yeah, he's a lot better at this than I thought he'd be," admitted the agent, and he threw his arm around Ryan's neck. "To think that he was just some outsider a few months ago trying to take us all down." Ryan couldn't help but look in his direction, only to find that Maxwell's sharp eyes were already trained on the sniper. More than that, they picked up on the incredulity in Ryan's expression. "Something on your mind?" The bite behind his tone was clear as day now, and the dark look on Cartwright's face sent a chill through Ryan's soul. The others, Kilpatrick and Wulfric, along with the entirety of the engineering staff,

"I guess a part of me feels as though this is just an excuse to do what we all thought he would when he came here," Ryan spoke candidly. It was enough to warrant a surprised blink from his compatriot, who seemed to experience a kind of realization of his own.

"It does seem a little suspicious, I must admit," the agent thought aloud, "but after fixing the drone network do you think he'd still try something? I mean, he is the King, after all." Ryan wasn't so sure that that meant anything. King Bryan, Ryan noticed, was an incredibly sharp master tactician, and one who had gone to war with the Kingdom perhaps a thousand times in the past. Now, he was nestled in the heart of the very nation he had at one time sworn to destroy. How was it that nobody else could see what was so plainly in front of their faces? Even still, Maxwell brought up a good point.

"I really don't know," he confessed, and Maxwell's eyes narrowed before he shrugged again with another pat to Ryan's shoulder. There was a little more of a press to the back of the young sniper's shoulder and a little pain that followed, and then nothing.

"Well, I suppose that's only fair, considering the deep heritage of patriotism that your family has demonstrated throughout the years." It was a compliment, but to Ryan it felt like much more of a pointed statement. Maxwell left him to go back to the rigorous cheers of the others, and Ryan took his sudden departure as an incentive to make one of his own. Little did he know that the King and his minions watched him all the same…

****

March 7th, 2085, 2:55 a.m.,

Lyla waited in the King's chambers and watched her restless leg bounce briskly against the floor. A part of her wondered what it said, what message in Morse code it sent to anyone who would listen. Did it tell of her frustration, or of her fear? Did it betray her uncertainty, or did it voice her anger? Could the decoder pick up on her love, or would they detect a spark of hatred?

The door to the chamber opened. King Bryan walked in as if in a dream, groggy and ready for his head to hit his bed. He looked up, and the moment he saw his daughter in the purple upholstered chair next to his scarlet and gold canopy bed, he realized that sleep would have to wait.

"Something wrong?" The King's question was as innocent as a man that mad could've made it sound, and Lyla gritted her teeth to keep from cussing.

"What are you doing, Dad," she answered. Bryan looked angry that she would even have the gall to question him.

"Nothing that you need be concerned about," he told her with a kind of parental force that conveyed every bit of "stand down, and watch your tone." Lyla understood the message, but dared to defy it.

"Oh," she began with an unbelieving inflection, "so I didn't see the a giant bomb on the inside of the World Trade Center tonight?"

"You shouldn't have seen that," Bryan said, frantic now, as if he knew that he had to do something horrible. "You should not have seen that!"

"Why the hell not?" Lyla shouted back at him, her eyes hot with the sting of tears. "You won't tell me anything! You expected me to just sit here without any answers? How long have you been planning this?" He shook his head, and she exhaled sharply. After everything, he still offered her no explanation. "Dad, tell me why there's a massive bomb in the World Trade Center." He shook his head and paced the floor anxiously like a child in fervent denial that he had done anything wrong. It was then that she saw how truly unstable he was.

"That is classified information," he yelled again, and pulled out his gun. He aimed directly at her face and watched Lyla blink away the tears. “You shouldn’t know anything about it.” His voice became so gentle, almost as if he was the confused one, like he knew nothing about the world. “Everything I do is to protect us—to protect you! You don’t need to know everything that’s going on. Just trust me and it’ll all work out, okay?”

Lyla couldn’t stop the quiver in her lip. She couldn’t stop herself from shedding tears over the man who raised her in gentleness and compassion, now reduced to a raving madman with a firearm. If he didn’t look enough like the Kingdom before, he certainly did now. For a moment, she looked at the muzzle of the gun that was held a few inches from her forehead. She thought to back away, to back down from him and just accept what he had become, but then she remembered that he’d raised her to be bolder than that.

“You’ve got a gun pointed at your daughter’s head,” she challenged, and watched the realization strike him like a metal rod. “How do you expect me to believe that this is your protection?” She was a lot calmer than she imagined she would be. She stood before him, his eyes soft again like the man that she used to know, and watched him pull the gun down. She smiled at him, and he at her, and then the world spun from the dull throb in her skull. He yelled at her, and for a few seconds she couldn’t understand a word of it. He hoisted her up, grabbed her by the face, and through hazy eyes she could only see the mania, for the man had been wholly lost to it.

“How dare you question me?” Her hearing refocused, and the growl in his voice as he smacked her face with his calloused palms only furthered the distance between this animal and the man she knew to be her greatest protector. "When I tell you something, you accept it. If I say stop, you stop. If I tell you to go, you go. If I tell you to shoot yourself in the foot, then dammit you ask me what kind of gun you should use. I am the King of the Reds, you are the servant. Your place as my daughter isn't enough to exempt you from my rule, so let that sink in before you start to puff your chest out at me again." He aimed the pistol at her left eye, fingered the trigger with all the intention of the seasoned warrior that he was. Beneath his hand he could feel her tremble with fear, and something about it made him feel good. As soon as she closed her eyes, he shifted his weapon hand a quarter of an inch to the left and fired. The bullet struck against the edge of her ear on the way to its burial in the wall. "The next time we have to have this conversation," he warned, "and I won't be so kind as to miss. Nod if you understand." She did it with no hesitation. He threw her down. "Now, get out." She ran, trading her father for whatever might lie on the other side of the door.

****

March 10th, 2085, 7:14 a.m.,

In the four days since the inaugural meeting of the Senshi Coalition, nearly everyone had moved to their proper place. Johannes Thornhill oversaw the assignment process of the Yoroi demolitionists and the neo-ninjas that Darius had trained. They had begun calling themselves the Violent Sands, a name that everyone who heard it could see the validity in. Erik Kincaid mobilized Esau Tillman and Levi Taylor to run training demonstrations for the Yoroi in the western region and the Southern Wastes while he did the same for the newer additions to their fighting forces in Johnson City. The Ballistics Squad, comprised of Orson Nucci, Karina Velazquez, and Drew McDowell, ran workshops alongside Bobbi Brynarr, Leroy Baptiste, Tony Landry, and Lex Ford about the nature of combining tactics.

Cal and Darius stood watch over their students and pushed them with the full intensity of the Dragons before them, and the boys seemed to escalate in their skills day by day. Even the Engineering Corps from the three factions collaborated with each other to develop new configurations for technology that already existed. It was something that Cal salivated over.

James, on the other hand, simply took care of Serenity, who was still too weak to get back into the fray. It was clear that whatever happened in Charlotte had changed her. Her team and their forces maintained control of the city, and Devin Dross had been dispatched to head up the day to day operations under the assurance that Serenity would resume command upon her medical clearance. She didn't say much to him, or to anyone for that matter. She just put her all into her recovery efforts. It drove her crazy during the first few days, but now it had been a full fifteen, and the stab wound had closed up enough to where she could handle a bit of light training.

"You really shouldn't push yourself too hard, love," James told her. It was odd for both of them to hear his voice take such a serious and deeply concerned tone. He had always been playful, sensual, intellectual, but never worried or scared. It was unbecoming of the son of a King. But then, perhaps this was just his willingness to freely express what he truly felt.

"I'm not," Serenity said brusquely. She checked her pistols and holstered them at her sides as she donned her Hanzo Gear. "It's not my first time healing from battle wounds, you know."

"I know," James replied quickly, gently, with a hand extended in an effort to comfort her. "I just—" his voice caught. She looked at him, an intimidating expression of curiosity locked into her face. He heaved a breath and stilled the shaking in his hand. "I don't want to lose you," he told her earnestly, and her eyebrows lifted in surprise. "I know you've hardly spoken to me since December because of what I did, and that is your right. But I want you to know that I wouldn't change a damn thing about what I did."

"I wouldn't want you to," she said, just as he became more passionate. He blinked twice, stunned by the sudden interruption, and for the first time in almost three full months, Serenity Crawford smiled at him.

"What?" It was all that could escape from his mouth, and it was met with a surprisingly girlish giggle from the former Scourge leader.

"You found a way to preserve my life when I wasn't able to see one. Thank you."

"So am I to understand that you forgive me," James asked cautiously. The sudden change in her expression mixed with how light and airy her voice was struck him as a trap that he would rather get out of than fall into any deeper. She shook her head as she stepped towards him in a way that reminded him of their attempted encounter in Johnson City. She reached around the back of his head as she pressed her body against his. "I think I'll take this as a yes, then," he voiced in a hushed tone. She smiled in the sultry way that he liked more than he could describe, lifted her lips as he lowered his, and then kissed him on the cheek instead. “Wait, what was that?”

“What do you mean,” she answered as she walked away from him and returned to her gear. She looked at the Reikiken for a moment and decided to wear it at her hip as well. After all, there was no shame in her allegiance these days.

“You can’t tell me that you’re still going to go train,” he complained. She smiled a wide smile, but sobered immediately as she turned back to face him. Now, he noted, she wore a matter-of-fact expression that exuded superiority.

“No,” she said as she folded her arms over her chest. “I’m going to the Medical Level first to see if I’m cleared. I won’t be training until after that.” James rolled his eyes, then with a face that was far less playful than it was a moment ago, strode up to take Serenity by the hands.

“We only just got back to being us,” he attempted to reason. “I’d like it if we could savor the moment before we jumped back into the heat of the war?” She gave his hand a sympathetic squeeze, and he immediately knew that for her, there would be no peace until there was. He smiled a rueful smile. “Fine. Just don’t take too long.”

“I won’t,” she assured him as she returned his smile. She ran her hand down his cheek, and then she was off.

****

March 14th, 2085, 5:43 p.m.,

Maxwell Cartwright knew how to go unnoticed. Years of training alongside Kyle Crawford meant that he had to be on the same level as that overbearing overachiever. A part of him relished in the fact that Kyle was dead. It meant that he was the number one contender for command over the entire Intelligence Corps of Kingdom Scarlet. Another part of him actually respected what the man was able to do in the Yoroi Territory, even if it did get him killed. Nobody could argue that Kyle was the first person to breach the Yoroi compound, but it was the showmanship that got him put in the ground and that was something that Cartwright would never allow himself to get caught up in.

It didn't serve him any purpose, anyway. He derived too much joy from being the shadow of an intended target. He knew that the latest one had no idea that he was being watched. It was true that Ryan hadn't done anything terribly suspicious that first night when he'd left their meeting with the King, but the fact that he carefully went through his clothes to check for any micro-comms that might have been placed on him. A smart move, but again, Cartwright knew how to go unnoticed.

That was why it was so easy for him to eavesdrop on the conversation he'd had with his father Alan. At first it came as a shock that one of the most decorated veterans in Kingdom history turned traitor, but knowing what he knew about the White Ruins Massacre made it easier to digest. The true surprise was that Ryan not only knew about it for months without so much as a word to the King, but that he told his father everything that they learned that night. Since then, he'd learned that insurgents had been helped into the city and that even now they looked for targets to bomb. He knew that they were the signal to the other factions, and that if their bombing was successful, it would likely spell out the end for the Kingdom as he knew it. He was the first line of defense in this scenario, and intended to do his job well.

"Can I help you with something?" The question came as a start to him. He'd been outside of the Atlas New York building for some time, and silently watched the blinds of Ryan's apartment from his car. He'd thought he'd gone unnoticed, and mentally chided himself for his recklessness. He looked up, prepared to make an excuse, only to find Lyla Ortiz with a look of pure disgust as she leaned against his car door and peered at him through the down window.

"Oh," said Cartwright, currently flushed of color. "My apologies, Milady, I had no idea that I was in your way."

"You're not in my way," she informed him, "I live here. I noticed you creepily staring at my building an hour ago. What do you think you're doing?" He was mortified. Of course it would be her that would notice him. He took the time to explain his assignment which was, under normal circumstances, classified, but he reasoned that the King's Right Hand would be a worthy exception to the rule. "I see…" her voice trailed off upon the revelation. "So, I live in the same building as a traitor." She clenched the pistol in her hand that Maxwell only just noticed.

"I would appreciate it," he started nervously, "if you would leave this matter to me. That is, aside from relaying it to the King, of course." She looked him dead in the eye as if he was insane to even ask, and that was when he noticed the black bruise above hers. His eyes filled with concern in an instant, and she looked back at the building.

"You know what," she voiced almost dismissively, "you got it." She took her hand off the car door and prepared to walk away when he called her name. She looked at him, a ferocity in her sunlit brown eyes. "What?" She was somehow more hostile, but it didn't faze him as much as he thought.

"I hope it isn't too much of an intrusion," he spoke gently in a vain attempt to quell her anger, "but I wanted to ask what happened to you." The question came so sweetly that Lyla almost forgot that the man had creeped her out. Almost. Her face flickered between surprise and a sternness that gave Maxwell a deep sense of regret. She pursed her lips, then heaved a sigh. He could tell that the question aggravated her, and so he braced for whatever prize he'd won.

"Let's just say that we should all be a little careful of the King right now," she warned. "Do me a favor?" He nodded once. "Get lost. You can come back in the morning when I'm in a better mood."

"Of course," he lied. He had every intention of telling her what she wanted to hear and then finding some other way to do what he did best: go without notice. She smiled at him in a way that he felt made her seem like the monster she was rumored to be, and leaned in so that he would hear her when she spoke.

"If I catch you out here again before tomorrow," she started in a slow pace as if she spoke to a child, "I'll put a bullet right between those pretty blue eyes of yours. Am I clear?"

"Yes, ma'am," he said with the utmost respect.

"Bye now," she bade, and stood to watch as he turned the ignition and drove away from the building.

****

March 14th, 2085, 5:55 p.m.,

Lyla considered where Maxwell's attention had been focused, and only for a split second did she contemplate turning over the traitor. It would be a good way for her to get back into her father's good graces, to mend whatever had snapped in his mind last week. Then she asked herself why she still had such an impulse to express loyalty to that man. What he did to her, her father never would've done. She gritted her teeth, looked up at the apartment, then strolled back into the building.

Since the time of the Second Civil War, Atlas had largely been unchanged. It still sported what counted as a modern look for back then, albeit with the latest technological advancements and drone access hatches on every floor. Artwork still adorned the walls, though nobody of common birth would've recognized the artists or the skill that it took to produce such work. Normally, Lyla would take the time to take it all in, to relish in a world that simply didn't exist anymore, but she needed to find this traitor and ultimately decide what she was going to do about his rebellion.

****

March 14th, 2085, 6:14 p.m.,

Ryan sat in his living room, still just as paranoid as he had been for the last almost eight days. He'd been careful about his coming and going, because he was almost certain that he was under Cartwright's surveillance. If he was careless, it wouldn't just mean the end for him, but for his father and mother as well. Even still, through all the paranoia, this was the most fun he'd had in a very long time. It was enough to make him question when he'd lost the joy in his job, but then again, the answer was obvious. Still, he was determined to reclaim some form of happiness. He just had to figure out how to get out of this alive.

A knock came at the door that put the notion out of his mind, and he marveled at how quickly excitement could warp into desperation in times of war. He reached under his small black coffee table and retrieved the pistol concealed between its solid top, then cautiously approached the door. He looked through the peephole to see a gorgeous young woman with caramel skin, brown sugar eyes and hair to match, and though her features were soft, she wore a hard expression. Lyla Ortiz.

"Let me in, or you're going to die," she said as calmly as if she talked about the weather. He did as he was told, and watched as she passed him over almost immediately and started ripping his apartment apart.

"Hey! What do you think you're doi—" he tried to yell at her, to approach her and intimidate her into settling down, but she pushed him aside like a shower curtain and continued her work. Before long, she had three small spherical items that glistened white and were the size of a grain of rice. He knew them to be micro-comms, the same kind that his brother had taught him about.

"You've been living your life on full display this entire time, it seems," Lyla commented, then crushed the microscopic devices. His suspicions were correct, which meant that the night his father came to see him most assuredly put them all in danger. "Seems like you realize the mess you're in. So, tell me, Captain Ryan Crawford of the esteemed Sharpshooter lineage, why I shouldn't put one between the eyes or, worse still, drag you in front of my father?"

Captain Crawford stammered at the question, which made Lyla raise her eyebrows. "I honestly don't have a good reason for you," he offered, which earned him a wry look from a woman he only just realized was a princess. He'd just noticed the bruise on her head when she snapped her fingers to recall his attention.

"Try again," she demanded. "Humor me." Ryan took a deep breath, then gestured to his blue sofa that, after her expeditious entry, was now out of sync with the rest of the room.

"I've come to realize that there's more to life than patriotism and loyalty to a political leader," he rationalized. She smirked as she narrowed her eyes.

"Hmmm, and that wouldn't have anything to do with a certain renegade sister, would it?" She was cool as she asked the question, and Ryan chuckled in a calm, almost defeated manner.

"Partially," he admitted. "It also has a lot to do with the fact that my brother died a fool's death for a nation that doesn't give a damn about him." There was a darkness to him as he said those words, a brokenness that dared put itself on display in front of her, and that she dared to connect with.

"And tell me, what did you think of the King's plan to 'protect' the Kingdom from the advance of our enemies?" The question compelled him to give a half-hearted chuckle. He was surprised with himself when he failed to apologize for the lack of decorum.

"It's insane," he said boldly, angrily, with the full knowledge that the woman before him was the daughter of that very King. "He says that the city is mostly outside of the blast range and that it would be safe to use those mines as a deterrent for the enemy, but…"

"The readouts aren't reliable," Lyla stated plainly as though she agreed. "Not to mention the giant one that was in the World Trade Center. The reports say that it was just a model for the smaller ones, but how believable is that, do you figure?" Ryan's brow furrowed, partially because of his own thoughtfulness, partially out of distrust. Everyone that had seen her knew exactly where Lyla stood with King Bryan, and speaking to her so openly could prove to be problematic later on.

"I don't trust it," he said finally, and watched as her expression softened. "Of course, you would know better than anyone what his true motivations are, though, right? After all, you both come from the Yaiba Insurrection, and both of you fought against the Kingdom for a long while before you came here to rule it." There was a little bite in that, but it just made Lyla smile.

"You would think that," she said with a little thoughtfulness of her own. "The truth is I don't know what motivates that man anymore, and whether or not I did is irrelevant. Fact is, I don't trust that Godzilla bomb, either. It looks like the King is determined to do whatever it takes to bring down Providence, and he wants to use New York as his personal ground zero."

"Hmm," Ryan said, "so what now? Am I supposed to trust you just because you spill some classified info and say all the right things like this isn't kind of sudden?" It was clear to him that she wasn't an intel op. She didn't care about presentation at all, and hadn't the slightest clue how to earn his trust. At least that told him that he wasn't a mark.

"No," she told him matter-of-factly, "but I have decided that I'm not going to turn you in to the King." The news was purely jarring to the Captain, and amazingly visible to Lyla. "Don't get me wrong, I came in here almost certain that I would snitch and earn greater favor with the King, but if I'm honest with myself, it's past time to depose him." She gave him the space to speak, but he didn't, and opted instead to carefully observe her and process what had been told to him. "You and your father need to go underground. As a show of good faith, I'll let you pick where."

"A show of good faith implies that you want something in return," Ryan pointed out. She rolled her eyes.

“Gee, I never thought of that,” said Lyla with venomous sarcasm. “I want your help, and the help of your connections from the other factions.” He laughed incredulously.

“Why are you acting like I’m the one running the show? My father’s the mastermind of all this,” Ryan explained. “Besides, if you think I’ll be the one to take you in it’ll take more than just letting us pick our hideout to get you through the front door.”

“Oh,” sang the King’s guard with another sarcastic burst, “you mean like using my position to talk Maxwell Cartwright into abandoning his post for the night?” Ryan blinked in confusion. “Don’t bother asking how. That information is only for trusted allies.”

“You know that’s only a temporary fix,” Ryan argued. “Cartwright isn’t the type to just give up without a fight, and he loves when his targets give chase.”

“Which is why you have to get out tonight, and figure out a way to get your parents to go, too. You have a very small window, and I suggest you use it wisely,” Lyla pointed out.

“And what can we expect you to do while we bide our time in hiding?” Ryan’s question was a valid one, and one that Lyla had expected since she made up her mind about what she was going to do.

“I’ll be the insider that your team is sorely lacking. I’ll relay developments in the King’s operations and throw them off your trail so they won’t find you until after you do whatever it is you’re planning to do,” she explained. She could see him think it over, and marveled at those clear green eyes. "So? Do we have a deal?"

"I suppose we do," Ryan confirmed in a sternness that echoed back to Kyle before him. He stood, and shook her hand as if to seal their agreement, and then with a degree of bewilderment, he watched as she took out her comms device and called Cartwright.

"Good evening, Milady," Ryan heard him say over the line. "Is something wrong?" It was strange for Ryan to hear Cartwright sound so respectful. He was a charmer by nature, and though he came off as snobbish with his incessant presentation of dignity, that, too was part of the charm. Here, though, he was just a man in service to the King with a clear understanding of his betters.

"Yeah," Lyla answered. "Your mark apparently saw us talking earlier and decided to get out of dodge."

"What? He couldn't have—" Maxwell started in a panic.

"Yeah," she interrupted him, "we don't have time for you to spin out of control. I need you and a team of investigators here within the next two hours. Take your time to assemble the right group, because if he slips through your fingers again, you might just have to answer to the King." Cartwright took a breath.

"Absolutely, and thank you for alerting me," he said.

"Of course," she replied, "I was told to stay out of it and leave the matter to you. I just hope that you don't disappoint." She hung up, then headed for the door. "Two hours," she told Ryan, and in the next instant, she was gone before he could hazard a reply.

****

March 14th, 2085, 9:11 p.m.,

King Bryan sat in the dark of the World Trade Center. The bombs had been dispersed throughout the edge of the territory and buried in the ground. He was amused at the foolishness of these people, and all he had to do was convince them that he had their best interest at heart. He chuckled to himself. Lyla had been right not to trust him, and Captain Crawford was right there with her. But it didn't matter. Nothing that they could do now would prevent him from enacting the ultimate plot for revenge.

"Thank you, Dad," whispered Jaden Piccio's voice from beyond the grave. It both chilled and soothed Bryan to the core, to know that his son approved, to know that he would finally be avenged upon the heads of all who were responsible for his death, even remotely…including himself. Bryan stared at the massive orb that remained in the halls of the World Trade Center and caressed its cold metallic side. The chuckle grew to a boisterous laughter.

"You're welcome, son!" Bryan shouted, and continued to laugh deep into the night. All of his greatest pains and worries would come to an end in only a few days' time, and he and his daughter would be reunited with his son. Soon.

Chapter Eighteen

March 17th, 2085, 12:25 p.m.,

John Hamlin entered the command center of Tactical Level X, a place that he had been particularly reluctant to visit since Emiko died, with an authority befitting of a Director. He was met with reverent looks of admiration from some and expressions of muted panic from others, but none of that mattered. They were here only five minutes after the usual staff went on their lunch break, so it would be easier for John to discuss with this group what had been on his mind without any irritating interruptions from his father or Vanessa.

Around the command center's central control terminal sat an unusual mixture of personnel from across Prevalence, but whose skills seemed to complement each other's greatly. Nearest him on the right was Esau Tillman, the stoic young right hand of Senior Agent Kincaid, and his associate, the aggressive and unpredictable Levi Taylor. On the left were the rambunctious Ryan Morrisey, the historically fascinated Teddy Grant, and the overly respectful Latrell McBeth. At the back of the room sat a timid Tony Landry and a seemingly indifferent but quietly fascinated Leroy Baptiste, two of Darius' subordinates from the Yoroi Alliance that had been brought into the Roan Mountain from their original duties for this particular meeting.

"I'm sure you're all wondering what I've called you here for," the Director began. "After looking through the personnel files from the three factions over the course of the last ten days, I've decided that you all would be the best fit." He left it at that, just to see the look of anticipation mount on each of their faces.

"The best fit for what," Ryan asked. He was always eager for a new mission, and this is exactly what it sounded like to him.

"Let me explain," John continued. "As we're all aware, the current King of the Scarlet Kingdom is our former ally, Bryan Piccio. Bryan served the Yaiba Insurrection for some twenty years, first as a warrior, then as a member of the Engineer Corps. Those of you who are from the Insurrection know exactly the kind of fighter he was."

"Usagi no Kamikaze," Teddy Grant supplied grimly. "He's the only non-Dragon said to have been on par with them. I could tell you stories of his most legendary operations—"

"There's no need for that," Master Hamlin interrupted. "I was there for the vast majority of them."

"Which means that you know better than anyone else what he's capable of," came Latrell with his arms folded. He was a very careful man, and whereas he could usually find the bright side in any situation, even he fell reserved in the face of being up against that kind of opponent.

"Excuse me," asked Tony, "but we aren't going to have to fight him, are we?" It was a valid question, and after a moment of looking around the console, John could see that it was a common concern. For him, it was unusual to an extent, but after years of seeing Bryan on the battlefield, it occurred to him that he'd been largely desensitized to his old friend's capabilities. For the people gathered in the command center, though, it was hardly the same. John inhaled deeply and for a moment he closed his eyes. He exhaled.

"No," he told them, "not at all." He felt the room exhale, and then the vacuum left by the now dissipated worry was filled with a deeper sense of intrigue. "Our mission isn't something that out in the open."

"What exactly is our mission," Levi asked with an air of suspicion. There was something that John kept hidden from them, and the fact that he'd beat around the bush for this long was already a cause for concern with such a group of warriors so unfamiliar with each other.

"Our mission is the assassination of Bryan Piccio," he informed them. Silence. Nobody knew at first how to respond to it. There were so many questions in everyone's minds. John decided to take the time to answer them. "We're all aware of the commando unit that's inside the Capitol as we speak and what their responsibility is. You're also aware of the divisions of air and ground forces that will lead the assault on the Kingdom once we have our signal and everyone is in position. What you haven't heard is what we'll be doing. I need you all to move with me as a shadow unit. Our job is to slip in and reach the palace undetected while the bulk of the enemy's forces are engaged with ours. Once we find a way in, I'll take Morrisey and proceed to the throne room. Everyone else will be dismissed to rejoin the main forces and, more specifically, keep any stragglers away from the palace at all costs."

"This," Esau started slowly, "is a tall order."

"I know," John assured him. He thought back to Yorktown, where Bryan told him his plan to destroy everything that John loved, starting with Darius. There wasn't a moment since then where he wasn't saddened by that exchange—or enraged by it. He knew that if they failed to bring Bryan down, to hit first and hit hard, they may never have a chance to do it again. And the truth was, John still hoped somewhere in his heart that Bryan would snap out of whatever heavy grief he felt and come back, but the reality was that that was childish idealism at its finest, and that he was the best shot they had at subduing the Kingdom's morale covertly. "I also know," he continued, "that everyone I've assembled here today is more than capable of getting it done." He looked at the time. It was 12:45, and as if on cue, Dre Hamlin appeared with a container of food.

"Oh, hell no," he started in a hushed tone that somehow managed to carry the full weight of his ire. "Tell me this isn't what I think it is, John!" John simply looked away from the elderly Lightning Dragon and returned focus back to the group before him.

"It would appear that we don't have the time to discuss the matter further," John all but growled in a low dragonic hum that sent a shiver through the meeting's attendees. "I'll touch base with you all when we get closer to time and we can go over more of the specifics of the operation." The makings of the shadow unit scattered as soon as they were given the freedom to do so, and as they ran for the door, Dre advanced on John with a kind of parental authority that the latter did not believe he possessed. "I take it you have an opinion," John grumbled.

"Damn right," Dre answered and tossed his lunch on the circular control terminal. "You're in here having secret meetings on our lunch break? The hell is that about, son?"

"What I need it to be about," John shot back. "What does it matter to you?" Dre turned away for a moment as he wiped his mouth with his hand, then turned back with a ferocity in his expression that John hadn't seen since the night the elder Dragon kicked him out.

"You know what, boy, I'm tired. I'm tired of trying to talk some sense into you. I'm tired of taking a back seat to your hurt feelings. I'm damn sure tired of letting you do whatever the hell you wanna do—"

"You forget your place," John interrupted, and Dre backhanded him. John stumbled back a step and, as if stunned, rubbed his cheek.

"You forget yours! I am your father, boy, and it's about damn time you understood that!" John chuckled softly.

"Oh, I understand," spoke the Director with sparks in his voice. "But what you don't understand is that stopped being my problem when you kicked me out and abandoned me twenty years ago!"

"How long are you gonna make me apologize for that?" Dre was as much a vessel for anger as was his son.

"Until you can build a time machine, go back, and stop yourself." John's tone grew cold in an instant, as if to say that he had no right to even ask the question. "Do you have any idea what kind of damage you did to me? You were my hero, Dad. I practically worshipped you from the time I was a little boy right up until that moment where you called me an embarrassment and you pushed me out against Mom's protests. And you think that that's something a piss-poor apology can fix? Back then, all I ever wanted to do was just be like you, my dad, the hero of the White Ruins Miracle and champion of our home. But you gave me every reason to want to be different from you." Dre's anger turned to biting sadness. He'd never heard John be so open with him about what he'd felt, but then, there were plenty of reasons for that.

"I didn't know how to process my own trauma from back then," Dre offered. "I thought I was protecting you from a hellish kind of life."

"I don't accept that," John said flatly. "You were the adult in that situation. You were the parent. Your job was to work through your own crap, not push it onto me."

"Yeah, well, you were the child and I was the parent. Your job was to listen to me the first time so that we would never have to get to this point!" Dre's anger erupted from the pit of his belly, and John just gave a hollow smile as he pushed past his father. "Where are you going?"

"To get ready," John answered. "Didn't you hear? I have a mission." Dre grabbed his arm and pulled him back over.

"I'm not letting you run off just so you can try to assassinate Bryan," he told him. The look in John's eyes looked almost reptilian: cold, predatory, cunning. Even so, Dre held on.

“You’re not gonna say a word of this to anyone,” John ordered as he snatched his arm away from Dre. Dre folded his across his chest.

“And what are you going to do to stop me?” The question was almost childish, but provocative nonetheless.

“Don’t test me, old man,” John warned, which made Dre raise his eyebrows. “I’m not above sending you to hospice care early.”

“Aw, you do care,” Dre teased with a legitimate smile. “Alright, then. When do you wanna throw down?” The question caught John almost entirely by surprise. He narrowed his eyes on his father and fixed his posture to look more intimidating.

“What are you trying to do?”

“It’s called a bet, John,” Dre explained. “You want a fight so bad, I’m gonna give you one. Not for free, though. How ‘bout if I win, you stay here and monitor the battle from this command center like the Director is supposed to do?”

“Fine,” John answered, clearly unbothered by his father’s challenge. “But if I win, you don’t get in my way again and you keep your mouth shut about this until after it’s all over.” Dre’s confident smile faded as his hazel eyes grew serious. Both of them stood with adrenaline in their veins and rage coasting atop it.

“Deal,” Dre accepted. “Meet me on Level C at 5 and we can get this show on the road.”

"All this time trying to 'protect me,' just to put yourself in danger like this," John said as he shook his head. "Fine; I'll see you then."

As John left, as Dre watched, the elder felt the knot in his stomach tighten and burn with sorrow and regret.

****

March 17th, 2085, 2:32 p.m.,

Serenity marveled at the work her team had managed to do in the time it took her to heal. Charlotte wasn't perfect, but it was at the very least a functional base. Hector and Tez had mapped out the wards and enacted defensive measures around the 277 and through Graham Street. The only way in for her was through extensive verification. She was immediately taken to the Charlotte Convention Center location, where they'd set up shop for a command center, and shown to her specific quarters. James whistled.

"Those subordinates of yours really know how to string together an operation," he said as he walked up behind her and began to massage her shoulders. She chuckled.

"I'm not sure that's what happened here. I think they were scared of being in the field without any experienced leadership and they turtled." James emitted a soft chuckle.

"I know the feeling well," he admitted. While he looked around, she headed straight for the communications console and tapped the frequency that her father had used to contact her. It was ideal for discretion, and the Kingdom wouldn't expect it unless Bryan figured out what was going on behind his back. The odds of that, though, were slim, and so with a smile Serenity waited for an answer.

"Hey," came Alan's voice. He was solemn, and waited a moment before he told her, "We have a bit of a situation."

"What do you mean?" The tone in which she asked the question perfectly reflected her military bearing and experience.

"The King put out surveillance on your brother and we were forced to go into hiding," Alan explained. "Your mother, too. We're alright, but God only knows for how long before we're discovered."

"What are your options," she asked with stone in her voice and expression. Alan thought for a moment.

"For now, the only thing we can do is plan our moves carefully. As of right now, we have an ally within the palace who'll make that a lot easier for us," he told her. Serenity's eyes went wide with surprise, then narrowed in suspicion as James looked over her shoulder.

"What ally," inquired the former prince with an air of supreme scrutiny.

"Lyla Ortiz, the right hand of the King," Alan stated flatly. "It seems that our friends in the Kingdom have been testing out chemical weapons and bombs on some of their citizens in a private facility. A few people were found dead on the same day that Serafina Leyva was taken out. It's starting to look like Good Ol' King Bryan has a plan to wipe out as much of your forces as possible."

"Go on," Serenity bade. He told her of the bombs planted around the Capitol's perimeter and how theoretically it would protect the Kingdom's innermost citizens from any attack by their enemies. "Did they account for our air forces?" The question stunned Alan.

"You have air forces?" He asked it without thinking, then immediately changed focus. "Never mind. We're doing some recon to figure out a counterstrategy, but you should know that he has a giant version of one of those bombs hidden in the World Trade Center. We don't know for sure if it's a model or if it's a live bomb, but once we have that information we'll get it to you and we can plan accordingly."

"Roger that. In the meantime I'll relay the intel you've given me up the chain of command. John will know what to do," Serenity assured him. The transmission ended as James and Serenity exchanged looks of worry.

****

March 17th, 2085, 3:25 p.m.,

Darius entered the depths of Level AA and checked in with the guards. There was a heaviness to his demeanor, and as he moved past the guards, he wondered what he would say.

The fact that the Holding Level only had one resident made it even stranger. In the past, or so Darius had been told when he was little, Holding Level AA had been used to house people within the Insurrection that had broken community law, as well as prisoners taken from the surrounding area that tried to break in. He'd heard that

Zahara Boyd once stayed there, back when they'd first brought her in from the initial Raid of Johnson City. She managed to earn her freedom by an extensive show of loyalty to the Yaiba Insurrection, and a close friendship with the former Kiryu, Raven Shahid.

The case with Alphonse Westershire wasn't anything like that. He was a prisoner because he took advantage of the kindness shown to him and tried to not only dismantle the Insurrection, but kill everyone there. Somehow, though, the Director saw fit to let him loose to train with yet more dangerous weapons and fight alongside them at the moment of truth.

Darius arrived at the cell to find the boy atop his bed, a knee bent with his back against a wall, arm draped over his leg. This was the kid that the Scarlet Kingdom had dubbed the Trojan Horse. He bounced a ball that he shouldn't have had against the wall over and over again, and pretended not to notice the Director's son standing at the door.

"Get your shoes on," Darius instructed. "We're going for a walk." Al just turned to look at his Sensei, then did what he was told. Within another few moments, they'd found themselves back at the power-lift and in total silence. Every now and then, Darius would look at Al, and when Al would notice, he'd look away.

"Look, I don't play for that team," Al said after about the fifth time, much to Darius' embarrassment.

"Whoa, hey, no," he stammered and staggered between a shocked and authoritative expression. He forced himself to calm down, and considered a proper address to the situation. Before he could say anything, his protégé spoke up.

"What do you think the Director hopes will come out of this?" Darius looked at Al again, a stern, almost John-like look on his face as they listened to the mechanical workings of the lift. Al looked up at his teacher, and for the first time, Darius truly saw him for the child that he was. He had no place in this war, and yet his involvement was completely out of his control. The Hiryu breathed a heavy sigh as his brow furrowed.

"Who can really say," Darius shrugged. "Knowing dad, though, he could just want someone to watch over you and keep you safe."

"Do you guys really think I need that?" Al scoffed. "I've been in the field since I was fourteen. I don't need anyone keeping tabs on me."

"Everyone needs that," Darius rebutted calmly. "Look, I have no intention of treating you like a child, but I do intend to treat you like a person. Whether that's what he had planned or not, my duty as your Sensei is to keep you safe both in here and out there." Al gave an unbelieving sound, and there was a pause for a moment as the lift came to a stop at Deployment Level A. They walked down the path, as if on the way to Johnson City. "So, why do you do it?"

"Do what," Al asked in return. Darius didn't look at him now, and kept his eyes on the path that, before he'd left, had been overgrown. It amazed him that so much had changed about the Insurrection—and Prevalence—in just a few months.

“You fight in a war you’re too young for as an intelligence operative, taking orders from people who would replace you tomorrow if it suited them. How do you do that?” Darius only realized that his disgust was front and center after he explained, but Al seemed not to mind. He could see that it was disgust aimed at the Kingdom more than at himself.

“That’s simple,” said the outsider. “It’s what my parents wanted for me. Darius stopped walking, and Al eased his stride to stand beside his master.

“So that’s it? You’re telling me that your whole life you haven’t made any choices about where you want to end up? Don’t you have the capacity to think for yourself?”

“Hey, don’t assume that I’m not thinking for myself just because I follow my orders! Aside from what I told you, I do what I do to keep my parents safe!” The words cut through Darius like fresh scissors through paper. Al’s eyes softened now as he continued. “Serafina Leyva took my parents hostage. She told me to do my job and report on the Yaiba’s movements and I’d get them back unharmed.”

“Oh, kid,” Darius started, and as soon as the words left his mouth, Al’s entire demeanor changed. His mouth opened and took a number of shapes, as if to form the starts of words that wouldn’t come out. There was worry in his eyes, panic in his brow, and Darius suddenly thought back to how it felt when he’d received news of his grandmother’s passing. The Fire Dragon knew that he couldn’t drag this out any longer. “Report came back about an hour ago about the Reds’ defensive strategy. They’ve recalled all forces and have mined New York’s perimeter with an array of explosives." The boy's face darkened with confusion.

"I don't understand," he was finally able to convey. "What does that have to do with my parents?" Darius refused to look at him now, because he knew that the rebellious teen and cunning warrior had made their leave, and all that remained was more of a broken child than what the Hiryu was prepared to see.

"According to our source, there were a number of civilians who volunteered to assist with military experiments designed to help the Kingdom's war effort. All of them were tortured extensively with biological and chemical weapons or mutilated beyond recognition," Darius carefully explained. He wrestled with himself and what he should do in a moment like this. Alphonse was a complete stranger to him, and while they certainly had the bond of master and apprentice going on between them, they hadn't nearly been at it long enough for his comforts to mean anything significant. Still, he inched closer to the boy and placed a gentle hand on his shoulder. "Your parents weren't kidnapped by Serafina, Al. They willingly signed on for that volunteer program. They thought it would help you. I'm sorry."

"How did they die," Al asked in his best attempt at sounding tough. "I wanna know, Sensei, please tell me." Darius paused for a moment to get his thoughts in order and deliberate if his apprentice should know or not. He let himself breathe.

"Your parents were severely cut up by Serafina, but they didn't die until a dead man's switch was triggered. Serafina Leyva is dead, and the moment she died was when your parents were lost to an explosion at the base of the neck." Darius elaborated it with as much care as he could have, but he knew it was the kind of news that couldn't be softened, no matter how gentle the voice who delivered it.

"No," Al sobbed over and over again as he sank to the ground. Darius knelt beside him, his hand still on his shoulder. Al, on an impulse that neither of them expected, hugged Darius with thunderous force. Darius, who had always had an aversion to being touched without permission, opened his mouth to protest, but decided against it. He hugged his student back, and offered whatever small comforts he could.

****

March 17th, 2085, 4:17 p.m.,

Aaliyah didn't know what to expect. She sat at the ground level rung of the bleachers on the side of the training ground court and watched as her husband prepared to fight her father-in-law. The audience was bigger here than it had ever been, and she knew exactly why. The only people in the Insurrection that didn't know about the drama between John and Dre were either newborns or newcomers, and many of the people within the faction placed bets on when it would finally come to a head. Yaiba men settled things with their Reikiken and their skill in battle, either through combat against the enemy or against each other in sparring.

This was the latter, and Aaliyah could see that these two were largely the same. The way they took to their one-armed stances in matching Hanzo Gear, the way they stared holes into their opponent with stoic eyes, and how they paced the ground like panthers on the prowl all showed a similarity that neither of them would openly admit was there. There was no referee, no mediator to this conflict of pride, and that's what it all boiled down to. The pride of the best warrior of his day and all the expertise that came with his experience, and the pride of the best that the Yaiba had ever seen. To make it more of a show, the usual metal trees that arose from the training ground floors were left alone. All attention was on the combatants.

Their blades crossed, patient and ready, the tips of either man's Reikiken pointed at the other man's head. Dre took the first move, and feigned a thrust at his son's chest. Without so much as a blink, John parried the move and watched his father follow the energy around to a cut at the waistline. John parried that as well, then moved in for a thrust of his own that was sharply deflected by a revolving block. For an old man, Dre could still move along the battlefield. John had to suppose that the Elder Lightning Dragon never really stopped training. John used the energy from his opponent's parry to swing down at Dre's leg. Dre awkwardly blocked with his sword in a reversed grip, and almost missed a necessary block to John's attack at his head.

Dre only narrowly managed to slip out from under the downward blow before his son could quickly disconnect and stab him in the face, then attempted a strike at the arm. The fresh Director casually pushed the blow to the side, but redirected it down. He watched as Dre tried his best to disconnect in a nearly unpredictable mix of elegant sidesteps and spins. John, though, was determined to keep their weapons connected. He felt each change of direction, each attempted attack, each expertly timed defense, and only when they were right in each other's faces did Dre manage a break.

Aaliyah found herself caught up in the precision and beauty of the fight that she almost forgot that that was what it was. Moreover, she nearly forgot the anxiety that it caused her in the beginning. While John had his issues with Dre, he'd only ever shown her the utmost kindness and respect, and while her husband never wanted to admit it, Dre was and had always been an incredible grandfather to Darius and Cal. She couldn't help but wonder if this match would settle more than just their political disputes.

Dre swung down at his son's legs with a level of force that made John doubt the man's age. He blocked just in time, then the other leg. Both men were hunched over from the combination of attacks, and on instinct alone, John flipped his aura sword sideways to stagnate an upward thrust from his father. Dre donned a look of fatherly approval until John pushed the blade to the side. Dre followed the energy and attempted to attack the seemingly exposed shoulder when John inverted his sword and kept himself safe. The look of approval returned.

John blocked his head as his father attempted to crash down on it and slid off the center line in position to strike back. His Reikiken moved for the midsection, but he was parried. He didn't care. He was tired of this, and resolved to pressure the old man and make him back down. He swung contrary to the initial flow and attacked the shoulder. He met a block and bounced off of it with a speed that made the crowd gasp, then redirected the outward swing downward. Dre blocked the strike, and again the Director shifted the flow into an upward swing at his father's abdomen. Dre extended his hand with his firesword held parallel to the ground and stopped the flow, but John disconnected in the instant the weapons met and stepped forward. The tip of his brilliant orange blade sped forward and nearly caught Dre off balance. John recognized it as the end of the battle.

Dre deflected it to the side as he teetered back, and John maneuvered his sword around into an elegant downward slash. It grazed the outer layer of Dre's Hanzo Gear and Dre fell to the ground. The fight was over, and with a begrudged look about him, the elder had to recognize that John had emerged the victor.

****

March 17th, 2085, 7:27 p.m.,

Leo felt a lot of things. He'd felt alone, even though he felt for the first time that he had a family that loved him enough to fight for him. He'd felt angry that Al had managed to fool him and betray him with such ease and what seemed to be so little a sense of remorse. He'd felt happy that he had a wealth of tech to play around with and the start to some serious relationships. He felt alien and at home, because of the ways in which his hard life as a nomad in the Southern Wastes tended to contradict the stability he felt here in the Insurrection.

It hurt him now, to think of those times. He barely remembered what it was like to have parents, didn't remember what it was like to have a brother. Then Al came along and changed that. They watched each other's backs a number of times, stole food from Scarlet patrols in the area, raided the battlefields for spare parts that they could sell or weapons that they could use to defend themselves. Maybe that was why he currently sought a moment with him on the Holding Level.

He approached Al's cell, fully intent to dig into the pain that he felt by the betrayal, prepared to give a speech about how they were expected to work together in the assault on New York, ready to demand that he answer the question of how he could be trusted in the heat of battle. Then he saw him. Al sat in his cell with his back turned toward the corridor and legs pulled to his chest as he wept. Suddenly all of the plans that Leo had concocted for this moment had gone out the window, and all he wanted was to be let in.

"Can I get a guard over here?" Leo shouted it into the empty hallway and startled Al from his misery. The spy turned his head to shoot Leo a look, but it quickly fell apart. Leo hated that it affected him. He was still angry about how reckless Al was, how little he'd regarded the lives of the Yaiba or even him. In this moment, though, all he saw was his scared little brother and he agonized over it.

A guard hurried down the hall and, for a moment, looked up at Leo. The young warrior aggressively raised his eyebrows at the bewildered keeper, and the man swiftly pulled out his keys and unlocked the door. Leo pushed past him and entered the cell, which only made Al turn further towards the corner.

"Here to tell me what a terrible person I am," Al questioned with more bite than what Leo had expected. It was like a stab to the heart to hear.

“No,” Leo answered with thoughtfulness in his voice, “nothing like that.”

“It doesn’t matter,” Al said. “Just leave.” There was a moment of silent expectation, but when the sound of Leo’s footsteps never came, the distraught teenager rapidly turned his head and slammed a fist against the bed as he asked, “Didn’t you hear what I just said? Get out of here!”

“I heard you,” Leo assured him coolly, which only seemed to aggravate Al more. He could tell by the tears that streamed down the angry young agent’s face. “I’m not going anywhere though.” Just those words were enough to make Al fall apart. He sobbed openly, and no longer cared if Leo saw him. After all, they’d seen almost everything of each other during their time in the Wastes, and the simple knowledge of that only filled Al with more regret.

Leo quickly approached him and pulled him into an embrace. He resolved that the strategizing could wait, and took this sudden vulnerability from Al to be an admission of remorse. Then Al spoke.

“I’m so sorry,” was what he uttered, and it was in that that Leo understood that he wouldn’t be going anywhere. Not so long as his little brother needed him.

Chapter Nineteen

March 20th, 2085, 3:33 a.m.,

Just a few more seconds and…there it was. The cameras that closely surveyed the World Trade Center were offline, but only for about thirty minutes. Lyla surmised that it would be more than enough time to get in and get what she needed. That massive bomb was too much of a wild card to take the King's word on its lack of authenticity. She hacked into the security system, and made a concerted effort to use her Yaiba slice training rather than her Kingdom credentials. Since the higher-ups were aware of their presence in New York anyway, it wouldn't be a surprise if they were the prime suspects in acts of espionage and terrorism.

It only took her a moment to deactivate the more serious security measures and plot her course to the innermost chambers. She knew that bomb itself was held in one of the old studios of 4 WTC, but the information pertaining to it would be held somewhere else. Had she been in the loop, this would've been a whole lot easier, but unfortunately the King no longer trusted her to do anything aside from get on his nerves. No, now she had to resort to the underhanded practices of her former faction to get information. It wasn't that she hated to retrace her roots, but she knew of an easier path and the fact that it was currently inaccessible to her was enough to warrant at least a small pout.

She kept her emotions in check, though, careful not to make so much as a sound. She didn't want to take the chance of her activities leaking to someone other than her current allies because she knew that the King would have her head if he knew. She took a breath and refocused on the facts.

The World Trade Center was an array of seven buildings. Office spaces, studios, a transportation hub, a museum. It was massive, and it was easy to get lost once inside. That was why the hacking was so necessary, and why Lyla currently made her way into building 4, where she knew the massive explosive would be. Never once did the weight of the place escape her. Shortly after the turn of the century, terrorists attacked the Twin Towers that stood in its place and almost 3,000 people lost their lives. The United States and other world governments took the time to enact steep security protocols that lasted for years in the aftermath, and an unrelenting fear lingered in the wake of the tragedy, only to give rise to a myriad of murders and instances of excessive discrimination. It'd been 84 years, and everything that the presidents of old and all their troops fought for had disintegrated, with one of the last monuments to that civilization held hostage under the threat of a massive attack by a maniacal King.

Lyla put those thoughts out of her mind for the time being. She carefully stalked the halls, watchful of every entrance and exit, masked by the Menpo of her Insurrectionist past, and almost there. She climbed the stairs because it was harder to monitor than the elevator. She picked the manual locks with stealth and skill. She entered the floor upon which stood the intel they would need to move forward. Just a little further and she would be able to get out unnoticed. She tried not to fixate on the clear glass of the floor that, in the daytime would magnify the light of the sun, and now only dealt in the steepest darkness. Her head darted in all directions as she watched for any signs of life and listened for the footsteps of staff security. Nothing. She moved on.

It took her twenty-five minutes to reach the computer console, and another three to break into it. She was down to the wire. The intel took precedence over everything else, and Lyla could only suspect that the moment she got in, a signal went out to the engineering staff—of which the King used to be a part. She inserted her micro-drive and did all she could to extract the schematics of every bomb built within the past four months, all with the hope that the big one would be included in the data.

Sirens stabbed through the silence of the dark. Whereas once that sound would mean the police, now it meant the something entirely different: Executioners. Lyla couldn't help but chuckle. It would take them approximately ten minutes to get there. With another 45 seconds left on the extraction, she had about seven to get out of the building unnoticed with the files in hand, otherwise it would be a fight. But maybe…

The micro-drive ejected. It was back in her hands and Lyla made a move for the stairwell. The moment the door opened she heard the ambiguous shouts of tactical movements. Security had been alerted to her presence, so there was no way that she would be able to head downstairs without sure incrimination and immediate extermination once the Executioners arrived. Lyla breathed out calmly and clapped her hands against her cheeks as she ran up instead of down. There was sure to be a door to the roof there, and if there wasn't, she'd make one. Anything was better than sitting around waiting for the King's secret death force to arrive.

Even still, Lyla couldn't help but crack a smile. This was more excitement than she'd seen since she rescued her father out west, and she was almost in the clear. The rush she got from it was enough to carry her up the rest of the stairs with ease, and to her relief, there was already a door to the roof. She broke the lock on it and burst through, but what she found there stopped her dead and brought her Reikiken to her hand.

"Out of all the people in the world, I never thought I'd be betrayed by my own daughter," King Bryan said with an emotionless chill. He sat on the wiring hub of the rooftop cooling system, his hands folded, his eyes as cruel as the King he'd killed, and his expression devoid of anything that could even remotely resemble paternal affection. "Well? Do you have anything to say for yourself?"

"Did you know I would come here tonight," was her only response, and the harshness of her tone surprised the both of them. It truly made him feel that she was an enemy. Sadly enough, she felt the same of him.

"I had my suspicions," he replied. "Ever since you lost your place and questioned my leadership skills, I wanted to see how much I could trust you. I gotta say," he said with a flicker of the old Bryan in his words, "when Cartwright told me you had a report to give me days ago that never came through, it broke my heart." She snorted a laugh that instantly drew his ire.

"We both know that you lost that a long time ago," she told him with tears in her eyes. "You're nothing close to the man you used to be. I don't even recognize you."

"So that's your excuse?" Bryan looked incredulous. "You have to watch your dad make some hard choices and suddenly you want to bite the hand that feeds you?"

"I was fine here before you came back into my life," Lyla yelled, then instantly realized her mistake. "I made my own way here in the Kingdom. I put a roof over my head. I fed myself, clothed myself, did what I had to do to survive in a place that hates me just because of the color of my skin. I proved myself—"

"To murderous racists, Lyla! These people are horrible when left unchecked," Bryan interrupted, and it was her turn to display unbelief.

"You can't even see it, can you? You've turned on your home, your wife, your family, and you've gone so far off the deep end that you're trying to kill them all! You say it's for revenge, that it's for some ultimate plan of retribution for what happened to Jaden, but do you think he'd want this?"

"Oh, the absentee big sister is gonna lecture the present father of what her little brother would've wanted! Do you have any idea how out of line you are?"

"No, someone needs to tell you what you need to hear, dammit!" She hastened toward him with authority in every step until they stood face to face, her brown-sugar eyes locked on his darkened blue eyes. Her voice was naught but a whisper as she told him what he knew all along but refused to admit to himself: "You like the power. Here, you're not the eighth best warrior like you were after Uncle John and the other Dragons. You get to call the shots, decide who lives and who dies, and you're using Jaden's death as a vessel to do whatever the hell you want."

"Enough!" Bryan's shout was all the signal Lyla needed to lift her Reikiken to guard her face, and it was a good thing that she did. The man that she at one time called her father had attacked her for the second time, but this time with an attempted blow to the head. She watched the sparks as Bryan's Reikiken slid down her blade, and when he moved for the shoulder strike, Lyla simply slid her sword under his and pushed it through in an elegant parry. The frustrated King used her deflection to wind up for another shot, and swung his weapon back at her in an obvious show of strength.

She pushed it back the other way, careful to step in as she did so to put him on the defensive. She knew that if he managed to get away from her, the fight would be as good as settled. He might've been in eighth place behind the Dragons, but he was still the eighth best soldier in the Insurrection before his defection. She couldn't hope to match his skills the way she was now. That was why she played defense. She pressed her firesword into his as she moved into him, but in swift order Bryan disengaged and ignited his repulsor boots as he drove his kyoketsu-shoge into the roof. In one second, he was in the air above her. In the time it took for Lyla to blink, he'd somehow gotten behind her.

She gritted her teeth as she spun away and moved to block, but it was awkward and choppy. He'd pushed her off balance, and when he saw it for himself, he swung at her with no particular rhyme or reason. At least, that was how it seemed. Each strike was so much the perfect counterbalance for her disorientation, and slowly Lyla began to realize that he was never out of control to begin with. He merely needed her to think that he was so her guard would be down. He moved to attack the legs, and when she moved to block he kicked to the side with the repulsors as he shot a kyoketsu-shoge into the cooling unit. He released in just the right moment, and attempted a cut from a different angle.

It was that ability, she knew, that earned him the moniker of Rabbit of the Divine Wind, and it was precisely the reason she had to fear him. For her young life, she got to watch him train in the various styles of Reikiken combat, master new techniques with the repulsors and the chains, and it seemed to her that he would never reach a wall that would stagnate his progress. He came in with a cut at the midsection that she barely had any time to parry, and she realized that there was no way to win or disengage from him long enough to escape like she knew she needed to do. He widened his stance, and with a brilliant blue flash from the repulsors, he rocketed towards her.

Lyla took a knee the second before he could decapitate her, and clapped a hand gently to his belly. A burst of light erupted at close range, and Bryan, for a moment, was blinded. He stumbled back for a moment, and Lyla took the chance to run at him and jump, both feet aimed squarely at his chest. She connected, and Bryan fell to the ground so hard that his head bounced against the concrete. She quickly rose back to her feet, aura sword raised high, and though she knew that she should've taken his head right then and there, the sudden swarm of Executioner footsteps assured her otherwise.

Gunfire erupted in her wake. A single tear slipped down her cheek as she raced for the edge of the roof and jumped.

****

March 20th, 2085, 9:53 a.m.,

The door opened, which meant that they could breathe easier. Alan rushed to greet Lyla as she came into the hideout, only to stop in his tracks the moment he saw her. She bled through her fingers as she pressed against her shoulder, and cracked a smile at him that made him question her sanity.

“Stop looking at me like that,” she told him. “I’ve been through way worse than this.” He shook his head as he ushered her in.

“Doesn’t make it any less horrific from where I’m sitting,” Alan commented. He raised an eyebrow. “You know how to stop the bleeding?” She nodded.

“Like I said, I’ve been through way worse,” she reminded him, then took his hand with the non-bloody one. She pressed the micro-drive into his palm. “Mission accomplished, albeit with a slight hiccup.”

“Yeah, well, hopefully we can do some good with the intel you gathered before the King can put us in the dirt. I’ll have Ryan take a look at what’s on this thing. You just make sure you don’t bleed out before we have a chance to get started.” She nodded at that as well, and before she could say anything else, he left her to tend to her wound. She found some old rags, ripped them up, poured alcohol on them, and gingerly dressed her wound with the due amount of pressure to stop the bleeding. It stung like a mother, but she couldn’t help but smile. She couldn’t remember the last time someone stopped to ask her about her, rather than what she could give them.

****

March 20th, 2085, 11:03 a.m.,

Ryan Crawford had never been so distraught at being right. The bomb that the King said was just a prop was, in fact, a live munition in and of itself, and it was one with enough firepower to take out the entirety of the Kingdom's territory. If the Senshi Coalition walked into battle haphazardly, then it would mean near instant death for them all. Just the thought was enough to send a chill down his spine. For the sake of his own sanity, he searched through more of the files and wondered just how much Lyla had managed to extract.

Something caught his eye. His eyes went wide with realization. These were the schematics. For twenty minutes he read over every possible detail of the weapon, how it was charged, how long before it would detonate after the initial amassing of energy, and of greatest importance, how to disarm it.

"Dad, come look at this," he called into the space behind him where the Coalition's commando team sat anxiously. Alan, who had been more than preoccupied with Lyla's condition, approached without hesitation. "I think I found what we needed."

"And what's that, kid," the old sniper asked of the young.

"The bomb is not only active, but it has a unique trigger mechanism. It's hardwired to pick up the detonation status of the mines placed around the Capitol's perimeter. If they go off, then the massive one at the heart of the World Trade Center begins to store energy," Ryan explained.

"It's almost as if it was keeping score," Alan muttered as he ran his fingers through his graying beard.

"Exactly," Ryan continued with more joy in his voice than he'd felt in weeks. "In theory, if the mines never detonate, then there's a chance the major one wouldn't either—"

"Unless King Bryan was deadest on killing us all in a blaze of glory," Alan interrupted. "I admire your optimism, son. Really. But I've seen the look in that man's eye. He'll kill anyone and everyone if he wants to, and while it may come off as a game to him right now, you never wanna know what a man like that will do when he's cornered."

"I know," sighed the son. "Except there's more than one way to disable it." Alan's eyebrows perked up in welcome surprise, then narrowed when his son adopted a smug look.

"Well don't just sit there," Alan prodded, "tell me something."

"The wiring on the bombs are their biggest weakness. Something with this level of intricacy couldn't have been done without advanced electrical engineering, so a powerful enough EMP, or even a medium-strength one at a close enough range should be enough to sabotage the damn thing." Alan gave it some thought, looked at his boy, then looked back at the computer screen. There was hope, and that was all that he needed to know.

“Sounds like the beginning of a plan. I’ll let your sister know,” he assured him, and clapped him on the back as a reward for his good work.

****

March 25th, 2085, 12:20 a.m.,

There was a stillness in the air, a moment of calm before the eruption of a hurricane, and John could feel it in his bones that now was the time. The last five days were spent updating the battle strategy for the siege of the Kingdom, and while he was convinced that they would be successful, he knew what the consequences would be if they weren’t. The knowledge of the bombs’ detonation mechanisms was enough to reassign a large portion of the Kabuto and Yoroi personnel to work the perimeter while the commando strike and aerial assault were to serve as a greater distraction than intended.

The Elders Council and the Yoroi Council were both happy to repurpose some of their units to work in their strengths, but John hesitated to stake pride in such an abrupt change of strategy. Nevertheless, what he lacked in confidence in the plan, he more than made up for with confidence in the people that would be watching his back while he confronted Bryan. He glanced over at his wife Aaliyah, the love of his life, who never failed to support him and take care of him when the trials of his job became too much. He wondered how she would feel about that flight. As much as he wanted to tell her of his part in this battle, though, he didn't. He knew that she would never agree to him putting himself in such a dangerous position, especially after the results of their last encounter. But it was as he'd said to the other leaders. This was something that only he could do.

He got out of bed and got dressed. There was still plenty of time before he needed to be anywhere, but he wanted to take the time to walk the halls of the Roan compound. After all, tomorrow was the day that the siege would begin. If he didn't come back, he didn't want to have the regret of a stoic departure in his last moments. He opened the door to leave, and found his sons standing at the door, their faces serious, contemplative. John closed the door softly behind him so he wouldn't wake Aaliyah, then turned his focus to his children.

"Hey, Pops," Darius said in a hushed tone.

"What are you two doing up so late," John asked in a tone that made them think back to a time when they were much younger, and much less in danger. The former Lightning Dragon could tell that it was almost too much for them to handle. "Sorry," he told them sheepishly. "Old habits. I just meant that you two should get all the rest you can. There's not much time left until we get started with the op."

"We know, Pops," Cal assured him. "It's just a lot, you know?"

"Yeah," Darius agreed, "the whole thing hinges on us and what we're able to do with forces we've never been in control of before. That's a lot of pressure." John smiled.

"I know," he reassured. "It's a lot of pressure for me, too. But this moment is too good of an opportunity to pass up. Walk with me." The Director started to walk the path of the Residence level. The boys followed, and quickly caught up to their father. They were silent for a moment, as was Level G as they passed by door after door, curious as to how many were unoccupied now that the war had dragged on this long. John glanced at them as their focus drifted to other places, and it was only now that he truly saw them for who they were. It was hard for him to believe that they were still just boys of eighteen. The battles they'd fought and the things they'd accomplished since their graduation duel had changed his view of them, though physically they looked almost the same.

"It feels so different to be back," Darius remarked.

"I would imagine it would," John granted. "You've been away since a little before the war started. Emiko was alive then." His voice grew darker, and the emotion of the loss returned almost completely. He cleared his throat. He made it a point not to cry in front of them. It was never because crying was beneath him, but because he knew that he needed to be a safe person for them to cry to. "Not to mention you've liberated the Yoroi Alliance." The change of subject was a welcome one. None of them wanted to think too much about the death of Director Ishikawa.

"I don't think it has as much to do with me as it does all of you," Darius pointed out. "Half the senior leadership in the Insurrection was wiped out and replaced, we're able to infiltrate Deep Red territory, and Cal has a new eye." Cal snapped as an excited gleam took his eye.

"I'm glad you brought it up," he said as he clapped his brother on the back. "I haven't told you about the Kiringan yet!"

"He'll see it in action when we're in position," John quelled. He knew his sons, and he knew that there was very little to stop Cal when he got started in a technical explanation. Moreover, it would've resulted in a demonstration, which meant a lot of collateral damage if the Lightbeams were to be considered. "I'm just glad to have you both here and in good health."

"Sounds like you been worried about us," Cal joked, and John shrugged while Darius snickered in what he thought was his father's blind spot.

"I always worry about you. Both of you are bright and creative and, if I'm honest, this life of combat is not what I had in mind for either of you," spoke the former Lightning Dragon.

"Ah but we're so good at it," Darius said as he slapped his father's shoulder.

"No arguments here," John was forced to admit. "Both of you have done more than I thought you would."

"Is that why we made Dragon," Cal asked with a bit more intensity. John looked him over, made it seem as though there was something to consider, and then shrugged in a way that either of his sons could only describe as anticlimactic.

"I have no clue," he told them honestly. "I didn't do the selecting. I just told the other Dragons to consider who they thought would be worthy such a leadership role. When I think about it, though, it's no wonder that they'd pick the

Hero of the Yoroi and the Metal Dragon of the Yaiba to step into their ranks."

"Don't forget about Lukas," Darius reminded. John smiled. There was no way to forget that boy, not when they put on such an interesting show during their graduation duel.

"Of course not." There was a lull in the conversation. None of them could really take their minds off of what the next day would bring, and now that they were all together again for the first time in months, they did all they could to avoid thinking about what it could. "Listen," John started up again after they'd walked for a while longer, "I want you both to know how much I love you. Neither of you has had it easy since you joined the Shadows and I wanted to tell you that I'm so very proud of both of you."

"Pops," Darius started with a calm voice that mismatched the worry in his eyes. "You don't have cancer, do you?"

"Yeah, don't be sayin' stuff like that," Cal urged. John stopped walking, as did they, and he pulled them into a tight hug.

"Nothing's wrong," he assured them, "I just want you to know." He let them go. "We should head to bed. Staying up all night won't make tomorrow any easier." They agreed, and reluctantly went back to their homes while John continued to watch over them with tears suddenly in his eyes.

****

March 25th, 2085, 10:44 a.m.,

The thunder of the heavy machinery could only be matched by that of every heart in the Coalition. The time had come. In a few short hours, they would arrive in Jersey City, and they would either realize their greatest victory or their most crushing defeat. Nevertheless, every leader had their marching orders and attended them with due intention.

The rearmost wave of the convoy were the Kabuto and Yoroi forces, save for those led on the ground by Darius and his team of elites among the Violent Sands. Their primary objective was to discern the location of the mines and disable them with EMPs. The Waste Raiders brought up the middle alongside the gold-clad ranks of Nash's forces. The former would evacuate the civilians while the latter gave them sufficient cover. There was no need, after all, for needless execution. At the front lines were those members of the Violet Shadows and Violent Sands with the most experience in head-to-head conflict, with specialized groupings ready to go as soon as the threat of the bombs had been neutralized.

John ensured that it would be. Cal's Kiringan would be able to pick up the thermal changes in the buried metals, then relay it to the command center on Level X. Dre would then report it back to the other leaders across Prevalence. While the new Kiryu, Leo and the Lightbeams would act as the air force of the Senshi Coalition, it would give John all the time he needed to slip in from the shore with his covert unit and find a path to Bryan. Darius would act in his stead and command the ground forces as planned.

The silent resignation to their roles told of the unparalleled stress this put on the entire Coalition, with the only one excited for all the chaos being Claire Sommerfield. It was easy to see, though, why the general consensus was that of a stubborn anxiousness. So many people had been killed in this conflict since the outset from all of the warring parties. John could hardly shake the images of Shonda, Manny, Raven, or Emiko, and those were the easier deaths to think about. When it came to Jaden Piccio, a young man he'd known since the day he was born and loved like his own nephew, he shook with a rage and sorrow he'd never known.

After all, it was only too easy for him to think about his own children. Had either of them died so far, would he be able to keep himself together long enough to secure a future where children didn't get drafted into military matters? He'd seen what the loss had done to Bryan. To his family. At the time the news came through, John judged his old friend for his attitude, but when he put himself in the same scenario, he doubted that anything different would've come about.

"Alright," the Director spoke calmly into the comms unit. Before departure, he made sure that everyone had tapped into the right frequency and knew the independent ones assigned to each of their mission roles. "Everybody listen up. In a little more than ten hours we'll arrive at our preliminary destination. Everybody knows what it is they have to do, so I'll skip the rehash over all of that. What we're about to do will challenge every single one of us at our core. It's nothing short of a full-scale invasion, and a win here isn't going to come to us without an almost inhuman degree of resolve. I can't speak to you from the position of a politician. I've never been very good at that," he said with a chuckle, then continued. "But what I can do is tell you what's at stake. Any of you who have had a desire to protect your family, or secure a future for your grandkids that didn't involve fighting, this is your chance to make that happen. Any of you who want more for yourselves than living in broken buildings or caves, it's right in front of you. Victory for us is more than just the end of this war, it's the freedom to rebuild in a way that benefits us all. All of us have taken enough losses. Let's make sure we get out there and return the favor." There was silence. It was expected, though. John knew that he wasn't the greatest at motivational speeches, and even now realized that his attempt had probably escalated the tension. Still, it didn't change the fact that he was right. He moved to silence his comms for a while, to regain his focus and prepare his mind, when he heard a response.

"Yes sir," Alphonse Westershire agreed emphatically. It resonated with him. John smiled.

****

March 25th, 2085, 2:53 p.m.,

Bryan stood with his back to the Court chamber as he stared out over New York. Even in the wake of his daughter's betrayal, he stood in the fullness of his power. He was beyond confident that whatever she managed to make off with that night was hardly enough to derail his plans, and if it was, then at least things would be interesting. He could feel Jaden's presence by his side, could feel the sureness of his victory over every person that had ever crossed him or played a part in the destruction of his family, and he smiled.

Bryan Piccio was a man convinced that his way was right. His allies had nearly fallen to naught, but that was fine since he had the expendable bodies of the Scarlet Troopers at his disposal. His Scarlet Streaks served as his last line of defense, though their supposed leader had been AWOL for days. Nevertheless, he was strong enough to protect himself, and figured that the presence of the new death squad was suited to be little more than an opening act for his guests upon their arrival. He chuckled under his breath as he ran his hands over the bullet-resistant top of his red-colored Hanzo Gear. He stood where none of his former comrades could ever hope to, at the peak of an empire, ready to purge the world of the disease that was the people of this continent and finally avenge his son.

"What a sad, pathetic little man you are," came a voice that he'd thought he'd rid himself of months ago. The footsteps approached from behind him, but before he could fully turn his head, there at his side stood the former King of the Reds, Shane O'Neill. His father. "You cower behind your mines and meat shields but have the audacity to claim strength. What kind of King are you?" There was a deep disdain in Shane's eyes that burned the depths of Bryan's being, but then in the instant that his anger reached its peak, he saw the decay in the old man's face.

"That's right, please, lecture me more on the proper uses of power when you didn't even have the power to save yourself from death," Bryan countered. "And anyway, what could you possibly know about me?"

"I know that you have other motives for all this that have nothing to do with your son," Shane started. The room warped, and there in the glass, upside down like a bat in a cave, the former King stood upon the roof with Jaden's throat cupped by a decaying hand.

"Let him go," Bryan ordered with authority befitting his position. Shane laughed madly, maliciously, and the room spiraled around them.

"You dare order me," the dead king spat defiantly. "Funny, given that you stand in this position only because of your inability to do the same!"

"Shut up!" Bryan shouted it like a toddler throwing a tantrum, unwilling to stomach the words of a corpse.

"You cling to your son only to justify actions that you've always wanted to take! You've been miserable for a long time, Mr. Piccio, and a part of you has always wanted to end things on a boisterous level to suit your darkest desires!" Bryan shook his head, tried to avert his eyes to the window only to find that the room had gone completely dark. "They say that if you want to see the character of a man, give him power! Take a close look at where that's brought you!"

"Sire?" The soft voice of Zachary Smithfield managed to reach him, and suddenly the volatile conditions of the room dissipated.

"What?!" The sudden snapping of the King was enough to make Smithfield take a step back in fear, and when Bryan realized what he'd done, he corrected himself. "What?"

"The Streaks have informed me that our enemies are inbound, with the Yaiba Insurrection nearing arrival in Jersey City. How do you wish to proceed?" Bryan, who was visibly covered in sweat, moved for his throne and sat down as he pondered the question.

“Let them gather as planned,” he answered forcefully, so as to disguise his weakness. Smithfield nodded obediently.

“Of course, sir,” he said. “And should I tell the engineering department to prepare the ballistic drones?”

“Yes,” Bryan ordered. As Smithfield bowed and made his exit, Bryan refocused his attention on victory. His moment had finally come, his desires would finally be realized, and no matter what anyone—living or dead—had to say about it, he would not be denied.

Chapter Twenty

March 25th, 2085, 11:30 p.m.,

Lukas crossed the threshold of the main room of the hideout and, after a look around, decided that he couldn't be happier that this mission neared its end. Dust lined every inch of the place, and all the light that they had was artificial in a way that was somehow worse than the cave networks of the Roan compound. Perhaps he'd been spoiled by the annex of Johnson City.

"Any news," Zayvier asked from a darkened corner near a boarded-up window. Lukas felt his heart nearly leap out of his mouth, but he swallowed and stepped further into the room. He noted that the rest of his team was there, and at his arrival, they all looked to him for their next steps. It made him nervous at first, but when he realized that his discomfort was not even a tertiary concern, he focused on the job he'd been given.

"Our forces are just across the Hudson in Jersey City. We've been given the greenlight for our unsavory activities," Lukas explained with more cheer in his voice than the moment warranted. He had to guess that it was a quirk that he'd picked up from his father. He shrugged it off. "We move into position at first light. They said that they'll handle the rest from there, so that means that once our job is done we need to get out of the way. Things are gonna get dangerous, so we need to flow with the public and regroup in the hideout. Once the main force has breached the Capitol, we're to rendezvous with them and hold the line around Central Harlem."

"Sounds like a plan," said Tareena. She wasn't exactly excited to get the show on the road, but she figured that the sooner they started, then the sooner they ended.

"Now," Lukas continued, "is everyone clear on who your blast buddy is if you get made in the field?" The question was more aimed at their allies from the Kabuto and Yoroi who were inexperienced at direct combat.

"I know that I go with Zay," Tareena confirmed with a bit too much familiarity. Her crush on him was as obvious to Lukas as it was to Zay, but neither raised any complaints since it was a safe bet that she'd stick close to him in the heat of the moment.

"I'm with Daxa," Jake volunteered. He saw her calm demeanor as a help, since this was the first time he'd been out in the field to such a degree. He was, by nature, a saboteur, and one that wasn't so used to striking in broad daylight. The nature of Kabuto warfare was to slip in undetected and lay traps that the enemy would only discover upon the attempted use of their equipment. For him, it was nice to have someone to cover him at the very least.

"And I got you," Aiden said in a somewhat amused voice. Lukas didn't know what to make of it, but decided not to focus in. There was too much at stake for them to get lost in the individual quirks of the team. He clasped his hands together and shot the others an excited look.

"Alright," he told them. "Let's gear up and get ready. The show's about to begin!"

****

March 26th, 2085, 7:45 a.m.,

The sky was darkened over the Capitol as a cold gust shot through the streets of New York. Already, the long-tainted rainwater poured onto the gray and black of the city while its denizens walked and drove in all directions. Among the many socialites and businesspeople, the elite and the commoners alike, the commando team hurried to their positions. Ryan and Alan had done everything they could up to this point, and resolved to lay low in the hideout since their family was wanted by the State. None objected, and while they chose the safety of the desolate Jazz Museum of Harlem, Lyla chose to wade in the shadows of the city with her watchful eyes on the battle's developments.

Among the intel shared with the commando team was a list of vantage points that snipers would use, each one near one of the high-priority targets. Each target had been properly outfitted with three Kibaku-shuriken in the twenty days since they crossed the border and stood ready for demolition. Lukas ran through the list in his mind again. The old JFK New York Kennedy Airport, now a drone storehouse. Columbia Barracks, the main housing unit for the Troopers stationed within the city. The United Nations Headquarters building, which had been converted into a training facility for Scarlet Kingdom soldiers. The Dawn King Shrine on 5th Avenue, which housed the main engineering facility. Madison Square Garden, the primary motor pool. Then the Stock Exchange, still the control center for the value of their currency.

"Is everyone in position," Lukas asked from a narrow alley between Broadway and New Street.

“Can confirm,” Daxa said, “with eyes on JFK.” Her comms went silent, and with little hesitation, the others followed suit. Zayvier kept watch over Columbia, Jake on the Shrine, Aiden on the Garden, and Tareena on the UN Headquarters. All members of the team were present and accounted for.

“Acknowledged,” Lukas replied. “In position as well with eyes on the money. Verify readouts.”

“All good here,” Jake whispered into the channel with more excitement than nerves now.

“Same on this end,” Aiden offered.

“And mine,” said Zay. Lukas breathed a sigh of relief. Judging from the reports of the Yoroi Liberation op, the Kibaku-shuriken were powerful enough when grouped together to cause some serious damage. Grouping three shuriken together at a specific point on a building was almost certain to bring it down. Even if it wasn’t enough of a blast to cause destruction, chaos was sure to ensue regardless, and that was more or less the point.

“Oryu,” Lukas called as he patched through to the Director, “Commando Squad Gamma is in position and ready to go upon your order.”

“Light ‘em up,” John responded, and switched off the comms. The time had arrived.

****

The first building to fall was the Dawn King’s Shrine. A cloud of black smoke wrapped from 5th Avenue around to 56th. The powerful spire that commanded the respect of the city’s citizens wavered for a moment, then collapsed. Debris fell from on high as the people below scattered with screams stifled by the toxic air, and while Jake was enamored with the power of the Kibaku-shuriken, his heart sank to see what carnage they'd wrought.

He hurried along as people ran on all sides of him, and effortlessly blended into the crowd of people headed west and north and south. Before long, the second bomb had gone off with such a force that the ground beneath him quaked to the point that he imagined it would give. Smoke billowed up from the northwest. Columbia. Jake didn't want to think about it, all the bodies that would have been buried in the rubble or the blood that had been pressed out of them like the juice from a grape. The screams of the civilians was almost unbearable, and before long he felt himself yield to the overwhelming sense of fear in the air.

Another explosion rocked the city from the southeast and more black clouds formed over the former United Nations, though Jake struggled to distinguish what he saw from what he heard. He never imagined that doing his job could warp his senses as much as it did. The screams around him grew louder, and despite his attempts to change direction, to get away from the people, he couldn't. There was no escape.

A fourth detonation to the southwest, but closer to where he was. It was the Garden, and as much as Jake thought it impossible, the sounds of crumbled concrete and twisted metal nearly deafened the roar of the people, even as it sent more into flight. He resolved that the only thing he could do at this point was to seek asylum, to run back to the hideout as best he could. He fixed his attention to that, and ran northward for Harlem.

****

Something in Daxa felt relief at the chaotic picture painted in the backdrop of a cold New York rain. She didn't think about the people caught up in each blast, nor did she think about the buildings that would collapse on top of each other and themselves. She thought of her grandmother, who desperately sought shelter from the bombs dropped over Johnson City back in December. She thought of the last time she'd heard her say "I love you." She thought of the silent sobs that she couldn't suppress in the months that followed. It was relief that she felt, and it scared her to be so beside her nature.

She tried to maintain focus here, tried to give herself a moment to breathe since the start of all this, but she just couldn't. Each burst of fire, each scream from the citizens that now ran for their lives without a clue as to what was happening around them sent her back to that moment where the last of her family was vaporized before she had the chance to do anything about it. How was it that she could feel that nobody could deserve that treatment and yet feel so content at the Reds' losses at the same time? She wanted to stop herself, from savoring it, from feeling that relief, but she couldn't, and it made her wish for the end of this assignment all the more.

The sudden ring in her ears told her that the Stock Exchange had been dismantled, and that Lukas' part in this phase of the mission was over. Now it was just her turn. All she had to do was press the button on her wrist and then…

****

Bryan's eyes were glued to the window as he watched his city go up in smoke. Smithfield stood closer to the entrance to the Court chamber than he did to the King, whose behavior, he had noticed, had grown increasingly erratic. The ground rocked again from the Financial District.

"What the hell is going on," shouted the King over the empty room. King Shane clapped him on the back as a smug smile crossed his blackened lips.

"Your power is slipping," the corpse all but sang into the Mad Rabbit's ear. "You spent too much time trying to rub your new position in the faces of the poor bastards you thought wronged you that you didn't notice how fragile it actually is, did you?"

"Drones," Bryan whispered, then turned to face Smithfield as he walked through the specter of his predecessor. "Get the damn drones online!" Zachary scrambled with the pad in his hands, which only drew more irritation out of the King. "Now!" The panicked sole survivor of the Red Engineers tapped a final key, and just as another explosion rocked the foundations of the Empire State Building, flashes of silver could be seen amid the all-engrossing black.

****

"Come in, Kazeryu," Daxa urged with a desperation in her voice. Gunshots cracked in rapid fire through the air, and it was all she could do to grapple from building to building with the kyoketsu-shoge.

“Daxa,” Lukas answered, “what’s—”

“Drones!” she shouted in interruption as she spiraled out of the way of the latest shot that was trained on her. The group of drones was indiscriminate in its targeting, and pelted the streets below with a hail of bullets. It created a perpetual cycle of screams and silence and shots and screams and silence and there was no time to look down, to save anyone else, because the repulsors at her feet already did all they could to change direction midflight. “They have drones and they’re attacking everything!” That shouldn’t be possible. Cal all but hijacked the KDN months ago and there’d been no evidence that the Kingdom was able to take it back. How did they—

A massive explosion took the East Village and the sky lit up red. The drones were cascading to other places in the city. That meant that there was no time for excessive thought or extensive deliberation. They had to get in touch with Cal as quickly as possible, otherwise the commando unit and most of the population of the city would be done for. The entire team was on edge now. Cal didn’t answer. The mine locations must have had his full attention. Lukas sighed.

“Alright, Dax,” Lukas started up again, “hang tight a little while longer. Where are you right now?” Daxa was too frantic. A drone flew up beside her and trained its gun on her face, but a swift slice of the Reikiken sent it on a downward spiral to the ground below. She looked around for any kind of identifying landmark.

“Union Square, I think,” she offered. “The Flatiron building is just a few blocks away!”

"Okay, that's good," Lukas reassured her. "Dive into the city a bit more so it's easier for you to hide. You need to catch your breath. Aiden, I need you to head in that direction and give Dax some cover. I'll head on over, too."

"Okey pokey," Aiden said neutrally, and just like that they had a plan set. All there was left to do was do their best to survive until help could come.

****

"There's too much noise in the city," Vanessa growled. Clearly she was dissatisfied. "I'm going in—"

"You'll hold your ground," John told her firmly. "We aren't in any condition to charge in, and if they detect any movement on the outside we'll have hell to pay. We need to give Cal enough time to determine the exact location of each bomb. If we move carelessly, we'll end up with a bigger problem on our hands." She gritted her teeth. She knew that he was right, and would've made the same call if she'd stayed in the command center with Dre, but she was back in the field for the first time since the Johnson City Raid, and she still very much wanted blood for what had happened to Raven.

"How much longer do you think that'll be?" Her forceful tone made John raise an eyebrow, and she stiffened under his gaze.

"It shouldn't be too much longer. Dre's been feeding the intel to the other groups by the update and Cal should be making his rounds to the other side of the island soon," answered the Director. It was satisfactory, but barely. The sound of gunfire and explosions that continued after the initial strike proved worrisome, though. It wouldn't be too much longer for the others to bite the dust if they didn't move fast enough. She patched through to Cal. No answer. He was still undoubtedly focused on the recon aspect of his mission. Vanessa tapped her foot violently.

The Kageryu decided to focus her attention on the commando squad. Two of the current Dragons were inside the city, and both of them had been students under her observation at one point or another. She refused to allow them to die so easily.

"Lukas, Zay, come in," she ordered.

"We're here," Lukas responded with a quickness to his voice. "Drones are attacking the city. Jake and Tareena have made it back to the hideout with Master Peters, but Aiden and I are still in the thick of it." Under normal circumstances where the shock could be allowed to register, Vanessa would've deigned to inquire further.

"What about Yadav," Vanessa decided to ask. "Is she with you?"

"She's being pursued by the drones. We're on our way to her position now. We'll hit back once we've assured her safety," Lukas explained. Vanessa looked back over the city, now enveloped in a foreboding mixture of red and black, of smoke and fire.

"Be safe," she whispered, and then the comms went silent.

++++++++++++++++++++++++++++++++++++

Finally, the last mine location came through, which meant that Erik Kincaid and Johannes Thornhill could do what they'd been itching to do since the start.

"Alright, everyone," Kincaid barked through the Kabuto encrypted channel, "time to do what we do best!" Nothing else needed to be said. The Kabuto saboteurs had already taken their positions around the island, and now that they had the intel that they needed, they felt confident enough to move in. Broken into teams of three, they found the bombs, gently outfitted them with enough Shock Pads to short-circuit them, and communicated their tampering back to command. The Yoroi, led by Johannes Thornhill, performed the twofold duty of arraying a network of electromagnetic pulse devices around the edge of the island, and creating controlled explosions to lure Scarlet command into a false sense of security.

In much the same way, the Yoroi positioned themselves around the isle of Manhattan and detonated explosives of their own upon the completion of the preliminary tasks. Within an hour, the signal had been sent. The real game was about to begin.

****

Lukas spearheaded the charge to Daxa, and burst through the city's skyline like a torrential gale. He had to be careful of his footing. The rain that pelted the city only intensified, though not enough to put out the charred bodies on the floor of the concrete jungle. The repulsors fired on full blast, and as he moved, he came under a large metallic cloud. He grappled up with the kyoketsu-shoge and added to his speed with the power of his boots as he spiraled through their continuous rain of fire and metal. Within seconds he appeared above the drones and began an assault all his own. There was no threat here, and he was free to split his Reikibo back into the twin Reikiken that joined at their bases to make it. He sprinted now, every other step augmented by the force of the repulsors, and his two fireswords burned lines through the drones at either side of him.

Holes opened up in the artificial cloud as he destroyed one after another, and soon they devised evasive patterns of their own. Lukas had to wonder how they could, what with the demise of the Red engineers, but it didn't matter. He spun and deflected and dodged as gently as a flowing breeze, and in between it all he slashed with the bladed titanium whips at his wrists and lashed out with burning aura. A drone rocketed at him with unforgiving speed that would've shattered his bones in an instant, but Lukas had the foresight to bound off the back of yet another with the heat-treated chains and rocket boots in expert evasion. Before he could rebound with an attack, he noticed a pair of figures below him that were still far too out in the open. Fortunately, though, he had the full attention of the drones now.

"Aiden," Lukas wheezed through the comms. It was hard to breathe and fight and fly and talk all at the same time, but it was more than within Lukas' resolve to do. "Get her back to the hideout. I'll rendezvous when I can."

"I don't like this," Aiden started.

"It doesn't matter," Lukas almost yelled, then coughed enough to scare Daxa and Aiden both. "Get to safety as soon as you can, that's an order!" There was no further conversation. Daxa took the lead and Aiden followed suit as they dove for a side alley and rocketed back in the direction of the hideout, careful enough this time to move out of sight. Now Lukas could dive back in with the full intentionality with which he did everything else.

He pierced another of the drones as he leapt into the air and used the extended chain as a tether. He blasted from the repulsors as he arched his body. The other drones started to swarm, and with his Reikiken extended he carved through wave after wave of them. The heat of his twin swords slowly infected the circuitry of the death machines, and their behavior became more erratic by the second. Their targeting was off, their shape began to distort, and the more the closer ones tried to fire on the Kazeryu, the more they destroyed themselves. Their explosions caused the heat to surge, and while it stung Lukas through the protective layers of his Hanzo Gear, he didn't care. All he was concerned with was the safety of the people with him. Besides, every advantage was his.

It was easy, he thought, to see the parallels between his father and himself. Just as Manny had done for him back in December, Lukas stood as the last line of defense between enemy drones and his comrades. Thunder boomed overhead and reverberated through the metal figures that surrounded him. He thought of the moment he saw his father die. A flash of lightning burst across their steel hubs. Internally he screamed, the horror as fresh in his mind as it had been on the day his father was lost to him. Then, he realized that he would not be made such an easy sacrifice.

The young Wind Dragon crossed his ankles as the repulsor boots fired, and with the bladed chains at his wrists fully extended, he spiraled among the drones to carve an opening for his own escape. When it presented itself, he dove straight down through the city, whipped through the skyline, and planted a few Kibaku-shuriken along the way. The drones, at least those whose sensors hadn't been completely fried, followed him in earnest, almost out of a sense of desperate obligation. He was careful to lead them down pathways that they'd already carved, through carnage that had already been affected on the streets.

He pressed his wrist, and the remainder of the waves in this portion of the city that traveled along his flight path were caught up in a three-ringed blast that brought entire buildings down upon the mechanical squadron. The strain on his body was nearly too much to handle, but he knew he couldn't stop. Still he pressed onward towards the hideout. He couldn't take the time to admire his handiwork or engage anyone in a one-word story. He knew from the explosions on the outskirts of the island that the main forces were about to close in, and it was wisest to be on the outside of the battle when that happened. More than that, he knew that if he stopped now, he wouldn't have the energy to make it any further. *Forward,* he ordered himself. All he could do was keep his eyes focused forward.

****

Ryan had grown restless. The rumbling of the ground told him that the Capitol had already gone to hell in a handbasket and their team leader was nowhere to be found. Already he had experienced a range of emotions. He was surprised that the operation went off without much of a hitch. The locations that his father had pointed out to the insurgents went down easy enough, but now so had a quarter of the city's population. He experienced a rush when the bombs went off, a burst of adrenaline when the screams poured in, and waves of relief as each member of the commando team walked—or staggered—through the hideout's doors. Now, though, there was anxiety.

The door opened again to reveal Daxa, followed closely by Aiden. There was some relief, but greater tension. Never in Ryan's wildest dreams had he thought it possible to rebel against the Kingdom to this degree. A part of him had to wish that their little band of rebels pulled through, because if they went down then it was only a matter of time before he joined them.

"You guys alright," Alan asked as he approached. Daxa fell to her knees from pure exhaustion. "What's going on out there?" That's when it occurred to her. They didn't know.

"Drones are striking across the city," Lyla said as she entered the room from the rear. Every eye in the room shifted to her, and a mixture of awe, incredulity, and irritation swelled between them.

"What, you knew about this," Zay asked with a sudden dark strength to his voice that gave Lyla pause. It was clear to her that despite her help, she was still a traitor to them, and the treacherous daughter of a traitor at that. She had to be careful, lest she find herself on the outside of the hideout and in the thick of the conflict. "Speak. Now."

“If you’re wondering why I didn’t mention it before,” Lyla started quickly, “it’s because it wouldn’t have made a difference.”

“How the hell do you know that? You don’t just get to play with people’s lives like that,” Aiden said with more attitude than any of his teammates could have expected.

“This group of drones operates on an older network that hasn’t been used since the 2020s. They don’t even carry the same firepower as the KDN, but they can still be just as deadly,” she elaborated to the dissatisfaction of the others. Zayvier sucked his teeth in abject anger. He tried to restrain himself only because there was a time where Lyla trained with him and Bryan was seen as an uncle to all the kids in the Insurrection, but it was clear that his patience wore thin.

“Skip the history and tell us how to take it down,” Zay barked. She watched him, saw his hand twitch, felt the tension escalate for a moment as his arm drifted just that much closer to his Reikiken. She was in danger, and while she had every intention of putting him in the place she thought he would fit best, she allowed herself to listen to the wise little voice at the back of her mind.

“Alright,” she spoke slowly. “As it stands, there’s only two ways to do that. The first is by a manual override. The problem is, only one person in the Scarlet Kingdom has the power to do that, and he’s sitting in the palace next to the King right now.”

“Well that’s just lovely,” Tareena interjected with sarcasm in her voice and her hands on her hips. “So what’s the other option?”

"You'll have to take the drones out themselves," she clarified matter-of-factly. Ryan and Alan exchanged looks, both with a degree of severe determination on display. The former, who felt as though his newfound freedom from the Scarlet Kingdom was threatened, was determined to protect it with all his might. The latter, who watched his son go through a challenging metamorphosis, was determined to protect him as much as he could.

Ryan left the room to gather his equipment and was back before anyone could question him. He didn't stop, merely donned the look of a killer as he moved for the main entrance.

"Where are you going," came the timid voice of Jake Parrish from the corner. Ryan glanced back at him and felt pity. It wouldn't have been hard to believe that he'd never witnessed that kind of bloodletting before, and wondered how traumatic it must have been for him to go out into the field and fight. Knowing that Jake did that, even at the cost of his own peace of mind, only strengthened Ryan's resolve. He turned back to the door, a brilliant smile on his face as he strapped his holsters into place.

"To lighten the load," he told them. "Can't let that Bautista kid have all the fun."

****

The irony was not lost on Bryan, seeing the Scarlet Kingdom alight under a red sky. It was almost therapeutic for him to see everything burn that the pathetic wretch that sired him helped to build.

"You think I care about this miserable plot of land? About the spineless people that have taken me for all the goodness in my heart," the dead King asked. It was enough to provoke a laugh that made his face shift between what it had been in life and that of the undisputed worm food he had become.

"What is it that you want from me," Bryan demanded. He was sick of this old man popping up and dissipating whenever he felt like it. He wanted his son. He wanted to see the face of the reason he was here, why he did all this, but he was met instead with a crotchety old man long past his prime. The Dead King smiled a twisted smile at Bryan that sent chills through him.

"Can't an old man want to see the successes of his only worthy heir," asked the villainous specter as he placed a decayed hand upon Bryan's shoulder. The current King slapped it away in disgust. "Oh, come now. Do you really still believe that you're better than me?"

"I know I am," Bryan yelled back, and the demon king laughed hysterically.

"You're the same as I am, son," he countered, then pointed out the window at the city ablaze in darkness. "Look at the joy you felt at the destruction you brought about! Think about how you felt when you beat your old friend, when you had him at your mercy!"

"Shut the hell up, man," Bryan roared. "You don't know the first thing about me! The whole time I've been here I've been solely focused on my revenge!"

"So you didn't enjoy killing one of your new subjects in front of all the others?" Shane's question made

Bryan stumble. "You took no pleasure in shooting Cecelia in the shoulder or putting your mouthy daughter in her place?"

"I've only ever done what I had to do," Bryan defended. "I wouldn't expect someone who's been steeped in the life of luxury for so long—oh, I'm sorry—had been steeped in the life of luxury to know anything about duty and responsibility to others."

"Is that what you call it?" King Shane smiled a wicked smile, as it was not his voice that asked the question. It was a softer intonation, gentler, more concerned than angry but not without a quiet rage. Bryan turned around to the unchanged face of Director Emiko Ishikawa. He didn't know whether to cry or yell. "You think your son would approve of what you've done here?"

"What my son would or wouldn't approve of is none of your concern!" The volatility that he felt could hardly be summed up with just anger or rage or animosity or anything so weak as that. "You ordered my son to go on that mission. You, Emiko, offered him up like a lamb to the slaughter and I should've kept him from it but I let him go. You know why?" Emiko offered no response. "It's because I made the mistake of trusting you, and for what? You wanted to bring down the Kingdom but look! I've done more in a handful of months than you could manage in the years since your old man died! I've manipulated, maneuvered. I've killed more of them in just this one day than they could ever rebuild from, and there's more that I have in store, so just sit back, watch, and keep your judgments to yourself!"

"Sire?" There it was again, the trembling voice of Zachary Smithfield, who somehow managed to enter the Court chamber unnoticed. Bryan shook his head, his eyes wide and expression almost deranged. Smithfield couldn't recognize the man before him, and it terrified him. "Who were you talking to? What was that that I heard you say?"

"No," the Mad King said with authority, though this time Smithfield didn't back down. In one hand he held the controls to the entire Auxiliary Drone Network, and in a holster behind his back and under his lab coat, he held a gun. "You weren't supposed to hear that, Zach," the King raged. "You weren't supposed to—how many times have I told you to knock before you come in?"

"You just bragged about manipulating and killing our people! You're a traitor!"

"It's not what you think, Mr. Smithfield, I assure you," Bryan told him as he took a step forward, hands stuck in a placating gesture. "Why don't we take a moment to discuss this?" The servant pulled his gun from its place at the small of his back and aimed it at the King's forehead. It caught Bryan off guard, but it surprised him more than it upset him. Even so, his expression changed to a deep exhaustion. "Fine."

Smithfield, in a moment of panic, fired round after round into the room and watched in horror as the King sidestepped them with a series of bursts from his repulsor boots. He drew his Reikiken, dodged, rolled, leaped into the air, slashed with a swing so fluid it made the firesword look like lava on a slope from the mouth of a volcano. Zachary mouthed, but nothing came out as his upper body slid to the floor. Bryan stood there, saddened at what he'd had to do. A gentle hand met the space between his shoulders and slid up to where his shoulder met his neck.

Shane smiled a proud smile, something that Bryan assumed had never even been seen by James or Nash, and said in a low, primordial growl, “That’s my boy.”

Chapter Twenty-One

John was increasingly unsettled as he still hadn't heard back from Lukas. He knew that there was only so much time that he could afford to wait, and in truth they were already a little beyond their opportune window.

"John," Serenity started, but he shook his head. He didn't want to move. He couldn't, in good conscience, call down an airstrike on Manny's son. Not after what happened in Atlanta. "John!" Serenity refused to be ignored. He looked at her, a tormented wrench in his face as he did, and to his surprise there was understanding behind her eyes. "We have to move now." He paced the ground and wiped his hand down his face as he bit his lip.

"Dammit, I know," he said. After a moment's hesitation, he reached out to Cal over the comms. "It's time. Begin your aerial assault on the city."

"Roger that, Big Dawg," Cal responded with his usual calm, "but, uh, we got a bit of a situation."

"The drones," John replied, "I know. Take down as many of them as you can and proceed with the original plan."

"Yeah, that's the problem," Cal elucidated. "We got drones all over the sky. We won't be able to break through anytime soon."

"Alright, give me a minute," John bade him with a tinge of urgency. He shifted his attention to Serenity and told her the situation.

"So what do we do," she asked, her face now intense and grave.

"We have to proceed with a modified plan," John reasoned. "We need the Violent Sands and the Ballistics Units to head in and take down what drones they can from below. Darius will lead the remaining ground forces with his Elites. You're gonna coordinate your efforts with Zahara and Claire." The second name caught Serenity off guard.

"Claire?" Serenity asked. As if on cue, the strong, brunette, pearl-skinned Queen Waste Raider approached from behind.

"Did somebody call my name?" The sudden emergence of Claire's devious voice made Serenity uneasy, but comforted John. The former Scourge leader looked her over. Claire was dressed from head to toe in camouflage with strips of metal tied to it. On her back was an RPG, and in her hands was an AK-47. Serenity couldn't help but think that the Raider Queen was the sole embodiment of Florida before its destruction in 2045. She looked at John, who nodded in the Queen's direction while he reopened communications with Cal.

"Cal, listen. Your mission just gained another level of difficulty. Find a way to disable the drones. If you can't get them all, then clear out as many as you can." He continued his explanation of the modifications to the plan while Serenity filled Claire in.

"Oh, this sounds like fun," Claire spoke loudly as she leveled a wicked smile. "Hell yeah, I'm in!"

“You got it, Pops,” Cal assured him with a confidence that could only be described as “Cal’s.”

“Good,” John told him. “Get to work.”

****

Waste Raiders, Kabuto, Yoroi, and Yaiba gunmen formed up, then fanned out. There were more than a single entrance into New York City, and they intended to storm the Capitol with all their might. The orders were simple: find vantage points, climb them, take aim at the skyline, and blast away.

“Is everyone in position,” Zahara Boyd asked firmly, a tinge of pure joy in her voice. This was a moment that she’d always wanted to reach, and now that she was at the point of pure, open, unabashed rebellion against everything that the Kingdom stood for, it was hard for her to subject her feelings to the due degree of military bearing.

“Aye, aye, Captain,” Claire bolstered through the comms. “Waste Raiders and Yoroi are locked and loaded at the Lincoln Tunnel entrance!”

“Then let’s move in,” Serenity urged. The communication ended, the commanders of their respective groups got the message, and between the Lincoln and Holland Tunnels, insurgents flooded New York.

****

This was bad. Lukas only managed to get away for a moment before the drones found him and blasted his hiding spot to smithereens. He fought them off, but only barely before his body nearly gave out. He made it to the top of a skyscraper on 87th Street before he collapsed. The drones closed in on him, and though he tried to rise to his feet, his body was spent. All he could do was feel the rain as it fell upon him, listen to the roars of thunder as they faded into the dull hiss of rainwater that immediately evaporated on his Reikiken. A tear fell from his eyes as he realized that he'd probably never see Daxa again, and a strange comfort accompanied it when he realized that he would be with his father on the other side.

The whirrs of the machines grew louder as they grew closer. Lightning flashed across the city, and though his muscles demanded that he give up, Lukas rolled over onto his back and strained to sit up. He resolved that he wouldn't die like some coward getting shot in the back, but he'd face his death with dignity as his father had done months before. The line of drones that had followed him now made a circle around the roof to ensure that there was no escape. The Kazeryu inhaled sharply, exhaled, then smiled as the water from the sky dripped down over his visor. He watched as they closed in around him, slowly and methodically as if they could think for themselves, and dared to look down his nose at the weapons of a foe that even now he regarded as inferior. Then he noticed a literal ball, black in color and mysterious in origin, drop from above.

In another second, the ball flashed a brilliant blue that rivaled the shine of the lightning itself, and emitted a sound so deep and terrible that it pained Lukas to hear it. He pressed his ears tightly as his eyes closed on reflex, but earned little comfort from either gesture. He could feel the sound in his bones. When it finally dissipated, Lukas noticed that every drone within a mile's radius steadily lost functionality. He blinked, confused, then panicked as he was lifted into the sky by a completely different machine that was startlingly shaped like a man.

"A-yerrr!" The sound was such a relief to Lukas that he thought he would cry. He'd been rescued, and by one of Cal's Lightbeams, no less. "You doin' alright, there, man? You looked like you needed some help."

"Oh, well that was just a part of the trap," Lukas joked with the biggest smile on his face. "I had 'em right where I wanted 'em."

"Sure, man," Cal responded through the android's vocal outputs. "Hey, I'm about to get started with my mission so I'mma gonna drop you atcha hideout so you don't get hurt."

"Ah, thank you, brotha," Lukas sighed. He told Cal where to pilot the Lightbeam, watched as more drones broke apart, and thought about what he would say to Daxa and the rest of his team.

****

Ryan ran through the broken bodies and pools of blood, the rubble and shattered drones that filled the street. There were so many people still alive that cowered under whatever shelter they could find, and as much as he wanted to help with that, Ryan knew what his responsibility was. Once the commando unit had done their part and their allies disabled the mines, it was up to him and his fellow traitors to disable the major bomb. The drone strike on New York was hardly expected, but as far as problems went, he didn't think that it would be that detrimental to the mission at hand. He could only hope that the unholy alliance of the other factions had found their way of breaking through like they said they would.

For now, the hail of bullets had subsided, and more curiously the swarms of drones fell from the sky to the ground. Something was happening above the city skyline, but he couldn't tell what. It didn't matter. He had more than his hands full with the job ahead of him. Not to mention that as a sniper, he was at his greatest disadvantage with his feet on the ground.

A war cry sounded in the distance and gunfire thundered through the storm and streets. It seemed as though their allies found their way through, and made a point to occupy any vantage point they could to open fire on the sky. An explosion disrupted the rest of the assault from a spot relatively close to his position. He heard the maniacal laughter break the silence as a brown-haired woman with glasses and a wicked smile fired another RPG into the air. Ryan shook his head and decided to get out of the way before the drones she shot down fell on him. He made a mental note to figure out who she was after all this was over.

Ryan turned the corner of 10th and 19th, where he found a car with most of its functionality intact. He unloaded his equipment and got in himself. It would only be a few minutes to the World Trade Center where they kept the bomb. All he had to do was follow Hudson down and then he could figure out the rest from there.

****

Maxwell Cartwright stood in front of the bomb with his hands in his pockets and a gun on his hip. He didn't care about the noise outside or the people whose blood now ran through the streets. He didn't care that the main forces had been pulled into the palace save for Argus, Felix and him. He didn't even care that the enemy forces had apparently breeched the city's limits. All he cared about was the fact that it was the combined treachery of Lyla and Ryan that had brought about this unfortunate compilation of events.

It was no matter. He had listened in on their communications for a while now, and knew that at least one of them should be on his way to them. After all, the bomb that the elegant spy eyed at present was as deadly as the pools of soldiers that joined together to flood the streets. The King had given them the order to protect it at all costs, and that was what Cartwright intended to do. Albeit, he would use it as bait first to flush out the traitors so that he could deal with them personally.

"Look sharp," warned Cecelia Kant, the newest member of the Scarlet Streaks and former muscle of the Scourge. "Sole transport inbound. It's him."

"Roger that," Felix sang into the comms. Cartwright could never tell what that one was thinking, and felt as though he'd put a bullet in him once things died down. He was a little too dangerously uncouth for Maxwell's taste.

"Keep your eyes on him and let me know when he enters the building but do not engage," ordered the spy. "I'll handle him myself." He didn't wait for her response. He simply clasped his hands behind his back and stared into the black surface of the bomb, ready for the battle to come.

****

King Bryan sat in his throne and looked excitedly out the window at the city around him as it threw itself into battle. He was beyond satisfied, overjoyed, even, that the citizens had been caught up in the chaos. They were meat shields that his troops could use to exploit the consciences of his enemies, and if they didn't, they'd die themselves. He wondered how long it would take John and the others to realize he'd already given the order for his army to deploy. It would only take them a few more minutes to prepare.

"What's missing, Bryan," Emiko asked him, much to his chagrin. He checked his tablet.

"The bombs," he realized. So many explosions had gone off around New York that he'd just assumed that some were his own. The report in front of his face proved him wrong. If the bombs never went off…

"It's only a matter of time before they come for you," Emiko completed. He looked at her, her mouth still stained with her own blood, her chest still a black and smoldering hole from her fight with Serafina. She looked at him and smiled with her cold, dead eyes.

"Run," said Smithfield, sympathy still in his eyes despite the gunshot wound in his head. "The Kingdom mustn't fall!"

"To hell with that plan," Shane spat, then placed a hand upon Bryan's back. Bryan took note of how comforted he felt by the gesture, and how much disgust he felt by the comfort. “Every Red King has stood their ground and fought. Are you a King?”

“Dad,” Jaden spoke before an answer could be offered, “you’re not gonna leave me, are you?” Bryan looked at his boy, the only one who still looked as he had in life, and smiled as a tear streaked his cheek.

“Of course not,” he whispered, then closed his eyes and took deep breaths. “Things are only just getting interesting.”

****

Mikki Sommerfield and Tony Landry were placed in charge of the evacuation effort, or rather it was to defend the evacuees from whatever fighting might take place. Hank Davis kept back at the entrance of the Lincoln Tunnel in Weehawken while Johannes Thornhill and Ezequiel Vargas worked in tandem with Nash O’Neill in an elaborate relay. Nash, as the former Prince, was their immediate establishment of credibility with whatever survivors were left in the city. He drove through the island with his subordinates and pointed them in the direction of the evacuation point.

Before long, people flooded the tunnel and Hank, with a team of Waste Raider noncombatants under his control, surveyed the new arrivals and got to work in the treatment of their injuries.

“This is awful,” Nash spoke broken-heartedly. For all of the misgivings he’d developed since his departure from the Kingdom, this was still very much his home. He grew up here, the laughter of children and the gripes of the elderly fresh in his ears, but now the only thing he heard was gunfire, barked orders, and the unsettling sticking sound of wheels as they drove through so much blood.

"It'll get a lot worse if we don't get the survivors to safety," Tony reminded him. The drones weren't as plentiful, but still patrolled the skies above New York with menacing presence. Tony knew they had a limited amount of time to work. They needed to get as many people out as they could, but they only had access to two tunnels to the other side. Even with the reduced population, there were still more than a few million people that would need to be evacuated. Tony gritted their teeth. They weren't sure how something like that could be done, which was why Nash was the one making his presence known. "Just keep bringing them our way and we'll do the rest."

"I'm on it," Nash replied. He and his troops shouted out in the hopes that some would respond to the promise of sanctuary, but few did. A lot more were too scared or too in shock to move around at all, and given the current state of things, Nash couldn't blame them at all. He opened his mouth to call out again when a rhythmic thunder pulsed through the air and ground. He knew it better than anyone else would, save for the men and women that followed him even now.

"Nash, what is that," Mikki asked with a tinge of worry in her voice. Nash released a breath he didn't know he held upon realization of the question.

"Soldiers," Thornhill told her. "Shifting to Operation Caravan. We'll hold them off as much as we can but there's a chance they'll be on their way to you soon. Be on your guard."

Mikki donned a half-cocky, half-nervous grin that reeked of her mother's influence as she said, "Finally, the moment I've been waiting for." She pressed a button on her hip and a light flashed on her forehead. Tony did the same, and with an exchange of looks they pulled out a pair of sai from twin sheaths on their hips. They'd learned that the sai were more than just melee weapons. Each one was equipped with a neurotransmitter device that plugged into most standard issue comms units. That neurotransmitter would convey the intended movements of the user through an air propulsion system in the hilt that allows for omni-directional movement of the weapon. The fact that they were heat-treated like the kyoketsu-shoge meant that they could withstand the use of a Shadow or a Sand.

It surprised Tony that they were excited for the possibility of combat against the Reds, and they didn't know whether it was because they wanted revenge for what had happened in the Yoroi Alliance months ago, or if it was because they'd been given a new toy to play with. Whatever the case, they opted to get their emotions in check. Right now, the most important thing to do was follow the plan and get the civilians to safety.

"Get ready," Mikki said as the sai in her hands fluttered to life and circled around her. "They're coming."

****

Ezequiel Vargas thought himself more of a diplomat. He was shrewd, stern, and typically unwavering unless someone presented an airtight argument that he couldn't outmaneuver. His battles were typically fought on a more intellectual terrain. That wasn't to say that he couldn't fight, however. The enemy emerged from 23rd and flanked them on the left side, and it was Vargas who spotted them and opened fire first. He thought back to his time fighting in the early days of the Yoroi Alliance and suddenly remembered the rush that he'd felt back then. A muted smile took to his face as the enemy struck back, and he and a small squad moved to break off from the main caravan to deal with them.

"Wait," Johannes Thornhill told him as he reached out a hand and pulled the elder back by the shoulder. Vargas turned and looked at the former envoy and freshest of the Council Members. He remembered the day that Johannes was born, how happy his father had been to parade him through the Clusters and teach him about the society that had welcomed him with open arms. He remembered taking Johannes under his wing when his father died in a demolitions accident and teaching him how to be a politician. Now, the same eyes that at one time looked at Ezequiel with unquestioned admiration looked upon him with deep dread.

"I'll be fine," the aged Ambassador reassured his former protégé, and pat the boy's cheek with a smile. "Mind your position and protect the innocent. That is our purpose here, my young friend." Before Johannes could reply, the Ambassador left their transport and joined up with his much younger squad.

Vargas took his position at the center of the formation while his soldiers volleyed with the enemy. They moved for cover behind a few trucks, and while two of their number fell to the enemy fire, the rest managed to get into position. More Scarlet Troopers emerged from all sides, clearly aware of their numbers advantage. The Yoroi Ambassador ducked as a bullet rocketed for him. He narrowly dodged, and only in the moment after a clear near-death experience did he feel alive for the first time since his ascension to power.

"Mind our flanks," Vargas commanded as he pulled two spherical objects out from the bag at his hip. He pulled the lynchpins with his teeth and tossed them at the growing crowd of enemies. He watched as a bullet split one of the projectiles and the entire western platoon was flash-frozen. Clouds of bullets emerged from the north and south as two more platoons sprinted towards their positions. "Hold steady," Vargas ordered with more passion in his voice than he'd heard in a long time.

They did as commanded, until another of his squad was picked off by enemy fire. He shoved a few Kibaku-shuriken into the hand of the soldier nearest him while he took two more of the Fuyukibaku and launched them in the opposite direction. The opposition shot the ice explosives long before they reached them, no doubt aware of what they would do, and pressed an advance. Vargas gritted his teeth. He returned focus to his firearm, and picked a few enemies off as he stood up to move.

He managed one step before his shoulder burned and a slickness took his arm in a way much more alarming than sweat. He'd been shot, and much to his displeasure, the bullet knocked him unceremoniously to the ground. There wasn't time for him to get back up, no time for him to fight back. His mind scrambled for what to do, because surely there had to be some solution, but then the last of his team was gunned down. Vargas bit his lip and cursed under his breath as he fumbled over some Kibaku-shuriken in his pack. He changed their settings from manual detonation to timed and launched them all over the area. He mouthed a prayer as the footsteps of his enemies grew louder in his ears and patiently awaited their arrival with a kind of peace that can only come from an insurmountable feeling of satisfaction with one's life.

The Scarlet Troopers gathered around the scene, and while they noted that Vargas was still alive, they paid him little mind. He was, in their eyes, little more than a frail old man who joined up with the wrong side. It was when they attempted to reach their command that they realized—for a split second—how wrong they'd been about him. The shuriken erupted in a ground-shaking explosion, and with his eyes closed and a bright smile, Ezequiel Vargas welcomed the end of a life well-lived.

****

Serenity smiled. Her back was quite literally against a wall as a number of her old infantry subordinates hunted her through the city. She let them chase her up to the Weiss Building, allowed them to believe for a moment that they'd had her cornered, even put on a bit of a show.

"Please," she pleaded with a fearful shake in her voice, "I have intel! I can tell you what the plans are for the capitol!"

"Well by all means," came the condescending voice of First Lieutenant Chase Gallaher, Serenity's former right hand. "Tell us what you know and we can have it dealt with." It took everything in her to ignore the smugness in his tone and expression. Something about it just made her feel as if she needed to remind him of his place. But she didn't. She merely sank to her knees as he approached her with a look of twisted joy on his face.

"Please," Serenity begged again, and let a tear streak down the side of her face. Gallaher dried it, softened his expression, and relished in the superiority that he finally got to lord over her.

"Shhh," he whispered as he stroked the side of her face. She didn't even bother to flinch under his touch. "It's going to be alright, just tell me what you know. If it's good enough intel, I might let you…live a little." Serenity knew that he propositioned her, and while her initial response was disgust and abject horror, she masked it and merely opened her mouth to speak.

"I—" she started, but before she could finish, his head exploded and her face was covered in a mix of his blood and gray matter. The enemy troops, stunned for a moment, suddenly came alive and aimed for her with disdain in their eyes. She launched her kyoketsu-shoge into the air and grappled up to one of the higher floors of the Weiss Building before she dropped a series of Shock Pads down all over her pursuers. "Code 1642, engage," she whispered, and when she heard the electrified shrieks of the Troopers below, she dropped a few Kibaku-shuriken onto them for good measure.

"I knew it," James all but hissed through the comms. "I knew that that slimeball Gallaher always wanted you, and in no savory manner at that."

"James, what do you think you're doing," Serenity replied all too calmly as she ran through the polished interior of the aged building. "These channels are reserved for combatants and combatants only." She was not amused with him, but at the same time she was.

"Well then it seems that I'm on the right line since I just saved you from what could've been a truly terrifying liaison with your former lackey." Serenity halted in her tracks and blinked in a stunned confusion.

"Wait, you mean to say that you took that shot?" She didn't know whether to be proud or deeply concerned that he was on the battlefield. "How the hell did you even get here? And what do you mean, 'saved me?' As if I needed any help."

"I didn't ask permission, if that's what you're asking, and by the looks of things you definitely needed mine!" She shook her head as she made for the World Trade Center.

"It was supposed to look like that, James, I was working them into a false sense of security! I've done it a thousand times," she explained rather loudly into the comms.

"Well I'm sorry for wanting to have my wife's best interest at heart!" Both of them fell silent as she broke through the glass and joined him as he sprinted along the rooftops. They'd never really discussed the possibility of marriage, and the only future they'd talked about up to this point was simply being together with no such formalities. Serenity in particular had never envisioned herself as the kind of person who would settle down or get married or have children, but James' obvious verbal blunder had suddenly changed all that.

"You said 'wife'…" She shook her head. That wasn't the topic right now and she had plenty more questions. "We'll come back to that later. Right now I want to know who in the blue hell let you loose with a sniper rifle."

"That would be me," bragged Claire Sommerfield. "You know how many of those things we have lying around? Shotguns, sniper rifles, AKs, hunting rifles, grenade launchers, RPGs, and so much more!" Serenity and James both felt as if she sounded like a crude saleswoman.

"He's never been trained for combat, Claire," Serenity informed her, and the Raider Queen burst into laughter.

"Oh, you mean you lied to me to get your hands on a gun and start spraying people? How very American of you," Claire jibed happily. "Next thing you know, you're gonna tell me you love it more than children!"

"Look, we'll talk about this later," Serenity growled, and Claire made a mental note to spy on that conversation later. "Right now I'm moving in on 4 WTC and could use some backup. James, rendezvous with me on top of the Four Seasons, downtown and we'll work out a plan."

"Sounds good," he agreed, and when the comms went silent, he breathed a sigh of relief.

****

John's heart pounded as the time drew near. The drones, while fewer now, still encircled the city as black smoke billowed upward. Every now and again, people would emerge from the Holland Tunnel, some bloody and wounded, others hard of breath. Hank Davis and his team diligently worked to provide relief to the refugees, but even with that working as well as it could, John still stood anxiously by the Hudson shore in Jersey City.

"Cal, Johannes, come in," John called through the comms network. "What's taking so long?"

"Scarlet troops have begun their attack on our forces. Civilian presence isn't enough to slow them down so we switched to Operation Caravan. We… we lost Vargas," Johannes informed. The news stunned John for a moment, because while he never really thought much of Ezequiel, he knew that the old bastard was a tougher man than most would have given him credit for. He could admit with confident sadness that it was a pain to lose him.

"What about the drones, Cal?"

"They don't work like the other ones," the Wood Dragon responded. "They got some kinda manual control mechanism so I can't just hack 'em and move in like before."

"So you'll have to destroy them all," John realized out loud. Time was drawing near. Without the support of the ground troops, it would be hard for the Ballistic Units to hold off the Reds all on their own, and the drones created enough of a buffer to render Cal's support veritably useless at the moment. "Then it looks like we have no choice. Hold the line for as long as you can."

"What are you planning to do, John," Johannes asked in a loud voice as more gunfire thundered through the air. John balled his fists tightly by his side.

"We're deploying the main forces," he answered with a low dragonic hum. He turned his back to the city, and with a nod to his established team, he moved deeper into the crowd.

****

Bryan couldn't help but feel the tension rise. His armies had been released into the streets, his drones dominated the skies above, and the city smoked with a kind of life that this Kingdom hadn't known for quite some time. He should've felt victorious, should've relished in the upper hand that came with a homefield advantage, but the mere fact that John was on the opposing team gave him pause.

The King and the Director had always made quite the pair. They'd liberated a number of bases and cities from Red occupation back in the days of King Shane, so the Mad Rabbit was well acquainted with his old friend's ability to strategize, just as John was with Bryan's improvisation skills. Whenever they fought in the past, though, it was always that strategic mind that reigned supreme, and it was that genius-level intellect that tensed Bryan's every muscle even when he knew that all he had to do was flip the switch to the massive bomb.

For a moment he considered it. It would really cost him nothing at this point to set it off and blow the Scarlet capitol sky high, but for the life of him he couldn't see the fun in that. He still had a plan to make John witness the death of his beloved son, to watch as the former Lightning Dragon's face twisted with insurmountable pain. If he blew them all up, there was no way to satisfy that plan. No, this situation called for a different kind of solution. King Bryan unholstered his Reikiken and watched as orange life breathed into it. He looked at the window to the Court Chamber sadistically, and slashed a diagonal into it before he jumped out into the dark sky.

It was time for the King to lead the charge himself.

Chapter Twenty-Two

Darius sprinted into the heart of the city as his forces followed closely behind. He'd already given marching orders to his subordinates in the Violent Sands, and while he knew them all to be capable warriors, he worried for them. He trained them, yes, but part of being a good Sensei was understanding what strengths and weaknesses one's students had. Darius knew that a major strength of theirs was their ability to work together. He didn't know how they would fair individually, but the one time they split up during an operation, Ina died.

Now was hardly the time to focus on that, though. This was war, and casualties were an expectation. If he was going to survive it, then it was imperative that he stow his emotions in the back of his mind and focus on the mission. Bobbi took the northern part of the island and had orders to protect the commando team hideout while her forces split focus between defense and evacuation of the area. Leroy took to the east to assist Nash's convoy with his forces, while Lex headed south to provide support to the bulk of Serenity's forces.

Darius would stick to the central part, and while he wouldn't be the one to storm the palace, he would provide the main opposition to the Red soldiers scattered throughout the streets. He lifted a war cry, and his troops did the same as they saw their enemy approach from the other side of 47th. Bullets began to fly, and while many of the Coalition soldiers vaulted to the walls of nearby buildings with their kyoketsu-shoge and repulsors, the wave of projectiles met the grounded troops at various parts of their bodies. Before the Reds could take pleasure in their minute victory, chains rattled as the blades at their front ends were launched all over. A few of the Red troops dodged, only to be met with the swift heat of a Reikiken or the cold steel of a katana.

Darius waited for his moment to properly engage, and took to a vantage point with Al, his apprentice.

"What do we do now," Al asked. There was something strange about his voice, as if there was a heightened sense of worry or uncertainty. It made sense for him to be conflicted in an assault on his homeland, but there was a determination in his eyes that told Darius what he needed to know. His anger had already taken hold.

"What we practiced," was all Darius offered in the way of clarity. "Which position would you like?" Al's eyes brightened as a borderline sinister smile took his jawline by storm.

"You know I work best when I can fly, Sensei," he said with a boyish chuckle. It was enough to unnerve Darius, that Al thought of war and espionage as some sort of elaborate game, but he resolved to recommend him for therapy once all the fighting was over and done with. Lord knew he would need it.

"That's fine by me," the Neo-Fire Dragon commented in his best neutral tone. "Just make sure you can keep up." The challenge was more playful than Darius typically was, and definitely more so than he had expected it to be. Without looking back at Al, he descended into the fray.

****

Darius moved like a flash of light through the enemies that were left, and his swift movements on the ground helped to relieve his struggling allies a bit. It wasn't much, but it was a noticeable change. Red light flashed along the street just before he could plant his foot on the sidewalk, and he blasted himself into a nearby alley with the full force of his repulsors. The shine faded, and upon his reemergence he tossed a few Kibaku-shuriken into the air where a small cloud of miniature drones could be seen forming. They hit their mark as effortlessly as he breathed, and with a slight tap to his wrist the metal stars exploded in a brilliant array.

"EMPs," Darius called to whichever suppliers were near, and without a word they tossed a wave of black disks towards the highest concentration of Scarlet Troopers. A few more enemy troops deployed the drones from their Thunderclaps, but before they could get very far, Darius and company executed the pulse command and stripped them of their power. They were useless, and Darius had as much of an opening as he needed. He charged straight forward, Reikiken drawn and ready. Bullets flew in his direction, but he spun off their trajectory with a burst of his boots and bounded up to the wall just as another explosive cloud flew at him.

He ran along the wall, cut through one of the Scarlet Dogs as he went, and flipped back to the ground in the middle of their formation. The sum of two-hundred enemy troops gasped in surprise as they trained their weapons on him. He smiled at them.

"You're surrounded," said their commander. "In the name of King Bryan and the Scarlet Kingdom, we demand your surrender!" Darius tightened the grip on his Reikiken.

"No, thanks," he replied with a smug look on his face. His heart pounded with an excitement that he'd never known. An image of his father flashed in his mind, and for a moment he wondered if the rumors of his exploits in Johnson City were true.

"Fire!" The commander's shout was well-received by his soldiers, who rapidly sprayed in Darius' direction from all angles. Darius, upon the utterance of the command, threw down a smoke bomb and ducked below their previous line of fire. He slashed out with his kyoketsu-shoge and whipped it in a circle. The first wave of soldiers fell beneath the cloud of smoke. He recalled the chain, and from a crouched position sliced wherever he saw a flash of light. One by one, the sound of metal against the concrete echoed alongside the shrinking boom of gunfire until, eventually, there was none left.

The smoke cleared to reveal the Hiryu back at the center of the formation and all of the enemy's rifles melted in two. There was a moment of confusion among them as some of them wondered if he was even real. Then, one by one, they pulled out their Thunderclaps and steeled themselves for battle. Darius' smile grew wider.

"Now this is more like it," he laughed. He pulled his free hand up to his shoulder and extended his index and middle fingers upward as his Reikiken slid along the ground towards his open side. The enemy fighters roared with their blades uplifted, none the wiser that they pressed on into his mode of expertise.

****

Leroy was more than a little annoyed. There was a wall of enemies between him and his objective, and while it was expected that the Scarlet Capitol would teem with enemy life, he still hoped it would have been easier than this. His soldiers ran ahead of him while he grappled from building to building towards the southern part of Manhattan.

"Almost there," Bill Jerrick came over the comms. He was excessively upbeat, but it wasn't difficult to imagine why. This taking of New York had been little more than a dream for so long, and now they lived it. Leroy figured that it would've been hard to suppress that kind of excitement. He, on the other hand, hardly cared. He just wanted to go back home and lay down in his bed. "Enemies inbound." The statement jolted Leroy from his fantasies of relaxation and forced a groan from the pit of his belly.

"Come on," he complained, "we just finished like a hundred of these guys." Bill laughed, much to the continued irritation of his Yoroi companion.

"It won't be too much longer. We're almost there," the Lightning Dragon comforted. Leroy refused to be assuaged, and resolved to exercise his anger on the enemies below. He dove from the upper levels of the city into the midst of the oncoming Troopers. He flipped forward and blasted his repulsor boots to cushion the landing, and the flames of the repulsors met with the face of one of his enemies only seconds before his boot did. As the man beneath his foot died, he blasted off of his face and flipped back into the air as he pulled the EMP pucks from the pack at his hip. They aimed for him, but before any of them could fire the first shot, Bill charged them from the front.

The Rairyu adapted to the form as seamlessly as John had, and stepped in tandem with the flow of the storm above. He stabbed, spun off the center line, cut at a diagonal, then pivoted with the grace of the Angel of Death as he split someone at the hips. He pulled his leg back as he turned and cut down through someone's skull. Suddenly, the entire formation of the enemy company focused on just the one man. Leroy grappled to another wall, bounded from it, then landed at the back of the formation. He stood with his hands wrapped around the Reikiken he had lifted over his head, and just as the first soldier at the rear noticed him, he cleaved down with a force that quaked as thunder.

Leroy countered the flow of energy as he stepped forward and split the next person up the middle. He spun the firesword over his head as he turned around and stabbed to the rear, then whipped it from the fallen soldier's skull in a wide arc that dismembered four people at once. The Lightning Dragon and the Haboob struck the enemy down from two directions until they met in the middle, nodded, and moved on with the mission.

"Alright, I admit that that was fun," Leroy said as they took to the rooftops again. "I still wanna go home, though." Bill cracked a smile.

"You're such a party pooper—"

"And damn proud of it," Leroy interrupted, then bounded ahead with a massive smile.

****

Lex Ford ripped his way through the city with no conversation. His strong style was more than what the enemy could handle, and somehow he'd managed to make it more aggressive than the others in his company would've expected possible. He ran ahead of the pack, not as concerned about his mission to support Serenity as he was steeped in the rush of battle. He tossed a round of Kibaku-shuriken into the oncoming crowd of Scarlets, and when they fell to the ground he slashed the midsections of the next wave, spun through their line, and cleaved down hard onto the head of an unsuspecting foe.

He whipped to one side and lopped off a man's head, then revolved around the body to slam his firesword down upon the head of another pursuant assailant. He tossed a smoke bomb into the face of another on-comer that violently exploded on impact. There was a cry of alarm from his sea of enemies that turned into a unified shriek of pain and suffering as the chains at his wrists rattled and slashed through the lot of them. Before long, he bolted down the road again and sprinted to the mark.

A burst of light whizzed past his head, and driven by instinct alone he blasted himself with just the force of his repulsors through the air and up to a nearby rooftop. He tossed EMP pucks of his own and activated them mid-descent. An array of silver orbs fell to the ground, and the enemies were forced to rely solely on their firearms. Lex, with his bright smile still firmly affixed to his face, sprinted and leaped from rooftop to rooftop, grappled up walls, and returned the gunfire with more shuriken.

The remote detonation of the shuriken was closely followed up by the arrival of his battalion, and before the remaining enemies could reorient themselves on Lex, they were struck down and their target was left free to move. As he approached the roof of the Museum of Ice Cream, Lex noted the sudden deployment of an RPG aimed squarely at the drones above. The projectile met its mark, and metal fell from the sky alongside the rain. It was enough to pique Ford's interest.

Before he could speak, the woman who held the rocket launcher looked over her weapon-outfitted shoulder with a look in her eye so cold that his feet were frozen in place.

"Who the hell are you," she asked brusquely. Lex raised his eyebrows as the corner of his mouth ticked up into a cool smirk.

"Lex Ford, Hamsin of the Violent Sands," he answered. "They sent me here to help you hold the line." He understood her to be the crafty and uncouth Queen Raider Claire Sommerfield, and was delighted to see that the stories of her bluntness and otherwise prickly personality were true. She smiled back at him, but something about it made him feel a little nervous.

"Thanks," she offered, "but we got this covered. Khursi!" All she did was call the name, and a young man that was more muscle than anything appeared behind her, as if he had been waiting for his moment in the sun. "Maul 'em." The phrase made Lex glance over to her incredulously, but he found himself more interested in what the young brute might do. His eyes drifted back over to Khursi, who smiled with an almost childish delight.

"Yes, Ms. Sommerfield," he yelled with enough deep enthusiasm to unnerve Lex. The bear of a young man jumped down to the ground and only used the kyoketsu-shoge he'd been outfitted with to slide ingloriously down the building's side. The moment his feet touched the ground, he clapped and looked up with his arms spread, only to catch the bazooka that his comrades had already dropped to him. He slung the heavy gun onto his shoulder like it was nothing, and when he noticed that it was preloaded with ammunition, he fired the rocket into the crowd of enemies.

Fire and smoke took hold of the city yet again, and Khursi took cover behind a large chunk of a broken building as the blowback of the explosion rippled out. He emerged and sprinted ahead, screaming like an overzealous child all the while, until a bullet from one of the overpassing drones dropped straight through his skull and he crumpled to the ground. Lex cut his eyes at Claire, who simply stood there with her arms slightly raised and a mildly agitated expression locked in place.

“Aright, alright, fine,” she said as a poorly-timed smile crept across Lex’s jaw. “I guess we could use some backup.”

“My troops are already at work in the surrounding area. All you need to do is keep knocking those out of the sky,” Lex replied with a chuckle as he pointed at the drones. Before she could offer a response, he jumped down from the rooftop and back into the battlefield below, determined to lay waste to as much as he could.

****

Bobbi Brynarr was level-headed. She was always the voice of reason, if not a somewhat timid one, and always sought what was best for the people around her. She was a motherly figure to many, despite the fact that she wasn’t old enough to be that for half of them, and a sister to most of the people she knew in the Yoroi Alliance. Today, though, here, she was none of that. As she blasted through the streets of New York with fire almost quite literally in the palm of her hands, she couldn't help but think about what it was like in the Clusters during the Anti-Rebellion Crisis. Friends turned on each other, family became enemies, and war broke out in a place that had always proved impervious to such barbarism, and all this because of the people that lived here in the capitol.

Her troops were more on the stealthy side than anyone else's, and resolved to lurk the shadows of the northern parts of Manhattan. They mined the area surrounding the commando unit hideout with a string of explosives, EMPs, smoke bombs, and Shock Pads, and waited on the rooftops throughout Harlem. It would only be a matter of time before the battalions of the Scarlet military moved northward, and when that time came, Bobbi had no doubts that they wouldn't need to raise a finger.

****

Deflection, then reposition. Downward parry into another enemy's leg. Head block, rolling parry, slash to the chest. Darius moved through enemies as a gentle breeze, and somewhere along the way, he lost himself in the tranquility of the movements despite the tumult of the battlefield. The moment one group fell, more would take their place, and the cycle would begin anew. Block the shoulder, then the leg. Parry upward, then flourish down into a block at the midsection.

It didn't take long for the Reds to figure out that they could attack him all at once, but when they all moved in to close off his movements, they realized a lot faster that he would shift his slowed pace to a much more erratic series of attacks. Slash to the face through another person's chest, change direction, cut down and flip. Swing up on the full revolution, block shoulder, snap into a head strike. Block head, spin under the connected blades, run the enemy through. Pull back, punch a hole in the enemy to the rear. Spin out of the move and plant feet with weapon hand fully extended and free hand raised above the head.

The Hiryu style was characterized by unpredictable offense, but done in such a way that the other styles of Yaiba swordsmanship could be seen as fully on display. Darius found that the easiest way to accomplish this was to rely on his strengths with his nigh-impregnable defenses, and switch to offensive measures taken from the other six styles. He found it to be freeing, as Hiryu was a vessel of his own personal expression.

The next wave rushed at him, and the former Rebel Dragon snapped his fingers twice. The show was about to begin.

****

Al read the signal loud and clear, and without a moment's hesitation, he dove into the battle alongside his master. His heart pounded inside him as his body spun once—twice—three times in the air with the firesword warped around him like an infernal ring. The former Trojan Horse landed, and though his bodily trajectory suggested that he would cut straight down, he somehow managed to cut out in a wide horizontal arc. Six enemies dropped from the single slash, then he reversed the flow of the blade to take down three more. A rather large enemy charged the apprentice senselessly, only for Al to vault back with a spin that carried his aura sword through his attacker's legs.

Just as another man sprinted for the boy, Darius did the same and blasted forward as he jumped slightly through the air. His back glided over that of his hunched over pupil, and the Master Dragon skillfully blocked the enemy with ease. He applied pressure to put his opponent on the defensive, then relaxed the pressure for an easy cut.

"Al, did you catch that," he shouted over the screams of the freshly downed foe. "Acrobatics is good and fine, but you need to diversify your move set a bit more if you really want to be effective." It was in this moment that Al could see how truly impressive Darius was, and was more than a little excited to have been matched with such a capable Master. He tightened his grip on his Reikiken and turned his attention back to the enemies as they swarmed.

"Yes, Sensei," Al shouted back as he dove into another line of enemies. He leaped into the air and slashed twice in a successful attempt to disarm and behead two incoming adversaries. The moment his feet touched the ground, he quickly moved his blade and body in a circle to deflect a series of blades, then jumped in one direction with a swift stab. While his body was still in the air, he twisted his torso to the rear and stabbed another overly excited enemy in the face. He retracted his blade, then spun through the air to hit a perfect Falling Leaf. His enemy crumbled before him, and before long he was able to match the fluid pace of the Dragon that led him.

In another moment, the two hundred soldiers that sought to block their path thinned to a mere dozen, and it was at that moment that Al spotted the strong, shadowy figure of a man in red clothing. Al blinked. His eyes closed to the ominous figure, and opened to see the King's face as clear as day, only inches away from his face. King Bryan looked mad, a disturbed smile from ear to ear across his jaw as he wound his Reikiken—now alight—for a decapitating slash.

A hand pulled the boy back only a second before the enemy's blade could rip through his neck, and Al hadn't even realized what had happened until he watched the hot orange light pass in front of him. By the time the image registered in his mind, Darius stood in front of him with his weapon arm above his head, his body angled low, and his free hand extended in front of him.

"That's my nephew," King Bryan growled, "reflexes as quick as his father's lightning. I have to say, I didn't expect you to come visit me."

"Yeah, well," Darius started, his eyes serious, his heart aflutter, his mind overtaken with a wave of mixed understandings and emotions and an overwhelming desire for something different but the steep realization that it was what it was, "It's not exactly a social call." He had so many questions he wanted to ask, but he knew that they would be a waste of time. One look in his eyes and Darius knew that the man who had been his uncle was gone. He exhaled with full resolve while Bryan smiled an unbelieving smile.

"Don't tell me you intend to fight me," said the King with the beginnings of a mocking tone. "All the trouble I stir up and they send a child after me? This is pathetic."

"Hey, I'm not a child," Darius argued. "I wasn't one when you left, and I damn sure am not now." The fire in his voice got Bryan's attention. The Darius of old would've been too scared of the Rabbit's skill to even remotely mouth off. Either he'd truly grown as a warrior, or he was in need of some dire reeducation.

"How do you figure," Bryan taunted. "Your reflexes are sharp, but you don't have a hope of handling someone as seasoned as I am."

"I don't know," Darius shrugged, all but stoic in his low stance. "One of us became a Dragon while the other was never deemed good enough to join their number." Bryan's eyes widened in awe, then narrowed in disgust.

"And here I thought that I wouldn't get a chance to kill a Dragon with John's ascension. Thanks for proving me wrong, kiddo." In an almost imperceptible flow of movement, Bryan appeared by Darius' side and raised his Reikiken high over his head. He brought it down, but the King was almost instantly deflected as Darius shifted to face him. Bryan redirected the push from his former nephew's blade into a powerful shoulder strike, but was just as easily moved by the Rebel Dragon.

Darius wouldn't allow for a third attack so easily, and slashed at the King in two wide arcs as he advanced aggressively. He was denied a connection each time, and had to swiftly turn and block to keep the madman away from his back. Al finished up with the stragglers from the earlier cluster of opponents, then stood by as he watched his Master go to work, unsure if there was any way to help but with the full desire to.

Bryan, on the other hand, took the energy that the Hiryu's block fed into his sword and turned it into an attack at the midsection. Darius only barely had time to meet it with force of his own and guide it to a less threatening position. He heard Al shift in his spot, but kept his eyes on the Mad Rabbit's movements. Bryan slashed in reverse to knock Darius' weapon from his hands, then followed up with a powerful downward cut as he sank into a seated position. Darius managed to hold onto his Reikiken only by moving his body according to its pull. He moved to defend against the second blow and succeeded in enough time to see his opponent blast into the air. Chains rattled as the blades of the kyoketsu-shoge rocketed down from the darkened sky. Darius jumped backwards out of their path, watched them ascend to their origin, and dodged again when they were thrust back down.

Bryan descended shortly after, his body angled forward and the tip of his blade positioned to punch a hole through Darius' chest. The young Dragon sidestepped the assault, and just when he thought to breathe he parried an intended shoulder strike that came in too strong to convey a friendly sparring session. He parried again, this time an upward swing, and stepped in to disrupt the flow of the next movement and come face to face with a man who could've just as easily been a second father to him. Now, as Darius stared into Bryan's eyes, there was nothing there but an intense hatred for everything this world held.

"Why are you doing this," Darius asked solemnly, though a flicker of his brow revealed to both of them the sorrow he tried so desperately to suppress. "I'm your family!"

"I have no family left," Bryan spat as he ushered a kick to Darius' chest. He adopted a reversed grip as his nephew—no—his enemy fell to the rain- and blood-soaked concrete. He smiled a sick smile at Darius, as if the moment he'd been waiting for had finally arrived, and raised his Reikiken as a moment of realization hit his intended victim.

"Hell no," shouted Al, who thrust his kyoketsu-shoge out towards the arm of the King, but he was too late. He missed, and the King's bright orange weapon plunged into the shoulder of the Hiryu. Darius screamed in agony, his eyes wide and what tears he expelled instantly evaporated in the heat of the aura sword. Al threw an EMP puck and activated it in time enough to stop the King's sword. Bryan made eye contact with the student, looked him over with an undeniable humor, and with a casual wink, he blasted into the air towards eastern Manhattan.

Darius was still. Silent. The rain continued to fall as gunfire and explosions filled the air.

Al rushed over to his master's side and frantically assessed the wound. Not too deep. From the looks of things, the Hanzo Gear did a lot to take the brunt of the attack, but even with those protections, Bryan was strong enough to force it through to the bone beneath the skin. Al was, for the first time in a long time, shaken to his core. His hands shook in his field of vision as he got on the comms.

"Director," he started, his voice weak like the child he never wanted to be addressed as. "Director Hamlin," he whispered again. For a moment there was no answer.

"Al, what's wrong," John said in a hushed tone, "did something happen to Darius?" Al was stunned by how quickly he knew.

"He's been…" his voice trailed off as he looked over at his beaten Master. "He's been stabbed."

"What do you mean," John asked, his voice more like it usually was.

"The King came out of nowhere and—"

"Bryan was there?" John's voice had become quiet again, like a distant thunder that warned of a massive storm. Al was scared to answer, but he didn't need to. "How bad is he?"

"He's alive, but beyond that I can't tell you," Al offered, and he could hear John breathe a sigh of relief.

"That's good," he assured him with more gentleness than expected given the circumstances. "That's really good. Get him somewhere safe. You can leave that 'King' to me."

"Roger that," Al said, and the comms ceased as he got to work.

****

Damn it, damn it, damn it, John thought. His plan was to get close to the palace, have his covert unit distract them or dispatch them (whichever came first), and slip in undetected so that he could assassinate Bryan, but the witty bastard was a step ahead of him. There was no part of this plan that went the way it was supposed to. Cal was supposed to have broken through a long time ago. The Scarlet dogs were supposed to have been put down by the Coalition forces, and Bryan's head was supposed to be in John's hands, but everything was wrong.

Even now, drones fell out of the sky only to be immediately replaced with more drones. The Ballistics Units were gathered in concentrations too high to be properly effective. The evacuation effort had been one of the first targets of the enemy force. Darius had been taken out of commission by the King himself. Lightning struck the ground behind him as he sprinted through the city. He deployed the kyoketsu-shoge at his wrists and ascended on the strength of his repulsors. The old plan had to be tossed out. A frantic chase for Bryan had begun. He tapped the comms in his Menpo and patched through to every member of the Coalition at once. There was a bite to his demeanor now, and he did what he could to suppress it before he spoke.

"Attention all forces," he started, his tone grim despite his best efforts, "Bryan Piccio has been spotted on the battlefield. I am in pursuit. Stay on target and remain alert. If you see anything, let me know immediately." Thunder boomed over the city, and as the sky echoed its anger, John allowed his rage to take control.

****

Bryan stood over the body of Johannes Thornhill with a great deal of satisfaction as he admired the split between his torso and his legs. The blood that seeped out of him washed away as the rain intensified, and all that was left of the evacuation convoy was the idiot, Nash O'Neill. The King smiled at the exhausted scowl on the former Prince's face.

"Something on your mind," Bryan taunted. "You might as well speak up, man. You won't have the opportunity to do so for much longer." He enjoyed this feeling. He thought it brilliant of them to house the refugees in their convoy inside the Bellevue Hospital. It was, after all, one of the most secure locations in the Capitol with a firm structural integrity. Still, it wouldn't matter in another few moments. His forces had already taken care of the majority of the enemy raiders, and Bryan was left to deal with the last of their little protectors. Johannes was the easiest to take care of, but he knew that Nash might be a little trouble, even as worn out as he was.

For a moment, it looked as though the former Prince would say something. His eyes grew colder and more intense as the rush of rainwater filled the silence. There was a chill in the air despite the heat of Bryan's aura sword, and thick anticipation loomed between them. Nash triggered the comms in his Menpo and muttered into the channel, "King Bryan spotted in the East near Bellevue. We need backup immediat—" He was cut off. Bryan had plunged the titanium blade of the kyoketsu-shoge into his throat, and watched as his blood spurted out with every dying beat of his heart.

"Well, so much for that," the King mused aloud. Thunder cracked loudly overhead. He thought it strangely amusing, as ominous as it was.

"All this killing," King Shane began with an air of condescension the likes of which only a royal could give, "just to let that boy live."

"He always was the sentimental type," Emiko remarked in an unusual show of camaraderie with her former sworn enemy. "It wouldn't surprise me if he remembered all the good times with the kid when he went to deal the finishing blow."

"I bet you'd just love that," Bryan said aloud. "How do you know I didn't have something more elaborate in mind?" They fell silent, Shane out of intrigue and Emiko out of horror.

"What do you mean," she asked in a dark tone that reminded him of his rambunctiousness in his earliest years of fighting. The King Rabbit grinned a wicked grin as he continued on his way to the southern parts of the island. The two voices made the mistake of believing that Bryan only had one plan to victory when in fact he'd put several into place. Admittedly, he intended to use them if things ever got out of hand and he started to lose, but now he simply didn't want them to go to waste. He patched through to the Scarlet Streaks.

"Wulfric, release the special drones to western Manhattan. It's time to show them how serious we are," Bryan spoke calmly into his comms. The King ended the call and cackled wildly, determined to end it all on his own terms.

Chapter Twenty-Three

Cal couldn't believe his ears, and nearly fell off the back of his Lightbeam. Darius had been stabbed? The very notion of it sounded ridiculous since he'd only ever been interested in defense. Sure, he could do more than that, but that was never where his heart was. Suddenly the presence of the ever persistent drones aggravated Cal.

"Aight, bet," he told the Director. "We gone knock this out and I'll come see about him." He knew that it was easier said than done, but he was determined that nothing would stop him from getting to his brother. "Kiringan, switch to Full Squadron Mode." The metal sphere in his head glowed a bright white that was only visible because of the darkness that swirled in the sky.

"Like we practiced?" Leo asked through their private channel. Cal looked him over and nodded. He'd forgotten about his apprentice the moment he heard about his brother, but it was nice to have him around. Something about Leo forced Cal to watch how he acted because he was, from here on, being watched.

There was a rumble beneath the shoreline that alerted the entire city. If things weren't as dire as they were, Cal would've smiled, because this was the sum of his projects on the Engineering Level back at the compound. For months he tinkered with the damaged metal and wiring of the old KDN drones, outfitted them with spare materials, and constructed 350 Lightbeams in addition to the seven that he had to start with. Kaneuji, who lauded the utility of the units and the vast differences in their functionality, took great pleasure in devoting all spare resources to the mass-production of the Lightbeams. The only reason the original seven took center stage up until now was that Cal didn't see a reason to bring in more. Now that had changed.

****

It didn't take long for the drones to take their positions over west Manhattan. Tony and Mikki hurried the last of their charges into the tunnel. There didn't seem to be any more refugees on the way, and the sight of the new drones started to make Tony nervous. Everything about their appearance was different from the earlier models. Whereas the first drones were more plane-like in shape, these were more ovular. They didn't have anything in the way of a gun, but there was a nozzle of some kind attached to the bottom. Something definitely didn't feel right.

"Looks like we're all done here," Mikki said. "I have orders to join back up with my mom. What about you?" Tony didn't respond at first. They were too fixated on the flashing red and green lights to think about anything else.

"We should run," Tony said, which took Mikki by surprise. "I'm going back with the evacuees. Davis might need help treating some of the injured." Mikki shrugged, unsure of what the fuss was about. She took her leave, careful to keep her sai active as she went. The new drones, conscious of her movement, followed after her, and left Tony to flee even faster.

****

John took notice of the new additions to his position and on instinct hit them with a few Kibaku-shuriken. He detonated them when he was out of range as he didn't want any surprises, but when they fell from the sky he noted the sharp increase in heat that lingered despite the near torrential rain. The only thing that he could think would burn like that without any flames was…napalm.

The Director became frantic, not for his own safety, but for that of the son that he knew was injured beneath the bombs. He sprinted across the rooftops, grappled across gaps, and spent every second looking for Darius, but he couldn't find him.

"John, what's going on," came Vanessa's voice from the other end of the comms. "You're going all over the place. Do you have eyes on Bryan?"

"I'm trying to find my son," John responded in a show of miniscule patience. "They have napalm drones, Nessa, and they're gonna start spraying them over this location. I need—" he choked up, cleared his throat, bounded to another building with all the force that his legs and his boots could conjure, and continued. "I need to find him."

"John," the Kageryu said as sympathetically as she could, "we can't do this now. I'll make sure that Darius is safe. We need you focused on finding Bryan and taking him down. If you don't, then all of this was for nothing—"

"Dammit, I know that," John snapped. "You can't just expect me to leave my son to get killed!"

"Bill and Callan are already on their way to his position," she assured him. He didn't calm down, but he was as close to it as he could've gotten. If there were people that he could trust his children with, it was those two. The fact that they were to drop everything they did to go after Darius was more than enough to give the Oryu some much-needed perspective on his present duty.

"Fine," the Royal Dragon grunted, and then began to move in the direction of Bryan's last-known position. "Get to him fast," he ordered all who would listen. Vanessa steeled her resolve.

"Don't worry," she assured him. "We will."

****

Ryan entered 4 WTC through a side entrance. He knew that he was being watched. After all, Cartwright was the one calling the shots with him now playing for the other team. Even still, he had two objectives. First was obviously to disarm the last bomb. Second, though, was to try and convince his old comrades to let him save their lives. He knew that the chances of that were slim to none, but he wondered if he could've lived with himself if he didn't try. First, though, he had to make his way through a darkness only illuminated by a what little sunlight could pierce the clouds and the drones that still blanketed the city. A flash of lightning ripped through the air in such a brilliant way that not even the destructive storm cloud of drones could hide it.

Ryan felt a greater sense of danger here, more than he'd ever felt in his entire infantry career. It was as if he had long expected something to happen, and the moment was upon him. He tread cautiously through the building, careful to spend time on the lower floors before he would head to the station of the final bomb. He knew that in the worst-case scenario, he was outnumbered and it would be wise to force his former allies to split their focus between multiple levels. He knew that, to some extent, he'd been under their watchful eye for some time now, and while he was sure that he was alone, something in the back of his mind told him that he wasn't.

****

Cal dove from high above in true Kiryu fashion, and thanked God that he'd had the foresight to make his Hanzo Gear resistant to high levels of friction. His body spun once, twice, three times, four, five, countless revolutions with an extended Reikiken for a Falling Leaf the likes of which the world had truly never seen. His Hanzo Gear burned in a similar fashion to the aura sword in his grips, and upon contact with the drones below, the heat disbursed throughout them brightly enough to knock a few of their circuits loose. The Wood Dragon continued to fall as his body uncoiled from the assault, and with the flex of his hand a Lightbeam came grabbed him and tossed him back into the metal cloud.

All over the terrain, the Lightbeams moved as the Seven Dragons in all their glory, using their own repulsors to create footholds in the air for their techniques. Only four of the Full Battalion Lightbeams abstained from direct combat, and were charged with providing support to the only humans amid this battle.

Cal cut through a drone on reentry, and when he went above the cloud again, pierced the shell of another with his kyoketsu-shoge to reel himself back in. He cut through that drone and the one next to it before he caught himself with the repulsors and pushed back up. He bounded onto the back of one of the death machines and jumped from one to another, careful to blaze a path of destruction with his Reikiken as he went. He turned, winked at Leo and smiled as he spread his arms. Leo, who surfed on the back of his own Lightbeam, watched with a start as his Sensei fell below the metal contraptions.

The upstart golden neo-ninja ran through a series of strong slashes and quick strikes as he moved for Cal's position. A line of drones raised up above the grey mechanical cloud and trained their guns on him. He just smiled as a bead of nervous sweat trickled down the side of his face. On instinct he impaled the one at the front of their formation with the bladed chain and pulled it toward him. As the spherical machine sped in Leo's direction, he split it effortlessly with the flow of his firesword as his body moved through the red-hot metal. The others began to fire, but Leo jumped out of the way and off the back of one Lightbeam onto another before he slashed his kyoketsu-shoge through the air. The former Lightbeam, freed of its former task, took to a higher altitude and blasted through many of the drones in the surrounding area.

Leo couldn't help but notice that the urgency that Cal had exhibited before was ever-present in his creations. The Dragonic Apprentice caught yet another in its optical sensor, but it resisted enough to provide the young warrior with a sturdy enough base to propel himself to. He kicked off the back of the Lightbeam and sped through two of the others that stood in his way. He landed on the top of a lower-flying drone before he chopped down through the third assault mech, then reversed the energy into a sideways cut that destroyed a fourth. Before he could move, the fifth drone fired on him.

He fall from the back of his Lightbeam, but it swooped down after him as he tumbled from the sky. Leo screamed, his body completely out of control as it turned over itself again and again, then stopped. The Lightbeam had caught up to him, grabbed him by the leg, and held him there for a moment so that he could catch his breath. He expected the android to turn him right side up again, but it did not. Instead, it flew upward, then accelerated, then tossed him mercilessly towards the previous objective. He screamed again, but was able to right himself as he shot through the clankers with a flip, a grapple, and a stabilizing blast from his repulsor boots that sent him back down. He slashed through a pocket of machines as he sped below what remained. The Lightbeam caught him again, tossed him up at an angle, and watched in wait as he cut through more as they appeared.

Leo breathed a sigh of relief, happy to have found a rhythm in which to work, but then he returned to his earlier worry. He had no clue where Cal had gone, or if he was even okay. The only thing that he knew was that Cal was alive. The Lightbeams would've shut down had he been taken out. He couldn't give all of his attention to finding him as long as the drones, which thankfully now dwindled in number, were in the sky.

Then he saw him. Just as Leo rocketed back up, Cal flew in the opposite direction with the smile of an amused child plastered to his face. Leo could breathe a sigh of relief, and as they flashed through the remnants of the drones as bright orange streaks, they started to see the end.

****

It took them a while to find them. Al had carried a barely conscious Darius quite a ways before Bill and Callan had arrived. Still, the fact that the Lightbeams had already taken care of the drones in the western part of Manhattan greatly increased their arrival time. The napalm drones that mixed in with the original batch had fallen to the streets below and even now ate away at the flesh of many Scarlets and Coalitionists alike. Al and Darius, however, were safely on a rooftop and out of the chemical's reach.

"This isn't good," said Callan, who looked at the bloody cloth wrapped around Darius' wound. He immediately moved to help Al support him.

"We need to get him to the evac zone," Bill said. "Should be a lot easier now than before."

"Not without some support," Callan rebutted. "We can't get him there by ourselves."

"Those seem like they'd be able to help," Al said as he pointed up at a lingering Lightbeam. Callan and Bill looked his way, and with a smile Bill tapped the comms.

"Hey Cal," he started with a cheerful ring in his voice, "you mind if we use this Lightbeam you got near us to get your brother out of dodge?" There was a long stretch of silence. Both of the senior Dragons and the apprentice worried that the message didn't get through, and just when Bill was about to try again, that was when Cal started to speak.

"No problem," he told them with a slight shake to his voice. He cleared his throat. "Yeah, just throw your hand in the air and hold up three fingers, then five, then one, then two. It'll register that as a countersign to a pre-programmed relief signal."

"Jeez," Bill commented, "you really thought of everything with these things."

"Appreciate his genius some other time," Callan urged. "We need to get Darius out of here fast." Bill was about to ask what the rush was, but when he looked up he noticed a wave of round drones with nozzles and flashing lights. They were different from the gunner drones, and Bill immediately recognized them as the napalm drones. He shot his hand into the air and followed the directions that Cal had given him. Three fingers, then five, then one, then two. The android immediately took notice and descended to their location on the rooftop. Calmly it assessed the situation, and took Darius from his two supports.

As soon as Callan had a free hand, he immediately patched through to Vanessa at command.

"Hey," he began, "we have more drones inbound and they're not gunners. We need a full evac of all forces."

"What do you mean," Vanessa responded in all urgency. "I can see it from here, Cal and his Lightbeams are bringing the drones down by the dozen."

"He won't be able to handle these," Bill chimed in as he stowed his Reikiken and pulled out Kibaku-shuriken by the fistful. "These drones are loaded with napalm. If the kid goes through them, he'll be lying in a heap just like the machine."

“Understood,” Vanessa remarked. The comms link went dead, and the three Insurrectionists stood ready with their explosives in hand.

****

Ryan took cover behind a support column. He knew for a fact now that he was being followed by someone, and it was about time he found out by whom. He could hear the footsteps gingerly plant in the shadows, the muffled breathing that ran steady as the rain outside, and the sound of his own heartbeat in his ears as the stalker approached. He didn’t know what would happen, whether they would be able to have a rational conversation or not, but the expert marksman took his pistol from its holster at the small of his back and prepared for either scenario.

The seconds that passed each felt like an eternity, and as the person grew closer, he only escalated in suspense. Then, he heard a familiar voice call his name. It was Serenity, and though he was surprised that she’d found her way to him, he was also happy for the first time since she left. He had her back, and she’d come to protect him. He emerged from his hiding place behind the column, his mouth formed in a smile, but the moment he saw her all the joy he felt was dashed against the ground.

He aimed his gun, his eyes darkened, and with a low growl that Serenity had never heard, he demanded of the man that held her, “Let go of my sister.” The man, who held her arm behind her back at a sharp upward angle, jerked it up and pushed her forward. She followed the silent direction and moved forward. “Stop!”

"Now, Mr. Crawford," started Maxwell Cartwright as his lips curled into a slick smirk, "I assure you that I have every reason to keep her in my custody." He watched as Ryan's finger moved from the length of the pistol to its trigger. He pulled out a pistol of his own and pointed it at her head. He could feel her breath quicken, her fear reach its peak as she stared death in the face as much as her little brother. The former leader of the Scarlet Streaks lowered his weapon. "You see," Cartwright continued, "your beautiful sister here managed to kill Killpatrick and severely wound Wulfric. Honestly, if her impulse control is this minimal I hesitate to think about what other ways she could get in trouble…" He let his voice trail off in a suggestive manner that was only augmented by the disgusting look on his face. He eyed her both disrespectfully and longingly, and neither of the Crawford siblings dared question what perverted thought ran through the man's head.

"Very bold of you to think you have a shot at finding out," Serenity snapped, and found the mouth of the gun pressed against her skull.

"Nobody asked for your opinion," Cartwright growled. "Whatever I want from you, I'll take when I see fit."

"Is that right," Serenity asked with a confident ring in her voice. All of a sudden she cared nothing for his aggression, his weapon, or his hold over her. She ducked below the muzzle of the firearm as she took hold of his arm and twisted behind him. He attempted to reverse the hold, but Serenity caught him with a sharp punch to the jaw, and he staggered away from her. Ryan took a sigh of relief, then fixed his own gun back on his old subordinate. "I'd love to see you try to take anything from me. The only reason I let you pretend was because I needed to find my brother."

"I guess that means we don't need him anymore," Ryan said coolly. Maxwell laughed somewhat maniacally as he dove behind a pillar. On instinct Ryan took cover himself, his weapon in ready position and his eye on the security mirror that betrayed Cartwright's position. Serenity remained where she was. There was no cover, no protection, but she didn't need to. Her Hanzo Gear was sufficient enough to block a pistol bullet. It would still sting, but she'd be able to move and fight. "What's the matter, Cartwright? You always made such a show of being the classy, honorable sort. Face your execution with some dignity!" Maxwell, who had been focused on Serenity, turned his attention to Ryan's position and fired a shot at the wall.

"Oh, like you reserve the right to judge me, *traitor*!" Maxwell ran deeper into the office space towards the back elevator. Serenity shot at him, both with her pistol and her kyoketsu-shoge in a show of coordinated brutality that made it hard to believe he somehow escaped with both leg. Before he could move to push the button, Ryan shot out the controls from his position, and when Serenity came in with a round of her own, Cartwright was forced to roll out of the way and dive under a nearby desk.

"You say I can't judge you, but you really make it hard," Ryan remarked with a wry smile that his former teammate couldn't see. "I can't believe you ran for such an easy out with the two of us here as your opponents."

“Makes it hard to believe that you ever rivalled our brother in the intelligence field,” Serenity added with smooth confidence.

“The only good thing about your brother,” seethed Maxwell, and the Crawfords tensed immediately, “was that he died before he had to endure the disgrace of turning traitor like the two of you.” Serenity was about to bound over the entire space on the power of her repulsors and rage, but was caught off-guard by the sudden emergence of a small blue and black cylinder. She took the cloak of her Hanzo Gear in her hands and shrouded her entire body with it, and when the cylinder hit the ground the room was encased in a loud bang and a brilliant flash of light.

Ryan was safe enough, though found that his hearing was momentarily dulled, but his sister was right in the middle of the floor’s entry way. The second Ryan felt the danger, he emerged from behind his piece of wall and saw Maxwell stand with his pistol aimed at Serenity, a twisted hunger in his eyes like a starved wolf with fresh prey in his sights. The youngest Crawford shot his enemy gun clear out of Cartwright’s hand, and went for another shot. Maxwell went for cover, this time back into the room and beneath the line of the surrounding desks.

Serenity emerged from her cocoon, a bit disoriented but otherwise unharmed. She couldn’t hear her brother call to her, but it didn’t matter. She instinctively looked in his direction, and when she saw his gesture to their surroundings it only took her a matter of moments to assess the situation for herself. Cartwright had slipped past them both, and now hid in the returned shadows of the room. All was silent now, and the Crawford siblings tread carefully between the rows of desks and chairs, unsure of where their opponent might pop up next.

****

Bryan stood with his face to the clouds. The drones fell, yes, but just as those would come to see their demise, the napalm drones would rise in waves to take their place. The Yaiba Insurrection and its friends wouldn't hold out much longer then, and once he had the assurance that they'd all been melted from their bones, Bryan would put an end to his own misery as well.

"Let's move! C'mon you lazy putzes, it's time to get the hell outta here," came the booming voice of a single woman through the thunder. "Word just came through; we have orders to evacuate! Napalm is gonna be dropping all over this place soon, so if you don't want your skin melted off then you need to get out as quickly as possible! Hey you! Stop your shooting and get to moving! If I have to tell you again, you'll be having a one on one conversation with Bubbe here!" She gestured to her RPG and the man to whom she talked fixed his face.

"'Orders to evacuate,'" Bryan repeated, a seething rage behind his words. "The hell they will." He entered a sequence on his wrist comms and almost in an instant, the drones appeared in wide formations that targeted the different parts of the island. The soldiers that ran the ground took notice, and as the napalm was dispensed through the streets, the screams of his enemies resounded to Bryan as a master symphony.

****

Serenity's eyes went wide when Cartwright took her hand and twisted the pistol from it. He pointed it at her head, only for her to duck and sweep the leg. The intelligence agent fired three rounds into the ceiling as he fell backwards onto the floor. He barely had the time to catch his breath when Serenity deployed her serpentine chains, her blade pointed at his face. He rolled out of the way and got back to his feet.

Ryan fired at him and missed. Cartwright covered the corner of another blocky pillar, then shot at Serenity. The former leader of the Scarlet Scourge blocked a face shot with the titanium blades at her wrists and rolled forward just as Maxwell had done before.

"That the best you got," she called out loudly. The effects of the flashbang from earlier still dulled her senses, and despite that, she was still more than a match for him. She smiled, because she really couldn't see how this man had ever once been compared to Kyle.

Cartwright searched for her carefully, though he hadn't forgotten about Ryan. He turned around, sure that the younger brother would have crept up behind him for an execution-style gunshot, but he was nowhere to be seen. Cartwright felt like a fly in the middle of a spider's web. Without much of a choice, he backed up towards the elevator so that he could keep his eyes on any point from which his enemies would emerge. The loud crack of gunfire erupted from his right, and on instinct he fell backwards to the floor just in front of the elevator. The second his back met the carpet, he was surprised to see a dark figure already in the air over him.

Serenity fell from the ceiling, her Reikiken poised to split him at the shoulders. Maxwell aimed up at her with the gun that he'd taken and unloaded round after round. She twisted in the air, so the only thing those bullets impacted was the shock-resistant gel lining of her cloak. He spewed profanities at her, screamed and cried, then fell silent as the aura sword burned its way through him.

The elevator door opened to reveal James, who went from happy to see her to appalled at the sight of Cartwright's remains. He spoke to the two, and while they couldn't hear his words they could see the urgency on his face as he pointed out the window. Drones dropped a white liquid all over the city, and they knew that they needed to get out as fast as they could.

****

Bill and Callan moved from rooftop to rooftop through the city, and only paused long enough to lash out with what they had left of the Kibaku-shuriken. They had split from Al, who already made his way back towards the Holland Tunnel to see about his master, while they did what they could to save as many Coalition troops as possible.

"I'm almost out," Callan said, his tone grim and his eyes inflamed from the chemical heat that increased its presence as they went. "The drones are gonna close in on us soon. When that happens—"

"We can't afford to think like that, Callan," Bill interrupted. He thought back to the moment that Dr. Masamune died. He saw the man as his father, and yet he had no real time to mourn the loss. He'd lost so much time with that damned amnesia, and when his memories had finally come back, he was summoned to go right back out to the battlefield from whence they rescued him. It was in passing that he'd found out how his other friends, all brothers and sisters to him, had met their ends. He had already lost so much, and couldn't stomach the idea of losing Callan, too. "This is not where we die."

Callan was dumbfounded. He knew just as well the losses that Bill had taken over the course of this war, and in many ways he shared in them. Even after all of that, Bill found a way to be optimistic, even though they could be burned alive any minute. He smiled. All they could do was keep running, keep blowing stuff up, and hope that they could make it out in time.

****

Bryan watched as two men of familiar body type passed him by, and his anger only grew. King Bryan had worked so hard—so damn hard—to kill as many people as he could, to rid the world of this conflict once and for all, and here they were blowing his death machines to pieces before a lot of the real damage could be done. He took a moment to take them in, then it clicked as to who they were and how they were able to make such an arduous task look like child's play. It was Bill and Callan, two of the people that made it into the Seven Dragons. They were the reason that he was overlooked, and more than anything, they spent all their time looking after John's brats that they left his to die in Midland.

"You're really going to let them escape," came Jaden's cold, whispered voice from just behind Bryan's ear. "They let me die!"

"I'm not," Bryan said with a tear in his eye. He recalibrated the drone commands and sent a squadron after his old friends. His anguished expression twisted into a dark satisfaction. "I'm not."

****

They were almost there, almost to the edge of the city. If Bill and Callan could just make it to the water, they could swim across the Hudson to the main encampment.

"We got incoming," Bill yelled. His heart raced as a kind of fear and dread took his mind in an iron claw and squeezed. Before he realized it, his breathing became staggered and heavy. "We need to get them off our tail!" Callan didn't respond, just threw the last of his Kibaku-shuriken behind him and set them to detonate on contact. The resulting explosion carried them forward just a little bit more, with Callan slightly ahead of Bill. Bill smiled a relieved smile as he took some more shuriken from his own pouch and tossed them at the emergent cloud of napalm drones. They exploded, and Callan was pushed ahead even more. Bill, on the other hand, took a stand on a rooftop a few blocks away from the harbor.

"What are you doing," Callan called behind him, a shakiness to his voice that he loathed. "Bill, we can't fight those things!"

"Go," Bill shouted back, his Reikiken in his hand and a ferocity in his eyes. "I'll hold them off as best I can. You get out of here!"

"No!"

"I can't lose anyone else!" Bill's words caught Callan off guard, and more than that pulled him back to stand on the same rooftop. Bill looked at him incredulously, and when he opened his mouth to scold Callan, the Suiryu punched him in the jaw.

"Don't be a child," Callan growled. "You have a wife and a son, both of whom have spent enough time without you. You can mourn all you need to, you can cry, but you can't ever forget about the people who need you the most. It's not me," he added before Bill could protest. "Your kid is gonna need someone patient and kind to see him through the kind of future you envisioned for him. So go. I'll take care of things here." Bill looked him over for a second and noted the outstretched arm. With a sigh of regret, Bill handed over the last of the Kibaku-shuriken.

"Callan, I—"

"Oh, my God, would you get lost already," Callan asked with a joking smile that was meant to put Bill at ease, but only made the moment sadder. Without another word, Bill sped towards the edge of the island. He felt one explosion, then another. A third one came, and with it the scream of his friend, but he dared not look back. All he could focus on—all he could allow himself to focus on—was Bri. His son, Ray. His home. His face hit the water only moments after the tears took his eyes.

****

John watched as chaos rained down all around him. He'd given the order to evacuate, but only half of the main forces made it out. Most of the Ballistic Units were gone, and the evacuation convoy had been wiped out as well. Everywhere he looked, more reasons to find Bryan quickly made themselves plain. He sprinted across rooftops from the west, back in the direction of Empire State. He figured that he could use the palace as a vantage point and look for the King from there, provided he could see his way through the madness. It was when he approached the Flatiron Building that he realized that there was a single person standing on its roof. It was a man. It was Bryan.

"Vanessa, has Darius made it out," John sparked into the comms. He didn't bother masking his emotions. The anger would've seeped through anyway.

"Y-yes," she replied. "Bill is tending to him now."

"Good," he spoke with a deep dragonic hum. "Keep all personnel away from the island. I have eyes on Bryan. Moving to engage." He shut off his comms, resolved to see this through on his own and on his own strength. He touched down behind his former friend atop the roof of the Flatiron Building.

"Took you long enough to find me," Bryan said without so much as a backward glance. John supposed that it came as a result of his confidence following their last bout. He made a note to remind him of his place in the pecking order. "And after I came out here just for you." He turned around now, and when his eyes met those of the Oryu, John could only see madness in them.

Chapter Twenty-Four

"You really think this is the time to make jokes," John snapped, and a crack of thunder boomed overhead. Rain fell hard, mixed in to no avail with the napalm spewed by the waves of fresh drones. Lightning spidered through the dark clouds as the distant sounds of moans and screams pierced the natural symphony with syncopated horror. "Look at what you've done."

"Marvelous, isn't it," Bryan asked as his sick smile grew sicker. "In a few short months I've taken down the Scarlet Kingdom and everyone else for that matter. You know, from a certain point of view both Emiko and King Shane got what they wanted, didn't they?"

"Emiko," John started, and did what he could to restrain himself with what little sense of practical reason he had left, "wanted a life for everyone, one where we could all be seen as equals! The only thing you've done here is go off on your own insane ideals!"

"And there's the flaw in her logic," Bryan rebutted. "Men are only equal in death, and that is exactly what I've brought about. You think I'm insane, John? You know what I've been through and how it's torn me apart from the inside out! And you preach to me from your warrior's indoctrination that I should be fine with the fact that my son is gone!" He grew quiet now, then smiled an eerie smile. "That reminds me. Tell me, how is that son of yours? Have you discovered what it means to lose a child yet?"

"How my children are doing is none of your business," John snarled, "and you'd do well to keep their names out of your mouth." He took a step towards his ally-turned-enemy and jolted when they were both knocked from their feet. An explosion erupted from behind the palace, some ways into the center of Manhattan, and a cloud of dust and debris moved out in a ring towards the island's edges. Judging by how little debris made its way to their location, John had to assume that it detonated closer to the northern part of the island. Then he realized where the commando team and two of his Seven Dragons were positioned. His face twisted in agony, then disgust as he realized the only group of people who might have suffered the brunt of the blast. Bryan laughed a wily laugh.

"What," Bryan chuckled as he returned to his feet and dusted himself off, "you thought your people disarmed my bomb? As if I'd let such delicate information leak to enemy forces. It's weaker than intended but still fully operational, even without the energy from the outer mines. I thought you would've known me better than to assume I would make it that easy, considering how long our history is."

As much as he wanted to, John couldn't afford to focus on the commando unit right now. He steeled his resolve as he narrowed his gaze on Bryan and said, "Yeah, well I would've thought you would've had better sense than to try and kill my child, but now it seems we're all surprised," John returned as he stood back up. "The sad thing is I know you won't stop, so I'm just gonna have to make you." He grabbed his Reikiken and immediately it came to life. Bryan looked down at the brilliant orange glow, then looked up and smiled. Both of them knew that there was nothing more to say. John couldn't convince Bryan to go back to the way things were and the King wanted nothing more than the death of every guilty party in his eyes. Words here were meaningless.

The Royal Dragon tucked his hand behind his back, then pointed his blade straight at the Mad Rabbit as a swift gust of wind blew rainwater all around them. Bryan slowly unsheathed his own aura sword and held it straight behind his body as his eyes grew bright with a burst of lightning. They circled each other for a moment, their stances firm and the water that hit the blades instantly evaporated and returned to the sky. Bryan leaped for John with a wild man's roar and a brutish attack at the head. John merely stepped back and parried the blow off to the side, and rolled his own sword underneath Bryan's in time for the sudden reverse of movement. Bryan carried the energy around to a shoulder strike that John ducked, and midway through the hard swing, changed the momentum to barrel down on the Director's back.

John blocked the move with as little effort as he'd evaded its predecessor, but Bryan used the resistance of the deflection to roll his blade in an arc towards John's face. The former Lightning Dragon spun out of the way and back into an upright position, but his effort to establish distance failed. Bryan knew him all too well. He knew that John liked to fight at a reasonable distance, and that if he could take up space then he would have a greater advantage.

The Mad King slammed his weapon hard against John's and pushed it towards his face, but John was crafty enough to move his body away from the blades and parry Bryan through to a position that better served the Yaiba leader. He fired off a few quick strikes of his own. Shoulder, then leg, then head, but when the last blow connected to his enemy's sword, he disconnected slightly and pushed the tip towards the space between Bryan's eyes. Bryan lifted one of his boots and fired a repulsor blast into the Dragon King's chest in an elegant backflip evasion, but whereas John hit the ground unceremoniously, Bryan landed on his feet.

His station only lasted a moment, because as soon as his boots touched the Flatiron roof, they emitted another blast that launched him high into the air. The Usagi no Kamikaze flipped, pointed his blade down, and descended with every intent to plunge the tip of his sword into John's heart to silence him once and for all. John rolled his body over his head to land on all fours as Bryan stamped his foot and sword into the concrete tile. The Dragon attacked with a swift kick aimed at the King's head, but Bryan turned away and was kicked in the back instead.

He rolled away from the sword and back to his feet, then rolled forward just as John exploded towards him on the repulsor boots and slashed at his head. Bryan picked up the Reikiken and defended his chest from the swift sideways attack that John dished out. John disconnected, and with the firesword angled upward at Bryan's face, attempted a stab. Bryan slapped him away, only for John to flip upside down on a blast from the repulsors and twist in the air. He struck at one side once, then twice on the other as he found the ground again. Bryan tried to take the opening at John's back only to be denied the kill again.

King Bryan couldn't remember the last time that John fought this aggressively. He was still calculated, yes, but there was supposed to be a degree of calm to him that fed into his elegant flow. Here, in this moment, he moved as fast and as angry as the lightning, and where there was an expression of fraternity in his eyes during his last bout, there was nothing but a deep bloodlust there now that Bryan couldn't help but fear. Bryan jumped back and took a guarded stance with his sword at shoulder level. He angled the weapon squarely at the space between John's eyebrows.

John stood in place, his Reikiken pointed down at the ground beneath him and his one hand still tucked behind his back.

"Seems you're back on your A-game," Bryan mused between short breaths. "You're a lot harder to keep up with than you were back in Yorktown, John." John smiled confidently.

"I was surprised back then," John admitted. "I'm up to speed now." He stood perfectly still, careful not to allow Bryan the satisfaction of a premature advance, and as he waited for the Scarlet King to make his move, John staved off thoughts of regret and sadness. He never thought that the day would come where he would have to take the life of one of the best friends he'd ever had, but it had. He never thought that Bryan would betray his family and John's, to the point of trying to murder a boy that he thought—knew—of as a nephew. Every worst-case scenario had become a reality, and yet John couldn't stop thinking of their past.

Bryan attacked, and it was like John had a flashback to the sparring match on Level C in front of their boys and Johannes Thornhill. Bryan feigned a stab, and when John moved to block it, he swiped at his former friend's midsection with enough force to sever metal from metal, but John somehow managed to parry the blade through as he revolved to his assailant's back. The King Dragon lunged, but was knocked aside by a powerful rolling block that echoed a manic laughter. Bryan pushed him on the defensive again with a downward diagonal slash.

Once again, Master Hamlin parried it away, but this time he tracked its length back to Bryan's hands, but he jumped away with a swiftness that felt all too familiar. It was like it couldn't be helped, as both of them felt that they walked through battles long gone by. Bryan thought to strike at both of John's shoulders in an unruly mix of speed and power, but already John had repulsed himself across the breaking concrete of the rooftop. Bryan casually blocked the strike to his head, then quickly rebounded with a sharp pivot beneath the blade of his one-time friend. John spun out, which established enough distance for him to parry the hidden swing through and bridge the gap again with a thrust aimed at Bryan's heart.

Bryan couldn't tell if this was fun or traumatizing. Here he stood, toe to toe with the best swordsman of the Yaiba Insurrection and a man that had once inspired him to do great things for the war effort. He thought back to their many missions together, how close he and Aria had been as they humiliated the Scarlet dogs of bases all over the lower East Coast. He slapped the stabbing blade off to the side with so much force that it took John with it, and carried his weapon around his head, into a downward slash. John sidestepped it and attacked Bryan's shoulder, but was quickly met with a hard shot from his enemy's firesword. They paused for a moment, and Bryan was reminded by the murderous look in John's eye that all that was over. They clashed, and the impact sent both blades quickly off to the side. Bryan wasted no time, however, as he shot out one of his kyoketsu-shoge in the hopes of catching John off guard.

When John dodged, he whipped the chain around in a plethora of directions to see if his old teammate could keep it up.

John recognized this attack pattern. It was what Bryan used during their fight in Yorktown, and just as he had then, the King Dragon proved to be more than up for the challenge. He sidestepped the first swing, then cartwheeled, then dropped into a back bend that turned into a back handspring, then again into a hasty parry with his Reikiken. He smiled, more confident now than he had been back then, and more willing to respect the work that Bryan put in just to be deemed an equal. Distance was Bryan's forte, but where swordsmanship had always been his weakness, there was no sign of that in this moment. John was being pushed further and further back, more so than he ever had before by any opponent.

Bryan pulled the chain back only to extend it again, the diamond-shaped titanium blade hungry for the blood of its master's enemies. John pushed it off to the side with the Reikiken, but this time knew better than to grab hold. Regardless, the Rabbit of the Divine Wind vaulted into the air with a tempestuous burst from his repulsor boots, and used the new tether to carry him forward towards John. He slashed forcefully through the air, but the overall motion of the blade was guided by a gentle push from John's weapon as he sidestepped. The Lightning Dragon Former struck at the shoulder, but Bryan slammed his blade into that of his enemy and followed up with a wild swipe through John's midsection.

John evaded with a cartwheel and deflected a secondary shot as he flipped. Once upright, he swiped from Bryan's hip to his shoulder but another hard knock to the side hindered any possibility of a connection. This time it was the Yaiba leader's turn to disconnect. The openings that he thought were there had faded with the change of Bryan's stance, and Bryan was less than eager to charge in recklessly as he had so many times. He couldn't help but think of their days in training, and how they spent so much time trying to one-up each other. A smirk escaped him as his eyes drifted off somewhere, but for all the nostalgia that bonded them together, there was that much more rage. John, who now remembered the deep worry he felt for his son who lay with a stab wound just outside New York, stabbed for Bryan's throat unsuccessfully, then immediately swung to the left leg. He failed to connect with anything more than his enemy's sword, then redirected the flow of his weapon up and across Bryan's midsection.

Bryan swept the weapon through, then reversed the sword's movements for a midsection cut of his own. He was parried in his own right, but only slightly. John twisted the blade beneath his enemy's sword and attempted a cut to the groin, but a hard slam kept him at bay. He flexed his arm, and the kyoketsu-shoge deployed towards Bryan's face at close range. The Mad King growled as he was forced to jump away, and watched as the brilliant titanium blade receded into the shadow of his cloak. Before Bryan thought to charge again, John tossed a smoke pellet from his pouch onto the ground.

The rain ensured that he would only have a few seconds of cover, and in that time he used the repulsors to vault over Bryan. Unfortunately for him, Bryan also had the idea to blast through the smoke. They met in the air and clashed as lightning struck the roof behind them. Thunder rumbled again as if decrying the madness that had swept the city. It was almost like God voiced his disapproval at such wanton death between two friends. John kicked Bryan in the gut to force a break in connection between the blades, and when he knew he was clear, he tossed three Kibaku-shuriken dead at the King. Bryan batted them all to the side and felt them explode behind him. He was knocked forward from the blasts, but with the skilled use of his repulsor boots, managed to land on his feet.

He and John stared each down, caught between memories from their past and the bitterness of the present, and the King couldn't help but notice that there was a sorrowful, almost pitying look in the Director's eyes.

"The hell are you looking at," he demanded, and gripped his Reikiken tighter. "Don't you look down on me!" He charged in to take John down with slash after slash, cut after cut, attack after attack, but each one was deflected, parried, retaliated against, or stopped in its tracks. Bryan yelled, unable to contain his frustration any longer. He wound up hard and swung at John's abdomen again. John had no reaction time to parry, and if he didn't want to be cut down he had no other choice but to block with as much resistance as he thought Bryan would put out.

The Director slammed his blade stiffly into Bryan's, and to their shock and dismay, both Reikiken shattered. Bryan hit John in the face with the hilt of his weapon, and punched the Dragon over and over again as he stumbled back. John caught his fist, then hit him with a headbutt that nearly took Bryan down. John ducked a punch and swept the leg, but Bryan caught himself on his hands and rolled out of the way of a downward kick. He hated this more than he hated the swordsmanship. He went for a tackle, but

John rolled out of the way, and timed his next kick so expertly that it caught Bryan in the shoulder on the latter's turn.

Bryan growled as he nursed the broken bone, but still tried to use his bear-like body to maul his opponent. John bent his torso to the ground as he raised his leg and kicked Bryan in the back. The King stumbled forward, just in time for John to kick the legs out from under him. Bryan landed on the broken arm, and when he cried out in pain it struck a chord in John.

"Alright," the Director said, "that's enough. Submit, and I'll take you in to stand trial for your crimes against Prevalence." He paused to give Bryan the chance to speak, to say something even closely repentant through the clenched teeth and the pain in his body. He mumbled something, but it was drowned out by another roll of thunder. "Speak up," John demanded as lightning flashed behind him. Bryan looked up just as it did, and noticed the darkness in John's face that made him seem as dragonic as his monikers would suggest.

"Drop dead," he screamed. In that moment, John heard all of the agony and confusion and frustration that Bryan had felt since the moment he learned of Jaden's death. He got up to finish the fight, unaware that it was already over. He launched a sluggish punch, but John dodged with little effort. "Over and over again I have to watch you look down on me," Bryan wailed as he attacked again and was similarly evaded. "In training! In war! In life! You tell me how I should accept it as the way that it is and I can't, John! And God I've tried so hard not to hate you throughout our lives, to focus on the good moments, but I loathe everything about you, from your arrogance on the battlefield to the way you parade around those little bastards you call sons! So you want me to submit? You want me to stand trial? Fine, I'll submit to you! I give up! Hell, I'll even agree to answer to your little Coalition, but only under one condition: I get to kill your two little boys right in front of your—" The animosity in his expression turned to shock as he realized the way that his throat opened. John stood over him, a look as grim as the reaper plastered to his face, and casually knelt down to get a better look into his eyes as they only barely retained any kind of light.

"Actually," he said with a tilt of his head and a deep dragonic hum that emulated the thunder overhead, "I changed my mind." With nothing more to say, John left the Flatiron building, determined to get back to Jersey City and see to his son's condition.

Bryan watched him go, then as his eyes lost focus and the world grew dim, all he could do was listen to the sounds of the rain and chaos as he drifted into an everlasting sleep.

****

John quickly realized that he wasn't out of the woods yet. The napalm drones still whirred about in the sky and dropped their payloads through the streets. To make matters worse, half of them had turned their attention to the rooftops themselves. John's movements were limited, and it would only be a matter of time before the machines noticed a survivor amid this dead city. He tapped into the comms.

"Attention all forces," he started, his tone solemn, but somewhat relieved, "King Bryan, Yaiba traitor and leader of the Scarlet Kingdom, is dead. The Kingdom has fallen." He gave them a moment to relish in their sighs of relief, their cheers of victory, the sobs that showcased their sudden release of tension. He cleared his throat, and things got quiet. "With that said, I'm still here and the napalm drones are swarming the area. I need solutions and I need 'em fast."

"I got you, Pops," Cal came in with a cheerful tone, no doubt proud of his ability to handle air force combat with the help of his Lightbeams and his apprentice. "Where you at? I can run a pick-up."

"I'm on top of an old office building off of 22nd, but a pick-up might be too dangerous. The drones might notice me and then converge on my position. It would be better if you dispatched a few Lightbeams to clear me a path." John could almost hear the gears turning in Cal's head.

"Makes sense," he mumbled. "I bet if I attacked from different angles with multiple Lightbeams, I can trick them into coming after me."

"While you're doing that," John started to suggest, "I need you to check the situation at the commando unit hideout."

"You must be talking about that shockwave from earlier," Cal filled in.

"Yeah," John exhaled. "Before we go home we need to make sure that we got all of our people out."

"I got you," Cal told him seriously. "Hang tight and I'mma get to work."

"Alright," John replied. He looked at the sky. Another wave of drones had begun its assault. "Just be quick."

****

The Lightbeams scrambled almost like real soldiers as Cal prepared them for flight. Almost half of their number had been drained of either their power or their fighting capabilities. A quarter of them had been completely lost to the first deployment of drones they were sent in to dispatch. That left him with about 87-88 Lightbeams that were still at peak performance. Cal had to wonder how well this would work out, but that time wasn't now. Now his only focus was to get people out. That was to say, if they were still alive by the time he found them.

He shook the negative thoughts out of his head and deployed the androids.

"Kiringan," he said to his left eye, "activate homing beacons." He hadn't told anyone, but he and Leo both (with the help of Sora Kaneuji) worked tirelessly to outfit all new equipment with tracking devices between training sessions. Fortunately, everyone in the Yaiba military was required to do Hanzo Gear maintenance after so many battles, which had been fast-tracked since the KDN bombing months ago. It was the perfect excuse for some illicit tinkering, and they would hopefully see the benefits of it now.

"You're not gonna go," Leo asked from behind him as he scanned the nearby medic station for any sign of Al.

"I don't need to," Cal informed him as he kept his focus on the city. "The Lightbeams work just fine on their own. I can be here and still do what my old man told me."

He saw John's position first, and sent the mechs in for the assist. "Speaking of, looks like it's showtime!"

****

John did his best to hold his position, and dispatched a wave of Kibaku-shuriken that detonated on contact while he thought about how useful it would've been for him to have had one of those Thunderclap things that Al had brought his way. The drones exploded at a distance, thought some managed to get in closer. Those he dispatched with his kyoketsu-shoge, and knew that once they made contact with the deadly machines, there would be no way to retract them without serious burns.

He slashed through the air in wide arcs, focused on his own survival and his wounded son on the other side of this mechanical horde. He would not be stopped. Another wave came, and with no hesitation he tossed out another round of exploding stars that fulfilled their purpose in expert order. The napalm payload of some of the on-comers splashed on the drones unaffected in the initial blast, and though they petered over to him, they ultimately fell below his line of sight. As they did, John couldn't help but wonder what that boy of his was up to.

Before long, though, explosions swept the sky in multiple directions just as a new wave deployed. Cal had finally gotten to work. The fresher drones, distracted by the explosive entrance, rushed to the different parts of the city to investigate. With his way now clear, John pushed himself forward through the rooftops alone, and only swung his kyoketsu-shoge to fend off the odd machine here and there. A Lightbeam took its place beside him.

"Need a hand?" The machine had a mechanical voice but still sounded like the boy who programmed it. John rolled his eyes.

"Boy," he started, and the machine laughed. "If you don't help me out of here…" John let the question of the threat linger, which Cal felt was sometimes worse than the actual threat. Even so, it was more of a joke than actual danger. John used his repulsors to hop onto the back of the Lightbeam, and just as Cal had taught him a couple of months prior, maintained his balance as they moved forward.

"Looks like we have more inbound," Cal said through the android. John looked back and saw that he was right. One group followed closely behind, while another cluster flanked them to the right. John breathed a sigh. Was it so much to ask for just a moment to breathe?

"Fine," said the Director. "Follow my lead." John jumped from the back of the Lightbeam and slashed through an oncoming drone with a kyoketsu-shoge, and just like before, the payload of napalm splashed and disoriented a few others in its cluster. As he sailed through the split, he kicked the air with his boot and blasted just a few inches over another drone. He latched on with one hand, dangled a bit, then the other, and watched as the others converged on his location.

"What do you think you're doing," Cal screamed through the mechanical voice box, which made John laugh.

"How do you think we fought the KDN back in the day before your fancy robots came out?" Cal had to admit that the question had always been in the back of his mind, but now hardly seemed like the time to address it. If any of that white stuff landed on him, that was it. He was done. The other drones sped towards him now, and John still had a childish look on his face, like he was about to outwit a friend in a game of skill. He jumped straight up in the air and bounded higher with the repulsors as the drones collided in a twisted heap of metal and goo. The napalm splashed, the machines fell, and John was left momentarily in limbo. “Any day now,” he shouted, and the Lightbeam rushed to grab him. John finally breathed a sigh of relief as the Hudson came into view. He glanced back at the Lightbeam’s face. “I can feel you judging me, you know.”

“Good,” Cal replied, “I am.”

****

The scans picked up a lot of pings from a number of homing beacons. Most of the signals were muddled, no doubt covered in a layer of hot liquid. It was a miracle that they were on at all. Specifically, Cal focused his attention on the northernmost parts of the island. He received intel that the commando base was somewhere in Harlem, some kind of museum, but the information came in so fast and the situation was so dire that he didn’t have time to internalize it. He switched his vision to one of the three Lightbeams that he’d dispatched to the area, only to find that there was very little left of what Harlem was. It was broken beyond all imagining, and it was in this rubble that Cal had the task of finding his friends, teachers, and allies from all over the Coalition.

The other Lightbeams cleared out much of the drone presence in the area, and even managed to locate the main dispensary of the drones at the old Yeshiva University campus. Cal wondered what the Scarlets thought colleges and universities were for, but put the thought out of his mind when he noticed some movement beneath the rubble. The Lightbeams began work on excavation, and that was when he heard muffled cries for help from two distinct and familiar voices. The androids dug deeper, though carefully, and eventually revealed the face of Lukas Bautista.

"Oh, thank God," he said, surprisingly cheerful. "I was telling Dax that if nobody heard us we would at least go out in a cool way."

"Daxa's in there with you," Cal asked through the Lightbeam. Lukas nodded to a space a few feet away, and immediately one of the other Lightbeams got to work with digging her out. It uncovered her mouth.

"Get me out of this hole," she yelled, and Lukas couldn't help but laugh. She growled at him, but he knew that she would see the comedy in it one day. The Lightbeam shook its head, and continued to dig Lukas out while its brother did the same for Daxa.

****

The moment John's feet touched the ground he sprinted towards the medic station. So many of the Yaiba, the Kabuto, the Yoroi and the Waste Raiders lay there with grizzly injuries, and a whole separate portion was allotted to Nash's men and the Red evacuees. Part of him contemplated how nothing would ever be the same now that the conflict was over, but it was drowned out by the overwhelming sense of dread that came with not knowing Darius' condition. More than an hour passed before he finally found his son, still unconscious with medical wrapping over the wound.

Hank Davis approached silently from behind him, and the only reason he didn't meet his end when he made his presence known was because John had no weapons left with which to strike him. He registered the man's face, knew it to be a friendly one, and the agonized trepidation was momentarily assuaged.

"Is—" John's voice caught in his throat. He didn't want to complete the sentence, because he didn't know if his lips would ask if he would be alright or if he was going to die. Hank placed a hand on his shoulder and offered a comforting smile.

"He'll be fine," Davis assured him. "He's a little banged up from the heat and the trauma, but the Hanzo Gear took most of the stab. He'll be able to move around again just fine soon enough. Just don't push him." Relief washed over the Director, who dropped to his knees as he thanked God for a crisis diverted. Tears welled up in his eyes, and Hank knew better than to stick around and watch him in such an intimate moment.

John placed his hand on Darius' chest and closed his eyes as he sobbed. All of a sudden, he felt Darius take a deep breath and move his hand to rest atop that of his father. John looked up to see a wry smile on the boy's face.

"Tell me that those are tears of joy," the Hiryu joked. "New York was a mess from what I can remember. Might've gone the other way."

“Look,” John said in faux warning as he wiped away his tears. He hugged his son. “I was so scared that I would lose you, kid.”

“What? Me? Never,” Darius told him with a quiver in his voice. He hugged returned his father’s hug as tears streamed down his cheeks. “I love you, Pops.”

“I love you too, son,” John said, and tightened his grip a bit. “I love you too.”

****

The headcount took hours, but when it was finally done, John gave the order to move out. They returned home with the knowledge that all of thc factions had suffered heavy losses. Johannes Thornhill, Zayvier Peters, Nash O’Neill, Claire Sommerfield, and Ezequiel Vargas were among them, as well as several of the Seven Dragons. Leadership was in flux, not just in the Yaiba, but across the board, and the Scarlet Kingdom was little more than rubble and fumes.

Its people were grateful for the help that they received, and while some still stubbornly assessed the Coalition fighters as terrorists, many more had to question the validity of that. It was strange, almost as if they had begun a long process of waking up from a drug-induced sleep. Before long, John gave the order to move out, and while he was hardly qualified to speak for everyone present, none argued with his decision to take charge. Barring the fact that he’d just led them to victory, everyone was tired and ready to go home.

He couldn't help but think, though, about what things could have been like had they been different. Would he have gone down the path of vengeance and volatile bloodlust had Darius or Cal been killed at Midland? And what if Jaden had survived? Would Bryan have still betrayed them somewhere down the line? John knew that it did no good to think too much of it. He just couldn't shake what Bryan had said in the moments before his death.

"Hey, Pops," Darius said as he clapped his father on the back. "You coming?" John looked around and realized that he was the only person left behind. He chuckled.

"Yeah, kid. Just got lost in thought," he said, and then realized that it was the wrong kind of thought. He'd spent enough time worried about the past and what it meant for the future if things went south and they lost the war. Now that they had won, he was determined to take his family by the hand and lead them into the future he'd always envisioned for them. He took some time to stew on that as Cal walked up next to him. He pulled his boys in for a tight hug. Finally they would all know peace. They had all earned the right to go beyond the mountains and live in the sunlight.

Appendix 1

GLOSSARY

- **Hanran no Ryu:** "Rebel Dragon." The Master Name given to Darius Hamlin.
- **Hanzo Gear:** Named for Hattori Hanzo, the legendary shinobi that saved the life of Ieyasu Tokugawa from Mitsuhide Akechi following the fall of Nobunaga Oda, the Hanzo Gear is composed of a hooded cloak filled with a shock-absorbent gel to resist bullets, a menpo mask that covers the lower half of the face and connects to a visor that displays necessary information, and a pair of kyoketsu-shoge. Standard-issue Hanzo Gear also includes a pair of repulsor boots that allow the user to cover greater distances, jump higher, change directions in mid-flight, and soften landings. The cornerstone of the Hanzo Gear, however, is the Reikiken.
- **Hiryu:** "Fire Dragon." One of the Seven Dragons of the Violet Shadows. The name is given to a dedicated master of the Hiryu Form.
    - Practitioners of the Form tend to be wild, but controlled. Their movements are ferocious, brisk, and powerful to end the fight as quickly as possible.
- **Kabuto Sanctuary:** One of the Four Factions of Prevalence. Pacifistic in nature, the Kabuto Sanctuary specializes in demolitions, espionage and sabotage. They philosophize that no fighting needs to be done if the enemy's equipment falls apart.
- **Kageryu:** "Shadow Dragon." One of the Seven Dragons of the Violet Shadows. The name is given to a dedicated master of the Kageryu Form.

  - Practitioners of the Kageryu Form prioritize disarmament of their opponents, wide swings and fighting in close quarters.
- **Kazeryu:** "Wind Dragon." One of the Seven Dragons of the Violet Shadows. The name is given to a dedicated master of the Kazeryu Form.
  - Practitioners of the Form prioritize a balanced approach to combat and can make use of a single Reikiken or, more famously, a staff made up of the two. The inspiration for the staff was taken from an old movie from the 1990s.
  - **Kibaku Shuriken**: A special type of throwing star outfitted with a remote detonator for more long-range combat capabilities.
- **Kiringan**: "Monster's Eye/Kirin's Eye." A piece of advanced biotechnology that syncs with the user's optic receptors and functions like a human eye, albeit with added features.
- **Kiryu:** "Tree/Wood Dragon." One of the Seven Dragons of the Violet Shadows. The name is given to a dedicated master of the Kiryu Form.
  - Practitioners of the Form take a more acrobatic approach to fighting, a trait that is greatly accented by the mobility of the Hanzo Gear. Their movements are forceful, aggressive and precise.
- **Kyoketsu-shoge:** Long chains with blades attached to the ends. The Yaiba Insurrection versions of the kyoketsu-shoge are heat-treated to resist the high temperatures of the Reikiken and diamond-shaped titanium blades strong enough to resist gunfire. They can be (and often are) used as grappling hooks.

- **Rairyu:** "Lightning Dragon." One of the Seven Dragons of the Violet Shadows. The name is given to a dedicated master of the Rairyu Form and exceptional leader among their peers.
    - Practitioners of the Form prioritize body economy, speed over power, and extreme precision. Rairyu users are noted for their elegant combat style, fluid blade work, and one-handed style.
- **Reikibo:** A staff made of two Reikiken conjoined at the hilt.
- **Reikiken:** "Aura Sword." Named for the heatwave that radiates from the blade, the Reikiken is the signature weapon of the Yaiba Insurrection. Thermal amplifiers in the hilt transfer heat from the user's hand through to the blade at much greater temperatures, which grants the weapon the ability to burn or melt through most substances with ease.
- **Sasori:** The Grandmaster of the Legendary Founders, Sasori-sensei was solely responsible for imparting the samurai and shinobi wisdom from which the Yaiba, Yoroi and Kabuto blossomed. It is because of him that there is still a chance for freedom.
- **Scarlet Kingdom (Kingdom Scarlet):** One of the Four Factions of Prevalence. The reorganization of the United States after the fall of its democracy that seeks to bring the other factions on the continent under subjugation. Rarely sees people of color as worthy of recognition on merit alone.
    - **Scarlet Scourge:** An all-female death squad of seven members, the Scarlet Scourge has gained a reputation in the Kingdom for being able to pull off missions that the general forces cannot. They are brutal, merciless, and determined to maintain the

station that they have gained for themselves. AVOID AT ALL COSTS.

- **Sensei:** "The one who has gone before." Sensei is a term used by the Yaiba, Yoroi and Kabuto in reference to anyone of superior rank, though not because of the rank alone. To be called "sensei" is to be acknowledged by one's subordinates as being wise as much as strong, and capable of leading one's students down the proper path. It is often interchanged with Master, Elder, or Agent, depending on which of the Factions one finds themselves in.
- **Suiryu:** "Water Dragon." One of the Seven Dragons of the Violet Shadows. The name is given to a dedicated master of the Suiryu Form.
    - Practitioners of the Form are noted for their purely defensive movements. They prioritize fluidity, timing, protection, body economy, and have an uncanny propensity to transform their defensive flourishes into subtle but devastating attacks.
- **Tetsuryu:** "Metal Dragon." A nickname formerly given to the newest members of the Violet Shadows that has been jokingly reassigned to Cal Richmond due to his affinity for technological developments.
- **Tsuchiryu:** "Earth Dragon." One of the Seven Dragons of the Violet Shadows. The name is dedicated to a master of the Tsuchiryu Form.
    - Practitioners of the Form are noted for their grounded stance, wide swings, and stunning movements that fluctuate between speed and power. These fighter intend to press the attack regardless of circumstance.
- **Usagi no Kamikaze:** "Rabbit of the Divine Wind." The Master Name given to Bryan Piccio for his unorthodox fighting style totally dependent on

coordinating his kyoketsu-shoge and repulsor boots to fast-paced and deadly results.

- **Yaiba Insurrection:** One of the Four Factions of Prevalence. The Yaiba Insurrection was the first of the factions to put the Scarlet Kingdom on the defensive through purely offensive means. Their victory at the White Ruins Miracle changed the perspectives of the other faction leaders, and established their Violet Shadows as a military force to be reckoned with.
    - **Violet Shadows:** The general military forces of the Yaiba Insurrection, named for the black and purple of their uniforms. The glow of the Reikiken often skews visibility of them, so they look like shades to enemies. Like the Yoroi Alliance and Kabuto Sanctuary, the Insurrection derives their military training from the Legendary Founders' samurai and military experience. When paired with their technological innovations, the Shadows prove to be more than a threat for those ignorant enough to challenge them.
- **Yoroi Alliance:** One of the Four Factions of Prevalence. Known for guerilla warfare and demolitions, the Yoroi Alliance has a stellar reputation for their trap mastery and impregnability. They are a very private, secluded faction that is extremely wary of outsiders.

Milton Keynes UK
Ingram Content Group UK Ltd.
UKHW010242230124
436511UK00018B/386/J